THE LAST JACOBITE PRINCESS

THE LAST JACOBITE PRINCESS

M.G. ANDERSON

Boyle
&
Dalton

Book Design & Production:
Boyle & Dalton
www.BoyleandDalton.com

Paperback ISBN: 979-8-90183-053-6
Hardcover ISBN: 979-8-90183-054-3
E-Book ISBN: 979-8-90183-055-0

Printed in the United States of America
1 3 5 7 9 10 8 6 4 2

To our parents who taught us
never to say margarine.

Prologue

The Black Horse
Sheepy Magna
Leicestershire
The Rectory, St. Neotts
18—
Dear Father,

Recently I happened across a village delighting in the singular appellation of Sheepy Magna in this country of odd names. A neighboring hamlet styles itself Norton-Juxta-Twycross, and the local capital is Ashby-de-la-Zouch of *Ivanhoe* fame.

The manse is decrepit, for the living has been vacant for the longest time. The parson's widow lives there alone with her cats, perilously I fear, for when the new vicar comes she will surely be rooted out. The church bell still works; to that I can testify for it woke me up at an ungodly hour this morning, but the rest of its fabric is in sad disarray. The roof is almost beyond repair, and the interior has the look of a pigsty in what once must have been a splendid example of the Conqueror's stamp on this land. So sad is the depredation of this charming village that I am convinced it were the model of the deserted village so memorably limned by your late friend Oliver Goldsmith.

Mistress MacPherson, the widow of the old rector and daughter of the previous, purports to be eighty-six years old but looks less than fifty, and is still a handsome relict of a more spacious era despite exceeding the biblical allocation of three score and ten. By common repute she is a witch, as was her father (hanged on a gibbet, flesh fed to the crows, etc.), who "returned" years later to haunt those who sought his doom, bringing in his train a Dr. Faustus, whose pact with the devil included a clause allowing him carnal relations with virtually all the infamous women who have disgraced the pages of history. Naturally her reputation keeps her in a lonely state, predisposing her to be garrulous when sympathetic company is at hand.

She has an extraordinary tale to tell, which if true is incredible, or if not is a brilliant concoction. One thing is certain: Years ago, terrible things inexplicable to either the laws of philosophy or our Age of Reason happened in this backwater. She has extended me the privilege of passing on her journal to you, and insists on doing so lest all these invaluable records are wiped out, as happened to the monastic journals in the reign of Henry VIII. She claims her chastity has been chased after seriatim, but then she is old, confused, and inclined to enhance every anecdote with the grace notes of fevered romance. Eccentric? Yes. Fascinating? Yes. Truthful? Perhaps. Any peeping Tom reading her story for vicarious pleasures may well end up a doubting Thomas. But if you believe in witchcraft, werewolves, and amazing serendipity then hold onto your hat.

CHAPTER I

My Birth and Improbable Origins

I was brought up in the plump-waist land of England that sits right upon the heart of our country, those damp Midlands, which afford a terrestrial Garden of Eden for the agrarian interest and rheumatics for the rest of us. "Came in with the drizzle," said the midwife who delivered me. A most reliable gossip was Mistress Smellie, with a way of making remarkable the most ordinary of occurrences. I don't think that was her real name, but it was her way of associating herself with that remarkable savant Doctor Smellie, whose gospel ensured the survival of England's babyhood, or at least improved the chances of the babes born according to his guidelines.

In time with the weather outside went the drip, drip running from my mother's nose when she gave birth to me, an incidental also relayed by that most reliable source. This effluence was a constant feature I was told. She died when I was but a nipper, and all I can remember is a thin drudge of a woman drooping round the hen house and yard, crossish, croaking and groaning. I can still see her thin, runny nose when she died complaining that the vicar would be late for her deathbed like he was late for all their bedtimes, and was more interested in the dairymaid's cowpox than in the demise of the most important parishioner in the village, to wit herself, and could they give her a clean mutch cap to greet the Lord, and woe that her linen should not be clean. She had come all over breathless when suddenly she sat up and shouted, "Where's me pattens, wench?" in case the approach road to the pearly gates was muddy.

Our Betty, her chambermaid, comforted her. "Mum, there'll be streets of gold where you's be goin'. You can wear yer silver slippers. Here, I've put them 'neath the bed so's you can slip into them nice and easy. But ye won't be needin' them for a long time. You's as healthy as a horse."

She was wrong. After these words of solace mother looked up said, "Mind the prince's dram!" and on that enigmatic note expired.

I don't think their marriage was a delight. But then, good sir, whose is? Her nuptials were not exactly made in heaven, although she had high hopes of gaining admission therein. I pitied St. Peter. I think she had him marked down to take over her husband's job, but with better timekeeping. Her husband, gentle reader, was my father, the tardy village parson.

As vicars go he wasn't a bad sort: solid-as-an-oak Church of England, forbidding any Hypocritical Tremblers (his all-encompassing term for deviant sects such as Quakers, etc.) to darken his doorstep. He preached a sermon every Sunday whatever the weather, and they were his alone, not culled from a book of collected sermons for use by lazy vicars. And he did have a good word to say about my mother. He told me that she was a disappointed person, whose life had not matched expectations. For one glorious night of her life she had bonded with royalty, which was on the occasion of Bonny Prince Charlie's solitary foray south of Derby. Their nocturnal frolic was said to mark the exact southern limit of his attempt to seize the throne in the Forty-Five. Few believed her story. Frivolity and loose living were not the first words you would associate with her. Nor was she considered one of the great beauties of England. But she stuck to the tale, and the episode provided something of interest. In case you are wondering, good sir, I don't take on no regal airs and graces. I was not the fruit of that amorous joust. I say that emphatically, but it has never stopped others from making the claim for me, so often that I was dubbed the last Jacobite princess by silly followers of lost causes, and after a while I did not dispute it. It did me no harm, nor did it profit me any.

On her deathbed mother muttered, "Hearken, lass, for I'll only tell thee once," then paused to let a great hacking cough surface. "Pass me thon watter jug." Stretching her quivering glass of physic over the pitcher she croaked, "The King!" and in a voice quavering and frail continued, "I hold the Secret of the Stewarts." This turned out to be a recipe, and I dare say a reward for sharing her bed with the bold chevalier with the white cockade.

Now, that slip of paper was supposed to have been passed on to me, the sacred keeper of the flame, even though I was never clear as to its purpose and very soon forgot about it, what with everything else going on. Was it the elixir of eternal youth? If so it had signally failed with the Bonny Prince, whose drink-sodden face showed the sad and relentless ravages of that which no man can avoid, not improved by his efforts to pickle himself in alcohol. Look at any of the later portraits limned in his gin-soaked dotage and see the ravaged face of the debauched cuckold. They say that lovers tend to seek their own reflections. Mother was said to look like the prince if he had been placed in petticoats, and that was why she became briefly the chosen one. But the face that won the hearts of the ladies of fair Edinburgh, or rather its duplicate in a twisted mirror, did no service for my mother. My memory of her face was rendered sharper by the portraits glowering down from the hallway of the vicarage, recklessly strewn by my father in his tormented grief. Like all paintings of ancestral worthies these tended to put visitors on their best behavior. She certainly had the look of the prince in his glory days, but while the chevalier was handsome, dashing and gay, notwithstanding a mite effeminate and birdlike, the features mirrored by her were beaky, mean-spirited, and Scotch miserly. The smidgeon of venerean strabismus which I inherited, and I am told adds to my charms, gave her the appearance of an Aberdeen peddler scowering the gutters for a bawbee. From her I also inherited my prim and proper ways and, what with her royal appointment, my occasional flighty caprices.

What was not realized at that stage of our history was that the young chevalier, in a moment of abandoned recklessness (an occupational hazard of princes), had given away the only extant copy of the Secret of the Stewarts on the assumption that the loyalty of his followers would guarantee the return of the parchment. But then his was the foolishness of youth rejoicing in its first full ripening flush, when all is possible and old age is something that happens to someone else.

To put the icing on the cake of his folly, he had decided to make a sport of gifting the mystery document by dividing it into three parts to reward three far-flung people. It would be amusing imagining the three trying to reconstruct the puzzle, for is not inflicting cruelty on one's subjects the other great sport of kings?

But all we inherited was the curse of the Stewarts as our patrimony. For what good is one third of a secret, and wasn't we worse off than having none at all? With nothing you may rest content, but with only a thirding you spend your life chasing after wild geese, ending up stuck in the marsh of their concerns, pestered by solicitations from afflicted relatives of whose existence, till your secret came out, you was sadly unaware.

My father's hobbyhorse was the young maids of the parish and their catechisms, which was much more compelling than the exploration of royal pedigrees and a possible claim to the vacant Stewart throne. Nor was he interested in hunting, thus leaving himself open to criticism by the local gentry on that score, but that breach of etiquette was granted a manorial indulgence since he was a stout two-bottles-a-day man like the squire himself. After mother died, and thereby all interest in opposition to the House of Hanover, he became absorbed in his own peculiar country pursuits.

He continued his interests in the spiritual welfare of the young maids of Sheepy. These actions were in the great tradition, for as the old saw goes, "Priests do love pretty wenches." Very noble, I thought, surrounding himself with measles, the King's Evil, and sundry afflictions of the impoverished, when easily he could have spent his time quaffing sack with the quality while pardoning their peccadilloes. I used to wonder when I passed the young maids why they sniggered. Jealousy I thought. After all I lived with father and knew for myself how staunch the timber of his moral rectitude was in supporting the family tabernacle.

All tipplers are tedious, stumbling about before finding their good rest under the table. My father, once underway on the festive road, would puff out his chest and, in a deep, rich basso profundo, start singing—at first hymns, ancient and modern, then jolly songs of the sea and the countryside. If he could have stopped there that would have been fine. But then he became maudlin, would slobber about my mother's grave and catechize me on how I must not reveal to a soul the Secret of the Stewarts.

Father would sit me on his knee, whereupon I felt his fruity breath wheeze over me. Whatever the concerns of a later generation this disturbed me not a whit. To me it was a normal portion of paternal affections, and as I was a lonely child, unstroked and unpetted in the main, these vinous caresses became my maternal hugs, and when he playfully rubbed his scrubby whiskers against my rosy cheeks, I confess I did not dislike it.

"Come, my pale and wan damsel. You shall be rosy and pink-cheeked, meet to match the dawn."

How innocent we were! This was before he made his daily acquaintance with Madame Defarge, or as he was wont to say, "What my Scotch friend Adam Smith calls the Maiden." This was a cheese-paring device used up North to shorten criminal lives by a head, and was his jocular way of referring to the routine task of attacking his daily harvest of bristles with the razor blade.

Some, at least, of the loneliness was of my own choosing. True the yeomen wenches were unthinkable as playmates for me; my father and his books were sufficient company. Most of the girls of my acquaintance were abysmally unlearned. I refer not to the common village Abigails, but the daughters of the quality, those coy young maids whose carriage and mode of dress were designed like gin traps to snare any man with the sniff of gentility about his person who strayed onto their game preserve.

One such was my neighbor, Mary-Anne Dixie, my youthful companion and, I suppose because she had no other rivals, my best friend, by which I mean we played pass-the-dice together on rainy afternoons. Her father was the local squire, who lorded it over Market Bosworth and Norton-Juxta-Twycross from his grand seat at Bosworth Hall. From an early age he took an interest in me, to such an extent that my father used to chide him about it in his own gentle, twitting manner. Mary-Anne's mother was a quiet, pretty, pale creature who kept in the background. There was talk of a youthful indiscretion, but then there always is in cases where a pretty wife is not flaunted like a set of silver at any social occasion. Originally a native of North Britain, she had been whisked off by Sir Wolstan in suspiciously speedy circumstances, a veritable blunderbuss wedding. Despite these rumours of *noblesse obscura*, her daughter, possibly the outcome of the indiscretion, and a truly ingrained snob, ignored the lady who to my mind was treated by the household more like an Abigail than as the lady of the manor.

At an early age, Mary-Anne had discovered her potential. In the land of the pale, long-boned Anglo-Saxon, she with her high cheekbones and almond eyes was an exotic. It was a handsome Spanish hidalgo washed ashore from the Armada whose seed, infiltrating the bloodstream of the local squirearchy, had created this pearl amidst the parish-pumps; or so she said, and I believed her. She had a habit whenever there was a reception or ridotto for the local beau monde to walk into the receiving room with a sudden swish of skirts and fan, as if her entrance was an entrancing thing in itself. I on the other hand tended to present myself as if I were a diffident mouse. "More like those damned skulking American rebels than a true British Grenadier," my father would laugh. I noted that despite her performance I could count on many gentlemen's eyes fixed on my person, if it is not too forward of me to mention. She was so snobbish that to be spoken to or nodded at during any county assembly by milady was considered a considerable feather in one's tricorn, as if a permit to court her was better than receiving a knighthood from those Hanoverian upstarts! Few of those so singled out for a week or two of heavenly torment reflected on the fate of the ancient Corn King, who after a year of frolics must die. There is no grave so clearly labeled as last year's fashion. But then I have noted that seldom do men so transiently favored reflect on anything beyond the brief, brilliant plumage of their passage.

Even father noted how she played with her eyes at everything in knee breeches. "She focused her coal black orbs at me." I thought it interesting that such a scholar as my father should notice the color of a girl's eyes. "We met in a spacious corridor, and she made as much ado in getting round me as if it were Anson circumnavigating the globe." He gave a portly chuckle. "She came at me with a winsome smile that read, 'Please, let me pass.' But underneath it said, 'I can make the Red Sea part. I can make you do anything.' Evidently I was cheaply bought, for when she came back again she smiled at me not."

Mary-Anne, despite the magnetism which drew in all the macaronis, coxcombs, and squires of the shire, chose to pursue the parson. Whether from an overabundance of youthful suitors who bored the petticoats off of her, or a genuine if misplaced affinity with the sturdy oak rather than the acorn, Mary-Anne's ambitions were decidedly fixed on Father, who refused to take her any more seriously than any other village infant he had dandled upon his knees. Like so many blessed by Nature's bounty, what she desired she, as a common rule, got. And what she didn't get, no one else might have. In short, if she couldn't have her playthings, she would stamp on them with her dainty feet.

Today Mary-Anne was coming. This could be a mixed blessing. If a third party of the breeched gender was present, I might as well be hung out to dry in the airing cupboard. Whereas if it was only us two she was all ears, even for my ungifted harp playing, that was until she felt the pangs of ennui, commonly arrived at before the hourglass registered the time to boil an egg. "Enough of this racketing!" she would shout as if I was the flibbertigibbet who had dragged her away from more important calls on her time, depriving the village of its benefactress. Then she would proclaim a desperate social engagement impossible to evade, flick her muslin Barcelony round her neck, and off she'd flit, leaving me feeling let down yet relieved.

No, the reason for my excitement today was that accompanying Mary-Anne was a young clansman interrupting a walking tour of the High Road to London, where he hoped to meet Dr. Johnson, he of the dictionary, and drink at this font of learning. In the meantime he was to act as tutor to Mary-Anne, a formidable assignation. James Cameron MacPherson's father was a Jacobite, who had been out in the Forty-Five, thus interesting intercourse was promised. According to Mary-Anne, he was especially worthy of note since several of his relatives had been hanged for cattle rustling outside Inverness Castle to the accompaniment of the skirl of Highland war pipes. With such antecedents how could anyone fail to be amusing? Mary-Anne had described him on such glowing terms that I wondered why she was prepared to share him out so early in the game.

The possibilities were threefold. One: she was bored already and was looking to palm him off on me. This scenario came to mind immediately. Two: there was not sufficient diversion in her immediate surroundings to amuse him, and she was anxious to unburden the load onto harmless, hopeless me. Since she never lacked confidence in the interest owed to her person, this was hardly likely. Three, a strong possibility: I was so dismally boring that she would shine in comparison. Seeing Miss Mouse would establish a norm of English womanhood for the heathen clansman, who assuredly had never met a lady in petticoats sans bare ankles and woolly plaid, and would thus be brought to realize that Mary-Anne was the absolute apogee of Sassenach maidenhood.

Mary-Anne had only one nag to spare, knackered old Nobby, on whom she was arriving by ride and tie. However, her style of doing it was all ride and no tie, pretending that she forgot to stop. "We was so engaged in looking at the flowers and composing little sonnets and odes to the swallows of spring." Thus she arrived as fresh as from a promenade round Pall Mall, coiffure perfect, while James, who walked, was tired and dusty. Still he didn't complain, so I surmised he was used to charging bare-shanked round boggy glens in the garb of old Gaul.

Before he finally arrived, we had sufficient time to cover essential ground. I admired her lutestring, she my best brocade; then, after summarizing the pros and cons of my outfit, Mary-Anne began praising the stranger breathily to get it out of the way before he came through the door. I still had not made up my mind whether she was trying to sell me the goods or allowing me to bask in her good fortune when the Chevalier de Ecclefechan was introduced by the maidservant.

He bowed briskly but agreeably. It was obvious at once why he was being so precipitously thrust on me. James was no roaring callant, five-cubits tall, built like a Highland stirk, with brains the size of a musket ball, shouting "Whae's fur Charlie?" to the unwary. No, this was a more delicate flower, of normal height and girth, perhaps a languid poet, but without the basic sartorial sense to attain that level of foppery. I had to admire Mary-Anne for her ability to pretend enthusiasm.

I poured some tea, which James drank quite as if he was used to the stuff. I detected no tremor in his hand as dish ascended to lip, as when an honest man is deprived of his grog. When we got down to conversation, he could hold his own on civilized topics. Despite Mary-Anne's attempts to steer our discourse to rapine and reiving, with which he was supposedly more familiar, he was happier talking about Adam Smith, David Hume, and other luminaries of the Hellenistic Revival, which was all the rage in the fair city of Edinburgh.

Mary-Anne was bored, ostentatiously fiddling with the ribbons on her poke bonnet. "Oh do tell us amusing things. My mind gets vexed enough with listening to Amelia and her Greek gibberish." Master MacPherson stirred his chocolate languidly, as if bracing himself before pronouncing a bon mot.

"When there are such charming creatures as yourselves to entertain, Greek gibberish is as"—he paused for effect—"as beautiful as any other gibberish." A mot if you like, but hardly bon. At least he tried. Now normally such a piece of gallantry would have Mary-Anne simpering all over the sofa, but she was clearly out of sorts. She stamped her feet and said, "Hence fly dull stuff. Let us have minuets, rigadoons, and the latest dance from France. Show us how to trip a gay cotillion. Tell us what garlands you have carried off this season dancing with the ladies of Edinburgh town. It is a town, not a Pictish fortress, is it not?"

Cameron smiled softly and almost painfully as he gently let her down. "That particular dance step was indeed a smash…" Here he paused. It was a slight pause, a hardly discernible break in his rhythm, as when a dancer makes a chasse instead of a step, and then he said quietly, "last year."

It was not often that I was given the opportunity to witness my socially dexterous cousin nonplussed. There was much ado and fluttering of fans from me as well as herself as I tried to remain unperturbed, but I fear a smidgeon of glee passed across my face like a fleeting rainbow, which was detected I am sure.

"Well then, what about a quadrille?"

"That's an excellent card game but we need four people."

"Oh...I know that. And if we need four, there's nobody here but lackeys and other such low people. If we invite one of them to play, we might start a revolution."

"So let me dance a measure or two of a minuet if that would amuse you."

"Oh, you make all our activities here appear such brummagem, Mr. MacCarriage." I knew this deliberate muddling of his name was a sure indication that she was not prepared to take his set down lying down.

"And as for you, Amelia, my charming country cousin who doesn't know the difference between a galliard and a haystack hornpipe, you have no need to take on so!" And finally, "No real gentleman of my acquaintance would expose a lady so to raillery. Nor would he be lacking in... what is it...bean sauce?"

"Perhaps you mean *bienséance*, good manners?" supplied James Cameron. For a moment Mary-Anne looked like Vesuvius in, what was it, LXXIX AD? Then, realizing she was bested, she subsided. Funnily enough, after this little exchange we all got on rather better. He smiled at me over his dish, and I smiled back shyly. Mary-Anne waved her fan about a lot and complained of the heat, looking out of the window as if some beau might spring up from the flowerbed to rescue her from this social no-place. Alas it was in vain, no one came, and she launched a desperate stroke to gain the upper hand, fluttering her fan round her décolletage, one of her standby attention-grabbing tricks, but it too failed. Cameron and I had no eyes but for each other.

Then he took my hand and hummed a few notes as he led me through the movement of the stately minuet. Behind his back Mary-Anne minced away in dreadful mimicry for a couple of measures. I was embarrassed for her rather than for him. James did not look stupid; she did.

When they left, he to hike and she to ride, I curtsied to his bow, whilst roses bloomed in both our cheeks. My heart gladly tripped. For the first time in my life I had a beau. Mary-Anne was furious.

CHAPTER 2

Animal Husbandry

Mary-Anne's father was the celebrated Sir Wolstan Dixie. Though by common repute mad, bad, and evil, to us as our neighbor and squire he was affable and nobly condescending. I saw him as a jolly old fellow, a sort of a cherubic John Bull, choleric, somewhat florid and puffy but warm-hearted, somewhat too partial to petting and having me dandle upon his knee, unobjectionable for a girl of twelve but not fitting for a maiden whose petals were just beginning to capture the spring sunshine. I was worried that I might be the cause of a seizure.

Knowing of my fondness for animals, and horses in particular, Sir Wolstan invited me to pass a morning with him inspecting the stables at his estate on the outskirts of Bosworth. His chariot would pick me up and deliver me the three miles, an unsought boon. Usually when I paid a call on Mary-Anne, the excursion provided my daily constitutional. How thrilled I was when the footman arrived at the door calling for Miss Amelia Wathes-Stewart. Father squeezed my hand warmly, but Betty, as she pressed my bread and cheese invention of the Earl of Sandwich into my hand, gave me the faintest shake of her head and with it a warning look.

Oh, go on, you say. How could even a country girl be so wet behind the ears? But there despite all my book learning I was daft as a brush. All these hours in the library sheltered from reality had something to answer for, as I was soon to find out. That my father, a man of the highest discernment and unimpeachable religious and moral rectitude, should hold Sir Wolstan in even loftier esteem, and generally bowed, scraped, and genuflected whenever the sunshine of his presence graced our humble cot, made me to think that in polite society the animal stall was the best venue for a morning reception.

Without as much as a peek inside the hall, I was whisked away toward the stables. As we strolled along the grove shaded by a fine growth of budding apple trees, I espied a line of beehives whose inhabitants, all busily humming away, diligently manufacturing honey, lent the scene a pleasant, bucolic air. So far were my thoughts unguarded that instead of minding where I was going and what I was about, I was absorbed in mentally checking the relevant passage in Virgil's *Georgics*, or was it the *Eclogues*, where the busy bees make their sweet ambrosia, or there again was it their sweet nectar? Oh was there ever such a foolishly distracted maid?

Phew! The gamy tang of the barn seized my olfactory nerves as if they was smelling salts. From behind me a lusty snort, as from a rutting stallion, announced the squire was about to speak.

"Ahem! You may wish to take off your kirtle to keep it fresh and clean," says my thoughtful host. I could see in the affability of his countenance and the boisterous twinkle in his eyes that he was eager to make the visit a signal success. I can see him now, even though the years have cast a cloud over my remembrances, his right hand tightly gripped round his embossed cane, his great round belly protruding forward like the bulbous warhead of a cumbrous ship-of-the-line, and teeth more suited to the stall than to the chamber. The puzzle of it was that there was a hungry look about him that disagreed with his well-nourished exterior.

"Such a pretty muslin frock. It would be a crying shame if it were ruined by the miasma of the sty." He had a point, so without further ado, and with all the innocence of a child of sixteen years, I slipped the pretty material off my shoulders and hung it on a bent nail handily posted outside the stable.

We went in to witness a stallion attempting to mount an indifferent mare. In the background, a cloud of bees was buzzing busily through the rafters. A peaceful middle-England scene. The squire's hobbyhorse was livestock, and he embarked on a detailed monologue about fetlocks, bridles, croup, swine fever, and so forth, for such was the staple conversational diet of the squirearchy.

"Place its toby into the inkwell, Amelia, if you please," he said. It was horrid, but being brought up to be obedient to my betters, I placed its prodder into the great slurping minge so that the stuffing could begin in earnest. I chose to keep my eyes averted, painfully aware that this was what country girls had to do, and thought no more of it than if they were baking toad-in-the-hole.

One of the bees, a great humble-bee, detached itself from the flock and came buzzing up to see what we were up to. It must have resented us, for without warning it dived toward the cleft in my bodice and stung me quite between my bosoms. Zooks! But it stung. I pulled down my shift to see the damage and espied a nasty red welt spreading right where my swan-like neck should be shown to its best advantage.

"Now I will never go to the ball!" I cried, dismayed.

"I say. Such a naughty pair of swelling boobies," says the naughty old man. And I realize now, years later, that the old squire must have thought that his anatomy lesson had borne fruit. For when I turned, his kecks were round his ankles, and a horrid red truncheon surrounded by underbrush was brazenly poking out from his shirttails. It could have been the stallion's younger brother. Silly me! For I thought ought of it, assuming it to be but a grown up version of the ever popular child's game "Dare or Double Dare," with the addendum of comparative pastoral anatomy, as my genial host endeavored to continue my agrarian education.

But all I was concerned with was gaining relief from the pain, which was now shrieking around my upper body as if sparked by Signor Volta's shock contraption. To that end, I rushed away into the garden in search of a docken leaf (thinking if they assuaged nettle stings, ergo they must do ditto to the bee sting), with Sir Wolstan hopping after me round the rose bushes.

If I were not in such torment I would have found mirth in seeing this choleric old gent of sedentary habits leaping about as if he were a fervent competitor in the Sheepy sack race, with rod and staff engorged to comfort me, swinging about like an enraged Mr. Punch. *Quel! Malentendu*! There was I, thinking him concerned about my painful plight, while he was off thinking I was leading him in a merry dance before succumbing to his embraces. With the squire hobbling after, roaring like Roger the bull, I scurried everywhere searching for a dock leaf, but as well look for a smallpox scab on a dairymaid. The garden—scraped, polished, and scoured according to the regimen set by Capability Brown, with lawn and flowerbeds fit for royalty to dine off—was hardly likely to be soiled by the presence of even one weedy docken leaf.

The cook! Of course, why hadn't I thought of her earlier? She had cupboards full of Gregory powder, brimstone, and old wives' remedies. Now tears were welling up with the pain of the sting as I rushed into the kitchen, skating over the stone floor in my pattens. The buxom lady looked aghast. I had forgotten my dishabille, and had only time to cry out, "Have you any remedies against the consequence of a prick?" when she screamed. Was my rash that ugly, or was it the appearance of my good-natured host in the doorway, his tadger on guard like a swollen barber's pole?

"Be off with you, you brazen hussy!" the Abigail railed. I left. I could see there was no help there. Then I heard from the kitchen, "I'm a good woman, I am, Sire, and I won't be baking no more rock buns in this house of Sodom no more. There's me apron, and if you can get another as bakes apple dumplin' as good as us then good luck to you, Sire."

The next I saw of him he was reeling outside with an apron covering his face, trotting and bouncing blindly around the courtyard, till finally his breeches tripped him up so he upended onto a mound of stallion muck piled outside the stable to sweeten the rhubarb patch. Seeing as how I weren't going to get any first aid here, and assuredly the visit was ended, I took myself off, not forgetting to remove my top petticoat from the rail. Then, remembering to waste not want not, I retrieved my Earl of Sandwich from the kitchen, taking in the spectacle of the noble knight of the county disengaging himself from the manorial midden. Roaring like a Turk he was now, as how he had been deceived by a conniving curate's child, and in consequence of her naughty games had lost the best cook in the county. He swore something awful. Most of these words were fresh-minted as far as my ears was concerned. I never knew the English language had so many distinct terms for the same thing.

Going home by Shank's Pony, I needed a breather, so took a break by the Three Tuns and under the shade of its old oak tree consumed my luncheon. My bee sting had lost its sharpness, and like all ills that come quickly to an end, the pain was soon forgotten. And notwithstanding all that had happened, I was still in total ignorance of that which made the world go round. Reflecting on the events of the day, I could see now that the squire would no longer regard us with the benevolence of yore. There was trouble brewing at the Manse, which boded no good for me and my father; but well sir, when I put down my crust I just laughed and laughed, laughing so much I could have died laughing.

A week after this I was in the library tussling with a particularly toothsome passage of Sophocles. The sun streaming in through the stained glass, filtered by the floating dust in the air, was transmuted into colored rays as if in an undersea grotto, transforming the spines of the tired old books into the gleaming bronze shields of Homer's warriors, the faded titles shining like golden filigree interlaced in the darker wood, a woman's work lightening the dourer handiwork of man, I ventured to suppose. I had little idea of the reality of the dark satanic mills in our North country where women were worked to exhaustion in inexpressibly horrid conditions.

I fingered my cotton frock in the quiet pleasure of useful activity. Oedipus, having stabbed out his eyes and being dragged all round the houses, had now arrived at Colonus. The story made little sense to me. Why shouldn't an old man stay at home peacefully toasting his toes in front of a nice warm fire? As usual my mind strayed to my own circumstances. Should I not be an Antigone accompanying my own dear father down life's weary byways? Goodness knows, ever since mother died he needed help. I usually put these maudlin musings down to weakness to concentrate, but I couldn't shake off the feeling that if I had been a more dutiful daughter, my father wouldn't be constantly landing himself in the pickle barrel.

Father's Achilles' heel was his love of animals. When respectable folk diverted themselves in games of cribbage, brag, or chuck farthing, he would be off outside, rain or shine, to pet lambs in the field and cows in the byre. When the beasts was to be taken to slaughter, the vicar would make his rural horseback rides to the sick and frail of his parishioners; otherwise his grief was not to be borne. As to whether he was the animal buggerer of spiteful legend, I doubt, but whatever his transactions with the animal kingdom were, they were multiplied and mutilated in the telling, like all country gossip, to become the transgressions that brought him to the gibbet.

For instance, on a Sunday when he was innocently shepherding his flock from the pulpit, the village layabouts made farmyard noises in which the sounds of sheep mingled with a chorus of cows. Was this a critical response to his sermons on St. Francis of Assisi, and they were objecting on the grounds that he was swerving dangerously close to the precipice of Romanism?

Another day, an impertinent whine came from behind the hedgerow. "Wooly back, ye was mithered by a wooly back!" I was jolted back from my musings to see Beth, one of father's milk-white dairymaids, on her hunkers mocking me. I was taking my stroll down the primrose lane between the Manse and church, thinking how sad was the Fall of Rome, even though so long ago, and just stared at this singular insolence, when she added, "Baah!" making it sound distinctly like vocal efforts of a little baa lamb. This went completely out of my mind, as anything said or done by these Abigails and Dorcases was dismissed as an event without a consequence, like snow in May.

Now this ugly scene came back, jostling out high thoughts, and that nasty hobgoblin Doubt set in. My thoughts turned to earlier today, when I caught him sneaking out of the house carrying a pair of Whittington boots, the thigh-high type favored by highwaymen.

"Father, why are you carrying an extra pair of boots?" I asked innocently.

"Silly girl, 'When weather makes you have a care, 'tis better far to have another pair.'"

This was too odd. I recollected happening on some of the village roughs talking lewdly about the technical aspects of 'sheep-shagging.' Suffice to say that when your sheep was caught, in order to keep it on station one places its hind hooves into the boots so that they might shake but not stir from the spot. I had to confess, on a couple of occasions, to sniffing the leather after he had returned from his wool gathering meditations, and observing the ripe redolence of sheep dropping. Even more suspicious was the odd whorl of wool clinging to the inside of the boot.

There was a rustle of cotton over linen. I was back in my study. Mary-Anne's hair was dusted with the Pulville pomade men use for powdering wigs, and she swept in announced by the sweet fragrance preceding her grand entrance. Mary-Anne had made her characteristic entree, totally wasted on me, for I have to say that more than ever she was merely annoying; but she was bored and wanted attention. I was at an unusually gripping juncture and wished her away, although perhaps I should not have made it so obvious.

"Mary-Anne, pray do me the honor of giving me space to think, reflect, and translate."

"Marry come up, good madam. Pray allow me to share your industry."

I showed her and she tried to be interested. Her ignorance, made more obvious by her pathetic attempts at pseudo-learning, I found more irritating than her fleece-brained giddiness.

"Why, your father could make something of that mumbo-jumbo in the twinkling of an eye. I think I'll go and search him out for you."

"Yes, rabbit! Why don't you go annoy him instead?" Knowing his rambles, I reckoned it would take all afternoon for her to ferret him out. Why she had taken to hanging round my father I cannot comprehend, because in her pea-sized brain he must be a dotard beside the young bucks in her train.

She was making great swirling circles round me. To what end I confess to being ignorant, unless it was to impress me with the perfection of her fine Holland linen. Certainly her gown and coats were as spotlessly virginal as herself. Getting no response there, she diverted herself to the gilded pier glass perched above the mantelpiece, and started flicking out her curls in the manner that had half the men in the village slavering and fawning, but for me it was as irritating as that final straw for the camel. "Mary-Anne, have you nothing better to do than fritter away your day in front of mirrors?"

She chuckled and showed me her very refined profile with that straight, somewhat over-ong nose, commonly considered her best feature, but whose minute downward twitch eliminated her from the canon of classical beauty. Her skin was darkly glowing like Wedgwood's best china, transmuted into ruby red by the dappled tints of sunlight. She looked at me archly, as if she had just discovered the Philosopher's Stone, and swaying slightly, teasing out her raven locks, started to intone: "Mirror, mirror on the wall, who is the fairest of them all?" And answering herself like an old toothless crone: "Not you, my dear, not you at all. But the girl with spectacles and books, why, she's the one with all the looks."

I had to laugh. It is not often you get such a compliment from the Aphrodite of Atherstone.

"Oh, cousin, cheer up and let's go visiting. There must be some gentlemen in this parish who are not mere lovers of husbandry."

Suddenly I was tired and my spirits drooped, as the weather, whimsical as always in our dear, dank Midlands, had withered away the early promise of sunshine, letting dark clouds fall upon the house, blotting out the sun's rays, enchanting only a few moments ago. I lost my temper, something I rarely did, flung my book onto the floor and spoke out. "I am out of patience with you. Why don't you go and get yourself tupped by Tom the cowherd, and then you can leave me in peace. Forsooth a rogering is what you are in need of."

Many times I have regretted that outburst, as uncharacteristic as it was unforgivable, although I wish I had a Gainsborough or a Reynolds there to capture her face, which resembled one of those ornamental goldfish in a lily pond, blowing petulant bubbles. The faculty of speech quite evaporated; she flounced out in her muslin, skirts rustling angrily in the breeze of her own temper, for as always she was dressed as for an afternoon engagement in the Pump Room at Bath rather than a damp day in the country.

There was a long interval during which peace reigned and I returned to the eternally blue Aegean, remote from the raindrops pattering on the pane outside. Something told me she would try and pester my father, and finding him would take up more of the time she needed to fritter away, but for now I was alone. I tripped my way through the maze of subordinate clauses set to trick the unwary, and at last the passage was mine. How I could feel for Antigone, responsible for an old benighted man blundering on his way to the grave. The room, the furnishings, the old grandfather ticking away, even the bottle on the mantelpiece faded from my sight, and I stood silent in a wooded grove on the outskirts of Athens long ago, listening to the rolling cadence of a tongue stilled ere Christ was born.

A sudden shriek jolted me from my reverie. It was echoed a second later by another louder, more penetrating scream that writers of Gothick phantasies would label blood-curdling. The third shriek had an air of studied horror, almost the affected refinement of grand opera. My book fell off my lap. I pulled up my skirts, adjusted my mutch cap, and, picking up my bonnet, allowed myself a little glimpse at the mirror (on the off chance that a handsome gallant was on the way to the rescue), and rushed out.

This impulsiveness I repented a yard outside our doorstep as my new satin slippers splashed through a puddle. Why had I not hesitated enough to don my pattens? Even my starched linen undercoat was mud spattered. The continuing shrieks guided me to the byre, and to where my life was to be turned upside down.

"Mary-Anne, what on Earth!"

"Miss Dixie to you, Miss Wathes," she replied stiffly, and I saw that we two were kissing cousins no more. Dimly I discerned in the shadowy reaches of the byre the outline of a clerical figure. There was no mistaking the button-up gaiters astride a sheep, like a jockey bound for a steeplechase.

Mary-Anne's fixation with father had developed into a poisonous rapture. She knew of his liking for the creatures of Noah's Ark. She also exaggerated alarmingly, and had, I am sure, threatened him with exposure to the rougher elements of the village unless he succumbed to her charms.

"It's not what you think."

I wondered what bounder had first uttered that immortal, unpersuasive line.

"I was merely out for a quiet piddle," he bleated. But whereas the evidence of his breeches was open to ambiguous interpretation, Mary-Anne's accusations were unequivocal.

CHAPTER 3

Rural Justice Dispensed According to the Laws of Edward II

The screams were heard all over the village, bouncing off the walls and echoing from the mouths of the village gossips. The first of the gallant rescuers was framed in the doorjamb, not the bravo of my dreams, but old toothless Jeroboam, the manse nursery gardener. "Lord, luv a duck!" was how that worthy summed it up.

"Or a sheep," chuckled Tom the cowherd, a sly, cross-eyed fellow, who was known to give a farthing to little boys to go behind the cowsheds.

Then old Jasper, the self-appointed village sage, usually seated on the bench outside the alehouse with clay pipe and pewter pot, popped his head in for a glimpse of all the excitement. It must have been of some moment for him to budge his fat arse. "Aargh!" he said in judgment, and I knew then that father's fate was sealed.

"Raise hue and cry!"

"Don't need to. We've caught the bugger red 'anded."

"Red arsed, more like!" This provoked the malicious, threatening chuckle of the lowest class enjoying a brief Saturnalia, when society is turned upside down and slaves become the masters.

"He's a disgrace to the cloth!"

"Throw 'im in't duck pond, the bugger!"

"He's a Jesuit, a buggerin' Roman priest!"

"Hang the bleedin' bastard!"

The winds of change had hit the village, and with a chill in my stomach I realized what it must have been like in one of Wilkes's Liberty Riots. The faces of humble folk I had known and condescended to all my life were suddenly convulsed by a red madness. Standing out in the midst of all the tumult, his dewlaps wobbling with the solemnity of his office, our squire, Sir Wolstan Dixie, brandished a warrant calling for a posse to apprehend my father and me also, as an accessory to crimes of buggery, sodomy, and sorcery. He must have scribbled the warrant in great haste, or had it prepared already. Oh how sweet is revenge when delayed, for there was no doubt in my mind as to why he was so keen to make this arrest.

They—the squatters, the landless laborers, the tenantry, and the squirearchy—all zealously united in this prosecution of the law, grabbed father, tossed him onto the midden, then picked him up and trussed him like a chicken. I saw him rather pathetically hauling his britches up, while stuffing a wobbly willy back into hiding. At least they allowed him to regain that shred of dignity before frogmarching him to the duck pond, where he was strapped into the chair and doused three times, coming up spluttering but alive, thus establishing beyond any reasonable doubt, enough to satisfy the requirements of any court in the land, that he was a witch.

The last I saw of him alive he was gasping for air and looking at me piteously for help. Even though they had slapped a scold's bridle over his face, there was no mistaking that agonized expression. The village worthies began a heated discussion. "Fry up thon naughty sausage!" said all those in favor of burning the offending object at the stake. "Let's string 'im oop and be done wi' it," riposted the impatient hangers.

The crowd surged toward the vicarage, shouting, "Burn the bugger's books and bed." They trampled through the orchard, overturning our modest hives, crushing our rhubarb and dahlias into the ground. *No more pies, no more floral table settings*, I thought absently. I was standing unnoticed on the sidelines, while a little birdie kept whispering in my ear, "Watch out, lass. You're next." For this was no ordinary disturbance but an ungoverned class revolt: wild, untrammeled, and very dangerous for anyone who sported *h*'s and *t*'s in their vocal baggage.

Crowds of villeins surrounded our house, shrieking raucously; appalling harridans screamed blasphemous abuse, while urchins tossed burning brands at the building, the flames lighting up their maddened eyes. "Thon vicar. Hang the bugger for buggerin' us sheep!" The thatch on the roof exploded into crackling flames. Our house was ransacked. Books were hurled onto the bonfire, their strange script marking them as the works of the Devil and his disciples. All my life's treasures consumed in an instant.

Someone shouted, "Seize the bitch!" They hesitated; mobs are only sheep turned nasty. No move was made toward me. Then, "She said my rhubarb pie were made out on nettles! It were good honest dung-fed rhubarb." This was the enraged cook, now turned agent provocateur.

"She turned my milk sour when she come a visitin'," screeched the crone who lived in the squalid cottage at the end of our lane.

Her sister, with a face as sour as her milk, screamed in corroboration, "An' she reads books! Novels!"

Strange are the ways of the mob, for this was the spark that set them afire. When I heard this, my heart chilled in fear of anticipation. And sure as eggs is eggs, it came. "Them cross-eyes o' her—they's the devil's mark."

I pished myself with terror, for I knew very well the penalty for witchcraft.

"A highway internment! On't gibbet!"

From nowhere, James Cameron MacPherson rode through the mob, bawling out, "This witch is mine. She'll burn! And suffer a highway internment without Christian burial!" He threw me on the back of his screw like a sack of potatoes. "No! She must be tried in a proper court; otherwise the whole village will suffer under pain of law. On a night like this it is impossible to establish witchery beyond a reasonable doubt! I will take her to the lock-up so she can't escape." His steed was spinning round, clearing a space and making me dizzy, while he made his speech to the crowd, then he galloped off to the farthest extremity of the village, carting me round the corner of the Wayfarer's Tavern. Quickly peeping around and seeing the coast was clear, he then dumped me onto the back of a hay wain, pushing me under the straw with no more ceremony than if he were stuffing a goose. If ever there was a more inconvenient time to discover you fancied a man this was it, and there was the flame of love surging in my heart, just seeing him astride Mary-Anne's nag. He slapped the pulling horse; the old cart creaked slowly forward.

"But where shall I meet you again, my handsome hero?"

"The Great Wen, at the Great Cham's Pineapple!"

"The Great Who?"

He ignored my query. "You'll find out. Now I must be quickly off to draw your pursuers away from their hare; for the moment the rascals have been foxed by my stratagem, my sweetest Amelia, pirate of my heart!" And then he melted out of sight. It was the nearest to an avowal I had ever heard, and so sweetly spoken. But as to the rest: "The Great When"—that must be a date of significance. "The big sham pineapple?" What to make of this enigma wrapped up in a fruit? But there were other matters demanding my attention, to wit, the angry voices surging past me on horseback, knowing they had been duped.

I wriggled my head through a bale of straw to stop me sneezing. With my nose protruding I had a narrow line of vision, which curiosity demanded I widen. Turning my focus back to the main square, I saw a sight that froze my innards. Looking back through a window of straw, I caught a glimpse of a black-coated figure swinging gently in the breeze from the gibbet. Crows were picking at his eyes. Tears filled my eyes, not just for grief of all that I had lost, but in the knowledge that, if I was Antigone, I had failed my Oedipus. It was my father.

The cart moved off, bumping sickeningly over the cobbles until they ran out at a ford across the brook. Here the horses stopped for a greedy wallow, placidly switching their tails to ward off flies as if they were there for eternity. Nothing was to be gained by stepping out to get the cuddies moving, for the lower orders were rampaging everywhere, burning anything belonging to anyone who could spell their names. I waited, nestling under the straw. Ragged, roaring rascals, whom I knew from my earliest years as stalwart, honest country bumpkins, scuttled past my wagon, bound on desperate measures. Fortunately they were not tempted to burn the hay wain where I lay in growing discomfort. Bits of straw were creeping under my clothes and threatening to bung up my nose. I waited, every long minute a ticklish torment, until darkness fell. The rascals had exhausted their madness and were now celebrating their triumphant day with enough ale and cider to send them into oblivion till next Saint Monday.

The usual evening rainfall had quenched the flames over the vicarage, making the possibility of entrance safe. Once again unbridled curiosity took hold of me, compelling me to creep back into the house. The blaze, which looked very spectacular from the outside, had been confined to the library and father's bedroom before being curtailed by the blessed Midland rain. I went up the creaking stairs to my bedroom, fished a key from its hiding place, and opened the strong box I hid under my bed. All my savings since I was an infant were there, hoarded for my trousseau. It wasn't much, but it filled my purse, which I secreted in my petticoat pocket. I cast a glance around me, stifled my sentimental tears, and left.

Our old horse was still in his stall, restlessly stamping the ground, his eyes wide with terror. Partly to calm him and partly to assist my urgent departure, I led him out of the stall, saddled him up, and trotted off. No one saw me; the pressing need for drink seemed to have quenched the revolutionary spirit. Soon day was breaking over the old grey stones of the church, anointing the Plantagenet spire with the golden glow of life. For no reason at all this cheered me up.

Clip-clopping over the Anker bridge, I reached the market town of Atherstone, where nobody was concerned with the commotion in Sheepy. The whole town was abuzz in its annual Saturnalia, the Atherstone ball game, a mad fiesta of fighting over a globe of stuffed straw. Silly, you say, but then wars are fought over more trivial excuses.

A foreigner coming upon this bedlam would put in a request that the troops be called out and the Riot Act read. Today the rowdies ruled the roost. Everyone and his neighbor was pressed into the High Street, with an overflow accommodated by the town's many taverns. Two gangs of roughs—one from uptown, the Uppies; one from downtown, the Downies—were fighting it out to place the ball in the other's goal. As a consequence of this desperate athleticism, so contrary to the inhabitants' accustomed indolence, all the windows facing the High Street were boarded up.

After a few false starts I practically gave Toby away to the coaching inn's landlord. He was knackered out and no use in this crisis. I cried when I handed him over, so copiously that the liveryman felt sorry for me, and paid over the odds for something fit for nothing.

"Don't waste your watter, lass. Here's a couple of sovereigns to you. A sovereign remedy, so they say, for life's troubles." He chuckled at his pinch of attic salt, then pressed me to take some supper. "Take yersel off to best room, and me missus will fit ye up wi summat as'll pep ye up, and some o' finest ale this side o' Burton to sluice it dahn wi."

I was quite without any appetite, but knew I needed strength and fortitude for what lay ahead, so I tucked into the steaming dish of shepherd's pie proffered by his good lady, who was clucking away at my state of tiredness and the disorder of my clothes.

"Here, luv, couple jars o' grog'll soon set you to rights." A pint of good claret sluiced down my neck, hardly touching the sides of my throat, I was so dry. This was merely a warm up, as a cataract of various vintages was poured into me to alleviate my parched throat. After this Lucullan banquet, I was fairly in need of fresh air, and here surely no one from Sheepy could spot me, so I tumbled out of the front door.

"Hark, hark! Make way for the toffee-nose lady!" A rascal with teeth like a castle laid waste bowed and doffed his hat with sneering effrontery. "Hey oop! wot's a grand lady doin' down here wi us common muck?"

They let me in but the air was not friendly. I had to smack at a couple of hands that were already sneaking up my petticoats. My money was secreted in an under-skirt pocket, and there was no way I was going to let a groper near it, but then I forgot about their constant tickling when I beheld a sight worthy of remark. A rosy-cheeked woman, whose face was wrapped tight in a tartan shawl, was holding up a child hardly more than a baby, shouting, "Eh there, Tom lad, here's our nipper over here!" She stood at the front of the press.

Tom, a monstrous yokel, strolled unimpeded to his lady love and held out the ball for the child to touch. "Lass, now our babbie's baptized." The strange thing was that during this touching ritual all was still and silent. Tom was allowed free egress to his wife and free return to the point of battle, where immediately the affray recommenced with renewed vigor.

I was moved to see this little rose of affection amongst so many unpromising thistles. *Good old England*, I thought. *Neither wonder these effete Frenchies can never beat such stout hearts of oak as our lads.* I began to sing:

"Hearts of oak are our ships.
Jolly tars are our men.
We will always be ready to fight
And conquer, again and again."

The crowd was looking at me sullenly.

"C'mon, lads and lasses, join in!"

No one sang. They stared at me as if I was a freak fled from the circus.

A sniveling whine surfaced from the crowd. "Why if it's not Amelia, the buggering vicar's daughter. Hey me duck, taint no tea and cream scones here." Some rascal from Sheepy had sneaked here overnight. Again hands were rubbing up and down my clothes like a posse of snakes. I could sense them whispering about me all around.

"Fancy a spot o' rough then, me ducks?" Malice was rising from the crowd like mist from a marsh. I was out of place and out of tune, and my silly gaffe had put me back into danger. Pulling up my skirts I scuttled back into the coaching inn and continued requiting my nervous thirst.

Thus it was providence, I reasoned, that led to me, the prim daughter of the vicarage, being nine sheets to the wind when the stagecoach en route to Coventry piled into the yard to take on board victuals and harness up a fresh team of horses. The other passengers were not thrilled with me joining the party, particularly when I needed help into the coach, requested a fine lady to shove her fat arse along the seat, and sang a rousing solo performance of "Rule Britannia" to the rhythm of the bumps in the road. I thought it hilariously funny, but my giggles were answered by steely silence, and from their glances methinks they had pickles up their posteriors, which perchance I may have mentioned to them. Thus we traveled in embarrassed silence, excepting for my unappreciated entertainment.

As a result it came as a relief when, just before Nuneaton, a masked highwayman leapt out of the bushes, introducing himself as none other than the bold Captain Farrell, the ferocious scourge of the Kings Highway, or at least the section of it between Tamworth and Coventry. Quite suddenly I was wondrously excited, for I was not unaware of his reputation as a gallant, and under my starched cotton skirts I squirmed with pleasurable fear. I knew, just knew, that he would be entranced by my maidenly charm, and would force me at pistol point to dance a galliard with him under the light of candles provided by the coaching company's lamps, while the coachee played a light bourrée by Bach on his post horn, and with that transient pleasure as a fee he would allow me to escape unscathed, jewels and honor intact. Under this scenario, notice, the role of my fellow passengers was confined to being a mute, adoring audience. On the other hand, he may have well thrown me over his saddle horn and taken me to his favorite tavern where, having been primed with a bumper of mulled wine, it would be off to his cave in the Dales to ravish me over and over again, with his companions in discreet attendance pretending not to sneak a glimpse at my dainty under-linen. And I would remain with him and enjoy a cut of his highway tolls for services rendered. Either prospect pleased in the odd drunken mood I was in. At least I would be able to look Mary-Anne in the eyes again, and cut some sort of half decent figure with her.

But when he got to me, he grumped when I curtsied to him, hauled away my Barcelony handkerchief, ripped the necklace off my neck, and went for my purse in a most ungenteel fashion. Maybe he was having an off day, for I noticed he stumped round the coach all crossish. It must have been his gout had got the better of him, so he couldn't dance a galliard with me, and the thought of losing out on such a prospect had put him in this liverish mood.

This was a very poor form of treatment from this gentleman of the road, and I wondered if he was feeling old or if standards were slipping in his line of enterprise. But then service is poor everywhere. My father used to complain you cannot get a reliable cowherd anymore, never mind a proper house-trained domestic. I swept back into the coach, slamming the door. Unfortunately my skirts got caught in the doorjamb, spoiling my display of affronted petulance.

A little bit further down the road I was still simmering with displeasure. When we were held up again I stayed in the cabin sulking, quite forgetting that I was dealing with murderous thieves and that the title "gentlemen of the road" was bestowed on them by an overly sentimental pamphlet press.

The door was flung open. Two coal-dark eyes blazed at me angrily.

"If you value your life you will dismount expressly forthwith, and be damned to the niceties of your dress, madam."

Well, I had never been called madam by a highwayman, and when I exited into the light of the driving lamps, and he saw the youthfulness of my countenance, the robber took a sharp intake of breath. "I do apologize, *mademoiselle*." He swept his hat off in a magnificently gallant sweep, till his head was practically scraping the shrubbery.

"Coachman, play us a tune on your horn. I wish to dance a measure with this beautiful maid." He swung me round gallantly till I felt quite giddy with the motion (and not without a twinge of emotion, for he had a most comely face).

"Well, robber, what is your name? It cannot be Captain Farrell, for he has already disrupted our journey, and most ill-humored he was about it."

"That's me dad. He is getting past it. I wish he wouldn't go about at night, what with all that damp. At his age he should stay indoors. His rheumatism doesn't half give him the gyp. It'll be the death of him, if he don't watch out. That is if he misses out on the Tyburn hornpipe." He laughed gaily. He was a charmer, this one, and no mistake. Then he said, "You must excuse me with all this family talk; it is so boring, but I suppose it's the least you have to put up with on the King's Highway, what with bugs in your bed, coaches breaking down, tediously garrulous companions, and me, especially since you've been robbed once already. Once a day is enough for anyone." Fancy getting this consideration from one who, when all is said and done, is nought but a thieving rascal.

"That's typical of him: selfish, no sense of family values, leaving me with the scrapings." He laughed, but seeing I was put out by his flippancy, he again assumed that winning countenance Mother Nature had gifted him. "My apologies again, my beauty, having to put up with insult and injury."

"What injury?" I was alarmed.

"Well, since you ask and the takings are so poor, I am going to leave these sad spinsters"—he pointed to my outraged but relieved companions—"and take you off to my den to ravish, enjoy, and generally plunder. Then, when I tire of you, I will toss you out the door, and flog you off to the highest bidder."

When he said this, my body was set upon by a strange nameless terror, but delicious not withal; the fear mingling with tiny particles of excitement was like the pinch of salt sprinkled over your breakfast porridge.

Without further ado he threw me over his saddle horn. The fine fat lady shouted, "And mind you move your dainty little arse when his gallant nibs shoves his musket up it!" and cackled with ill-bred glee. Oh to have had the last word! The insult borne on the breeze was like caution thrown to the winds. No vicarage tea party for me; my fate was in the lap of the gods.

We sped along a muddy path, Black Bess Junior's hooves drumming through the mud in a great gallop to throw off my pursuers, who showed no great zeal or activity in rescuing me from the jaws of death or worse. But then inertia is oft the middle name of these yokels. My father once had the greatest difficulty in persuading a thatcher to come out and mend our roof, and we had to spend a blustery Christmas with rain dripping into our mulled wine, and that in a time when the country was groaning under the iniquities of the Speenhamland system, and the poor was whingeing and croaking about lack of employment and the harshness of the landed classes. Well, they could all go to the colonies and hang for all I cared. You see I was bitter after their treatment of my father, topped by their indifference to my misfortune.

"Where are we bound for?" I whispered in his ear, kissing the little wheat germ planted there in the process.

"Why, Lunnun Town, my sweetmeat, where your face will be our fortune." It was nice of him to be so candid about my potential for whoring and his reaping its rewards. How my life had gone from following "the cool sequestered vale of life" and keeping "the noiseless tenor of my way" to being a die tossed about by rakes in a gambling hell, my tale will tell. It seemed wisest to go along with the vagaries of the tide and hope it would all come out in the wash. So it was off to London for Dick Farrell and me to seek our fortune like Dick Whittington and his cat.

CHAPTER 4

Alone in the Great Wen

"Here, lass, with them flagons up front. Over here wi some of that porter, if you will. Me mouth's abaht as dry as a dowager's drawers. We can't be waiting till tides be turned."

After many adventures, I found myself as a bosomy barmaid at the Pudding Tavern, deep in the Hundreds of Drury in London Town. It must have been just the ticket for me since my cheeks bloomed and I began putting on weight in just the right places. For the first time in my life I was a lady of my hands. I learnt to add very fast to count up assorted orders and translate the louis d'or, doubloons, and kopeks my nautical customers palmed off on me into shillings and pence. I became a dab hand at clearing up the pots, tankards, and trenchers shorn of the fortifying comestibles that sustained the inner man. I learnt how to change and clean the sheets (or the straw of our less fortunate clients) while fending off the ardent gropers without offending. Most important of all, I was to be able to pour the ale from tap to pot, keeping a high level of froth without any spillage, while allowing the patron a bonny vista of bosom. My instructions were to lower my décolletage slowly, as the night progressed, to the point where a fair maid might be expected to blush.

I had no idea that my tits were such a great draw or a landmark in South London, but they soon became a minor tourist attraction, lending their attached owner a morsel of celebrity status. "Aye lass, I be thinking o' changing t' pub sign in thy honor, wi Two Puddings 'stead of just the lonely one." Mother Red Cap, mine hostess, commented on my cotton frock held together with a drawstring. "When thee wear that, lovey, like that"—she pointed to my dropped drawbridge—"takings take off."

When late in the evening I became hot and slackened the string, it was as if the castle was being besieged, and the amount of beer purveyed would have filled a moat. For a lady as precious as myself, you may have thought this would be bothersome, especially since I was used to a life of ecclesiastical retirement. Surprise, surprise: I found myself enjoying it and thinking, if this be life then it ain't half bad. I recollect looking up sharply, as I was pouring the amber nectar, to find a man gazing transfixed at my knockers, and it was him that went red with embarrassment. A proper sporting gent he was, with his satin weskit and beaver-pelt tricorn. By the looks of him he had more brass jingling in his pocket than all my regulars put together. For a passing moment I thought I knew that face, but it was soon occluded by smoke, pushed aside in the press, and forgotten about, while I was fairly glowing with the maidenly pleasure of being admired not for my brain, which seems to attract leechy bores and tedious pontiffs, but for my bonny bosoms, which drew a warmer crowd. A passing thought that the witch finders from Sheepy were still on my trail. No, he was too well dressed for that, but it occurred to me later it might have been one of the eccentric elixir hunters who kept popping up in the village from time to time, as regular as the harvest. They were a nuisance, forever prying through our windows and even sniffing into the hut of easement.

The alert reader may notice I had quite forgotten about my handsome James during my short excursion with Dick, my rascal lad. I make no apology for my inconstancy beyond saying I was a mere seventeen, a village virgin, gape-mouthed at the wonders of the world's greatest parish.

Beforehand I had been too much of a skinny wight for him to take much amorous interest in me. Dick didn't put it quite like that, but if I wish my grandchildren to read my journal then I have to render his Billingsgate digestible. I thought he might begin to take a fancy to me, noticing I was repelling boarders upstairs and downstairs and all round the clock. But no, I was naive and had not learnt the great lesson in life that women are like any other object in this man's world; the price goes up when availability goes down, and if I had kept him at bay like a panting dog, I would have been his one incorruptible love, whose portrait he would carry in a locket, together with my maiden hair, when he went on his midnight rovings, and so decline to dance a cotillion round the coach of any shameless hussy he met while at work.

The further I left behind the sheltered precincts of the vicarage, the further went its sensible precepts. I was foolish and hotly eager to cast off the trip wire of my virginity, so one night while I was slaving away under a veritable Trevi Fountain of ale, disbursing foaming tankards to the parched multitudes, and he was spending the evening fooling around with other damsels, I said to myself that I was ready to get acquainted with his spanker, and reenact Dido and Aeneas's love fest in the cave, my bedchamber taking the part of the cave.

I put on my prettiest gown and let down the drawstring at the speed of sailors dropping sheets in a gale. I noted that beady-eyed gent of more quality than our usual riffraff being more than averagely beady-eyed with me, but put it down to the randiness of the seasoned timber and thought no more of it, beyond the passing fancy that I had seen him before.

As I wiped the froth off the last pewter mug, I gave Dick a nod and jerked my head up the stairs in case he thought the carnal act was to be consummated across the beer-soaked tables. He grinned in an affectionate manner and my heart lurched.

In the light of the candle I stripped down to my silk chemise. As I shucked the last of my irksome petticoats, Dick groaned like an old, sad dog, and I knew that for once I had enslaved a man. I lay back for his invasion and my conquest. For this, I thought, great armies have gone to war; slimly shafted Nicean barks have slid down greased slipways into the great blue briny.

Something was in the way. The randy sod had forgotten to remove his breeches. There was now an embarrassing hiatus as he tried to pull his kecks over his shoes, so eager was he to get at the goodies, meanwhile the epaulets on his jacket brushing against my breasts were giving me rope burns. At last the moment was ripe, but all the maneuvering and wrestling had substantially diminished my ardor. I was at the stage where I would put up with it if he could get it in, but any further delay and I would say amen to that.

Wouldn't you know it but there was a knock at the door. This was not your polite, timid knock that you might expect when Mother Red Cap had closed her doors to Jack Sprat. No, it was a rough hammering such as you would get from the bumbailiff.

"All right! All right! We ain't got no lack o' beer for thirsty boys." I opened the door angrily to see three hard-looking ruffians making ready to break the door down. These were no ordinary bumbailiff catchpoles. The two Bow Street Runners and the beady-eyed gent, who had raised the posse of the fleet, entered without a by-your-leave, pushed me roughly aside, not even removing hats, to haul Dick, John Thomas and all, off the bed.

"I might have known we'd catch youse in a whore house!" Shouted the puzzlingly familiar man. At this rate, without trying, Fate would have me branded a spinster forever living on parish charity. Despite his disarranged clothes, Dick put up a ferocious fight, smacking his fist into their faces, stomach, and ofttimes the wall.

"He's as slippery as an eel, this rascal 'ere!" It needed all three to subdue him, each of them pulling at a limb. That meant he had one limb free, with which he landed the man with the beady eyes a tremendous crunch in the goolies (rendering him *hors de combat*), who then fell to the floor screaming in a falsetto that would have brought the roof down at Covent Garden. The other two, taken by surprise, or possibly being opera lovers, relaxed their grip on Dick. That was all he needed. He broke away, dealing such a solid kick to the other bailiff that he too was compelled to retire from the fray. Dick ran outside the room, whereupon he took off over the landing and was off up the street before you could say Handel's Largo.

"Don't you move, you black-eyed witch. We's a coming back to put you in Newgate too!" Belatedly I recognized the beady-eyed gent as none other than the constable of Sheepy Parish. My, was I in deep trouble.

I could hear Dick clattering over the cobbles and the three in hot pursuit, raising the hue and cry, shouting, "Stop thief!" and "Good citizens, seize the rascal!" But the good citizens were otherwise engaged, for not a soul tried to impede the escaping malefactor, who yard for yard was steadily eluding his wheezing pursuers.

At the end of the street sat an enormous steaming stew of night soil. Evidently the Finders of Gold had been less than punctilious in their calling, for it hadn't been shifted for weeks. Dick, who was more athletically disposed than his pursuers, reckoned one quick leap over the pile would take him clear away. He leapt. It was a splendid Olympian leap. Unfortunately, just as he launched himself his breeches, which had not been firmly secured, took this opportunity to obey the laws of Mr. Newton and dropped round his ankles, resulting in him piling head first into the manure.

The gasping constables sauntered round the pile, and even insisted on him tidying himself up before they made their arrest. "Get that shite off you, lad, afore we cuff you. It's a flippin' liberty you're taking, expecting us to arrest you in this state. What would me wife say, goin' home in that stench?"

I hadn't been as inactive as my observations would suggest. I blew out the candle in my room and walked down the stairs to enjoy the splendid vision of Shagging Sheila (so styled by her less industrious colleagues), framed in an aurora of petticoats petalled akilter, womanfully servicing an overzealous client in the doorway. I could tell by the long-suffering look in her eyes that it had been a long day.

"Sheila, you look tired. Why don't I lock quim to cock with your patron, and you go and have a nice lie down in my room?" In case you did not know, whores, nannies—whatever name of shame you give them—are helpful to others in their guild, and so she wasn't too surprised.

With a sigh of relief accompanied by a sucking sound from I don't care to know where, Sheila detached herself from the customer, saying, "Bless you, me ducks, I need fortnight's holiday and a long cool-down on the River Thames before I start this game again. Which be your room, lovey?"

The customer, nothing loath to have fresh meat, leapt on me in the standing position, throwing my petticoats over my face, effectively masking my identity. "What's with them pantalettes? Where's thy pretty little minge, you tease, you? Why, it's as dry as me dusty attic dahn there." At this point the stalwart men of law pushed past us, knocking my client way to the ground before he had docked and before he could instruct me in the Great Secret, thus easily giving me the opportunity to slip away. The gull, who was drunk as a lord, was incapable of stopping me. I didn't run at first because I wanted to hear the hullabaloo as they tried to arrest Sheila on charges of witchcraft. By Gad! That lass put up a fight! I nipped down a back alley and started to run when I heard a shout from the hallway.

"Get a candle!"

"Fore George! Why, the witch has changed her shape!"

"No, we got the wrong lass."

By then I was well on my way.

The Bow Street Runners were not the only ones interested in my welfare, I discovered. Splashing through puddles along the Highgate Hill Road, I espied, posted on a tavern door for the benefit of those as could read, an intelligence:

Thief, Female, seventeen years old,
Noted vagabond branded on left buttock: V
Highwayman's moll calls herself Amelia Wathes.
Pretends to gentility.
Fond of Latin tags and quotations from Classics.
Wanted in Midlands on warrant of Sir Wolstan Dixie, knight of Garter, JP, in connection with sorcery and witchcraft.
Devil's mark on part of body, invisible in daytime.
Do not tackle on your own, as she is armed and extremely dangerous.
5 shillings reward dead or alive.

There was a picture pretending to be me, showing a very mousey-looking girl with weasely eyes, if such a rodentiate mule be possible. Totally out of proportion from the rest of the artist's concept was what looked like a pair of steam puddings set out to storm the front of my blouse. Seeing yourself as other people see one is often not a pleasant experience, and I don't know which offended me most: the portrayal, the description, or the measly reward—not even a quarter of a guinea being offered for such a dangerous malefactor. Obviously there are items in my story which I have chosen to slide over, and when I have a moment will get down to telling you, but now I saw I had better make tracks quickly, unless I wanted to be whipped behind a cart on my way to Bridewell (that repulsive prison for reprobate women that stank of the dead dogs floating down the Fleet Ditch into the Thames) or, even more likely, hanged as a cutpurse.

I was yet a novitiate in the ways of the street, but intent on learning fast. First I had to find where was James Cameron MacPherson, whom I had lost sometime, somewhere, during the Great Fire of Sheepy, and missed more than my heart could tell. What was the meaning of his riddle? Quite soon after I arrived in the capital I discovered that the "Great When" was not a date but the Great Wen, a sobriquet for London Town. Likewise, when I recalled James's original plan to meet up with the great Dr. Johnson, he of the dictionary, I realized the "sham" was the Great Cham, an unofficial title assumed by the great man, and the Pineapple was the sign above the tavern he frequented.

When you are ensconced in the teeming center of the world's greatest city, nothing is far away, and if you are going away you are going nowhere. Or, in the well-known apothegm of the Doctor, "He who is tired of London is tired of life." But I digress. The Pineapple was merely two streets away from my hideaway. So one night, in order to take my mind off the impending event at Tyburn, I decided to call on this local, as dressed up as I was capable of in my poverty.

From the outside, the ordinary tavern did not appear much, certainly not what one preconceived as the greatest fermenting ground of the intellect since Plato set up his academy under the shade of the groves of Athens. Nor when I entered was the interior anything to write home about, except there were more cobwebs and dust than in most traveler's rests, and the landlady had that moody, don't-mess-with-me stamp to her features which seems to be the hallmark of mine hostesses up and down the kingdom. There were a few idlers at the bar, snuffling at their clay pipes and pewter tankards. Seeing me they perked up, for what with my mantilla and quilted farthingale, indeed my very feminine presence, I was a boon from heaven, as fodder for their low, common (but absolutely non-Johnsonian) mode of jesting.

I spied a young man sitting all on his own, moodily twiddling an empty glass, evidently out of pocket. "James!" I shouted, and ran towards him quite without dignity, bumping my flounced skirts against the surly customers.

"Amelia!" he cried in rapturous reply. "Marry come up! It's wonderful to see you." He gave me the most energetic hug, and at once I was transported back to my dear little Sheepy, and for some reason my innocent priggish nature made a brief reappearance. "Why, sir, we are not as yet betrothed!" Which was in a manner of speaking, "Hands off! No liberties if you please!"

"Oh, I do apologize." He unhanded me, but I laughed at my own dullness and stamped my feet.

"Oh, James!" And that was all. For now I cried and cried with pent up emotion and happiness. I swear, if one of those Fleet Street priests, who could have you married in minutes, was sitting at the table, Cameron and I would have been spliced in a trice. James grabbed me round the waist and tossed me about as if I were a woolen doll, till I was dizzy. His eyes were shining as if he were in Paradise Garden, and then he cried with floods of Gaelic tears that matched, I am sure, one of his dear highland burns in full spate.

"Some say you are being chased by bizarre treasure hunters for a curious scrap of paper that tells all the secrets of the universe, but I don't believe them. It would be a scrap of paper bigger than your father's Bible. Amelia, we have to get you out of here. There is a hue and cry afoot. You have thrown off the Bow Street Runners once, so they are going to make sure you don't escape them again. You have seen the notices?"

I nodded dumbly. Our joy was stifled at its outset.

"We must get you out of here quickly. They say you are a witch with a book of cabalistic spells and curses."

"But where shall I go now?"

"My dearest lass, 'tis not for now, but for much longer," he said with the saddest air.

The next morning we happened upon the Tyburn Oak, or rather the mob picked us up along the Edgeware Road and dragged us along in their tidal wave like poor wretches sucked to their doom by the Solway Current.

Neither of us was familiar with London, else we would have given that area a wide berth. As it was, we were on the spot to witness young Dick do his Gallows Jig. The scaffold itself, the old Tyburn Tree, was sited in the middle of a huge square, packed full of the most vile, high-smelling mob you've ever been downwind of, all in a convivial mood for the jollity of dispatching a fellow being. There were children twittering about like abandoned sparrows, or ferreting around in gangs of cutpurses—one stealing, the next passing the goods on, and the third absconding. That this was also a capital offence was cheerfully forgotten.

"Pies o' mutton, sweetmeats, mince pies!" A lady entrepreneur with brawny arms, a visage as swarthy as a Turk, and a moustache a cavalier might envy was bawling out aggressively in the midst of other criers, all vying to out-shout each other. Bloods and macaronis were hanging out of wayside inn windows, laying bets on how long each victim would twitch. Fancy coaches and chariots were parked in a ring; within were gents and ladies of quality arranging their dresses and fussing with their patches, rouge, and hairstyles. One lady bore an extraordinary coiffure: a man of war of the king's navy complete with masts, cannons, and figurehead. It would need an Archimedes to calculate how she would exit the coach, for it was like the ship in a bottle problem. But I'll no more harp upon this string, for now along came the final act.

There was no fancy coach for the culprits. A great cheer broke out when the cart containing the three wretches appeared. Each one was sitting on his coffin, a noose around his neck, while an unkempt priest read an uplifting text to which none paid a blind bit of notice, as the three were chatting to each other without any terror at their approaching doom.

Dick was in the middle, dressed in a fetching white outfit. On the scaffold he was very brave but pale-faced. His last speech was not bad, though delivered with a certain amount of stage nerves, understandable in the circumstances, as he steadied himself for being turned off by the New Drop. The crowd, sensing a brave 'un, gave him a rousing send off.

He looked around in the mob and, catching my eye, implored, "Pull my legs, Amelia," then leapt off the ladder. His neck made a crunching sound as he jerked on the rope. Immediately two rapscallions jumped out of the crowd and, seizing him round the knees, swung back and forth from those juddering limbs, making his last request unnecessary.

I should have done as he bid me. We had often joked about this saying and how, because of the occupational hazards of his profession, it was inevitable that I would have the last laugh on him, and laughingly I had promised to perform this humane but grotesque act. But on that day my blood was chilled, and my limbs refused to move forward. I knew any center stage movement of mine would bring out the bailiffs, so I stood back, denying Richard Farrell, a true gentleman, his proper valediction. I whispered to James to hide me, and then disappeared into the anonymity of the crowd. As a lover I was a disappointment, but as a coward I lived on.

Now I saw the truth of James's urgency concerning my departure. That evening we made shift to the Last Sight of England, an insalubrious dockland tavern noted for its quality of clientele, described by a connoisseur in these matters, Admiral Hood, First Lord of the Admiralty, as the scum of London, the flotsam and jetsam of Thameside. But if I wanted to escape the Runners it was no avail going to an assembly at Ranelagh Gardens or some lady's salon to sip chocolate while discussing Voltaire and Rousseau.

"One berth, one berth only, Mr. Sawney, that'll be fir the wench. Besides, I can't be doin' wi proscribed Jacobites on board. Nah, do ye want it or not? It's free for the winsome girl." This one-eyed, very villainous skipper looked me up, looked me down. "Aye, the artist hath caught you to the very tee." Thereupon I disliked him immediately, which should have put me on my guard, but I was young and foolish—how often we use that excuse. More to the point I was desperate to get out of the squeeze that I was in. I was in double trouble: hunted as a Jacobite and harried as a witch.

"And we sail on evening tide. I can see as you're in a hurry, lass. Ye've got Newgate stamped all over yer gizzard." Nor was our Palinurus one to inspire confidence; he had pirate written all over him, and I wasn't sure I might not be called upon to pay midway over the Atlantic, where a refusal to do the rascal's unsavory bidding might end me up deep in the drink, as supper for the sharks. But he was the *deus ex machina* that was going to get me out of this jam. One thing I had learnt in my accelerated education into the world was to let the future look after itself.

And now this odious villain, offering me free passage to the Indies (or was it the Americas), gave me a leer that would make Cleopatra shiver. My New World geography lessons had been deficient, and I had only the haziest picture of eagle-feathered savages and rum and molasses plantations, but I knew they was all well beyond the Sheepy Parish constable's long arm, so I accepted without seriously asking why this generous offer was mine and mine alone.

I had a last supper of bread and soup on Old England's soil, spoilt by my tears salting the hot liquid, and in two hours I was on board. Under the setting sun the Great Tower of London glowed with homely warmth, as if the very stones were saying, *come back, all is forgiven*, providing me with yet another moment of regret. Then the sun dropped behind the tower, whereupon the stony façade abruptly put on a chilly front, and I thought of Anne Boleyn.

As night fell the tide was in our favor, and we were slipping out of the Thames sea-road and into the channel. I had clung tightly to James on the dockside that evening, shedding a flood tide of tears, when he promised he would come to join me, but he made that promise with the jaunty assurance of one making a rendezvous to meet in the Pump Room at Bath, and secretly I wondered if that other siren, literature, was calling him back to London Town. I consoled myself with the known fact that Scotchmen display feelings as conspicuously as the heathen Redskins I was about to encounter.

CHAPTER 5

The Snowbird Legend

There was an insistent rustling on the deerskin fabric of the tepee, as if a hungry, straying fox was nuzzling around the village for fodder. An urgent whispered voice cleared up the mystery. Doe Eyes sighed and huddled herself beneath the blanket to try to bring back sleep, but in vain. Why did Little Rabbit pester her so early in the morning? She must know how much it annoyed her man, a brave not famous for the length of his temper. Almost as if he could echo her thoughts, Great Owl grunted, rolled from her side, and reaching from under the blanket, picked up a pot and hurled it at the wolfskin door. Lucky it did not contain the breakfast broth, Doe Eyes thought, and lucky it did not break, as it bounced harmlessly off the hide door to be smothered by a pile of soft skunk fur. The pot, a fine clay piece engraved with figures of warriors roistering and maids demurely fetching water, had been lovingly painted by Doe Eyes's great aunt, who was a weighty figure in the village and one of the rare female elders whose voice was heard in council. It was a wedding present. Her aunt was one of the few people in the tribe she feared. Explaining the breakage would make for an unpleasant interview.

"Come quickly, Doe Eyes. The whole town is all a flutter. Everybody is up! You're missing all the excitement!"

"Missing what?" Doe Eyes sleepily unknotted the tent flaps. She squinted out. The sun had not yet begun its ride across the sky, and the mist was still snaking tendrils round the tepees, *wigewas* and lodges. A heavy dew lay over every tent and cooking pot in the village, and even the dog watering the path had a damp look. A few cooking pots were bubbling over smoky, spluttering fires that were struggling to keep going. Most fireplaces were unlit as yet; their firing-up flints lay idle by cold ashes.

Doe Eyes yawned and then half rolled out of the tent. She squinted at the daylight still vying with the morning mist, then fell back in again to put on a fine doeskin tunic and a silky-smooth fox-fur coat, ostensibly to ward off the chill morning air, not forgetting to apply some paint to her face and a spot of soot to her eyelashes and brows. Who knows whom you might meet on the street in your morning promenade? Doe Eyes was not exactly vain, merely very careful. As the prettiest squaw in the town she had a reputation to maintain, and sure as the rain came from the sky, she meant to uphold it.

This little celebrity she enjoyed was the main reason that Little Rabbit was always pestering her to bond together as a blood sister by taking the bleeding ceremony. Still, Doe Eyes tolerated her adhesive friend. Why? There is always something enhancing about having a disciple, particularly one like Little Rabbit. Owning her was like having your own spy network. There wasn't an autumnal dried leaf crushed by illicit lovers that wasn't heard by her. Any back-tomahawking about Doe Eyes was reported as soon as uttered, so swiftly that any challenges to her position of tribal beauty could be rooted out before the pretenders had time to put on their daily war paint.

They had now reached the center of the village, a plaza lined by large beehive huts, the dwellings of the village quality, with a platform in the center fronted by a painted, stone-ringed fireplace for ceremonial bonfires. The whole area was dominated by a baleful totem pole, whose ferocious images were a persistent reminder of their ancestors' adherence to the tribal gods.

In English terms this was the equivalent of the mossy Saxon crosses in our marketplaces. Beyond this sacred precinct was the pomerium, a palisade of wooden stakes marking out the urban territory from the little agrarian area and the wilderness beyond. Her friend was right; most of the village was there: all the squaws certainly, plus a scattering of old men dotted about on the fringes of the crowd, sitting disconsolately in their blankets, wearing that uncomfortable look that men take on when in a place of women. All were silent, staring in astonishment at a singular spectacle.

In front of the platform stood a huge stranger, clad in a dingy sheepskin. Around his neck was what looked like a copper torque, but from close up showed itself as an angry red weal. Dangling underneath this scar was the cross of the White man's carpenter god. Above his moccasins were the absurd clerical gaiters of the pale-face witch doctors. A grey shaggy thicket of beard framed his face, but not even that curio could draw attention away from the eyes, the great, wide, staring eyes of the loner, one who had been out a thousand days in the wilderness. He was the enemy, a White Eyes, a *Shemanese*, but his skin was redder than any of the redskins, redder even than the pot hurled by Great Owl earlier. It was an angry redness, the red rash got by the paleskins exposing themselves to the copper sun, ready to burst out into great, watery blisters, while his body under the skin, utterly unlike any Indian's, was soft and podgy like an unhappy old squaw's. Nevertheless the man stared around without any fear or indication of pain. In his arms he was carrying a lumpy bundle of rags.

He spoke. It was in English, but an English totally at variance with the few White trappers and traders who cautiously approached the tribe's encampment. No one could understand what he said, but what he meant was unmistakable.

"I have been called many names but I stand before you, Lorenz Dow, castaway, preacher in the desert. Formerly I was abased and accused of the Devil's work by the Devil's spawn, lower than the lowest of the low Hypocritical Tremblers, but now cleansed by the wilderness, as was Our

Lord. I have seen the light and seek redemption amongst the heathen. If you wish to cook me into a stew, or put me to terrifying tortures to avenge yourself against the all-consuming White Eyes, now is your chance. I only ask one thing if I die. You!"—he suddenly stuck out his finger, shouting so defiantly that even some warriors started back—"Make sure a message is got through to a proper Englishman, no papistical rascal or American rebel, and tell them that I died an honorable martyr, worthy of an entry in Foxe's Book of Martyrs, or at the least a footnote. And that village in England which treated me so utterly shamefully, may it hang its head in shame."

Here he nodded toward his impromptu congregation and waited. No one moved. "So you are not going to eat me. I understand. Old meat is tough and stringy, and mine is all fat." He sighed as if disappointed, then returned to his main theme. "I have cut all ties with the Romanism, paganism, nonjurors, and popery which led me astray. To cleanse myself, I labored in the wilderness amongst thee, the heathen and the beasts of the field, like St. Anthony of olden time beset by wicked temptation." He pointed to the sad bundle of rags that lay in front of him. "This is she, the she devil! She who hath led me into temptation."

The bundle of rags, up till now mute and still, groaned croakily in the language of the *Yengeese*, the English. "I need a bath!"

The warriors made the sign to ward off evil, for here surely was the devil disguised in the shape of a paleface girl.

"Yea, though I live amongst the beasts of the field, yet I am no St. Francis, but liken unto John, who baptized in water not in the flesh of beasts!" His voice had risen thunderously, frightening the squaws. The braves stared stonily ahead. "My head has already been placed on a platter, and I give you Salome!" He pointed at the pitiful heap of rags, by no stroke of the imagination adding up to seven veils, which lay there woebegone, incapable of moving a muscle, far less striking a provocative dance. "Take her." He kicked the bundle toward the fireplace and strode off, swallowed up in the dark recesses of the forest whence he had come, and was seen no more. A legend had been born.

The bundle stirred and then coughed violently, stirring up some of the soot from the fire. It was a squaw, although it was difficult to make her out properly, for her hair was like a thorny bush in early springtime, and her skin like those who mined in the earth for flints. Under the muck and soot there was a veritable archipelago of running sores and bruises covering her skin, while her clothes were so tattered it was difficult to say if they were made for the back of the pale people or Indian. She pulled back her hair; the crowd saw the eyes of a hunted, frightened animal. Under the heap of muck and slatternly dishevelment, cowering and shivering in the cold embers, the women, always more discerning than any man, saw a beauty none of them could match. Suddenly a winter chill snapped at their bones. Her skin was ivory, as white as the elusive snowbird that slipped away silently every year, heading for the white mountains of the cold northlands. If she had not had the high cheekbones and the almond eyes of the purebred Indian, she might have been labeled Shemanese, White Eyes.

The squaws began searching around for cudgels to beat her, then sorted themselves into two parallel rows an arm's span apart, setting up the gauntlet, the traditional hostile reception for strangers. Two withered hags grabbed her and threw her down at the entrance to the line. Another old crone spat at her, and the dribble dangled on the end of the girl's matted hair like a slimy pearl, to be quickly joined by a volley of spittle. Under this fire the girl covered her head in the dust, her frame trembling with frightened tears. Doe Eyes, when she saw that skin the color of pale honey and the figure that was pure sculpture, knew her day was over. She picked up a hefty birch branch and marched toward the huddled figure intending to break bones.

The old chief, who had been watching silently from the back of the crowd, stepped forward. The crowd parted in silence. He stood behind the girl, facing the mob, and with his bare hands he wiped her face and shoulders. He stared at the silent, smoldering harpies; no one moved. Then he took the blanket off his shoulders and wrapped it round the girl in an unmistakable gesture.

"Touch this squaw, and you touch me. From henceforth she shall be my daughter. Ever since Little Petal died my lodge has been empty of the sound of laughter. My *neewa* is barren and no papooses spring forth from her loins. This"—he pointed at the inert heap lying beneath him—"is the answer to my prayers from the gods. The strange, bright fire-man who delivered her was truly the messenger of the Great Spirit, Wishemenetoo."

With that the great chief picked up the girl and carried her back to his lodge. Just as they passed Doe Eyes, the girl caught her eye; then, curling up in the chief's arms like a helpless lamb, she put her arms round his shoulders and gave him a simpering little buss on the cheek, while in the same blink of an eye she winked at Doe Eyes. This orphan of the storm was not without guile. Doe Eyes's heart sank into her moccasins. The chief turned toward the Furies. His face was as a stone as he intoned, "She comes as a stray bird from the pale winter country. She shall be called Snowbird." All the while village elders were clicking and shuffling thread-strung wampum beads into new alignments. Thus the chief's decree was properly recorded in the tribal annals.

Snowbird had no interest in the local braves, finding tedious their courtship ritual, which consisted of leaving a dead turkey outside her wigewa. This she was supposed to cook before carrying to the brave's lodge, symbolizing her acceptance of the proposal. Her adoptive father was forever complaining about having to dispose of their rotting corpses. "Why don't you just accept one of them before the great, fan-tailed bird becomes extinct?"

Irritated by unnumbered Lotharios pestering her, Snowbird dreamt up a scheme that would deter all but the most infatuated. She invited contenders for her hand to participate in a competition guaranteed to reduce the number of aspirant suitors queuing up outside her dwelling.

Beyond the village was a ragged, sawtooth mountain with a great bite snatched from its middle. In the center of this bite was a rock needle on which the morning sun rested. The crags were sharp and steep, hopelessly insurmountable. The one who climbed to the topmost pinnacle of this mountain, the Seneca Rocks, could claim her hand. This was enough to ensure perpetual spinsterhood, as no one had ever managed to scale this deadly precipice. Despite the dangers, many young-bloods took up the challenge, so instead of removing turkey carcasses from their lodge, her despairing father now collected the fallen bodies of battered braves for handing over to angry relatives. And instead of a befitting humility, the princess displayed an unpleasant arrogance when the funeral processions wound their way past her tepee.

Not unnaturally, since Snowbird was responsible for the whittling down of prospective husbands, the other squaws had taken against this outsider. Like smoke spiraling from a tiny spark amongst the crackling leaves that uninterrupted will destroy great forests, nasty rumors spread to account for the lightness of her coloring. Up till then it had been ascribed to her being the orphan of a *kitchokema*, a great chief from the great snow country beyond the forests in the North. Now it was whispered she had the pale skin of the White Eyes from across the mountains of the rising sun, who were destroying their hunting grounds (a rumor that dared not be spoken aloud except in murmurs in the forest). The squaws preferred to talk behind her back, for even without her exalted rank she was a formidable controversialist, and those who had tackled her in the past tended to retreat discomfited.

It was late spring. The first shoots of green had chased away the dull grey of winter, and the trees were heavy and ripe with leaf and blossom when a young man from over the hills and the great prairies of waist-high grasses, far away to the west, blundered into their territory in pursuit of game. He stumbled onto the edge of the river—a branch, a mere budding twiglet of the mighty Potomac that starts its seaward journey from these mountains. At this point the stream is a mere stripling, gamboling over rocks and trees in a spirited torrent, but here and there it slows down, catching its breath with a deer wallow, these little pools of calm, reflective water which provide superb bathing. The one in question, an oasis of azure under the spreading canopy of great oaks whose shade cooled the water, was the princess's favorite retreat. Snowbird, as was her wont, was bathing naked, and the snowy complexion of her skin was open for all of Mother Nature's creatures to delight in.

She was enjoying the cool waters, dappled by the lacy patterns of the leaves overhead which filtered the warmth of the sun, humming a little song and laughing to herself at her own private whimsy. What it was we cannot tell. We might guess it was over some poor infatuated fool falling off the rocks, but speculation would be unfair. The brave from across the Great Plains with the waist-high grasses stood transfixed. Never before had he seen such a creamily perfect body. Even being here was blasphemy, but he was unable to draw his eyes away, and he knew at that first smitten glance that his life had just embarked on a dark and dangerous passage, and his actions were fated as the heroes in a Grecian tragedy.

The boy moved forward. A twig crackled underfoot. The princess spun round in the water and caught sight of two black eyes staring out of the bushes. How dare this man spy on her! Her face turned dark with rage. The brave stepped forward, apologetically splaying his arms, and the girl stopped just as she was about to let fly a few choice words. This man was no skulking turkey-leaver. Here was a magnificent brave with a body hewn out of sturdy oak, with a face a princess might die for, and even his words of apology, though brief, were eloquent.

"I am very sorry," he said, and then stopped speaking, realizing the girl wasn't listening but staring abstractedly at him, as a stargazer watches the waxing and waning of the moon. No sooner had she taken him in, as slowly as the sun rolled over the great Blue Mountains, than it dawned on her what her spoilt little life had been missing…a feeling, an emotion she could not name. When she later recounted her morning adventure to her intimate companions, she said it was as one with the sun's first light exploding onto the blossom of a cornflower. They informed her that she was suffering from a malady for which there is no known cure. The heartless princess was lovestruck.

Quickly Snowbird sank beneath the surface of the pool to cover her shame, but the water was so clear that no contour of her body was spared. Like a diaphanous night rail the blue-green tint added enticement to enchantment, irresistibly compelling the young buck to dive into the pool, an impertinence that normally would have earned him a tomahawk cleft across his skull. But today the princess, equally afire, swam round him in circles, leading him on as if she were an enticing minnow. The more they swam the smaller became the circumference of the circles, until they were swallowing tongues in the center of the pool, bobbing up and down from surface to depths.

After a while they had to stop to catch their breath. They stared at each other till, realizing the magic of the moment could not go on forever, the boy asked her name before introducing himself. Nookeesa had a sunny, relaxed smile and a charmingly amusing way with himself. They were just at that first exciting stage of getting to know each other—Snowbird telling him in an animated way about the turkey mountain outside the *takatchemoke* wigewa, Nookeesa lying that he had never seen a naked squaw before and could he have another glimpse at her *massih,* to which impertinence she was playfully slapping water over his face—when a hunting party, happening to pass by the pool, burst through the undergrowth and saw them. Naturally they assumed the worst.

The hunters stood aghast on the strip of wet sand before the deer wallow, their moccasins slowly sinking in the mud, all spears pointing at the malefactor before shouting in unison, "This is forbidden! This is the gravest sacrilege! Who is this outsider who despoils our naked princess? He is *cut-ta-ho-tha*! Marked for death." Three of them leapt into the pool and floundered toward the brave. He was too slippery for them, squirming away like a slippery fish and, with a prodigious leap, bounding out of the river. But within a spear's length the stranger tripped over a root, allowing one of the hunters to smack him on the back of the head with a stone-bladed tomahawk, a *casse-tête*. They dragged the unconscious brave, dripping blood, clear of the poolside, and bound him with leather strips on the sandy bank. One of them said, "Make the knots very tight. He is slippery." Snowbird was screaming, "He is not cut-ta-ho-tha! He honors me more than the turkey killers. He is mine! He will be my *wahsiu*, husband." She stamped her foot like the spoilt child she was. "And I want him!"

"No, little pretty princess, this is way beyond your reach. He must die! The Great Spirit has spoken many times about the fate of strangers seeing that which is forbidden!"

"But he just happened by."

"So he just happened to pop into the princess's pool? That's what they all say, Highness." They laughed with the throaty, judgmental laugh of the pious on Sundays.

After tying up Nookeesa, the hunters frogmarched him naked through the village before throwing him into the sacred council house to lie on hard earth softened by clean patches of straw. The pious worthies, muttering ritual responses to ward off malignant spirits, tightened his bonds by dipping them in vinegar. The pain of the knots cutting into his wrists kept him awake all night. Finally they tied a thong round his neck, attaching it to one of the chamber's pillars. During the long night he was constantly fed deer meat and rum, and the calumet pipe given to him was constantly filled with the sweetest *kinnikinnick* the village had blended: everything as laid down by tribal custom, the traditional Last Supper for the condemned. Two squaws attended to him on every watch, for it was feared that one alone might take pity on the handsome prisoner and release his bonds.

It was a chilly, damp daybreak when he was hauled out in front of the council of elders, without even a blanket to mask his nakedness. In view of the spectacular nature of the case the council house was packed. Notwithstanding the heat exuded by the great crush of humanity, the ground was still damp, and the morning chill penetrated every corner of the great lodge. The elders felt it in their bones, and could be heard blowing warm breath into their cupped hands. The first hour was spent lighting up the calumet and passing it around in formal ceremony, the old men wrapped in their blankets, staring at the prisoner. The blank intensity of their gaze would cow any prisoner, and even Nookeesa, as brave as any, felt his spirits wavering against those eyes that held no pity. He was bound hands behind back and attached to a stake driven into the ground by a long leash like a dog.

When the trial began, Snowbird testified that it was purely by chance that they met at the pool. The lad, wanting to cool off after a long journey, leapt into the stream, and it was only at this point that he noticed her. The pool here was so narrow they could hardly avoid having a conversation. All else was pure invention and overwrought imagination on the part of the hunting party. The elders, who in their long lives had experienced similar encounters, nodded sagely, the smoke from their pipes dancing lightly in the air, softening the severity of the moment. But then she went on.

"They were all envious because they had never had the opportunity of seeing such beauty as mine," she said haughtily, tossing the magnificent black mane of hair over her shoulder. "Their squaws are all shapeless cows, bloated by childbirth!" An angry murmur arose from the hall. The foolish princess had overplayed her hand, completely throwing away the sympathy of the tribe. A quick discussion ensued, out of which it was determined that the intruder be put to death for defiling the royal person. There was no dissension.

The judgment of doom was pronounced. It was ordained that he who had committed a blasphemy would be tortured with pegs driven into this chest before being burnt at the stake. There could be no exceptions to the ruling laid down by the tribal ancestors. Nookeesa showed no emotion, even though his bowels ran cold with terror. Snowbird screamed with horror, ran up to her father, and pleaded for Nookeesa's life, saying nothing shameful had happened, that they were just getting to know each other, and they just happened to be in the water. There followed an old-fashioned argument familiar to any father who has indulged his pretty princess and lived to regret it, and to any daughter who has had to butter-up an old-fashioned parent.

"What's wrong with him?"

"We don't like strangers making themselves free with our daughters, especially the daughter of a chief, who must be above suspicion. That's what's wrong with him."

"He wasn't shaming me. We were just getting acquainted, honest!"

"Honest?"

"Honest." She made him a set of melting eyes that even the stern patriarch couldn't resist. "Anyway, why do you want to kill the first boy I really like?"

"Why don't you like the men of the village? Why do you have to look over the hills and valleys for your own precious stallion?"

"Because they are all dull, and their only wit is laughing at your feeble jokes, while he is new; he is exciting." At that point the girl beat on the old man's chest, and with a wheedling simper added, "And strong like you!"

"I wish you had a mother. I am sure she would know what to make of you."

"Daddy, you know I lost my mother far away across the mountains a long time before I met you, who have been father and mother to me."

She was spoiled of course, the apple of her stepfather's eye, and would get away with murder if she cajoled enough. In the end the chief, who had the casting vote, spoke with the dignity of a monarch and the eloquence of a word wizard, reminding the elders that her method of selection of suitors, or rather their elimination, was depopulating the village of the lifeblood of the nation, braves, who would be essential when it came to the inevitable trial of strength with the *Englishmanake*, which promised to be a far more pressing problem than that of espying a naked squaw. Surely they had all had forbidden glimpses of buttocks when the women were defecating in the morning. If her daughter married this bold young man, who seemed a worthy addition to the tribe, then this problem would be settled, and the stench of rotting turkeys would be removed from his lodge. His voice went up a pitch at this point as he spoke with feeling. It was a subtle speech, eloquently teasing out their minds to make them forget their former ire, and flattering in that it drew on their combined sagacity to conquer their anger. Snowbird's father, Seneca, was not the kitchokema, the great chief, for nothing. The old men puffed their pipes and nodded approbation. Seneca had made some excellent points, but still there was the tribal law to consider.

It was the youngest elder who came up with a compromise. "Let the young brave be no longer cut-ta-ho-tha. Let him seek his bride under the same rule as our braves. Let him try to ascend the mountain. If he fails, which is the most likely outcome, he will die. Justice will have been done according to tribal law, and the Great Spirit appeased. If he succeeds it will be *unsoma,* an omen of good fortune; the lad will make a worthy addition to our warrior band, and the chief's headache with his willful daughter will be relieved." And that was the speech that finally carried the day.

So the young Nookeesa was suffered to live with the proviso that he undergo the rock-climbing test. In vain Snowbird pleaded for him to be excused, saying he wasn't a local, therefore wasn't aware how dangerous it was courting her. But the stern old chief, who had counted coup a hundred times, knew he couldn't get this one past the council, and she could beat on his chest and give him cow eyes till kingdom come, but the tribal law was inflexible. When this failed, she pleaded that Nookeesa had got blisters on the way over the mountains, and the sharp rocks would impair his climbing style, so the trial of skill would be unjust, but old Seneca was as unmoved as the rocks that bore his name. However he did manage to hear a plea for an adjournment. Nookeesa would be given a month to live in the village, allowing time for his feet to heal, to check out the configuration of the cliff face, and to see whether the village life suited him and vice versa. Most importantly it would test whether Snowbird would not weary of him, as in the past her affections had been short lived.

In the meantime, the stranger had to undergo the trial of the gauntlet, as did any intruder into the village. All the disaffected suitors and jealous squaws lined up, armed with the heaviest clubs they could find, to give him the sound thrashing he deserved. Some were especially sore, as they had been deprived of the spectacle of burning at the stake. Nookeesa calmly looked at the crowd sadistically screaming for blood, then did the most astonishing thing that impressed all. Instead of running through the clubs raining on top of him, he nonchalantly strolled down that tunnel of hatred, gazing directly into the eyes of the maddened beaters, some of whom shied away from his eyes and lowered their clubs. For the most part the blows still came hammering down in torrents, but many of those who had come to beat him ended up by praising him, clacking their clubs together in applause, and the running of the gauntlet ended as a triumphal march through an archway of clubs held aloft in salute. Nookeesa had made his first good move.

The day of the mountain trial was eagerly awaited by the whole village as a well-earned respite from the toil of their daily lives. There would be feasting and dancing fueled by kegs of *tizwaz* and flasks of rum sold illegally by one of the few White traders to visit the village. All the villagers were rooting for Nookeesa. He was a handsome, likely lad, who had made himself popular with all in a very short time. Besides, if he was successful he might take away the arrogant madam to his wigewa beyond the hills, and it would be good riddance to her, her airs, and her tantrums. But now, to add to the drama, another had entered the lists, making the ascent a race to the death.

CHAPTER 6

The Mystery of the Unloved Stranger

Nookeesa's name was Chippewa for "swift waters," a tribute to his swimming proficiency, but his opponent, blessed with the unfortunate name of He-Who-Makes-Skunks-Run-Away (usually shortened to He-Who), said the name Nookeesa referred to the volume of water passed by the youth. "For he fills a cooking pot every sundown."

This disliked, unwashed brave, eking out his existence somewhere out on the fringes of the village where the pi-dogs snuffled through piles of steaming garbage, had been captured in a raid on another tribe from beyond the Great Lake of the Winter, Lake Erie. He hung around lodge fires till chased away, but occasionally some pitying soul gave him scraps the camp dogs had spurned. Nobody wanted him, not even as a slave, but he wouldn't leave even when the squaws threw piss pots at him. In the end they accepted him as a necessary blight, a shibboleth to help ward off the smallpox, which was currently raging through the Red man's settlements. In time the most abused squaws accepted him as one of theirs, and they let him help wash the dishes in the creek, clean the latrines, and fetch wood and water. But when he attempted to join hunting expeditions, the braves laughed and threw mud at him.

"Wae! Offal stench, you would frighten the animals away." When they went on the warpath, he was allowed to collect dispatched arrows, and they went so far as to give him a special quiver for his harvest. "Stay way back, for we cannot fight when you sicken us." But fire the arrows? No! Although sometimes they pushed him into the front line in the expectation that his odor would repel their Mingo enemies. No one was exactly sure why he was there, but then, no one cared.

His home was a sad lean-to down by the river's edge, where the smell of animal dung mingled with his unwholesome bouquet. If you happened to go down to the river bank in the evening and chanced upon him, you might hear him muttering to himself in a tongue unknown to any Indian from the Blue Hills, or to the Dutch or English trappers who occasionally passed by when following the beaver. Some said it sounded French, but the voyageurs who canoed down the river when the leaves fell said that if it was French it was the strangest pidgin they had heard, and no, they didn't understand *rien*.

The stranger remained a mystery because no one was interested enough to delve any further into his origin. Eventually stories sprang up. One French trapper recognized the patois and said that it was French, although of a barbarous kind that would jar on the ears of the *habitués* of the salons of Paris.

In fact, the outcast was a Creole from the islands, offspring of a mulatto and an indifferent plantation owner, who had given away the unwanted child to a band of pirates. After a while these brigands, realizing they had no use for him, threw him into the sea. Instead of being eaten by sharks, the unfortunate found a floating spar and clung onto it for grim life, for oddly enough, those who have least to hope for from life are often the most tenacious in keeping hold of it.

A favorable tide then beached the boy somewhere in the Carolinas, where he was chanced upon by seekers of rare seashells, much sought after as currency. Believing such a being washed up so mysteriously must be in possession of powerful magic, they took him into their bosom, fed him, fattened him up, and gave him his very own temple. In short, they adopted him as their tribal god, but after a couple of indifferent harvests and trouncings by neighboring tribes, they sold him off in disgust as a slave to another group of wandering Indians.

The bad harvests continued. The luckless tribe was reduced to eating slimy blackened potatoes fried up with grass, and the remnants of the tribe were virtually massacred by their neighbors. The survivors quickly repented of their precipitate action, and frantic efforts were made to find the god they had so sacrilegiously expelled, but he had slunk off into the wilderness, and from there, after more misadventures, he ended up in the Seneca village.

The unpleasant aroma of which the Indians made great noise was the exhalations of some desiccated pomanders, manufactured at Chantilly, which he had managed to hold on to through thick and thin and whiffed at every occasion; although getting fainter every day, it was a means of clinging to the tattered dreams of what might have been. But don't believe everything you hear, even when it is in small print. I learnt later that this outcast among outcasts had as many fantastical antecedents as great chiefs had feathers in their war bonnets.

On one memorable occasion, after hitting the tizwaz pretty hard, he was afire to boast, and pounced on a luckless brave casually walking around the township, pounding him on the chest, saying, "The father of the despised He-Who was a Franco-Italian noble of the highest blood, a trusted courtier at the court of Bonny Prince Charlie, the heir apparent to the throne of Britannia in Rome and Versailles." The captured Indian, enduring this fantastic rubbish, nodded frantically, with ne'er a clue what he was talking about, at the same time peering around to see if there was a way he could slip through the tepees to escape. "What is more, he was entrusted with the Secret of the Stewarts, that is to say he stole the only copy of it from Charles's room when the prince was in his cups."

Vainly trying to suppress a yawn, the Indian felt compelled to ask, "So what is this great secret you talk on about?"

"The great elixir of love and life. Take one mug-full every night, and you will live as a youthful brave till you are a hundred, and your totem pole will be firm and a formidable delight for the ladies, never bending nor wilting."

"Bit awkward in the daytime. And how come, if you are such a great ladies' man, the squaws all throw piss pots at you? And furthermore, why, if you are such a blue-blooded nobleman, are you living in this pissy little Indian village with leaky thatched roofs, and not in your precious Versailles? Now, let me out of the way before my squaw beats me up for forgetting to put meat on the table." So saying he pushed his way past He-Who and departed.

The brave missed out on the most enthralling part of the outcast's alternative biography, whereby his father was found out stealing the recipe, had the parchment ripped out of his hands, so he was left only with the bottom third, then further blotted his copy book by getting caught between the blankets with the mistress of the Cardinal of Lorraine, whereupon his departure from the court was swift. Shortly thereafter he was sentenced to be a galley slave in King Louis XV's Mediterranean fleet. The galley was captured by Barbary pirates, and the outcast's father was given the choice of joining the crew or walking the plank. It was hardly a difficult choice for a man of so few scruples, so he joined and swiftly rose in the ranks to become first mate. In this capacity he was allowed to swive a beautiful, captive Creole noblewoman over the taffrail before she was thrown to the sharks. But in their brief conversation prior to the act, he took a distinct fancy to the lady, and held at bay with his cutlass the rampant crew insisting on their turn. Wisely, I think, the captain allowed her to be kept on board, declaring her the rightful property and plunder of the first mate, and the result of that tryst was none other than our outcast. None of which spared her from spending her leisure time scrubbing the decks.

But of course nobody was prepared to believe such palpable nonsense, even after hearing how the pair married and lived happily ever after on a fine estate in the West Indies, till that unhappy day when pirates made off with their only child, the now strapping He-Who. But then why should they believe him, for He-Who made up stories of royal courts, and other fantastical fairy tales, such as his lectures on the magical properties of queen bee honey, to which only the trees bore witness, and he boasted he could speak Gullah, French Creole, Italian, and several Indian dialects. (He also claimed to speak Magyar, Russian, and German, but to assert this would stretch the indulgent reader's already strained credulity too far.) Nor did they learn that he was there in the village for a purpose. Through the pioneer's grapevine came a tale of a White woman in this valley who was in possession of the Great Formula of the Stewarts. There was only one White woman in the Seneca valley: the recently adopted chief's daughter, so pale of complexion she was called Snowbird.

Even this outcast dared to dream, and dream he did of the unattainable. He had caught sight of the Princess Snowbird, gorgeously accoutered with bells and buckskin fringes, strolling round the encampment with her retinue. One glance at her and he was smitten. So to the profit motive was added amour, strong enough to risk life and limb on the cliff face. But it was a sorrowful, painful love, for he realized right away that this creature of paradise would never be for the likes of him, the despised outcast. Since then he had harbored an unhealthy passion for the princess, and made a totem pole every night in his pit to the image of the girl.

The advent of Nookeesa, however, afforded him an entrée. If foreigners could try for her hand, the logic of tribal law now determined, so might social rejects. And He-Who felt that he, the despised dark horse, had a good chance of taking the prize, for he had dreamt up a devious way of downing his rival and winning without taking too many risks. He put his name down as a candidate for the princess's hand in the time-honored fashion, standing in front of her father's lodge and howling at the moon. After waking up all the neighbors, he threw down a rotting turkey he had pinched from another brave's wigewa, then strode off into the dark, kicking the feral dogs out of the way, subtly adding to the general cacophony. The princess, when she heard about his challenge, gave a dismissive cry of "Pfoof!", thought no more of it, and ignored him more than ever when they passed in the street.

CHAPTER 7

A History of Early Mountaineering in North America

The night before the ordeal, Nookeesa heard something creeping into his tent. Whatever animal it was actually snuggled up to him under his musk-rat blanket. Was it a raccoon, a fox, or, judging by the way it slithered, a poisonous snake? Slowly his hand inched toward his tomahawk. He grasped the haft and slowly raised it up, ready to strike. The snake was wrapping itself round his nethers. Wait! It was warm and soft, and moving deliberately toward his member. If it bit that off, there would be little point in entering the contest. Poising the blade carefully, he brought it down stealthily to mark the target, raised it again. Now!

There came a girlish giggle from under the blanket when an unequivocal warm mouth was applied to his arousal. "So, this is how you welcome your lover, with a casse-tête, when I come to give you my all?" she gurgled merrily. "You who are prepared to perish for the sake of our love."

Nookeesa muttered a relieved curse.

"I am making an equal sacrifice on the altar of true marriage."

Nookeesa nodded, well aware the penalty for adultery was death.

"At the very least you could make an investment in the future of our family, even if you are not present at its realization."

This took a bit of working out, but realization brought a chilling reminder that put Nookeesa off. "I cannot take advantage of your compliance," he said rather stuffily.

"You think spurting your essence into me will weaken you?"

"No, I have enough and to spare, for I am a true warrior, but I will not because honor forbids mingling of flesh and fluids before marriage."

She wept. She sighed and even turned slightly nasty, revealing her true colors for the first time. "No true Indian would refuse. Have you been preached at by the missionary White Eyes's god in a bun? They alone are particular about this marriage sacrament." Presumably she had sampled a pioneer's hot cross bun at some time, thus creating an instant but errant theology, which included a fitful grasp of the doctrine of transubstantiation.

The Chippewa laughed, tucked in his breech-clout on top of his torrid lover's testicles (for the princess really was delectable), and went outside to be at one with the voices of the night. The water from his proud phallus made a great arching fountain, and his steam rose up to mingle harmoniously with the rest of the nocturnal moistures.

"*Ohehwa*!" From the watered bush there came a muttered imprecation. Nookeesa went back to his tent thinking the gods of the place had given their blessing to his knightly quest, but it was He-Who, jealously spying on the lovers, who had been subjected to the warm spray, which the village elders later pronounced as poetic justice for his *pockva-no-madee-way*: name-calling.

The day of the trial could not have been more splendid. Early mist evaporated in a weak, pale-pink sunshine that triumphed over the fog and blazed its bountiful gifts over the tepees and lodges, encouraging the villagers to come out early, while the dew glistened in the grass and the river shimmered and burbled over the smooth grey stones of the streambed. Nearly everyone turned out for the event, apart from a few carping old widows whose bones refused to move and the inevitable brave crippled in the never-ending clan fighting (who was left behind and ignored, as was the normal run of things), for the climb provided a break in the seasonal grind of the village, a sleepy backwater not normally given to fiestas. There were cheers for Nookeesa, for even though an outsider, he was physically brave, with an easy, open personality. The two contenders placed corn stalks in front of the totem pole to appease the spirits of the mountain. He-Who was greeted by a hail of buffalo dung chips hurled at him. He did not care. Years of being a social outcast had made him immune to insult. Also, he had refined and tested his plan so thoroughly that his confidence was strong.

Old Seneca gave his benediction: "Great Spirits, bless these thrice-brave braves. May he who has the heart of a mountain lion, the swiftness of a gazelle, and the suppleness of a squirrel win the hand of my beautiful daughter, whose beauty is like that of the great snow mountain, which lies beyond the setting sun, and who like the mountain is just as daunting to approach, and will not help the maid with the pots and pans." A swift, icy glance from the aforesaid maiden cut short this line of eulogy. "May he who is not quite so neat or swift of foot tumble to a swift and honorable death. May his tepee in the land of the sky be filled with beautiful, ghostly squaws, who equal the living one in beauty but surpass her in obedience." The ambivalence of his send-off puzzled the audience, leaving them not quite clear whom the old chief thought was going to get the best of the bargain.

They were on their marks. Both carried round their shoulders ropes of strong twine to slide down from the summit. Tension rippled through Nookeesa's frame as he knelt on the starting stones. He-Who appeared to the onlookers almost recklessly nonchalant. A blanketed old man, who wore his cheek scars with pride and who had counted coup many times, turned to his neighbor, saying, "The evil smelling one wears the smirk of the cat that has slurped up his brother's cream."

His friend nodded. "Count not your scalps before the battle." They both nodded sagely, their pipes bobbing up and down in step. At the very least He-Who had the advantage of being on his own ground, and through months of watching the suitors plunge to their deaths, he was able to exactly pinpoint the crucial spot where they all fell off: a jutting overhang about an arrow's flight below the summit. Most, even the clumsy oafs who tripped over the squaws' cooking pots, could manage to make it to that point. Trick his way past there, and the princess and all her goods, chattels, and secret formulae for the elixir were his.

A tomahawk flung by the Great Chief, the sachem, thudded into the ground, and they were off. They started at a lung-bursting gallop, but after a short sprint slowed down to the steady trot of the long distance runner. Simultaneously they hit the icy waters of the upper Potomac in parallel racing dives; swiftly surfacing, they swam like sleek otters, then waded the last section to the bank, the broiling white waters churning through their thighs plowing onward in an energy-sapping sprint. Both threw themselves gasping on the further bank, slurped down some water, filled up their leather water bags, then, standing on the flat stones at the water's edge, hands on their knees, they gasped and forcefully sucked in their frantically hammering breaths before beginning the arduous climb up the steeps.

Nookeesa was the first to get started again, scrambling over boulders, through tangled undergrowth, and into the trees. The outcast grabbed at Nookeesa's legs, pulling him to the ground before kicking him and taking the lead. Nookeesa leapt up, following in hot pursuit, now about five paces behind the leader. He desperately tried to keep pace, even while gasping and doubled up in pain from the kick. His opponent, though at first glance weedy-looking, was fit, fast, and wiry, the fiery spirit of the fed-up loser providing that extra kick. Through pine and beech trees and jumbled boulders the size of houses they ran, slipped, and slithered. Nookeesa was passing a decaying oak when a dagger flew by him, grazing his head and almost ripping off his ear before thumping into the wood. The searing pain made him stagger back, and an involuntary cry escaped from his lips. He-Who scampered upward, steadily widening the distance between them; soon the morass of impenetrable forest and foliage hid him from his pursuer.

Nookeesa collapsed on a boulder, his chest pumping and wheezing like a bellows. He was lost. Up above were a number of possibilities: rills of old watercourses and shallow gullies. He plumped for the one directly in front of him, and after scrambling up fifty feet, his way was blocked by a thicket of brambles. He slid back down on his backside, his buttocks cut and bruised by the rough earth and rocks. He was back at square one. Where to go next? In his mind he saw his enemy sitting smugly on the summit block. If he picked the wrong route he might as well give up the chase. He sat down and considered. He-Who wasn't so far ahead. He could hear him cursing and shouting, so he too must have lost the way, and was blocked in a thicket of some plant with razor sharp thorns that stuck to him like an unhappy lover. There were a few more minutes of thrashing about futilely by both parties, but then the immediate problem of follow-my-leader was solved when the outcast leapt out at him from the bushes, his body ripped and torn from the brambles, his face contorted by savage desperation. Even Nookeesa's sculpted body, the very icon of the noble savage, was disfigured by scratches and scars. They glared at each other, their breath coming out like horses galloping.

Slyly Nookeesa outlined his scheme. "Listen, outcast, our quarrel is not with each other but with the mountain. If we fight to the death here, even the winner will not be strong enough to climb the slick rocks. We need every last ounce of strength to deal with the demon that lives on the summit. If not, both of us will be the losers; only the spirit of the mountain will triumph, and the wench, our prize, will remain triumphantly smug and virginally untampered, and will have a good laugh at us. What is more, a new generation of poor lads will needlessly fling away their lives while she sits in her palatial wigewa, laughing her head—and other more interesting body parts—off. Let us go our separate ways, and let fate and climbing skill alone decide. If both of us survive then let us tussle on the summit, and the champion may throw the loser to his death on the spiky rocks, and grind the arrogant bitch to kingdom come."

The outcast thought about it, and like everyone else making a pact with the devil suspected mischief, and like everyone else reckoned he could in the last resort play dirtier than the other. "Agreed," he said, and no sooner spoken than he began scrambling up the rock, eager to gain every second, every inch of advantage. Nookeesa followed closely, letting He-Who do all the hard work of pioneering through the brambles. They scrambled over scree that slid as soon as a moccasin was placed on it, and through waist-high foliage they plowed separate paths that slowed them down considerably. The outcast quickly got wise to Nookeesa's sly strategy, so he deliberately hung back and sneaked in behind him. Lying in second place meant using far less energy in battling the bushes. Nookeesa tried giving him a kick, but the outcast pulled back out of range and laughed.

Finally they arrived at a broad flat rock separating the forest from the vertical rocks. To their front, like a giant fortress rising out of the earth, towered the summit buttress of the mountain, impregnable and unyielding. Gasping and panting, they glared daggers at each other. To their right the rocks were still vertical but rent by a stony chimney wide enough for a man to squeeze in and haul his way upward. This seemed to be the way to the top. However, their boldness had been preceded by a subtle mix of caution and thorough planning. Both had made a secret reconnaissance of the route and knew that the apparently easy way up was a cul-de-sac blocked by an impossibly exposed wall. Both had seen hapless braves fall off from that spot.

The twin competitors had prepared themselves well for the ordeal. They wore soft deerskin moccasins whose soles gripped the rocks like barnacles on a fishing vessel. In their training on lower crags they had learned to rely on balance rather than hauling themselves up by main force. Now their chests were rippling in and out like taut tribal drums. The competitors stared at each other as if hoping the other would give away the secret.

It was He-Who who broke the silence. "There is only one way up. One path. One warrior goes alone. If two warriors go they will meet again sooner than expected in the great hunting ground."

"Well spoken, but if I go first, you'll pull my feet away to win."

He-Who said, "We can sit here arguing the toss forever, meanwhile the princess, eager for her wedding night, might lose patience and choose another groom with less fuss."

"An excellent point. Why do you speak good sense when you are such an awful fellow."

"Hah! Why do we not smoke a pipe on this weighty matter?" He-Who fetched out a pouch of tobacco and a long calumet. "Let us relax and consider while the village gets restless." Far below the villagers were milling about in confusion. Like spectators at any blood sport they wanted an outcome, one way or another. He-Who coughed decorously. "We could both go down and tell the princess to—"

"And both of us would be shooed out of the village forever as pariahs," replied Nookeesa.

"You can get used to it," said He-Who dryly. Then, clicking his fingers decisively he said, "Why don't we lead alternately, making a bond of blood that we will not trip the other, and it does not matter who goes first on the last pitch, for that is where we die. I go first: I have a chance of winning, but then I fall off, and you see where I went wrong and make no mistake, so you can rejoice tonight in your nuptial lodge with your shining reward."

Nookeesa could see the sense in this and nodded. "You have pondered wisely. But how do we decide who gets first lead?"

He-Who picked up a stone, put his hands behind his back, then held out his fists. "Pick!"

Nookeesa's fingers did a quick dance before choosing the empty hand.

"He-Who goes first, first."

The pariah attacked the rock with determination. On his training excursions he had learnt how to jam his hand in the cracks. He trod as lightly as the panther waiting in the tree, balancing on his toes, his moccasin slippers licking round nodules of roughened rock so small they were just visible to the naked eye. He made good progress till the final obstacle; an overhanging block as big as a tombstone glowered over him. He bridged out—his feet balanced on either side of the crack, making use of tiny corrugations to support him—and thrust in a hand jam, pulled on it diffidently, then quickly reversed the move as his hand, slimy with sweat, was slipping out. He reversed back down till he reached a precarious resting place. He-Who was sucking in air, his heart thumping like war drums; he swiped his hand on his breech clout and went at the rock again, pulling with his left hand on the sharp vertical edge of the block. His legs lost contact with the boulder and he was swinging vertically, his arms straining to hold himself on. He made a grab for the top of the block, pulled up; his legs regained contact with rock, but now were shimmying and shaking. He quickly pulled over, then swarmed and shuffled like a sea lion on top of the boulder till safely settled on the ledge. Relaxed, he looked down, smiling smugly. "C'mon then, favored one, let's see you do it."

So the truce was short lived, Nookeesa thought as he clambered up. He had watched every move of his rival and copied them. Yet he was nowhere near as smooth-footed as He-Who. His legs were beginning to quiver like a plucked bowstring, and his fingers were turning from bone to butter.

"Take a look down now." Nookeesa was at the tricky move where his legs were swinging free; without thinking he looked. As far as a hawk could fly without alighting there was nothing but air beneath him. He panicked, puffing and panting, but then taking a firm grip on his nerves and forcing himself not to look down again, he grabbed the top of the block and swung over the obstacle resolutely. However, in doing so he clasped each hold so tightly that he was totally spent. Nookeesa flopped onto the platform like a salmon swept up onto a riverbank, his arms and legs quivering as they had never done in the most ferocious battle. He lay for a while to recover his composure. Fortunately his pitch was a mere stroll across a ledge. Even so he took his time and was extra wary whenever he was forced to make an exposed move across one of the rocks.

Another difficult groove faced the pariah, but he secured his first handholds firmly, placed his feet confidently, and flitted up the ragged crack as elegantly as a dancer. His opponent watched, desperately trying to commit every move to memory, noting that there was only sheer rock on either side of the crack. But the brave, instead of hugging the rock for security, leant back so that his weight was comfortably on his toes, and instead of making long strenuous strides he took little steps, using every wrinkle and cranny to proceed upward, rocking his body weight over every new hold while his hands were used to maintain balance not haul himself up, all done with a smooth, unhurried, upward rhythm. Nookeesa couldn't match him for style or grace, but he overcame the pitch by sheer determination, fearfully trembling at every move till he pulled himself heavily onto the stance.

They were now on a platform broad enough to support a large wigewa. Their vantage point was superb. Down below, the river snaked in and out of the trees, murmuring gently as it romped gaily over the stony shallows to debouch into the emerald pool where Nookeesa and Snowbird first met. A tomahawk flight farther brought fields of Indian corn surrounding the village, rippling in the faint breeze, making a ring of gold as in a Byzantine icon, which set off the brightly colored lodges and wigewas of the band. The whole village was out waving and cheering on both contestants. Belatedly they recognized the daring of the outcast. In the background the Appalachian hills, soft, indistinct, but beautiful in the morning haze, stretched into a blue infinity.

Nookeesa waved down at the onlookers before turning to face the challenge in front. The way ahead was blank except for a huge, moon-shaped crack so prominent it could clearly be seen from the ground. He looked to the left—nothing. To the right were some faint holds, but they faded out into the abyss. So it must be the crack, although its outer walls were bare. The outcast was studying Nokeesa's face for signs of fear, then he grinned again, and in a mockery of a White man's courtly bow bade him proceed.

Nookeesa went up a few feet. His hands and feet shuffled around indecisively. He-Who was sitting calmly, enjoying his pipe, as if he was watching an exhibition of tribal dancing. "This is where many braves fail," he observed chattily, a remark that did not ease the other's fears. Nookeesa put his hands in the crack and leaned out so he could see what lay ahead, and to get a spot of leverage he pressed his feet high on the opposite wall. That was easily done! Tentatively he tried again, and by sliding his hands up the crack and shuffling his feet up the wall, he found he could move easily. Toward the top his left hand was getting sweaty and slowly slithering out of the crack. He looked down, panicked, and lashed out at a hold on the lip. Swoosh! His feet went from under him! Frantically he threw his right hand over the top of the crack. He scrabbled about. There was nothing there! Then magically his hand caught a root. No time to wonder if it would hold him. He pulled with the last of his strength at the plant and swung his feet into the crack. They jammed; they held. A moment to grab his breath, and he hauled himself onto a ledge choked with tree roots and flakes of rock. His heart was thudding so loud he thought his chest would burst.

The outcast leisurely tapped out his pipe and, copying Nookeesa's method, ambled up the pitch with annoying ease, neatly skipping up the wall. However, he admitted, "You set a cunning path!" so he must have found it harder than he made it look. Then, He-Who going first, they scrambled through a mess of trees and broken chunks of rock that provided a natural staircase, till they were stopped by a huge chunk of vertical white granite that at first sight appeared seamless. After that lay the summit. Approaching it close up, they discerned a slim, jagged crack bisecting the wall. With luck thin fingers could jam the crack, but what was there for the feet?

"There is no other way. Nobody has reached the top of the crack. This is where the last ones fall. It's your turn."

Nookeesa, mouth dry with nervous tension, was unable to speak. He stepped forward and went at the first section of the wall. To make the expedition more daunting, the crack was lined with a sliver of damp moss, which wept whenever his fingertips clutched it. By strenuous jamming and splaying his feet flat against the rock he made a few feet of progress, but he knew he wasn't going to make it, and with his heart not in it he stood no chance. Defeated and depressed, he slithered tenuously back down to the boulders. He turned to the outcast, who was sitting snugly with his breech clout doubled over to act as a cushion. "Your go now."

"No, you get three attempts. I wouldn't want to deprive you of your chance to get the girl. Besides," he yawned, luxuriously puffing at his pipe, "I am comfortable, and I wish to smoke all of my kinnikinnick before I perish…if I have to." He gave a high-pitched chuckle. "You, too, sniff and take pleasure in it. Make this a good day to die."

He paused to let out some smoke. A self-satisfied smugness was written all over his features. Nookeesa had an insatiable urge to kick him in the face. Common sense alone held him back, and the need to focus his energy elsewhere.

"Go to it. I know I can do it. If I take over now, I will have the princess, and you will have disgrace. Make your two attempts. When you don't get up you will die a glorious death. When I do I will win the bride.

Whose will be the greater prize only the gods can tell." It was neat; it was logical, although Nookeesa would not agree with the final summary.

"I too need the rest." Nookeesa sat down on the ledge. The two deadly enemies sat sharing kinnikinnick in their pipes, chatting idly, savoring the tobacco's sweet aroma and the beautiful view to the west of the blue hills vanishing into the distance, as the condemned might enjoy the last glimpse from the scaffold. It was especially poignant to Nookeesa, for there was his road home, and the Great Spirit was letting him have this last look at it in its full summer-afternoon splendor.

He-Who tapped out the last of his ashes. "Now go! Think of the delights of *your* princess in her bridal array." He leant on the *your* with heavy sarcasm. This gave Nookeesa the spur to attack the rock. He made a few tentative steps, but it was clear that mentally he was still not committed. He pulled up on a jam, warily lifting his feet from a narrow ledge to an exiguous smear on the rock. Every muscle in his body was tensed. Water from the spongy moss spat out on his face.

"This is the spot where Heaving Wolf fell off."

Nookeesa almost jumped out off his holds in fright and haplessly slithered back down. His feet jammed in the crack were battered and squashed in its narrow fissure, the backs of his hands bloodstained and ripped. He was trembling. "It is impossible!"

But the relentless He-Who taunted him. "Go! Remember the beauteous melons of the princess await the smooth touch of your fingertips!" He rose up and said, "Listen. She is not for me. I should mate with pigs and hedgehogs. Go up and be counted a hero amongst your tribe. I will stand beneath you and perhaps hold you if you fall."

Whether he believed it we shall never know, but the sneering voice put the steel back in him, and with his courage recharged, a nervy Nookeesa started up the crack. At his previous high point his legs started dancing, almost knocking him off the holds; his fingers and forearms were already weakening.

"Hold still!" commanded He-Who, grabbing Nookeesa's feet to hold them tight against the rock. He-Who had two bags slung round his waist. From one he fished out a huge chunk of bear grease, and quick as a flash he slapped it onto the underside of Nookeesa's moccasins. "Go for it! For your princess!"

Nookeesa made a desperate, flaying lunge for an obvious handhold. He caught it, but his arms were shaking and almost numb with the acute strain. His strength was going rapidly. Quickly he shifted his feet to a friction hold, but his moccasins were as slippery as an eel in the hand. With a swoosh Nookeesa's feet shot off the sloping holds. Slithering and sliding, he tried to place them again, but it was hopeless. All his weight was on his arms, but under the sudden immense strain his biceps melted into butter, and slowly, desperately, his fingers uncurled and gave out. He was off! Wordlessly, Nookeesa plummeted, his body somersaulting backward to perish on the boulders hundreds of feet beneath.

He-Who saw the full extent of the fall and let out a bellowing war whoop of victory. The cry bounced off the rocks, echoing back and forth down the Potomac Stream till it died in a faraway whisper.

There was no hurry now. He-Who sat down amidst his gear, then drew a hallucinatory plant out of his pouch and chewed away, feasting his mind on the joyous humping that was to be his reward tonight. At length he put his hand into the other pouch and plastered hand and moccasins with sticky pine resin, his secret weapon. Thus glued to the rock, he mounted the last few feet to the spiky ridge easily. His hands touched the summit stone. The first touch by man, he reflected. He stood up, sat down, considered doing a handstand, then thought better of it, contenting himself with the long trumpeting yodel that was the agreed signal for the victorious suitor, adding the incomprehensible "*Vive la belle neige—avis et mariage*!" Around the summit rocks a hawk lazily circled the mountain, its wings barely flapping as if it were reluctantly applauding. Down at the Indian town, Princess Snowbird fainted.

A sour miasma advanced like a cloud to herald for the bride the arrival of the triumphant groom to claim his wedding night. With great ululations and the supping of vats of tizwaz, the nuptials commenced, while at the foot of the rocks the bloody body of poor Nookeesa was left forgotten. The elders of the village puffed at their pipes and nodded in solemn accord. The great sacrilege had been met with fitting retribution. The traditions had been vindicated. Surely the gods would smile on the nation again. In addition, the bleeding of the bride and the maintenance of her sworn vows would appease the Great Spirits, ensuring many seasons of happy hunting. The ground thundered with the thumping of wooden phalli on the drums clasped tightly between the knees of the groomsmen. The village squaws arrayed their Hiawatha in the smoothest of buckskins and softest of feathers in readiness for her defloration.

"Are you ready, Maid of the Snowy North? Are you ready to pleasure a warrior about to be a prince?"

A thin bird sound, halfway to a whisper, not Snowbird's usual imperious voice, replied. "Be gentle, conqueror of Seneca. I have a tender quiver, and it is as yet sealed." Then in something akin to her normal tones she said, "Go down to the river and bathe before crossing this threshold, you whose smells make the skunk seem sweet. But stay! Before going, drink this honeymoon potion, my lord and master. It will add sweetness to your undoubted strength." She passed him an amphora containing a ferocious brew, strengthened by adding subtle herbs sufficient to knock out a horse.

He drank, and then stumbled down to the riverbank, crashing through bushes and colliding with trees. "*Excuse moi, monsieur*," he said and giggled on realizing his mistake.

As soon as he was gone far enough for his aroma to be out of range, the princess threw a dog-skin blanket over her back and crawled out of the tepee. Scuttling on all fours round the back of the tents, she paddled off disguised as a cur. No one noticed the oddly-shaped stray dog, for they were all huddled round the campfires in the comatose phase of drunkenness, watching the burning logs spark and jump with the philosophical detachment of those becalmed by alcohol. At the edge of the village she stood up, looked back at her home for a while, then moved off toward the saw-toothed mountain, the dog blanket, draped over a bush, the only evidence of her passage to a more ethereal realm.

When she disappeared from this Earth, onlookers swore that, at the moment when the heavens opened up in protest at this sacrilegious marriage, a bird was seen to emerge from the roof of the tent, a snowbird, which circled the wigwam twice and then sped northward to rejoin the Great Snows.

CHAPTER 8

The Last Jacobite Recalls Drumossie Muir

I had entered this strange and wild country by way of New York, where half the population conversed in Dutch, another quarter French, another German; the rest spoke a kind of Mummerset English, incomprehensible till I caught its strange lilting rhythm. I had landed sick as a dog after throwing up all the way across the Atlantic, thus failing to endear me to my shipmates, who were all heartily glad to see me gone. My wall-eyed ship's master had kept me in his cabin at the start of the voyage, presumably in the hope of debauching me when I was napping, but chucked me out onto the deck after I had spewed up over his best waistcoat.

As quickly as he could he disposed of me, selling me off at the dockside as an indentured servant in a gentleman's boarding house to pay for my fare. As he said, I couldn't cook, couldn't sew, was too nice to wash soiled clothes, so I might as well lie on my back and watch the sunsets. But good luck to the first to enter me, as I would likely puke over their staff of office—that was how he put it. I wasn't sorry to see him go either. He was a brute of a man, without any vestige of charm or any redeeming feature. It made me feel sorry for his mother.

In those first six months I was no use for anything. My infirmity altered its nature from the seasickness to the seasoning, which afflicts all those who make the passage from gentle England to this horrid climate. The boiling heat and humidity of summer do for many during this period. For me it was like being in a steamy laundry room when the door is locked, and for several weeks I felt ghastly. However, the gentleman who ran the boarding house early on saw I was good for nothing, but was kind enough to give me a letter of recommendation to another boarding house.

"Ye should be ashamed o' yersel, lassie!"

Standing over me breathing self-righteousness was this tree trunk of a man dressed in plaid, sporran, and kilt, decorated with the gaudy tartan of the royal Stewarts.

"Tarted up like a wee hoor selling yer wares to any Caleb aff the streets! Aye, ye'll be sitting on yon pretty wee arse on the stool of repentance soon enough, when the Guid Lord catches up on ye, or any decent minister if there were one in this place o' Babylon, this Sodom, this Gomorrah! And on the Lord's Day too!"

I was used to this style of approach so I took another sip of my chocolate, extending my pinky delicately so if he had any savoir faire he would spot a proper lady, a trainee courtesan from the palace of Saint James no less, and not the sort of common *hoor*, as he so finely put it, with whom he would customarily have conversation. I directed him to Bathsheba, who specialized in religious maniacs and had all sorts of costumes available for priest, bishop, nun, or Auld Nick himself. (*Nota bene*, how tactful I was in refraining from enquiring how come he was here himself on the Lord's Day.)

"Second door on the right upstairs, Caleb yourself, and mind you pray with your clothes on. There's a lot of chills going around just the noo." I said the last bit just as a tease, you know. "And mind you keep the lock on your sporran," I added naughtily.

"It's no wise tae be pullin' the tadger aff o' Angus McOgg MacPherson, ye ken."

"Oh, I'm terribly sorry, I took you for one of our regular customers." In truth I was a teeny bit intimidated by this haggis-devouring giant. He seemed to be an Old Testament prophet brimful of righteousness, fire, and brimstone, as much a fish out of water in this den of sin and iniquity as a vicar's daughter. *Hello*, the thought struck me, *we're birds of a feather.*

I put on a winning smile. "Pray, take a seat and rest before commencing boarding." I had had it up to my décolletage with slimy ne'er-do-wells with their oily, common humor, who had nothing better to do to pass the time between appointments than attempting to engage me in intercourse, and felt that with this Celtic warrior by my side I would be spared their unwelcome pleasantries. He was handsome in a foreboding manner, with a craggy face that had been around a bit, and those eyes—those grey, all-seeing eyes—were the perfect weapon for ferreting out delinquency.

"Whit are ye daein' here, a lassie like you?" He could see at once I was not the usual run of trollop who spread her legs at the first sound of chinking silver, so I told him with a fair approximation of the truth that I was a distressed genteel lady whose father had been cruelly persecuted for his religious beliefs, and I had landed in this locale by an unfortunate chain of circumstances. After all, this was America, and I knew enough about the country's puritanical peculiarities to see that an account of his being hanged for shagging livestock would not go down too well with the pilgrim fathers.

"Tch, tch, ma wee hen, that's a terrible tale you're a-telling me noo. And ye'll be wondering whit I'm daein' patronizing this place of fornication?"

As a matter of fact that had occurred to me, but I couldn't help butting in pedantically, a fault of mine that used to be criticized by my less studious companions. But there was something about the manner of the man—rude and untutored like the rest of them, as he appeared on the surface—that encouraged me to think on the schoolroom. From there it was but a short step for me to wax lyrical. "Fornication: now that's interesting. In Ancient Rome, you know, ladies of easy virtue plied for custom under the *fornices*, or arches, of the portico of the Theater of Pompey. For it was a nice shady spot to trawl, as the rich and famous were wont to take their post-prandial constitutional through the gardens, sauntering by the statues of Praxilites and Phidias stolen from the Greeks. Ergo, the word pops up more than a millennium and a half later!"

For a moment I regretted my know-it-all impulse when he looked at me flabbergasted. This habit of mine had shaken off all but the most ruggedly determined approaches I may have had in the past, which were then diverted to the less academically strenuous Mary-Anne. Breathlessly I continued while he stared in wild surmise, as if words might deflect him from pouncing on top of me. "It was the first theater in Rome. By putting a statue of Venus on top, he exploited a loophole in the law, making it a temple, giving license to the licentiousness underneath the arches as it were. You might say I am the kin to that statue of Venus, an icon of respectability in a theater of..." I stopped.

"My Goad! A lady of the classics, a bluestocking, drummin' up trade in a hoor hoose! This New World o' oors is truly an amazing place!" The last phrase he sibilated like the steady drizzle of his homeland, and I found myself warming to the man. "Ye ken."

He steadied himself and became business-like, ordering up a dram which he downed with much greater expedition than it took him to prise the groat out of his sporran. He made a grimace and let go the bottle. "Ach, this must hae crossed the Atlantic in a bucket full o' sheep-dip." He looked at the label vaunting its manufacture in the Cantuckee highlands. "Aye, sometimes ah never learn." Despite that, another was ordered up and swiftly disposed of, but remembering himself he asked me if I wished to partake. "But nae, lassie, gentle-folk like you are mair at ease with yer chocolate."

Actually I was dying to sling some version of the fiery craitur down my throat but cancelled the thought as possibly striking the wrong note. Very dimly I could see my ticket out of New York.

"Why am I here? I'm looking for a woman. I'm a widower and I need a woman. But no one that spends her time lying flat on her back, but one that can cook and scrub and also keep hoose and kens which end o' a musket is which."

"Why have you come here, then?"

"Why? I'm desperate. New York is full of sequestered ladies, unhappily fallen, and some of them read the Bible." He took a good look at me. "Anyway, you wouldn't do. You've led too soft a life. Besides, a man wid rather hae a guid dinner on the table than a housewife that speaks Greek."

"What makes you think I would be interested anyway?"

"No hard feelings, dearie."

We talked for a bit about this and that, finding that we were both mildly stimulated by each other's company. I dropped into the conversation my expertise in the art of pot scouring acquired when incognito under the Dog and Roger roof. And I was sure, given a cookbook, I could bluff my way into a man's heart, as the old proverb has it.

"You know, I can bake a pudding as well as translate Epictetus."

"You dinna bake puddings; you steam them."

"Shows you how much you know about puddings."

He looked at me steadily. "You look awfy frail for the frontier."

"Well, I managed to run a household in the backwoods of England." I was stretching the truth there, but who's to tell? "I don't see how yours can be much harder."

He glanced shiftily around the room as if coming to a decision, while making sure there were no witnesses, then said, "Noo, let's get down to serious talk." Meaning a drink to keep our throats well lubricated while we were blethering. "Whaur does a man get a drink in this town?"

I didn't point out that he was well tanked up already, recognizing that this was purely formulaic and now serious negotiations were about to be placed on the table. He ordered a bottle of Canary from the girl with the broom, who was hovering about with her big ears twitching. This time he provided me with a convivial glass, and then hitched his head forward furtively as if he was going to tell me gold had been discovered on his land. "Ye're no a republican democratical atheist like the rest of the crew in this misbegotten land?"

"What a strange question to ask. Of course not! After every meal I always put in a request for God to save our noble king."

"Then let's drink a toast tae His Majesty."

Right away I knew what he was up to. "Why not?"

As always in America, a dish of dusty water was standing in the center of the table. He tipped his glass toward me and softly intoned, "The king."

Drawing the glass over the surface of the dish, I wafted it back and forth two or three times to make sure he got the message, locking him eyeball to eyeball with all the force of my twinkling green eyes. I had him. "The king," I echoed in response, and added, "My Bonny Charlie's noo awa."

My little trap snapped shut, and his mouth once again fell open. "The King Over the Watter. The true king, the House of Stewart! How could you know?"

"Family connections, you know. I'll tell you later if we get better acquainted."

"Ah weel, that's as may be, but if ye come, I'll no be tampering wi your tits. It's a huswifie I'm after, no' a hoor."

Don't hold back for my sake, I thought. Now was not the time to act precious. I saw this man as a lifebelt and would hold onto him with every bone in my body. I gripped my chair tightly. *Go very cautious here. With careful handling, this broken-down, mad Scotch preacher could get me out of my involuntary servitude in whoredom.* I decided to tickle his self-esteem like a poacher guddling trout. I could tell he thought me a bargain. A little more Herodotos, heaped on with Pindar, and he was deliriously happy. I was home and dry.

"It seems we are both satisfactorily accommodated." I held out my hand. "Call me Amy." Amelia sounded much too soft-scented for the rugged frontier. And so I said farewell to the stews of New York.

And that is how I came to be a frontier lady in the German Valley, not a long-rifle shot from Seneca Rocks in the depths of the forests of Virginia. The house was well sited above the busy banks of the Northern Potomac. Our neighbors were a mixed band of Mingo, Iroquois, and Shawnees, peaceful enough for the present. It was not a plantation mansion, nor was it a slum. It may have been a log cabin, but it had one merit that held it above others of the same species: My new master had made a very Calvinist effort to keep it clean. There was a broom, and he had not been afraid to use it. The sheets in the household were made of linen and they were still white, not the mildewed grey beloved of inattentive bachelors. The woodwork, the walls, etc., and the furniture (not Chippendale but serviceable withal) had been polished till it looked like it had been holystoned. I found later that it was common hereabout to exaggerate one's wealth in order to snare one's woman. A great manor house with a platoon of servants turned out to be a one-roomed hovel, with the lady of the house acting as chief skivvy and bottle washer, and then doing overtime duty as musket loader when pestiferous Indians came a-visiting. But then, fair's fair you might say, after my cullying him by misrepresenting my culinary skills. After all, one pudding doth not a banquet make.

Still there was an inescapable air of somber masculinity about the furbishments, which was unexpectedly muted by a circlet round the outside of the building of what appeared at first sight to be huge, lemon-colored turnip lanthornes similar to those children make for All Hallows

Eve. On closer inspection the lemons turned out to be covered in hard nodules. This was the hedge apple, a fruit inedible to humans, a string of which hung round the cabin and was reputed to keep at bay witches, warlocks, and all manner of unspecified evil spirits. I was surprised Angus would buy such a cock-and-bull story, but as he said, "When you're dealing with the great unknowables, Amy"—and here he pointed to his buckskin fringed jacket thrown over the best chair on the property—"this man takes nae chances."

Angus also liked to read and talk about what we read. When he showed me his library I was astounded. Where had he acquired this treasure trove? It was as if an explorer in the desert had come upon the pagan parchments of Alexandria. Apparently a naive Methodist minister attempting to convert the savage Shawnees had been deprived of his vital appendages, plus his scalp, plus his library. His books had been considered devilish fetishes and were about to be consigned to the fires when Angus came upon them and managed to persuade the savages that they were worth saving, probably saying that they contained big magic. There was nothing he could do for the charbroiled corpse, but at least he could rescue these tokens of a greater civilization. The Indians had no problem wishing these accursed relics on the pathfinder in exchange for a bottle of whiskey (and very naughty was Angus for giving liquor to the Indians).

Angus was a very fair man, who was as good as his word and didn't come battering on my door of a night to ravish me. In fact his total abstention on that front made me wonder if the seasoning and humidity had diminished my attractions. When I looked in the yellowing fragment of glass purloined from some extinct pioneer wife's wardrobe, I had my answer. A sorry Medusa stared back. Limp and soggy in the heat, my coif was a bad-hair nightmare, my fashionable pallor as far gone as the winter. Like any country slut I was brown as a berry, and those plump little Sunday-School-teacher cheeks were now tight and drawn. I was the wine that did not travel well.

Despite this he did not demote me to in-house drudge but showed me his needs, so that quite soon I became a passable housemate after the custom of the country. For example, I could rustle up a very succulent possum stew to satisfy him and his voracious mates, who grabbed the bowls and wolfed the mess down without a by-your-leave till they gave a chorus of gratified belches that sounded like hogs rutting. But then that was preferable to their conversation, a series of bellows, yelps, and slaps on the knee that would have had the good Dr. Johnson turning in his grave, even though he was yet extant and still at the letter *O* with his dictionary.

When I was not on form, on the infrequent occasions when I was moody and moping (every second day according to my salty tongued Scot), he would make me another tea from the sassafras bush.

"It's a spring tonic, Amy lass, excellent for thinning out the sluggish blood after a long, dull winter lolling in front of the fire."

Once again he was right, and a cup or two of this made me quite the sprightly thing, and as he put it in his pithy way, "a wee bitty of a blether."

Like all lonely people he wanted to talk, and fore George, did he have a seasoned listener. He, like the rest of his ilk, had come out in the Forty-Five. Captured, he was transported to Virginia, but instead of muttering, as many did, that they got second best to the hangman's rope or, best of all, having their innards skewered at Drumossie Muir, he put his best foot forward and made the best of things in this Novus Mundus.

Out of doors he moved soft as moss on moss and had culled a botanist's knowledge of every tree and plant, though with names unheard of at Kew Gardens. He knew his way round woods and Indians, and taught me a thing or two about woodcraft. In case you are wondering if this is a very lady-like activity, let me tell you. If you want to survive on the wild Virginia frontier, whether you be laddie or lady you'd better learn which end of a musket the ball comes out.

Nothing could compare with those early mornings when I woke to the fire crackling, the smell of the resin off the pine wood spitting and hissing as it dropped into the flames, and him smiling as he pushed a pewter mug of wood-smoked tea into my hands. I took my first waking breath and drank in the stillness of the woods, broken only by the cawing of mockingbirds. Then we strode out into the bright morning and saw above the line of green the great blue vault of heaven broken only by a few puff-clouds lying lazily on the hilltops, waiting to be dissolved by the sun. Down in the valley, the north fork of the tiny Potomac bustled busily over its bed of rounded stones. We sat on old tree stumps and watched the beavers at work (gnawing at trees to make their great dams) and at play (wallowing up and down in their slides as children at the fair), and then we padded upward for the game on the hilltop, our moccasins scarcely stirring the grasses. Holding his finger to his lips for silence, Angus would point out a broken branch or a tuft of grass feathered the wrong way (indicating the passage of a deer), then before I could say "Charles Edward Stu—" the long-rifle was up on his shoulder, there was a sharp crack, and a deer was downed.

"Venison for the next fortnight, aye, Amy?" His back against a tree and rifle loaded and ever at the ready, the Highland laddie was crouching on his honkers, skinning and trimming like a master carver at Versailles to make ready for the carry. Angus carved the meat neatly into bricks, placing them carefully into the skin, which he then stitched up into a backpack such as soldiers carry. The larder was well stocked up for when his bottle comrades came round to eat us out of house and home. Deer was prime, but bear stew was his favorite, and we would spend days trailing after traces of bruin. Why, I don't know, as that animal cornered was ferociously dangerous, and the heavily greased meat seemed hardly worth the trouble, needing sugar smothered all over the roast to make it palatable let alone digestible. But to his pals it was a great coup, and the best sport was to be found in its getting, so I guess that had to be the point.

Sometimes when we were roaming over the hills in what I thought was an aimless fashion, Angus would stop, take in a feature of the landscape—a hill, a bend in the river, things not discernible to me—and if satisfied by what criterion I knew not, he would chip on the bark of the nearest tree the letter *A*. *He's a bit old for that*, I thought, expecting next an arrow, a heart, and the letters *AM*; I really didn't know what to think till he burst my self-conscious bubble.

"That's me laying my legal claim to the land."

"But surely the land has belonged to the savage Indians since the time of Noah?"

Angus looked at me as if I were codding him, then laughed. "You haven't been long on the frontier, Amy." Thus ended our discussion regarding the laws of property in North America.

Occasionally when wandering where the Blue Ridge Mountains melted into the smoky distance, we would come across groups of Indians doing the same: hunting, setting traps, or just staring into the yonder. At first—seeing them daubed with paint like diabolical woodland phantasms or the horrid Green Man, whose image used to scare us back home—they terrified me. Angus whistled at them like a skylark, whence they came over for a palaver consisting of lots of staccato grunting supplemented with a rapid patter of hand signals, like the hand shadows against the walls we made to entertain our friends on wet days. Then they sat together to share a pipe, or calumet as they were wont to call it, and grunted about the hunting prospects, where to set the best traps, etc., just as you might talk about the village cricket prospects in England.

These calumets, varnished in tobacco stains, were intricately decorated with pagan demons, and some of them had the dual functions of casse-têtes, or tomahawks. One of the pipes had two stems, which they stuck up their nostrils. Disgusting! I felt sick and had to turn away when this was lit up. Fortunately I was not asked to join in the pleasure of the smoke. As we had just killed, my man offered them some meat, which they gobbled raw on the spot, making me wonder if they had eaten the past fortnight. It was difficult to gauge which was the more revolting, the smoking or the eating with its accompanying panoply of sound, their table manners calling to mind our squire of Bosworth, the ineffable Sir Wolstan Dixie.

Even though there were any number of Scotch trappers haunting these backwoods, I was taken aback to hear the Indians speaking phrases in Gaelic intermingled with their pidgin! But still you can imagine my amazement when out of the blue a gravel-voiced old brave, who had wintered hard for at least sixty years by the look of his wrinkled visage, said, "What quoth the guid doctor on the Scotch and their porridge. You ken the yin aboot other countries using it for the horses, but in Scotland it sustains the populace." Faster than the flash from his musket pan, Angus shot back the riposte, "Aye sirrah, but such horses! Such men!" Which I believe was first used by...but alas, my memory fails here.

At times Angus would start maundering on about his wife, something that he was not inclined to do except on a night when the storm clouds exploded and we remained wet for a week. It was upon such a night that Angus let me in on his story. His normal stentorian voice was as dull and listless as this dreary night in November, with the rain pishing down and the sun promising to be shy of us for a good four month.

"It was an English laird that snatched her away from me, and for my sins I let him. The sun had sunk and risen again on a cold dawn on Culloden Moor after that fateful day, the sixteenth of April, the year of our Lord, seventeen hundred and forty-six. There was a bitter east wind that was picking up some rain and sleet, and I was lying downcast in the heather, wet and wounded from a cowardly Sassenach musket ball. Mind you it could have been a Scot. There was many a traitor knave who fought on the wrong side that day. I could hear the noise of the dying: those doing it of their own accord, groaning, and those being helped along by an English bayonet, screaming defiance or just screaming. In the distance I could hear the regular crash of musketry. The firing squads were busy obeying their orders from Stinking Billy and enjoying it, too, the base bastards. I was wondering how they would dispatch me, by steel or by lead.

"'Up on your feet, ye Erse-speaking bog trotter, ye!'

"I said, the name's Angus McOgg MacPherson, Sassenach.

"'Oh! See, we have a right one here!' The dragoon sergeant yelled to his fellows. 'These Highlanders, rag tag and bobtail, all they have is their pride. Look at him, a pretty mighty thing he is now. This one's a cripple. Give 'im a musket to lean on—an empty one, mind you. He looks as like he wants to fight that battle all over again, and I'm too weary for that. That was yesterday's business, ye kale-eating rascal! All bets are off now.' The sergeant, evidently a man of high wit, had all his troopers laughing heartily.

"'And he'd beat you too! With claymore or musket, or tear ye apart with bare hands if ye let him!' A high-pitched cry came from behind a heather clump. My Fiona had run from her sheiling two guid Scots miles away to rescue me. 'He's a man, and he's a Scotsman!'

"'Can we as take her wi us to inspect heather, Sergeant?' called out a soldier from the ranks, who looked about sixteen. The sergeant said, 'Sure, a bit of rapin' the local scrags on the side is your due after yesterday.'

Fiona screamed and leapt on the sergeant, kicking and biting him. 'Get her off me!' he said. 'This one's a right bloody shrew, wot needs a right good arse-tanning.'

"Their officer—a young sprout of a major, I reckon, for he wore a crown on his shoulder—had ridden up, his horse whinnying and snorting while he sat straight-backed, all pomposity, as if all Scotland had a bad smell. 'What's this deuced row about, Sergeant? Can't you shoot these damned rebels without such a fuss?'

"The sergeant said, 'In a jiffy, sir, with no problem, but this one's whore is as raising a loud objection, banging on as if it was Houses of Parliament.'

"'I'm naebody's hoor; I am my Angus's wife, and proud of it!' She threw out her bosom in defiance. The officer began to take an interest in his surroundings, as Fiona's heaving breasts were gaining his attention. Frantically she threw herself on her knees in front of his horse. 'Let him be! Take me in the heather, but let him be!'

"'Get on with it, sergeant. We haven't all day for these ragged-arsed rascals. I have an important engagement. I am dining with Lord Cornwallis tonight.'

"'Mustn't keep 'is lordship waiting,' the sergeant muttered and winked at his mates, who threw me up against the wall of a half-burnt-out croft.

"'Load! Present! Fire!' There was an angry snap of triggers, a crackle and flash in the pans, but no crash of volley. The deluge earlier that day had dampened their powder, so they misfired. A pity that had not happened afore the battle. The officer must have taken that as a warning not to mess with the divine scheme of things, for he told them to hold off, kicked his spurs into the horse's flank, then sauntered up to Fiona, so close the horse was snorting down her blouse.

"'Throw her in yonder brook, my bonny lads.' This they did expeditiously, then dragged her out by the hair and flung her onto the heather before the major, who ran his whip over her as if he were stroking her flesh and became entranced by her soaking dress, now as translucent as a spider's web.

"'A bonny Celtic thistle, this one. Take her to my tent, lads. You boys will have to get your mutton elsewhere.'

"She saw the look in his een and said, 'You can rape me or you can have me willing. Kill my man and it will need all your braw gallants to hold me down. Spare him, and I will follow you to the end of the world in a white petticoat. Ye have a Highland gentlewoman's word on it.'

"I can still see him now, slavering with lust and calculating, what's one more dead or alive prisoner now. He placed his whip under her chin, forcing her to look up into his eyes. 'Ye know, by Gad, you are too bonny a lass to be spread out over the heather. Marry, come up. Why yes, you will marry me. Surely only a papistical kirk on the hillside sanctified your bedding with yonder sheep-shagger, and I am in want of a wife. Why, if you learn how to behave, I shall show your beauty off at Hampton Court, I shall, and by George, I shall be a squire to be reckoned with. Spare the Scotch rascal, lads. You, Mistress MacHavers, or whatever you are called, have the word of an officer of King George as guarantee for his life. And, sergeant, make sure these damn muskets fire properly. We still have work to do. Now up you get, lass.' And he howked her onto the back of his cuddy.

"Fiona, looking as proud and bonny as on her wedding day, whispered to me, 'Adieu, my love.'

"'Don't shoot him! But keep him nice and raw with that cat o' nine tails, for the Americas,' the men guffawed and kicked me on my way.

"She pleaded and pleaded, 'That's not what I meant.'

"'Learn the King's English,' he sneered. 'That's what I meant!' And to his troopers: 'Turge the rascal well, boys, but keep him in good shape for planting tobacco for those damn tea-drinking Yankees.'

"We had a son. He will be about your age now. Aye, Amelia, it would be a braw business if you could meet him. For age hath withered my needs, and you are in want of a lusty rutting lad."

Well, there you go, thinks I. My cabin door will stay unbroken.

"An auld couple frae the Kirkton looked after him, and for all I ken they still do." Angus stopped and gazed into the fire. He looked old and tired.

"Och, awa to our beds, Angus, my fine man. We need to be on the heather braw and early the morn," said I in affectionate mimicry.

And so to bed.

CHAPTER 9

Pride and Prejudice Among The Shawnees

The local tribe, the Shawnee, were camped just beside us by the bend of the creek which flows into the Potomac. The latter empties into the sea by way of a great bay, where the new Federal Town was to be built, and which according to advertised promises was to be a fourth Rome, greater than Moscow, the Turkish town, and old Rome itself. Our situation vis-à-vis the natives was cozy and neighborly, with little in the way of tension and misunderstanding. My Angus knew no racial prejudice against the copper men, dealing with them as equals if not masters in the ways of the wilds. From them he had learnt everything about trapping, food, and medicine. "And make no mistake, Amy, they make excellent teachers: much mair patient than my dominie at home, who would skelp you as soon as look at you. For example, see this buckskin pouch with the wampum beads decoration." I turned the object in my hands. "Go on. Open it and tell me what it is."

The pouch was stuffed with bits of fluff and leaves, and had a pleasantly woody aroma. "Oh Angus, it's that herbal tobacco of yours that makes you smile away the day."

"Ye daft wee besom. Your imagination gets you higher than these trees, Amy. This is medicine, powerful strong medicine. If you—God protect us—suffer a musket wound, I'll clean it out with these"—he indicated the herbs—"and then I'll stuff and seal the wound with these here buzzard feathers. Here!" He pointed to the furry contents. "It's a capital remedy. You can learn an awful heap o' knowledge from the Indian. It's listening to him without getting your scalp removed that's the hard part." To my surprise their primitive herbal remedies worked whenever I was forced into sampling the medicines they drank. Perhaps it was the horrid taste that persuaded you into rude health.

Although Angus liked and trusted the Indians, he had no illusions about them as noble savages or as preservers of the great temple of nature. "The Indians know about the woods and keeping the game herds from disappearing because they need them to survive, and they are canny enough not to wipe out their own seed corn. But their law is survival. They'll smile at us as long as we trade 'em guns and rum. But come the day when we overrun their hunting grounds and take what's theirs, don't be surprised to wake up with your throat cut and in need of a new peruke."

We took great care not to trespass too much on their hospitality by treading on their land uninvited, despite the fact that the Indians dropped in for tea as casually as Lancashire weavers. They were quite capable of sitting outside for hours on their haunches until we took the hint and asked them in, not before checking that all our valuables were stowed away safely. And quite soon I became comfortable with their company, even though they did stare at me something awful.

A White woman was a wonder to their world, and visiting with them is a big thing in their neighborhood, very formal and ritualized, with an interminable amount of time taken up with such imponderables as the passing round and puffing on the sacred calumet stuffed with their kinnikinnick tobacco that to me smells of tree bark. But we are all the same at bottom, call us civilized or call us savages. What price a Buckingham House Levy to Angus's Saturday night levees, bar the ocean betwixt us plus some dainty Nankeen china tea sets and a flunky or two thrown in for good measure?

Ofttimes their slatternly squaws were brought along to scowl at me, assuming me to be a bought wife, a supplementary purchase when frontiersmen went on their annual shopping expedition. Not a bad system when you think of it: better than purchasing sight unseen hideous drabs shipped across the Atlantic in packet boats by despairing parents, reducing the poor woodsman to drink and the hope of an early grave for his bride through too-arduous childbirth. When the Pocahontases learned that I was merely a hired hand sleeping in a cold, lonely bed, they took pity on me, smiled, offered beads of wampum shells, and volunteered to braid my hair that I might be more comely and thus induce a long-knife brave to offer up a retaining interest in his stone wigwam.

"Thank you," I said, wafting my hands with elegant politesse, and meant it. If I ever got home again the wampum would come in handy as an amusing bauble to impress Mary-Anne. For the pipe I never acquired the taste and would only pretend to suck on its spittle-strewn stem before hurriedly handing it on, as in the game of pass the parcel.

One of the squaws never stopped fussing over me, constantly fingering the fabric of my dresses and caressing my cheeks as if they had magic properties. She was incessantly whispering and giggling to her mate, a sad-eyed piece but the only serious looker amongst the bunch, who gave the impression that she had been dragged along for the ride. The fidgety one was a proper chatterbox, perpetually getting scolded by her friend.

"Rest your babblings, Little Rabbit. You know what a serious thing it is to slander people. What a fishwife and *pockvano-madee-way* you are! Before long one of those you have wronged will have your scalp adorning your tepee, and where then will your tongue be? Pale Amy does not want to hear the tales of our parish water hole, and will think us all tedious rustics." I translate loosely.

But I did listen, for fascinating things were going on down in the valley, with a familiar ring about them, making me think life is much the same the world over. The French I'm sure will have a word for this.

It was in one of our tea parties that I learnt about the chief's daughter. I had only a few snatched phrases of their lingo, but I could tell that she was beautiful by the caustic tone in their words when the homely ones spoke about her. Her little social circle was very exclusive, and my squaws, who must have belonged to a lower echelon of society, could not break into it, that is except for Little Rabbit's friend, Doe Eyes, who had the requisite looks to gain entry and so must have created some enormous gaffe to have been blackballed. Her Regal Highness Snowbird's snobbishness did not endear her to the polity of squaws. Her way of mincing around, flaunting her wampum, and generally putting on airs put me in mind of Mary-Anne, when I remembered the time I was cut out of her society as a result of the alleged sins of my father.

The ill-favored ones became daily more friendly as, despite my pale skin, an inescapable form of ugliness, I was a rival princess with an alternative court where they might socialize without feeling ostracized and do all the things that go on in any court, such as parade around flaunting their fashions, at the same time plotting and backstabbing like billy-o. Round my star they swam like wondrous gaudy planets in giddy and unpredictable orbit, and the log cabin, to the untutored eye a squalid and rude hovel with possibilities, became a Versailles to Madame Princess's Tuileries.

Quite frequently, about once a fortnight, say—I have to be careful here for they didn't count in weeks, and I quite soon lost track of the calendar—they would invite Angus and me over for a powwow, or parliament, with lots of grunting and calumets going full belt all round the campfires till it resembled Mr. Watt's steam factory, unproductive except for enough blethering to keep Sheepy busy for a fortnight. Snowbird never once put in an appearance. I liked to think that it was because my reputation had gone before me, and our rivalry, egged on by our various supporters, ensured that unconsciously we avoided each other like heavily backed prizefighters in the early rounds of a bare-knuckle contest, weighing each other up without coming within sparring distance.

One day they held a great feast to celebrate the start of a new hunting season, a date on their calendar as important as our Easter or Christmas. The maidens and men, dressed variously in the skins of bear, deer and fowl, elk and antelope (in other words all the fodder of the forest), danced and shuffled to the music of pipes and drums round the great fire in front of the totem pole; consider it if you like as standing in for the altar in Lichfield Cathedral. The music was wild, wanton and warlike, making the scratchings and scrapings of the orchestras of petty German princelings piffling in comparison.

In my bosom I could feel the stirring of strange and unfamiliar passion. I was not alone. In the gloaming of the firelight, uncannily reddened by the reflection of the copper faces of mine hosts, there was a glowing and a glimmering in each and everyone's eyes. Tonight the village would be a woodland Gomorrah. The effect of the insistent drumbeat knew no ethnic boundaries, for Angus's eyes gleamed with a faraway look as a single dewdrop of sweat trickled down to the tip of his Gaelic beak and hesitated before it plunged and sizzled in the fire.

He stirred, made some remark about it reminding him of the ceilidhs, fiddles, and the great war pipes of his youth, and started tapping his feet to the rhythm while humming a variant on the tune "Diddly Dum Dum." He was so intent on this humming business, taking it so seriously that I couldn't help asking him about it. He said that the great piping family, the MacCrimmons, treated the humming organs, mouthpiece and throat, as a musical instrument, and there were frequent dum-diddly competitions between the clans when they weren't busy stealing and fighting amongst each other, which festivals were generously lubricated with claret for the upper classes and usquebaugh for the humble tacksmen.

Normally his musical taste was homespun. As we tramped over the little bens and braes of Virginia he liked to croon wistful Scotch ballads such as "Barbara Allen" or "Parcel of Rogues," a musical indictment of the rascals who sold out Caledonia in the 1707 Act of Union. All these Scotch ditties about lost battles, lost loves, and limits set on mortality made for a doleful tramp over the heather. When he saw me downcast, he whistled and hummed modern melodies such as "American Taxation," "Chevy Chase," "Children in the Wood," or "Springfield Mountain." Being American, these were upbeat and optimistic, and brought a spring to my step and a glow to my cheek. He even made me laugh, telling me the most popular dance in the Scottish Highlands was called "America," which was like musical chairs without the chairs. At every round one person would drop out till there was only one left, who had to stay to mind the sheep in the glens when all the lucky folks had danced away to America.

We were breasting the highest ridge in the area when down below the spiky rocks of Seneca Mountain came into view. It was odd being above those fatal spires where so many of those boys who had striven to find love were rewarded with death. The unexpected sight of these forbidding stony turrets abruptly thrust into the forefront of my mind all the recent tragedies that had been prompted by the affectations of one silly highborn girl.

These melancholy reflections elicited a sigh from my breast, to which Angus said gruffly, "Wheesh lassie, ye'll scare awa the deer." Despite the Indians' dance to placate their Artemis, venison had been tough to hunt of late. A well-meated buck would keep the larder stocked for a fortnight, and just then I was hungry. I spotted our deer at about a hundred yards, placidly munching away at some berries without a care in the world. Poor innocent thing! I raised my musket to take it out. The powder was loaded, the shot was rammed home, and the hammer was cocked; the deer's shoulder was in my sights when whoosh—an arrow split the air by my chignon and brought him down.

A brave hidden behind a bush just where we were standing raised himself up on his haunches, waggled his finger at us (expressing I know not what, unless it were an apology for jumping the gun), then, looking quite sheepish, went out to claim his prize.

He was a fine, handsome warrior, and I could feel myself blushing as my eyes took in his muscled copper skin. I had forsaken my frilled, brocaded dress because of the brambles. For a moment I regretted my practicality, but I have to say I looked quite the thing—winsomely Ganymede-ish in my soft braided buckskin outfit—so perhaps all was not lost; moreover my skin had taken on a soft, honeyed complexion from so much exercise under this North American sky. Could this be the Nookeesa whose recent arrival had caused so much of a stir in the Indian encampment, and whose bold physique had set the shrewish princess's heart in a flutter?

We introduced ourselves to this Lothario of the woods. "Hi, and how are ye?"

"I am Nookeesa, and I'm lost." An unusual admission for savages, who are generally loathe to confess to any failings. He sat back on his haunches in the Indian way of saying he was all set for a chinwag. Without any encouragement his life story came pouring out, the vital chapter when he took that fateful dip in the pool duly noted. We nodded, the story already familiar to us, as was their romance, the staple yarn round the campfires for months now. As my staunch Scotch friend put it, "They were in want of a guid war to give them something else to blether aboot."

We glanced back into the bushes to espy the most glorious pair of fawn-like eyes I had ever clapped eyes on, belonging to the most beautiful girl, Indian or English, I had ever seen—and I had looked into the mirror many a time and oft. I could only see the top half of her face; the nose, the mouth, the chin were all blocked by the abundant foliage she was shyly hiding behind, as though she were playing peek-a-boo. So finally the beautiful Snowbird and I confront each other in this neutral setting. She jerked like a deer when she saw me, as if recognizing me as someone she owed money to, but it was so quick I wasn't sure and dismissed the thought, for more serious perceptions were shaping up. I saw; I sighed; I had met my match. Her perfect, cone-shaped bosoms I could meet pound for pound. Her legs were long and lithe. These were no problem, as mine were the best pair outside of horseflesh (or so I had been assured by the pony-fancying gentry back home), but that heart-shaped face was bonnier than any I had seen in the flesh or mounted in a frame, in palace or castle. She moved with a balletic grace that emulated the creature of the hills we were bent on destroying. Here, far from the feminine factions of the village way down in the hollow below, beauty looked upon beauty and found the reflection pleasing. No longer need our eyes make an aesthetic adjustment to accept mediocrity. Our friendship was sparked by that first relieved glance. After all it was as conceivable that I would chase after her Nookeesa as she would beard in my den my bearded buckskin Angus.

Nookeesa was to turn out to be a most singular Indian, and the word "savage" hardly applied here; and after all the stories put out about the Indian princess, the last thing I expected to discover was Snowbird's maidenly modesty, which I found both amusing and endearing. Whenever we were engaged in intercourse, she would never look boldly at me but assumed the very picture of meekness with her head fixed upon the ground, as though she was masquerading as the humble retainer, or she didn't want me to look too closely at her for some other unfathomable cause. After all it wasn't possible we had met before.

We reached the cabin. Angus invited our friends in. "Please welcome to our humble abode," an unnecessarily accurate description. They took us at our word, and grunted with pleasure at the invitation. Nookeesa made a deep rumble from his belly and stroked his tummy in anticipated pleasure. It was an evening that we had thought to pass in solitude, but now we had guests. So why not make a party of it? They were delighted, and Angus proudly served up a new bottle of his precious nectar, which "I've been saving for a special occasion, and what could be more special than a princess come tae dine wi us humble folks." He realized that his brindisi might have trod on a pair of toes, so dexterously amended his toast to: "And what could be even more special than when princess meets princess." Honor was satisfied. Meanwhile the liquor in question was slipping down Nookeesa's throat like a waterfall over a cliff, and Snowbird, sitting in her shady corner, was not lagging far behind. They laughed uproariously whenever Angus displayed some of his Scotch wit (no, not an oxymoron when laughter and whiskey gang together) and they formed an excellent audience for Angus's tall and getting-on-taller stories, which I regret to say I had heard quite sufficiently already, thank you, but joined in the applause for good fellowship's sake.

All night long the cabin echoed and re-echoed to a glorious bacchanalian uproar. Soon we would be running out of the precious spirit, but luckily some old claret came to the rescue, plus Angus's devilish home-brewed beer. By the time we had drunk it nobody noticed that what it lacked in flavor was compensated by too much sugar. So it fizzed and popped and gave us enormous headaches the next day. What with the Indians' presence it must have resembled the first Thanksgiving, although in this instance we had saved the Indians and not vice versa; nor, I suspect, would the Puritans have been amused by our imitation, which was more boisterous than religious.

Here I saw another side to my Angus. With these rude unsophisticated people he was charming and amusing without the unbending condescension of your average paleface. He rejoiced in their company as if they were the Prince's own boon companions, displaying his learning so easily and pleasantly that each one of his guests felt that they were doing Angus the honor of their company. More and more I saw my father in this Scotch hunter. They both had the same joy in honest company and with it a pleasure in teaching of the Classics, which they both loved in their own weird and individual way.

It was during one of those hospitable, jocular evenings that I felt the pangs of homesickness. Sitting by the fireside, knitting socks and repairing clothes, thoughts of home and father inevitably came to mind. Conjuring up his image in my imagination, I wondered: Could I have saved him? Was I so seduced by my friendship with Mary-Anne that I had let her take the initiative on that fateful day? The tears bubbling up behind my eyelids obscured my vision, so I made a wretched hash of my woman's work. To make the evening more heartrending, Angus was waxing bibulously eloquent on another might-have-been.

"He'll be aboot your age, lassie. Wa's ma Blearie, he'd be a bonny fechter. The twa o' ye wad blithely gang together. I could see the baith o' ye dancing the altar twa-step ain bonny day."

No doubt the tears coursing down his cheeks as copiously as one of his highland burns were not impeded by the substantial drams of the fiery craitur he had supped, but I have to say I was not unmoved by the picture he had just limned, although I cautioned myself that any son of Angus—left to rot in some smoky black house, fighting off midges and hiding in the heather from the Sassenach policeman back in the old glen—would hardly be the cultured gallant I had hoped for in my dreams, a man to fill my father's place in the manse.

Possibly to take their minds off his forthcoming trial, Snowbird and her handsome friend took to dropping in to tea, for cress sandwiches, to eat my home-baked scones, and to provide an audience for the recitation of the poems of Rabbie Burns. To me this stuff could have been Hebrew, but it was all the rage along the valley of the Potomac just as much as it was in Edinburgh salons, or so I was told. And here the pair of lovers began their first halting steps in the English tongue. I couldn't help but giggle, for Angus was teaching them braid Scotch, although the girl's accent by some weird twist of fortune emerged with a plough boy's unmusical lilt. "Ye wee glaicit besom!" doesn't half sound strange coming from the mouth of a full-blood Chippewa warrior complete with face paint and eagle feather war bonnet. And in the meantime Snowbird and I began to take to each other slowly and cautiously, as if still not sure how much of a threat the other posed.

CHAPTER 10

Culloden Replayed

It must have been a month after this encounter. It was a pleasant, balmy evening, and we were sitting back replete and happy after a trough full of groundhog pie, me thinking I could never look these poor, innocent creatures in the eye again, even when on a cold winter's day they were prophesying an early spring. I had just quoted Dr. Johnson's withering observations on Scotch men and their country, giving me great amusement. Old Angus was content to indulge me in this good-natured attack on his homeland. "If it tickles ye, lass, let it be, but perhaps the good doctor was observing through very English spyglasses, and did he not deign to visit thon benighted country and found it worth the trouble?" We were talking about this rather than discussing the affair of the mountain climb, to take our minds off the tragedy. We had just heard the news of the accident, which distressed us greatly, as did the thought of how we would get on with Snowbird's new beau, of whom we had heard much and liked little.

But the best laid schemes of mice and men gang aft aglay, as the Scotch poet was wont to say, and a great mischief was on hand to try my sorely tested spirit. Like all thunderclaps that set your life to splinters, this came without any warning on a sleepy summer's evening, with a dreadful pounding on the door more urgent than even the most ardent suitor could summon. Taken aback, we stared at each other open-mouthed, all thoughts of gallimaufry fled away, hearing desperate cries for help in Scotch Gaelic and Lallans. Unless these were fervid Jacobites, who else would wish to disturb our peaceful evening in this wise? Now guttural voices pleading told me that Scotch was not their mother tongue.

Opening the door we found two shivering wretches on the doorstep. One was Snowbird trembling like a leaf with fear; the other was a battered and bleeding Nookeesa.

"But you're dead?"

Snowbird practically headbutted me aside and stepped in.

"Quick! The whole village is after us for breaking sacred customs in front of the tribe and creating a great sacrilege, the punishment for which is burning alive for the man and a quick execution for the princess with the tomahawk club, if she is lucky. We are *cut-ta-ho-tha*: damned. The outcast is leading the hunt, for I have chosen, you see, to disregard the rules of the competition, taking the loser instead of the cheating winner. But I think I have also abdicated." Hysterically blurting this out, Snowbird then stopped and gasped before restarting breathing. There was not much need or time for further explanations.

"How come we thought you was dead? And you was married off to the outcast, living sort of happily ever after?"

She was short of breath, practically sobbing. "I lay there because it is our fate as females to submit to whatever the father of our country wills for us. Then I thought that whatever is inevitable ought to be delayed in case the Great Spirits change the course of the heavens and make the stars stand on their tiptoes. I fed the outcast jugs of tizwaz as a nightcap, stoking him up for the plowing of my virgin furrow. He slurped it up greedily like a man in the desert. My best hope was that he would fall asleep or have a sad worm instead of a stout totem pole. After a couple of dozen jugs—he was a greedy man—which I strengthened with my patent knock-out, he couldn't have rogered a rabbit, never mind a great princess, for he fell to a-snoring." And here, mindful of her late greatness, she sniffed haughtily.

"In my grief I left the tent and wandered into the night. At first I went to the pool where we first met and I was captured by my warrior's magic." She stopped and stroked the wounded object of her affectations. "The gods must have loved me that night, for they guided my next steps. I thought of my folly in condemning so many young braves to be eaten alive by the mountain, so I wandered up the slopes ridden by guilt. Then I saw him caught in the branches of a tree, wrapped and swaddled in thorns and thickets. Of course he must be dead, but he was still bleeding. And glory be to the tribal gods for a miracle to one so undeserving (I mean me not him); the same humble plants, which had caused him so much pain on the way up, had preserved him, and by tangling him up saved him from hitting the ground on the way down. So truly there is a purpose to everything in God's garden, even brambles. Gently I uncoiled him like you would a papoose from its bundle, dragged him down to the border of the village, and scuttled on all fours to Little Rabbit's wigwam, where I managed to get potions and poultices, at the same time fending off her more and more insistent questions. And then I repaired him," she said proudly. "He was a gift to me, just like the Christian God's gift to the Holy Virgin. So our ways have been destined to walk the path together. I prayed to *Inu-msi-ila-fe-wanu*, the Great Grandmother Spirit, knowing she would understand this virgin's plight." She pointed to herself in case there was any doubt. "We fled. And now we are here," she finished simply.

Behind them in the forest we could hear angry shouts of hot pursuit. If they thought the White man could protect them in his lodge, Angus had no such illusions. "We can hold oot for an hour or twa. Ye are going to run yon path together, else yer life is going tae be shortbread: short and sweet. Ye maun tak tae yer heels, and fast." He gave me a worried look. "Amelia, I never met a sweeter, bonnier lass than you. I'll never see you and my laddie dander down yon Almond banks together. Ye go with them, for sure they'll tear us all limb frae limb if they catch us."

"But what about you, Angus?"

"Nae Scotsman will say that Angus McOgg MacPherson was found wanting. Here I'll stand as my ancestors stood on the banks of the Bannockburn. Now go in God's name. Go, hen." Even as he was saying this he was stacking his flintlocks by the door, speedily pouring powder in them. At the last moment I tried to cling to him, but he pushed me off, not roughly but kindly. "Here, lassie, toss off a bumper for me at the White Cockade, off the Grassmarket. And if ye find ma son, well guid luck tae ye baith."

This tavern was, I knew, his favorite watering hole in Edinburgh.

"Here, ye maun tak these." And he flung a pair of muskets at Nookeesa and Snowbird. "Ye'll hae yer own tomahawks." They both nodded. At this point musket balls were heard whistling through the trees, and one thudded past our heads and embedded itself into the wainscoting behind us with a violent crack.

"Wheesht a minute! Amelia, take this!" He tossed out an old leather bag tied up with a leather lace. "I kept this for a rainy day; it's no raining the noo—it's pouring." It was a heavy bag clearly filled with silver. No time to inspect now; that would keep for later. "Go! In God's name. Go!"

We needed no other invitation. We took off.

In a trice we were up the hillside, chests heaving with exertion. Down below us in the besieged cottage I could hear Angus shouting to the uncomprehending Indians, "Awa wi ye Sassenachs. Remember Prestonpans, ye red lobster bampots! Ye'll no forget Angus McOgg in a hurry!"

Eons after, by the light of my own guttering fireplace, when I stare at the wood, cracking and spitting like the vanity of boastful men, thinking of this moment after the weariness of a life crowded with the chicanery and cowardice of those men supposed to protect the frail sex, I cannot but smile at his magnificent madness as he re-created that other great folly at

Culloden. Oh, Angus, you were the roughest, dearest, gentlest man that I would never embrace. And I touch my lips to you in heaven.

There was no doubt Angus's heroism saved our lives, for he held them off long enough for us to make our escape. From his barricaded stockade he pounded round after round, veritable fusillades of grapeshot into the enemy, as if a platoon of the Gordon Highlanders was encamped within.

Cresting the ridge I caught my last glimpse of the cabin, now a great red bonfire of crackling, exploding wood. All the homeliness I had tried to build in the last year, the little trifles that add up to a home, placed on tables and bedsteads: all gone. Our vegetable garden was now filled with dancing, shrieking Red devils trampling everything underfoot. I hoped and prayed that Angus had gone down long before this moment. I had no illusions as to his fate. Not so long ago Colonel Crawford had been burnt at the stake near here.

Nookeesa tugged me away, urging me to hasten, signaling frantically with his hand, hissing, "Let's go, lassie." We ran on. I noticed that both Snowbird and Nookeesa had lost the plasticity of expression they employed when speaking English, and now their faces resembled the ancient stone idols of fierce Babylonian gods. Momentarily it flashed through my mind: Are they suddenly my captors?

We continued through the woods westward, which was nothing if not perverse since civilization lay to the east, but as it was evening perhaps it was better to follow the sun. We pounded upward on the slippery path, always hearing those diabolical shrieks, sometimes fading, sometimes nearer. My dress was catching on every bramble, holding me up and leaving a trail of threads that even a tenderfoot could follow, never mind a Shawnee tracker. I kept tripping, and at length fell down in the mud, where I lay weeping in despair. An arrow landed, quivering into the tree in front of me. I am dead, I thought, and all because I politely invited some aboriginals for tea and cake.

A tomahawk went thunk into the tree just below the arrow. Their shots were getting better and nearer. I screamed and tried to get up. Nookeesa hauled me onto my feet and threw me forward on the path. We crossed the ridge top. Ahead was a gully pointing sharply downhill. We scrambled down on our bottoms till we landed with a splash into the streambed that marked its foot. I pulled my skirts up to avoid the muddy banks.

"Stay in the river bottom," Nookeesa ordered.

It was cold and numbing on my legs, but it seemed sensible to obey and not to make tracks in the mud. The stream twisted and turned so that every bend was out of sight of the other. Our pursuers split up: one group going downstream, the other following a bramble-crammed buttress uphill. At least they were confused as to our whereabouts.

We hit the valley bottom and immediately joined another stream system. But the muddy banks on either side were now limestone cliffs, which effectively trapped us in their cauldron. The stream beneath our feet broadened and began to foam and froth. The current was pulling more insistently at our legs. In front of us we could hear the blast of raging waters. Then we saw boiling, thundering rapids straight in our path. We had surely reached an impasse. But Nookeesa with his rock-climbing skills led us up the rocky bluff that bisected the cliff. The hem of my skirt kept slipping down, masking my footholds. This was impossible! I started crying aloud in fear as I slithered about at the foot of the cliff, too timid to commit myself to upward progress. Clutching a slippery hold, terrified, I prayed aloud to the Lord, reminding him that God was an Englishman, imploring Him not to let his little compatriot daughter fall into the hands of the heathen nor into the cauldron beneath.

In this strange, dangerous setting, Snowbird actually had the impertinence to laugh, and I said, "She laughs, who put us in this pickle." An ignoble sentiment to let slip, but I plead guilty. Nookeesa couldn't contain himself enough not to smile even in this dire time. He shuffled crabwise across the rock, down to where I was perched like a frozen parrot, and ripped the dress—petticoat and all—off my back, leaving me with only a distressing collection of unmentionables to cover my nakedness. I finally burst into tears. I say finally, but the tap had been turned off and on all through this dreadful event. If death and torture was not enough, I the virgin daughter of a decent minister of the Church of England was about to be dishonored in my final moments.

My concerns on this score were out of place. My lacy cotton pantaloons were more suited to crag scrabbling than a billowing frock, and my petticoats and overdress were put to use as a rudimentary rope to haul me up the cliff. We reached a ledge two thirds of the way up, and behind a thicket parted by Nookeesa we entered a hidden cave he had discovered on his hunting trips.

Without so much as an adieu, my damask and silk dress, the last relic of my career in New York, was consigned to the river below the falls. However, this watery dispatch served a good purpose, as the splash drew the Indians' attention. They came babbling away amongst themselves to the foaming pond and, seeing the garments billowing before being submersed in the froth, concluded with much ululating that we had been drowned in the rocks beneath. Judging by the volume of their caterwauling it was good riddance to bad rubbish. Honor was justified by the chase, and the angry gods appeased by the watery sacrifice. As they went away they were chuckling. I had never heard an Indian laughing. It was a strange, gurgling, giggling sound. I deduced they were talking about her, and saying not very nice things.

Inside the cave Snowbird reddened; at least she had the decency to have some sense of shame. Even in the half-light I could detect a change in her complexion, and she sent off our departing host with a gesture of surprising vulgarity for a princess. For safety's sake we had to remain put for the night, and a distinctly unpleasant one it was, I can tell you.

For those who sigh after the delights of untrammeled Nature's Realm, here is the story of that long, long night. I froze and shivered in my severely diminished nocturnal attire and had the dubious pleasure of listening to that pair keeping themselves warm by rogering the night through. And if you believed that Indians are emotionally undemonstrative you were never more mistaken. Snowbird groaned, wailed, and hollered her appreciation as they thrashed away at each other every hour on the hour. Of course it was their honeymoon; I forgot. Where they got the stamina from after that chase, goodness knows. Perhaps I was jealous, but then I hadn't realized how much fun that unconsecrated sacrament must be. Snowbird was certainly an appreciative recipient, but judging by the drumming of feet and the war whoops coming from Nookeesa's mouth, it was one of those rare Christian pleasures where it is even better to give than to receive. With that philosophical insight I finally fell asleep.

We emerged next morning to one of those glorious dawns that are a feature of the frontier: the sky a milky blue and a positive aviary of song birds overhead with their dawn chorus. Only the three of us—stiff, starved, and cold—were grumpy. Without breaking our fast we took up our westward trail. The two savages broke into a cantering lope, while I dragged myself forward, exhausted and increasingly resentful of their interference in my pleasant situation. I noticed that their cross-cultural friendship toward me had diminished once their kinfolk left off their life-threatening activities. It was not a neighborly, happy troika that galloped through the never-ending forest. They grunted at each other in their barbarous tongue, then turned to snarl at me, accusing me of sloth and general unfitness. "Lazy, fat-bellied white lard, move your bones." And there he had touched on a nerve. Nothing in my upbringing had ever induced me to break into more than a mild trot. Perspiration was as unfamiliar as a visit from my Dublin aunt. My most energetic exercise so far had been my stepping out in a slow minuet with the highwayman.

By a mountain stream I stopped to slap water on my face while they had a short powwow. Nookeesa concluded that, as we were not out of the woods as far as trouble went, we should try and hit a pioneer settlement on the Ohio River, for all the tribes (through their mysterious communication system) would be aware we were outlawed, and open season declared on our scalps. This plan perked me up, for now they would have to take me a bit more seriously as their passport into the White world.

Hardships were nothing to these two, while my lack of food, lack of sleep, and lack of proper clothes weakened me so much I was dragging along pathetically, which for some reason gave them perverse pleasure; they sniggered while I bumbled from bramble to bramble, frequently landing my arse in a freezing puddle while they jogged confidently along the nigh invisible trail.

CHAPTER 11

Paris on the Ohio and Snowbird takes French Leave

For two days we headed through the forest toward the great Ohio River, passing several small settlements hugging the shores of the Kanawha River, whose settlers seemed to be barely hanging on to their lives. Each and every one of them was keeping a weather eye out for imminent Indian attacks, all with their muskets primed and ready, stacked by their plowshares. At Briscoe's Settlement, which consisted of maybe a dozen shacks and the same number of tents, a jumpy customer in a tricorn hat decorated with eagle feathers greeted us. His eyes were constantly swerving round the horizon, long rifle crouched at the ready, when he warned us, "Indian attacks, they be pretty bad this year. Delawares, Wyandots, Mingo, you name it—they's not particular whose scalp they take, long as it's white. And say! These two lovebirds you got with you, I'd be watchin' them, for ain't they two birds of a different feather? That woman's a high yaller Frenchie if I'm not mistook, and the man's pure cigar-store Injun. No ma'am, don't sleep without a loaded musket by your pillow, and good luck to youse. Ye asking me what to do? Don't stop runnin' till you hit the Frenchies' place across the big river." His wife, pitying me, gave me an old dress and mutch cap, which had belonged to their daughter, long since murdered by the Red man.

For the first time in America, I was excited to be visiting a specific locale. I had heard much about the fabulous city of Marietta, that North American Parisian paradise founded by aristocratic refugees from Madame Guillotine. Dotted playfully around in the suburbs were plaster-cast, mock-marble shepherd's cottages a la mode of Marie Antoinette's creation in Fontainebleau; elsewhere great Palladian columns frolicking with putti and cupids, armed to the very teeth with lovers' darts, overlooked the Arcadian hills, misty and tantalizing in the distance. By the great chateaux, reminiscent of one emerging from the dawn mist in the Loire Valley, haughty damosels tittered and miscued their croquet strokes to have them nudged back to order by their languid beaux, who looked forward to tickling their balls through the hoops left in delicious disarray by the picnic's aftermath. After a year amongst crude frontier people, compelled by cruel circumstances to travel with the most uncouth of companions, you could not imagine how much I was looking forward to all the treats of polite society.

Arriving anywhere on a rainy day is liable to dampen first impressions. The whole town had the dank, dilapidated glower of a wet Sunday in a Lancashire mill town. I used my execrable French to secure us lodgings, this being the first priority before going sightseeing. The auberge where we took refuge was what was called an American hotel, where the spirit of companionable democracy took precedence over the European's class-conscious desire for privacy.

Once we had time to take stock of our situation, and I had time to inspect the miserable collection of shacks that lined the riverbank, I saw once again how the world was not up to the challenge of my imagination. When I spoke French, the rude Acadians laughed and spurted forth rivulets of tobacco juice. Their French was that of the voyageur, not of Versailles. To make it worse, many of the trappers were not French at all, but of raw Scotch ancestry like my dear, deceased friend Angus, and their French was less pidgin than sparrow. Discourtesy was their byword.

They delighted in being grossly offensive to our Indian brave, whom they treated as a plantation negro, spitting on him and pushing him into the mud, of which there was a super-abundance. To me they were moderately offensive. Only to our Indian princess were they entirely sweet, neither laughing at her nor jostling her off the sidewalk. To her they were courtesy itself, sweeping great bows and making space for her to pass by, capping these outbursts of charm with offers to show her the temples of Diana and Selena on a moonlight stroll.

To this young lady these gestures were manna from heaven. She lapped them up, strutting haughtily to and fro on the Main Street, promenading a la Madame de Pompadour, twirling her wampum beads across her cheeks as if they were an opera fan, while making coquette's eyes to all and sundry in breeches, culottes, or even kilts; or you might find her holding court, curled up on the sofa in the hotel parlor, monopolizing both couch and conversation, occasionally breaking off to pat down her finery. Her suitors, seated or standing, all waited on her command while their dish of tea went cold. Her almond eyes darted about the room restlessly, eager to move in for the kill, and when she spotted anything that took her fancy, Snowbird would beckon with her index finger beguilingly, and there would be the lucky gallant who would take her arm for the evening (and regret it the next morning when he turned out his pockets).

Naturellement, she abandoned her buckskin and beads with the utmost celerity, and when she finally made her metamorphosis the effect was unbelievable. All who encountered her that day when she emerged from the milliners, a butterfly on a bright spring day, just gawped, speechless. She had no money, and when she attempted to pay with wampum beads the owner was discretion herself in rejecting those charming *trouves*, saying she had no idea of the exchange rate and feared she might possibly undervalue these items that she was positive were of a rarity not likely to be surpassed in this area. Then she gently introduced Snowbird to the concept of credit. The lady of the establishment had little doubt that with her charms the princess would soon retrieve any liabilities she might accrue.

Now that she was the most scintillating newcomer in town, I came in for a deal of secondhand attention. Luckily I was not too deformed of face or feature to be an embarrassment, and became a moon to her great sun, getting the benefit of her discards, of which there was a great number, while she was busy sorting out the municipal pecking order. As things fell out it was mainly the rapscallions who came back for more, since she was so hurtful in her rejection that the more sensitive souls tended to wilt away, not returning for that second bite of the cherry, which was me.

It was the Indian campsite all over again, except that Nookeesa (or "Newquay," as the settlers called him) was reduced to the part of Buttons, a role he didn't relish but which Snowbird subjected him to mercilessly. He had to be on hand at every moment—to fetch her fan if she was in need of cooling, or her muff if she was in want of warming, to attend to every draught that tickled the princess—and had better wash his hands when warming her chocolate, and no more stirring it with his fingers. I do not know when her passion for Nookeesa faded, or why, because he had acted splendidly on our forced march, but it had vanished as surely as the morning mist when the sun gets up. As she explained to me in a mishmash of tongues: "*Je suis toute passion.* My feelings are French, and he's *comme le vin* that does not *marche bien.* In the village he was adequate, *mais ici*"—she gave a genuine Francophone shrug—"*avec les Blancs* he is ridiculous," rounding it off with a dismissive twirl of her pink parasol.

Not knowing whether he was coming or going, Nookeesa took to following her around with great mooncalf eyes, which infuriated milady, now displaying something of the chilling snobbery reminiscent of Mary-Anne back home, dismissing a redundant suitor. The constant clamor of their quarrels was driving me out of the boarding house and wishing them a good riddance, for after all it was their nonsense that had killed off Angus. But in fact she turned to me as an ally, saying she would rather take refuge in Sheepy Magna than ever again associate with malodorous Red men. I must have oversung the praises of my native heath, for I knew that in her current state of high-handedness its simple charms would rapidly stale.

When I warned her of this possibility, she sniffed and said the company of any Englishman, no matter how lowborn, would be more pleasing than hanging out with a savage who couldn't tell a scalp from a periwig. Nookeesa blanched, not knowing how to react, for if he acted like an Indian he would only be proving her point, while he as yet did not yet know how to parry an insult with a jest.

Meanwhile, whilst playing the fine lady indoors, out on the street any Indian who was unwise enough to cross her path and try to hit her up for a subvention for old times' sake got a kick for his pains from a pair of dainty but finely pointed booties, followed up (if the poor rascal was not nimble enough to escape) by a smart jab from the point of a most fashionable silk parasol. Civilized usage? Well, as I said, she caught on quickly.

One event struck me as rather odd. Our waiter at table that particular evening was not French but straight out of the backwoods English—or rather American, as I must remember to say nowadays. She had already ticked him off for failure to arrange the complex cutlery setting in its correct format (rather specialized knowledge for someone just come to town from the Stone Age). Now, counting our check, the garçon was reckoning in pounds sterling, as was customary here in the back of beyond, and then translating the sum into Yankee dollars in order to collect the cash. It had been a confusing night, as some of the guests had paid in Russian kopecks and others in French louis d'or, mingled with a rash of Spanish doubloons. Not unnaturally the poor lad got confused, but Snowbird, instead of being patient (never having had to learn this virtue), turned on the boy and chided him in quick and very fluent English of the East Midland variety. "Oi, stupid! Didn't thy mither shows ye how to count! What d'ye reckon fingers is for?" The poor lad shied away as if kicked by a horse.

Marry come up! Where did that come from? But the suspicion and the moment passed, for at that instant in walked a dark, handsome stranger, and our former lady of the faded buckskin and wampum beads came over all coy. The wretched boy thankfully withdrew, and said adieu to our tale.

Offers of marriage she received by the cartload, but to none did she pay the slightest heed. She laughed as she used the proposals for kindling, reserving the loudest shriek for those attempting to express their sentiments in poetry. That is with the exception of one. This was the dark French chevalier, whose dress, though of the frontier, was impeccable (Beau Brummel's second cousin, forsooth), although contrary to foppish custom his skin was not powdered white, but was so burned by the sun he could be taken for an Indian. However, it would take a bold boyo to tell him that, as he looked every inch a killing gentleman, and could pip an ace of hearts at twenty paces. I had witnessed him doing this when he entertained the company in the hotel lounge, and had no wish to see him do the encore on a human heart. This little demonstration acted as an aphrodisiac on her, for there she was flushing like a flibbertigibbet parlor maid behind a wildly fluttering fan when he found his mark. This Monsieur Jean was just up her street—mad, bad, and dangerous—so she laid it on with a pitchfork. A risky experiment indeed, as he didn't look the type to take no for answer, and if she was reluctant to let his Cupid darts gain ingress, well, let's say she hadn't been warned.

The man was at ease with everyone; whether Black, Red, or chalky White he knew the right thing to say and when to say it. How can I describe a gentleman of so many textures, who would not have been out of place being received at Versailles, but who managed a perfect balance on the slippery slope of fashion, so that while always perfectly attired there was ne'er a trace of foppery? If the loutish frontiersman wished to mock, one glance at his cold, killing eyes discouraged all but the most stupid, and many who had started out with drollery were soon stuttering groveling apologies. But this was rarely done, as his knowledge of backwoods lore engendered respect, as did his readiness to challenge with sword, knife, and powder any who disputed his cut of cloth or honor at the tables. He was acquainted with the customs and dining habits of the Shawnee; he had read Tom Paine; he had dined with Voltaire and knew enough of the Norfolk system of crop rotation to pass an idle hour with Farmer George at Windsor. He possessed one painting by Fragonard and a sketch by David, so he said, and I believed him. He could play the clavichord and, with equal virtuosity, the frontier fiddle. In short he was dangerous as the devil and as sweet as an angel. This was the man who had Snowbird's card marked, and she was on the brink of succumbing to him.

"Would mademoiselle care to saunter in the moonlight down by the Petit Pont d' Avignon and watch the moonlight shimmering on our pseudo Seine?"

To this nonsense Snowbird simpered like a village virgin and consulted her engagement book. "*Mais oui, monsieur.* If your ardor is not too pressing, allow me but a moment to make myself presentable to *tout le monde.*" She flitted upstairs for an extensive powdering of the nose and general titivation. Poor old Nookeesa, poor spurned Red man: Join the rest of your tribe of rotting turkeys in oblivion. He too ran upstairs, but it was too late. Mademoiselle gave him a look that told him he had joined the history books.

Snowbird came rustling downstairs, radiant and triumphant in her finery, wearing a hat adorned with ostrich feathers. Jean took her arm like the gallant *gentilhomme* that he was and led her away.

The Frenchman had a canoe weighted down with stones and sunk in shallow water by the banks of the Ohio a quarter mile north of the town. He could have said it was a caravel to transport her to the mystical Orient, and she would have believed it, so silly was she for him. "'Tis a day for beauty, and a day for pleasure. Let us take ourselves and a picnic basket up the stream. I know a spot, *un joli petit arbor*, where the brilliance of the flowers might possibly serve as a fitting setting for your radiance, although I fear they will be merely adequate in comparison to your pulchritude. I insist you allow me to paint your portrait and sell it later in London, Paris, or maybe even Philadelphia if the Congress would cease being so damnably colonial—if I can bear to part with it. If you abandon me, *Cherie*, I will not relinquish it but keep it in front of me as a reminder to commit suicide, after I have cleared up these little matters with *mon dieu*." What mortal woman could resist this overpowering barrage of garlicky Gallic charm delivered by one so sweetly perfumed, a factor worth noting amongst these raw and ofttimes rancid frontiersmen, who rarely saw a bath and had never heard of a tablet of soap?

He escorted her to the creek bank. Easel, brushes, and palette were already stowed neatly away. Snowbird daintily lifted her skirts up on entering the canoe, revealing an ankle and calf most of us would die for. To add to the tone of the proceedings, a Black man carried her valise to the boat, whereupon he was handed a *bon cadeau* by the voyageur. The Negro tipped his hat, gave the birch bark hull a shove, and off they paddled into the middle of the stream. Or rather he did all the work; she, nestling under her ubiquitous pink parasol, her skirts spread out so you could see the delicate lace work on the silk, concentrated on looking pretty. On the sandy riverbank a little crowd of disappointed admirers gave her and the frog a sporting cheer. Nookeesa, sitting alone on some bleak, river-washed stones, wept.

The early morning mist into which they vanished hung heavily over the river, the only sign of their passage being the diminishing splash of oars as they paddled upriver. They were never seen again.

There were tales, of course. They had been ambushed by Mingoes and, after a horrible tribal rape, had been burnt alive together, finally embracing each other on the stake. The Frenchman had married her and taken her home; later both were dispatched by Madame Guillotine, holding hands on the scaffold and displaying an aristocratic insouciance that even the most rabid revolutionaries reluctantly acknowledged. A further refinement on the gossip came when news filtered through that gallant Jean was no more than a voyageur on a spree, who liked expensive clothes and expensive women. He stole her away upriver, but was stopped in midflow by a Shawnee arrow. Snowbird, now irrevocably damned as a White woman, was sold into slavery to a Mingo chief, from where she joined the ranks of oblivion. The canard that she really was a white woman was easily accepted. Just look at her suspicious origins and her too-speedy mastering of idiomatic English and French. Anyway, there were enough White women kidnapped by the Indians to fill a fleet of canoes and make that variation on the theme plausible.

Much later, a fantastic rumor rippled round the frontier that the Frenchman was none other than the diversely scented He-Who, all cleaned and togged up. But even this ardent suitor had had enough of her and her high maintenance carping and demands, so that after a few weeks of being her hair stylist and personal groomer, he sold her as a slave to a band of Wyandots up on the Muskingum River in Eagle Feather's town, and good riddance to the lady.

As each tale came in wilder than the last, I wanted to say, "Stop!" And whenever I saw somebody starting a sentence with, "Did you hear the latest about Snowbird," I would run away clutching my ears. Whatever version of the story we believed (and you had to take them all with a pinch of salt), we knew she had come to no good end. I was sad for her, but have to say I didn't wear mourning longer than was dictated by fashion. She was a beautiful but bad woman, and no one's man was safe with her in the house, so she no doubt deserved to share the fate of Cleopatra, Messalina, Lucrezia Borgia, and other naughty ladies from the past. Perhaps if I were aware that she had been abducted I would have paid more attention. As it was I was left to moralize on the fickleness of royalty, especially after her initial declaration of passion for sadly reduced Nookeesa and the price we all had to pay for it, especially now he had been tossed aside like a once-treasured, raggedy doll. But as I said, all this comes later on.

To save money when we arrived we booked one room only. Anyway, there was only one room to spare so it was Hobson's choice. Mistress McGillevry, our landlady, a Spartan Scot, was prepared to put up with three in the room on the well-founded basis that three is a crowd, and where gooseberries grow love will not flower. Although she did say when she pocketed our cash (after a minute inspection of same, which included a solid bite of the coin), "And nae hanky-panky, mind."

I don't know what she made of Nookeesa. Presumably she thought he was a Negro page boy, a very fashionable accessory in London, whom the two of us took turns to employ. When we undressed or attended to our toilette, we told Nookeesa to get under the bed. However, after Snowbird took French leave, the picture altered. Mistress McGillevry's moral outrage gained a head start on the claims of hospitality. That afternoon, as we were still getting over the shock of our desertion, there came a knocking at our door.

"You twa open up. I'm no haein' this. Now yon frilly hoor has shot the crow, the twa of ye will be skelpin' weel together. I'm no haeing my hoose turned intae a den of debauchery. So oot ye gang."

"But we don't do anything. We put a bundle, a bolster, in the bed betwixt us, so no hanky-panky."

"Dae ye think I was born yesterday?"

"But Newquay's like my brother!"

"Yer brither wi yon complexion. Pull the ither one." The door was opened up. The landlady stood back, arms folded as if she were sizing

Nookeesa up for a bout of wrestling; it slowly dawned on her as if she was seeing him for the first time. "And him, he's no darkie!" Her voice went up in pitch in anger and alarm. "He's an Injun! A Red savage in my hoose! Oh my God! I could have been scalped in my bed! Get oot o' here this instant."

We left a note on the dresser explaining our sudden absence to our fickle friend. "*Quelle dommage. Il faut partir.* So sorry we had to leave." No elaboration necessary on our togetherness in this crisis, considering the treatment she had been meting out to Nookeesa in the last fortnight; but note, I wrote it in French as a sop to her recent interest in matters Francophone. We picked up our stuff and trailed in a desultory fashion down the stairs and out into the street.

"And don't think ahm no goin' tae tell the boys aboot this, ye wee hoor!" Mistress McGillevry said. By the boys she meant the local Caledonian society, of whose company I could say enough was enough. "And you, ye black, red villain." Her voice picked up even further into a gruesome shriek. "A scalping's nae good enough for ye. They'll fry ye in hell!"

We fairly scuttled through the town. Just outside the town limits was an old red barn that looked as if it hadn't had much recent usage. "I'm tired. Let's stop here the night," I said. And so we fell asleep on a rough straw bed, just like the princess abducted by the gypsies in the old song. She must have had finer straw than us for she slept soundly, but that of course is a song and must be pithy and rhyme so I reasoned.

Dusting the straw off in the morning after a scratchy, sleepless night, we considered our options. They weren't great. We had outstayed our welcome in Marietta, and if our landlady made good her promise of a visitation from the local Caledonian Society, it could be fatal for both of us. For no logical reason they were eager to blame us for Snowbird's defection.

Now they pretended that she had misled them into believing she was White, thus allowing them to switch their ancient racial prejudices against us, a supposed mixed-race couple. We sat around listlessly twiddling our thumbs in the straw, letting the day pass, and now it was evening.

"Ye know we might as well shift ourselves. At least we don't need to pack," I said.

"Where do we go?"

"Dunno. Somewhere. Far from here." Somehow overnight I had become the leader of the team. There must have been something in being the vicar's daughter. I walked to the door of the barn. Hanging on a nail was an old rusty spur. Not an obvious place to put an odd spur, I mused. Could it have been put there deliberately? Well it must have done at some time. Shades of Robert the Bruce getting a plateful of spurs for breakfast. I took it as a hint for us to get out of town fast. "Let's go!"

A glance down the road in the dusk and I thought I could just discern red glimmering torches searching houses; the old fiery crosses calling the highlanders to clan warfare must have been dusted off and brought out of their cupboards.

We ran till we were way out of town and holed up in a wood, where we stayed all the next day and the following night. Around noon (it must have been, for the sun was shining directly above, piercing the foliage in the tree) we heard a dog barking and tearing back and forth through the wood as if to pick up a scent, followed by crashing through the undergrowth. We froze, and I tried to burrow myself in a ditch. The mutt stood above us barking its head off, then we heard: "C'mon Rover, let's git along. Iffen you be so loud, Mom will find us." The voice was high and fluting. It was a kid playing hooky from where he ought to be—kitchen duty, working in the fields, or at school. We peered out to see a young lad, hands in pockets, fishing pole under his arm, whistling without a care in the world. His high-pitched, tuneless whistle faded away into nothingness. Nookeesa managed to forage some weeds and berries, which he claimed were edible.

They didn't look appetizing, and they tasted worse, but chewing the disagreeable mush took one's mind off more unpalatable matters.

If the good citizens had been following us they weren't showing too much enthusiasm for the project, because we never saw hide nor hair of them again. I don't think they were overconcerned about our racial solecism. For after all, what was in it for them? And as for the fiery crosses—merely a colorful sunset.

CHAPTER 12

The Chief Brings Home a Bride

We hurried back into town and headed for the put-in by the Ohio River bank. Our luck was in. There was nobody about. The vigilantes were probably sleeping off their hangovers, and best of all, a voyageur's canoe was bobbing about in the shallows, fitted out with paddles, tent, and enough furs to make for camping in style and give us money from trading the goods in afterward. This was the first lucky break we had.

Our canoe slipped into the stream like scissors cutting silk. The setting sun's bright copper ball hung over the trees on the western shore, its light dampened by a gauzy sheet of mist hanging over the branches, illuminating us as if we were center stage. We slid into the shadows to be unseen, but there was ne'er a sound to be heard save for a solitary dog barking to be let in to its master's cabin. At first we jumped at any creak or ripple, expecting to see trappers leaping into canoes in hot pursuit, but there was nothing save the water lapping against the hull and the dog's plaintive cries getting fainter in the distance, a reassuring measure of how much water we had put between us and Marietta, which would never be Paris on the Ohio.

The sun was peeking through the trees on the Kentucky side of the river, splaying tendrils of gold that shimmered on the little waves, when we put in at the Shawnee town, where the Scioto flows into the Ohio. An old lad wearing ragged, greasy buckskin, which smelled as if the dead animal was still in situ, hauled in our canoe. He tipped his head in salutation—"*Bonjour, jolie mademoiselle.* Hey, Injun laddie"—and stuck his quavering hand out, hinting at the great service he had done us. "How's about helping an old chiel wi his breakfast dram, your honors?"

I dropped a couple of roubles into his hand, knowing it is seldom foolish to make a good first impression. He squinted at them, put them in his mouth to bite on, and then, satisfied they would be acceptable, said, "*Merci*, sweetheart. I'll see it's spent wisely." He stood for a minute, shaking his shoulders as if he were inwardly debating a weighty proposition from Herr Kant, then said, "Be honored if ye'll jine me for breakfast."

Off we went to a smoky log cabin packed with his raucous chums, some ensconced on logs filling in for benches and some sitting on the dirt floor, all busily scoffing down plates of pork and beans with great wedges of sourdough bread doing the honors as cutlery. Whisky jars were emptied and recharged at a healthy rate. Invited to have a swig of his morning refreshment, I took a cautious sip. "Ye'll find nae better poteen between here and old Dublin Town," I was informed, meanwhile a cannonball exploded in my head. The taste was indescribable. The neighbor who had generously invited us to share his dram laughed at the expression on my face. "Never have tatties been put to better use."

I thanked him politely, at which he took a good long look at me, slowly nodding his head up and down.

"You're not long off the boat, lass, I'll be bound. Wi manners like these you might be the vicar's daughter." When I told him, he muttered some incomprehensible oath, and then, "What brings a lass like you to this abandoned portion of the world?"

After hearing a severely truncated version of my story he said, "It's like what happened to thon ither lass." It seems that everyone on the frontier knows everything about everyone else's business. "There's this Frenchie

Creole girl, see. Seems her best friend and her lover was cheatin' on her. Then this gent comes along, invites her on a picnic to take her mind off being deserted by her two best friends in the world. But this French-speaking, perfumed skunk was a White slaver who touted her round the tribes— Iroquois, Seneca, Delaware, and so forth—to sell her off to the highest bidder."

It could be none other than Snowbird doing her Parisian coquette act.

The old voyageur chuckled, as people do when talking about another's ill luck. "Mademoiselle, monsieur, *le deux* were—how you say it—whoring behind her back. They left her *deserte* and *pauvre*. But she is not *Française, mais Anglaise, d'une petite ville Quatre Hommes Coeur*."

So it just shows how gossip can turn the tale around and how successful she was in pulling the wool over people's eyes with her French routine and her honest Injun eyes. But get this. Here's the punch line: So she was not French at all but English from a place called Four Men's Hearts. Now, how possibly could an Indian squaw know about a piddling little hamlet, a dozy little nothing place a morning's stroll from Sheepy? I for one had never mentioned it. Surely not?

It was then that certain things began to click. Behaviors that made Snowbird almost the doppelganger of dear, nasty old Mary-Anne—her way with suitors, her looks, her nose stuck high above the human midden, her gestures—how could I not have spotted it? I remember her dismissing He-Who by slamming her hand down as if she was slamming a biscuit lid shut on a naughty boy's hand; what was that but an exact replica of Mary-Anne's gesture? How had her complexion changed so? Then I remembered Snowbird making a great deal of the restorative properties of blackberry juice on the skin, her slipping into English and French as easily as she donned the garments of an English milady. No squaw could have done it so easily, could they now? How could I have been so dim? Well, there's none so blind as those who don't want to see. But then how had she gotten herself across the Atlantic? And why would she have wanted to get herself across? She had plenty of worlds to conquer in Leicestershire, and only those who were desperate made the crossing voluntarily. What if it were true? But there again such coincidences were only possible in these novelties we call novels; perish the thought.

We re-embarked and were ceremonially launched with a warm endorsement of cheers and good hearty pushes from the patrons of the inn; turning a corner we were drawn into another, slower world. As I dipped my oar languorously into the water and watched the snared marsh weed slide off the oar like a sad salad, my mind tripped up a beat, just as dancers do when the fiddler tires of solemn old songs and strikes up a hornpipe. And all around spring buds were blossoming in their meadows.

To our front, families of turtles dived off the banks into the water; some (the wiser ones) lay lazily on a log. Maple seeds dropping from the air whirligigged in neat formation like columns of dancers; a goose piped away northward; sandpipers sported then flitted away, hovering inches above the stream, their wing tips lightly flicking the water's surface. A muskrat frolicked in ever decreasing circles; purple and white phlox flowers lined up in shady bowers encircled by yellow butterflies. We stopped and picnicked under the shade of a rock bridge complete with its own waterfall. Rough-winged culdon, purple martins, and great majestic herons glided downstream afore our bow as if they were admirals of our one-boat fleet. It was here in this cauldron of Nature, not in Marietta, that we were presented with as sublime a prospect as any dreamt up by the brush of a Watteau or a Fragonard.

Again we took to the placid waters. I shuffled lazily in the boat and let my toe trail in the water. This was my attempt at being seductive—my first, I hasten to add. "Newquay, what do you think of me?"

"You are a very nice lady. Much nicer than Ice-Bird princess."

"No. I mean do you think of me the way men think of women?" I slid my hand lightly under my bosoms to underline my point. Naughty me! What was I thinking? For a moment I thought the boat was going to capsize.

"No! No, Mrs. McAngus! I don't think of it! You are not like them."

There was a long silent spell. I determined not to break it to force him to say something, anything. What a naughty tease am I.

"You are like the great lady who wears white robe and wimple—'frigid nun,' the men in colored skirts call you. Men steer clear of you for you know too many things; you can beat men at own game if you care, but you do not wish, for you act like the clever mouse that never sleeps but lets other get stuck in traps, and so you get to keep the big cheese."

I resolved then and there to be the mouse that turned. I asked, "Could I ever be like that other regal rodent shrew? You know who I mean."

He laughed. "You mean like a dog in heat!" He tended to take things literally. "Never! You are much too nice; you are a very bashful maiden. No bitch in heat howling at moon." He laughed again, choking it off abruptly. "See! Now I talk too much and we must row."

"Why must we row?" I queried, enjoying the languid moment and reluctant to replace it.

"War canoes come toward us mighty swift."

"Say 'swiftly,' not 'swift.'"

"Swiftly! Woman who talks too much, just paddle swiftly and not argue!"

An arrow slicing the water beside us put an end to further discussion. I looked back to see a sight to freeze my innards. Satan's own spawn. Twelve war canoes were stroking powerfully toward us, all filled to the brim with bronzed warriors.

"Pull!" Nookeesa shrieked. I practically pulled my shoulders out of their sockets. Our bowsprit shot high out of the water. It was to no avail. As if drawn by some infernal contraption of James Watt, their boats swept toward us with a rhythmic, steady determination.

A shower of arrows sprinkled the water on both sides of our canoe. *With a bit of luck,* I thought, *we might yet make it to the Kentucky shore.* I looked hopefully at the bank. Straight in front was an inlet shaded by trees, which might just give us a hiding place. By straining every muscle we could get there and run ashore. Nookeesa saw it and turned the canoe toward the bay, which turned out to be a brackish pool spotted with floating leaves and scum that slowed the canoe almost to a halt. It was a forlorn hope, and it died on the instant.

Three canoes slid out of the shallows under the trees and cut across our bow, their backwash almost overturning our canoe. An arrow winged across the sky and landed with a shuddering thud on the woodwork of the canoe, pinning Nookeesa's hand to the gunnels. He screamed, and I was sensible of a terrifying spasm of shock and a warm wetness spreading through my under-linen.

There was a screeching crash as one of the Indian boats rammed into ours, and a horrible painted savage leapt into the bowsprit. That face daubed with green and red woad was a fiend, a totem pole of murderous savagery. He held aloft a stone casse-tête poised to smash my skull like an eggshell. His flesh stank of a hundred hyenas; his muscles oiled with panther grease were as tight as whipcord. Now I would know what it was to die.

There was a violent crunching shock, and our world turned upside down. Our canoe had crashed head on into a stout oak tree, and the bow jolted upward, throwing the Indian into a tangle of overhanging boughs. The main branch, flexed like a longbow, sprang back, catching hold of his necklace of teeth and dragging him up out of the canoe; his feet were peddling madly. The necklace snapped, and his neck was caught in the branches, throttling him. He grunted like a bullfrog, his feet wriggling as the life was choked out of him in what I hoped would be a horribly slow death.

In that instant another canoe collided into ours, knocking me into the water. I went down and had enough sense to swim under the boat and head out toward the Ohio side, which I knew was Indian territory, but it was no moment to be discriminating. The water was freezing, but luck was on my side, for its murkiness gave me enough cover to get into the trees.

I scrambled to the shore and looked back. That last look was enough to make me hate the Red man forever. On the other side Nookeesa was being hauled to the ground, and they were slicing away at his skin as if they were skinning a rabbit. In their frenzy, their interest was completely bound up in the torment of this hapless man, one of their own kind. His screaming could have raised the devils out of hell, and amongst that litany of terror I heard him shrieking, "Amy! Amy! Help me! Please!" which turned my bowels to water.

I saw I was looking at the mirror image of my own death if I didn't rapidly get away from that spot. I felt my hair standing on end; I was rooted to the spot, but knew I had better make an exit before my scalped hair became a conversation piece in some squaw's wigwam.

I scrambled up the muddy trace of a deer path from the shore as fast as my skirts would allow, but they were getting snagged on thorn bushes from which I had to constantly wrench them clear. A great shrieking banshee howl erupted from the Red devils on the shoreline. They had seen me, and now turned their attention away from Nookeesa to me. A stone axe whirred through the air and thudded into a tree hard by my right shoulder.

I was making encouraging progress, for the path, slimy and steep as it was, afforded my pattens more purchase than moccasins, whose owners kept slipping on their bottoms, and then sat howling with impotent rage before standing, slithering and stumbling onward. But what hope had I, a lass adrift on an alien landscape, against these warriors on their home turf? I kept on running along the trail, which was becoming steadily steeper and slicker. My skirt caught again on a patch of brambles. I pulled at it, but that just snagged more cloth. I tugged and I tugged till I finally ripped it loose, but that hesitation was fatal. The drumming of footsteps on the ground told me that the race was lost. Crying like a baby I ran on, but the tears in my eyes blinded me, for I ran full tilt into a tree root that lay across my path, tripped, and fell flat on my face.

I jumped up, but was again flattened to the deck, this time by a huge warrior. I spat full in his face, but that did nothing to quench his lascivious grin spread over the ugliest features you could ever imagine, with the contours and texture of a misshapen potato with nose, chin, and mouth sprouting up as angry excrescences. He had me fixed on the ground, belly to belly, his arms pinioning mine. Three of his comrades came up and had a little verbal set-to with him. "Leave something for the rest of us." At least that is what I assumed their conversation was about from the lewd gestures they were making.

Some sort of agreement must have been reached, for the others settled down to holding me down on the ground, each taking an arm and a leg apiece. A newcomer loped up and took his tomahawk out of its scabbard to sharpen it on a flint taken from a buckskin pouch on his belt. Dully I wondered whether my hair was being styled for the grand opening, or if its removal would provide a celebratory post-party moment, or there again, perhaps even be removed as if in consummation at the moment of the grand climax of the event which was swiftly to follow. Dully again, I realized it wouldn't be long till I found out.

My assailant howked up his breechclout to reveal an enormous warlike tadger bigger than I had ever seen in nightmares, bigger even than Neddy's, our amorous plough horse back home. And was it imagination, or was it really steaming in its hot red crudity? Mind you, my experience of any sort of exposure to this particular organ of affection was insufficient to form an authoritative judgment, and it might have been the teeniest periwinkle. The point, as they say, was academic. I tried to comport myself as a true English maiden and my father's daughter. Doubts about that last thought rose up to confound me, but I amended them to a daughter of the manse, and prepared to submit to a fate worse than, and then death itself.

My skirts were thrown up, pantalettes ripped asunder, and in pure terror I pissed myself. The face that I was looking at was that of hell itself. There was no noble savage here, only barbarity lit by fiendish ecstasy. My thighs were brusquely thrust apart. He undid the wrapping, then my breasts were uncased and mauled by calloused hands as if they were cows' udders.

The bulling machine stopped in mid stride. I glanced up into the trees; interspersed by a corona of golden rays was a giant figure with the shoulders of an oxen yoke, upon which sat the death-dealing face of the basilisk. Did I realize at this moment that this was to be my savior? The reactions of the others should have told me. He grunted what were evidently words of command, and the three holding me down by my shoulders and legs leapt back and stood aside sheepishly. As it happened, Whingwy Pooshie and I would rub along pretty well together, but at the moment I did not know this and felt only such a blissful feeling of relief that once again I wet myself. This time my suitor got the full gush of it, which wiped the grin off his ugly face, or so I supposed till I saw his eyes popping out and him rolling over. Neatly bisecting his skull and shoulder blades was a bloody cleaver.

The chief rapped out some orders in an icy voice, and without hesitation the three accomplices knelt down in a row facing the river. A huge chap whose hairdo resembled a witch's coven waddled up with the gait of one who has too many muscles for normal ambulatory progress, carrying a casse-tête whose blade was the size of a whetstone. The executioner turned to the chief, who gave him a slight nod, then, grunting a few words to the condemned, he walked along the ranks and, with a sound like cracking walnuts, administered the coup de grace. Exposed to so many horrors in such a short period, I couldn't even scream. All that came out of my palpitating voice box was a dry gasp.

"Stand up, White wench! Let's see what our brothers have given their lives for! Mmm! I see it is to taste your pallid flesh." The chief looked me up and down. "And I understand why," he said. "And yours is as yet unbroken?" It was less a question than a statement. It was a wise man that could tell all that at a glance, but that was his way, making instant judgments, which on reflection were usually correct. I stood up and tried to stop shaking.

"Mmm! She is like the willow in the wind, but—" He paused as the connoisseur does when appraising the fine china in front of a crowd of amateurs at the auction. I noted the feathers on his war bonnet reaching down to the ground and turning gently in the slight breeze, changing their tints to suit the mood and the light like Chinese silk. "She has good bones for mounting and will make strong papooses; therefore"—he paused, making sure all heard him—"she will be mine. Take her back, taking good care of her, and tell the squaws to prepare her for my lodge." Then he strode away dismissively. I had no time to thank him; anyroad I was too dazed to speak, what with the abrupt change in circumstances. The others stared at me, and you could understand their perplexity. Supposing I had now some standing in the community as the squire's lady (or at least lady friend) I began issuing orders of my own. They weren't too sure of my position; for one thing I was using the tongue of the Seneca Indians, all but incomprehensible to them, and a moment ago I was tribal enemy number one; now I appeared to be the king's new favorite. Not desiring an appointment with the chief's hatchet man, the braves scurried about to comply with my instructions.

"Release the brave Nookeesa and repair what's left of him."

They untied him, all the while looking quizzically at their chief to see if he countermanded the order. Nookeesa was in a pretty sorry state when thrown in front of me, scared and very resentful. His chest, which had been flayed raw, resembled a lobster. It must have been agonizing, although of course he gritted his teeth and refused to let on; but at least he was alive, and in the end there was nothing a liberal application of badger grease couldn't cure.

The next few days are confused in my memory. We tramped up hill and down dale, across a forested landscape. There were oaks, walnut trees in profusion, pines galore, sycamores and elms of immense size. Some measured at least two cubits across the stump; some were clumped together at the root, clustered like a family. From the parent tree sprouted two, ofttimes three others, and sometimes another generation, the grandchildren of the original spreading sycamore emerging merrily on top, and finally there were the countless pawpaw trees. At last we broke out from the panoply of the trees into the sun, coming upon open flat land, and we crossed immense plains covered with grasses so tall you had to jump to see above them. But my escorts seemed to know by instinct which way to go.

And there were flowers: Rousseau's children of Nature, sprouting liberally everywhere, purple, yellow, blue, violet, and pink, unabashedly expressing themselves in their coloration, truly an American efflorescence. That together with the sun and the impeccably cerulean sky lightened my mood, edging out the darker hues of fear and uncertainties.

Goodness knows how they kept to the trail. To my naked eye it was nigh invisible except when little markers popped up on the path, like broken sticks arranged in an arrow to indicate a change of direction, or a stone with another smaller stone sitting on top like a fresh-baked bun, saying "don't go there." Under a big parent tree lay a tight circle of stones enclosing a delightful floral arrangement.

"Oh! What a pretty posy!" I cried, throwing my hands up in the air.

"Be silent!" I was enjoined ever so severely. One of them made a bowl-like motion over his stomach, as if a man with a big fat belly was lying in wait for us, while another nodded in concurrence and, picking up a walnut, waved it about, pointing at the river, signifying I don't know what. Whatever it was we had to make a wide circumference of the area, creeping through horrid bogs and thickets in complete silence, inflicting horrible damage to what was left of my clothes.

After my first fright wore off, I became very hungry, so I signaled to my captors by rubbing my tummy and licking my lips that her ladyship was in need of dinner. They stopped, checked that there were no enemies around, then split into groups, leaving Nookeesa and me under the charge of Bear Claw, a cheeky, hot-blooded brave who kept circling me to gain the best angle to find any apertures in my clothing, while pointing out the tent pole in his loin cloth. "Look at me. Hee! Hee! I give you plenty of this when you want it," he said, and waggled the implement, which in my very limited experience seemed hardly worth writing home about. But it was all teenage bragging. The scene by the riverbank warned him off trying anything more physical, although he kicked Nookeesa every few minutes just to show who was in charge. I found that with my scant knowledge of Shawnee I could just about understand what they were saying. Theirs was just a variant dialect with the same relation to the mother language as Scotch has to Shakespeare.

The Indians had divided themselves up into hunters and gatherers. The gatherers returned earliest with piles of wood and kindling for a fire. The hunters came back empty handed except for some grubs that were wolfed down. Happily they did not invite us to share that revolting lunch with them. There was a deal of good-natured chafing about their failure to fill the larder, which did nothing to still the angry rumbling in my stomach. It was in my mind to chastise them about their poor showing as providers, but in the end I decided not. It was early days in our association. They were walking very warily about me. If a fancy woman starts throwing her weight around, she makes enemies who whisper in the king's ear when his ardor is on the wane. (I don't need to remind my more historically alert readers about the fate of Anne Boleyn, a most tactless—then headless—lady.) Nor did I want to get the reputation of a shrew before I had even entered their camp. Besides, the big chief was not here to act as my protector, and anything might slip twixt cup and lip. For instance, I could be eaten by a bear, which would indicate carelessness on their part, but there would be no one around to gainsay them.

At this moment there was a dreadful growl and roar, and a huge brown bear started a trundling run straight past the grub-eaters, who were arguing loudly over the choicest morsels. It was heading for the nicest, whitest meat in the restaurant: *moi.* I screamed. The hunters leapt to their feet. An arrow whooshed. The bear stood up on its hind legs, gave me a plaintive look, lay down, and died. And the neatest warm hearthrug was lying at my feet.

The Indians started whooping and dancing. Unlike English menials they didn't need a boot up the rump to get them started, so in two ticks they had made sparks by chipping flints they carried in pouches dangling from their loin cloths, reminiscent of the highlander's sporran, and before you knew it the kindling was glowing healthily. Two of them sat in front of the pile of tinder, puffing and blowing to coax it to light till fragile little flames appeared; they then fanned the smoldering kindling with a blanket till it caught fire. Meanwhile others were skinning the bear, slicing it, and sticking the slices on sharp sticks for roasting. The fat dribbling off the meat exploded with a soft whoosh into the fire. The bear steaks smelled delicious, and my lips salivated in anticipation. When the meal was ready, the Indians used sticks to spear the meat and get it out of the fire. As there were no knives and forks to hand they used their hands to greedily pull off strips that were either raw or burnt, piling the food in their mouths till they were bursting.

It was then that they noticed us lying there, silent and starving. I thought for a moment they had been under instructions to keep me trim for the chief, but judging by the way they now scurried around, I realized they were just like your average man—selfish and forgetful. Later I found out that Chief Whingwy Pooshie had given strict instructions that he liked his women well-meated, possibly quoting Rubens at this point. There wasn't much flesh left on the bones, so we were left to gnaw the scrapings, but they gave us a sort of soup of liquid bear fat. And then, strangest of all things, they tapped the tree behind my head, and out came a syrupy liquid, which they added to the soup. It was delicious, and for no reason at all my spirits perked up, and quite soon after that, or so it seemed, we arrived at our final destination.

CHAPTER 13

Anne Boleyn Comes to Town

The town was by the riverbank of a tiny insignificant stream that went by the charmless soubriquet of the Mad River, which may or may not have been a fitting term for its citizenry. It was sited on a fine piece of bottomland filled with neat fields of broad beans, sweet potato, and Indian corn, all unfenced as far as I could see. All the necessary jobs of planting, watering, and harvesting seemed to be the responsibility of the squaws. The males sensibly confined their activities to politics, which encompassed smoking, gossiping, scratching themselves, the speedy downing of vats of tizwaz, and then the belching and trumping to clear their bellies, which they seemed to enjoy enormously. *Plus ça change, plus la même chose.* The town, Wapatomika, was one part of a conglomeration of villages, none of which could be seen from afar because all the buildings including the town hall were shrouded by oaks, elm, and magnificent sycamore trees, a sensible arrangement which kept out the chill of the cold in the winter and provided a desperately needed cooling shade from the worst of the summer heat, which was unbearably hot and humid. Never did I miss Old England as during these dreadful dead days of August, or as they called it, the Frying Moon.

There was the usual smoke from cooking fires, the squalling and caterwauling of little children no different from anywhere in the world, and then the smell, which was awful. You could tell a brave's breakfast from the aroma radiating from his skin not his breath, but the odd thing was that after the first few intakes of breath you began not to mind (and quite soon not to notice) the bucolic bouquet.

Now as to the village itself: On the outskirts there were tepees: tent-like hutments just like our charcoal burners, a cone made of sticks with a skin thrown on top. These temporary affairs belonged, I believe, to the lesser sort, the undesirables, just like our squatters and cottagers. Further in, the streets were laid out in orderly grids, and each plot was filled with a beehive-shaped lodge done up in mock Tudor style. I mean by that the structures were supported by wattle and daub. Many of the more prosperous villas were decorated with vegetable gourds hanging outside, which were the habitat of house martins. *Why*, I thought, *it's like England, where the more sophistical quality keep pet parrots for their amusing conversation.* But it was not for any frivolous imperative of fashion that the birds were kept. The villages were plagued by all sorts of flies, of which the birds ate upward of two thousand a day, thus substantially reducing the insect nuisance around the house. And we think we're clever. If you can't teach your grandma to suck eggs, don't expect to outsmart the Indian on his home turf.

Right in the center of the town was a magnificent lodge with all sorts of addenda and appendages thrust on top, rather like our Tudor mansions back home when they are "improved upon" by some misbegotten modernizer. This was the chief's lodge and my future home. Much to my surprise I came over all excited at this, like a bride back from honeymoon being shown the mansion of which she is about to be mistress; and I began planning carpets, curtains, fripperies, and furnishings, and which servants I would have to get on the right side of and which I would have to boot out if I was to be a proper lady of the manor. Truly I was naive beyond stupidity.

However, I was immediately hustled into another smaller building by two bossy squaws clucking like mother hens, tut-tutting over my garments, which they shucked me out of most expeditiously. They rubbed me all over with what looked and smelt like table wax, after which scrubbing I felt gloriously clean and refreshed. My clothes were dumped in the corner, presumably to be thrown in the municipal rubbish tip; but no, later I found bits and bobs of my apparel turning up in odd corners of the camp. One doughty warrior, whose spear was adorned with the feathers and scalps of subdued enemies, topped off the whole effect by having a blue silk ribbon and a frill from my pantalettes tying off a gruesome skull.

I emerged tricked out in buckskin, which I swear was softer and sleeker than satin, and around my neck instead of pearls I wore a necklace of wampum beads. It was evening, and as I was escorted along the village streets, the Delaware ladies, in contrast to the savage critiques of the Shawnee town, were now applauding their own handiwork. In the soft glow of the campfires I felt like any bride, inexplicably radiant with happiness. There was a hum of approval from the generality gathered round the flames. It amazes me continually that in any society that I have been a party to, the shallows always win over the silent streams running deep. The squaws nodded all friendly smiles and then returned to making bread by crushing and kneading acorns from the white oak till they formed a sort of flour, which they then broke into rolls to be baked in an oven of red-hot stones. And you know, I honestly couldn't tell the difference between these and the floury cobs we breakfast on at home, except the butter and marmalade that we slather so greedily onto the bread (at least in the houses I was wont to visit) were missing.

Just as we were approaching the threshold of the domain of the great chief, my steps began to drag. Oh critics, shake your heads, but life is written in great clichés. Why my reluctance after the initial excitement, you may well ask? After all I was marrying into the landed gentry, the dream of any curate's daughter, and this one a hero to boot; and isn't every maid already half in love with a hero? Why, this man had rescued me from the very worst of mortal perils. Any sensible girl would have swooned immediately in his arms. So shake a leg, girl. Get in there before he changes his mind and picks someone the family knows something about, not an article that might have fallen off the back of a Conestoga wagon.

Well, to answer my own question, there were two points at issue. One, he seemed a mite older than I had anticipated in a lover, and if fate had ordained for me older men (whom I hasten to add I had a partiality toward out of fond remembrance for my own dear, dead, reprobate dad), I wondered in the words of the old song whether he had got a ding doram to do his fallorum, or the other way round. Secondly we didn't really know each other, did we? I mean we hadn't actually spoken to each other. I may have screamed and heard him throw off a command or two in a series of masterly grunts, but the two of us had never got round to a conversation even as basic as a chitchat about the weather, which can tell you a thing or two about a person. We had hardly broken the groundwork for a more lasting relationship, and all of us know too many people who have rushed into disastrous marriages based on a momentarily coordinated fluttering of hearts. On top of which there is the obvious question mark about him being a savage heathen with a less delicate skin tone than mine. Well that I minded not a bit. What the people at Sheepy Magna would say about the dark-hued foreigner with the eccentric dress sense I took not the slightest heed of, and you can understand why. You see, touching his swarthiness, I went along with the rabid Scotch poet, Burns: "a man's a man for a' that." Although I have to say I was not a hundred percent on his side about rank being "but the guinea's stamp." Being a bit of a snob myself, the fact that there were many feathers in his bonnet, indicating membership of the upper landed gentry, was definitely (and even Mary-Anne would have to concede this) a feather in *my* cap.

For those of you accustomed to the wedding rites as conducted by the Church of England, the ceremonies of the Wyandot Indians may come as a surprise. For whereas the first, when stripped of all the satins, dresses, and hullabaloo, is merely the witnessing of a contract (until death us do part); the second tears through all the steps from fancying one another, picking him out from the crowd, to courting, the contract, and the consummation, all in one splendid party. So if you are the impatient type, become an Indian and live happily ever after with a pipe, a wigwam, and a handsome hunk of Mingo manhood, oiled and muscled, all set to gratify the blushing bride.

Before I describe the solemn mass, I need to say a word about the church, which it wasn't, but that's the best English approximation I can come up with. The building was a huge wooden edifice with all the features of a church except for pews; mind you the faithful seemed happy sitting on the packed earthen floor, an arrangement that wouldn't go down too well in England. The pillars supporting the roof were ranked along the aisle, but instead of bearing hymn and psalm numbers were decorated with cartoons of men hunting, winning battles, and all the varieties of rape and pillage perennially celebrated by manhood—rather on the lines of the columns acclaiming the mighty deeds of the emperors, recently unearthed in Rome and Pompeii. The windows, set high up under the roof, were made of stretched animal skins instead of stained glass, polished so smoothly as to be translucent. They provided the motes of dusty sunlight that feature in all churches of whatever hue and faith, which I like to think shows that we are all connected spiritually.

First of all, I was led in by a procession of braves carrying burning torches, which gave a reassuringly homely touch to the ceremony, just like the link boys in London lighting the way for fine ladies in their sedan chairs. Then in filed the squaws, whereupon the braves lined up opposite the solemn-looking maidens, who were trying their best not to giggle. There was a certain amount of shuffling, as in musical chairs whereby you jostle and elbow your way in to get yourself opposite the tall, dark, and handsome lad you fancy. The music, by the way, was provided by a chamber orchestra at the fireside, which made up for its lack of violins with drummers, pipes like flutes, and cow bells arranged harmonically, led by an old man who kept time by a sustained groaning and wailing. If someone else took a shine to your chosen brave there followed a session of undignified pushing, shoving, and (in the worst cases) eye clawing. But it all seemed to work out for the best in the best of all possible worlds, for each of them ended up with someone they were happy with. As a method of choosing a partner for life it is probably as good as any other system. Remember, amongst the tribes life is short and violent, so you are best to grab what you can while you can, and unusually it carries the advantage of being a lady's choice. Say what you like; in some ways they are more progressive than us. Mary Wollstonecraft, what say you now? Here in this Stone Age community the rights of women are vindicated. Possibly I am reading too much into this.

When the dust settles, your man faces the fire, places his hands behind his back, and to seal the deal you grab hold of his hands and don't let go. After the choice has been made you have to explain your pick, and to seal the contract the brave gives his verbal endorsement. In our case it went like this:

Me: "You have the heart of a lion."

Chief: "A lion cannot mount a pony."

Me: "Don't quite get that. Anyway you have the strong arm of a warrior."

Chief: "Surely 'tis not an arm my bride needs to warm her wedding night?"

Me: "Oh! I get it now. The church bell's rung." I clunked my head and then, pointing to his surging breech-clout: "You have the tadger of a grizzly bear, I'm sure. That is to say I am no judge; being the vicar's daughter, I have only seen one on beasts of the field."

Chief: "That's more like it. Now you are getting into the spirit of things. Your breasts are ripe and huge like melons, and your *massih*, your mossy bower overflows with sweet honey."

Me: "Hey, hold on. That's going a bit too far. Okay, I am going off the script here. Your blood is like the racing stallion. How about that?"

And so on and so forth. And so to bed.

So it was with some trepidation that I finally tripped over the bridal bower. My introduction to tribal life was a lot more gentle than Nookeesa's by the by. The poor boy made the acquaintance of tribal customs by having to run the gauntlet. It gave him a very sour face when I encountered him next morning, while I looked replete and happy.

I lived with Whingwy Pooshie for many moons. On the whole it was a happy time for me and as good a learning experience as could be got amongst the dreaming spires of Oxford. The hardest part of my life was time spent chewing buckskin to make nice soft moccasins for my beloved, but I soon palmed this off onto an older squaw who had still managed to retain some teeth. Whingwy Pooshie, like all sugar daddies, didn't mind indulging his child bride, and anyway my imposing on lesser fry showed the bossy regal touch which up to now had been kept in low profile. The thought that I had merely traded one big red virile member for another was dispelled the first night in the wigwam. When I arrived there I assumed that I was to be taken bestially, and the best thing that I could do was to submit with a good grace and lie back composing poetry to the rhythm of the rood as nice girls are supposed to do.

Whingwy Pooshie welcomed me into the bower, all tastefully decorated with incense, burning candles, sweet smelling herbs, and vegetables. With a nod he invited me to take my ease on the bed, a bunk piled high with soft doeskin pallets and even a satin counterpane, which judging by the style of the needlepoint had been stolen from a French woman at Marietta or Gallipolis. Whingwy Pooshie sat down beside me, patted me in a friendly way, and smiled. After all the stories I had heard about the rapaciousness of the savage I was, to put it mildly, astonished, and all my fear vanished with that friendly smile.

He tucked his legs under him and settled down to smoke his pipe, decorated rococo fashion with lots of snakes intertwining with beasts of the field. The tobacco was actually sweet smelling, making it tolerable for the squaw sharing the wigwam with the smoke, not like the awful mundungus the lads smoked in Sheepy. I had heard of people smoking after intercourse, but before? This was ridiculous. Then, after a few deliberative puffs he turned his head to me and winked, something I had been told Indians couldn't do.

"Sleep good, pale beauty from beyond the Bitter Sea," he said, or rumbled rather, in a mixture of broken French and English. "Welcome to my lodge in the woods. From this night on you will be my squaw, under the protection of my right arm, and no harm shall come to you. You will be fed and pampered by the junior squaws. If anyone harms a hair on your head or looks at you, you know already how they shall answer to Whingwy Pooshie's wrath." Well, that was nice. No more worrying about bills and tinkers coming to your door. I could see that he fancied me, but even then I had an inkling that when my cheeks ceased to bloom and the first wrinkles came on like the winter weather it would be down the ladder for me, munching the next ripe little pumpkin's moccasins.

Whingwy Pooshie really was a fine figure of a savage, with a pleasant personality for a heathen. So a fate worse than death plus home comforts along the bonny, bonny banks of the Mad River seemed a fair exchange for continually legging through the brambles chased by zealous Scotch Calvinists or vengeful Seneca Indians. As I looked upon his rippling pectoral muscles and his fine intelligent forehead, I thought, *Things could be worse.* A delicate shudder of languor stirred like an ebb tide through my body. My fortress was about to be invaded. What else could I do but shut my eyes, lie back on the soft pile of bedding, and think of England.

A few minutes later I opened my eyes expecting a vista of huge hairy red meat looming on top of me, breathing all the rampancy of the pitiless Delaware nation, with a battering ram for a tadger. But no, my man was sitting contentedly on the dirt floor, still puffing away at his fancy little calumet.

"No! No! My little spring lambkin, fret not thy little quim. Your loins will not be rendered asunder by a big Red man. The days when I mounted like a great stallion are long gone. Too many moons have passed when I have been lonely in the blanket. My squaw has long departed and waits for me in the happy hunting grounds. Desire has wilted as a cornstalk after the great rains. No longer do I even salute the totem pole. But my people"—he shook his head at their misplaced compassion—"they see only my loneliness and say I have been a widower too long. A chief must plough a lusty furrow, and so to please the crowd I have to copulate with a young and passionate maid. They have watched you with searching eyes and know that you crave a strong steed and are beautiful to boot."

This last was a face-saving concession. For even in the candlelight he could tell I was put out of countenance at being labeled a wanton slut like any village milkmaid.

"But what is loneliness to them I call solitude, and now I enjoy the peace and quiet of my wigwam. You, my pretty little doe, are my prisoner and my possession." He put this so sweetly I couldn't take it amiss. "I need from you silence both within and without the folds of my tent. Silence and good cooking: Give me that, and life will be good in a land teeming with game and warm hunting lodges and rivers where a brave cannot swim but for being tickled by trout. And do not forget now and then when the moon is full to howl like a coyote, signaling your pleasuring at my masterful mountings. If your squaw friends ever find out you are unbulled—No, I see you doubt that you will have any friends, being so White and clumsy; you have none now, but soon they will be queuing outside your lodge to be your gossip friend at the watering hole—I will trim your pretty little neck from ear to ear." He smiled as he said this to show that while he was deadly serious he was still a proper gentleman, and I had better take him at his word.

Well, sometimes you get in life what you least expect, and despite repeated attempted rapine, pursuit, and plunder of my person, the wide world seemed to be conspiring to keep me virgin to the grave. I couldn't give it away. Notwithstanding my outstanding natural attractions celebrated by limners and minor poets on the banks of the Anker, swiving me was about as enticing a prospect as spending a wet weekend in Wigan, and this during the early days of the Industrial Revolution.

Looking back on it, I think I began to fancy him when the tomahawk stopped the homicidal rapist right at the point when meat was to meet with sweetmeat. Relief had swiftly become affection. But love began to knock at my heart when after his housewarming speech I knew I couldn't get him. And we always want what we can't have, don't we, ladies? Now, settled in the comfortable, familiar surroundings of Sheepy, I realize it was but silly infatuation sparked by my taste for the exotic.

I tried everything to get Whingwy Pooshie fancying me, from curling up like a cozy little egg to wriggling and writhing as if I was the snake in the Serpent Mound, a sacred tabernacle in the woods which did as the local Stonehenge for the Indians. Remembering the witch ways of Sheepy, I said the Lord's Prayer backwards in a vain endeavor to hex him. I even thought of getting one of the old crones in the village to put an anonymous spell on him, but that would have blown my cover so I put it out of mind. However, I took to watching them hex lesser gentry plagued with flabby rods, and tried to copy their formula, but I must have got the recipe wrong for nary a totem pole was raised in my honor in this house. I was flummoxed. I remembered my father and how he liked home comforts. So I came over all domestic, laying out pipe, moccasin, and favorite deerskin rug to welcome him home after a hard day's warrioring, which activity consisted of chewing the fat with Old Hat, the medicine man. As a personal face saver, I decided that one of his displaced squaws must be popping the leaf of false Solomon's seal into his evening cup of tea to dampen his desire, a strategy the Indians employed chemically to the same purpose as the lambskin armor devised by Monsieur Condom, which functions for us Christians physically.

Hearing people talk energetically and earnestly in a foreign tongue, one always assumes the best, viz, that the discussion will be high-brow and high-flown—that the topic settled on might be the putative existence of phlogiston, the theory of concentric spheres, or that the world was hollow and open at both ends (all the rage in the colonies). It came as a disappointment when I broke through the complexities of their grammar to find that Old Hat and my man were chatting about how there was so much rain, why their squaws couldn't dry their towels properly, and how old Stick-in-the-Mud was too drunk to find his wigwam last night. On another occasion they chatted about the state of the economy and the disappointing harvest from the oak trees. They used the acorn for bread making (as I think I have already mentioned) and cooking oil, and the inner surface of the bark is often employed as a textile for clothing.

Once in a blue moon their discourse was raised to philosophical heights, as the following bon mot shows, which I overheard when trying to roast buffalo on a stick, just as we roast pork on the spit at home. (The result tasted too heavily of wood smoke to be enjoyed, and soon after I was relieved of another wifely duty.) Whingwy Pooshie was blethering with one of his cronies, Red Dog Who Mounts Coyote, who was grunting contentedly on his pipe. "Squaws come in all sizes: good, bad, and ugly. The good ones are no good because they are ugly. The good lookers are no good because they are lazy, or trouble. But"—and he took a long, satisfied pull on his pipe as he said it—"the calumet is always reliable, never fails to please."

Chief Whingwy Pooshie retorted, "You might say squaw is always squaw, but a good calumet is a smoke."

Red Dog grunted in agreement. "Good. Good."

To improve my chances in the mating game, I manufactured some makeup out of berries and herbs, but it was no go. I ended up looking hideous—pallid with red splotches splattered over my face. My husband stared in astonishment, then asked me kindly, "Why are you wishing to become lady witch doctor?"

So I gave up and began to believe the lack of nocturnal activity was due to the miasma arising out of the muddy waters, inhibiting carnal affections. (Despite Dr. Jenner's vaccinations and poor little Robert Phipps, his guinea pig, the miasma theory of disease was still very much in vogue in England.) Would the tribe have continued in residence here if they knew the connection between the climate and the braves traipsing around with leadless pencils, I wondered? To add to my puzzlement, papooses kept popping up everywhere like snowdrops. I wished I had the Stewart formula for eternal youth with me to drop into his tizwaz, for this surely would put the iron back into his droopy spout. There was little I could do, so once again I became the meek female to whom I had vowed adieu. But I was stuck. Divorce Indian-style was out of the question, as that ended with the squaw being done to death for adultery. So I resigned myself to being an old maid, using the old excuse for doing nothing: waiting and seeing whither life's great current would drag me, which is a sure recipe for being caught on the hop.

Now and again Whingwy Pooshie went out on raids, partly to keep his warlike faculties in trim but mainly to hold back the palefaces who were dribbling across the Ohio River. The numbers were small, but it was like rain in Tamworth, a semi-permanent drizzle. I told him the instructive story of Canute and his quarrel with the tide. He nodded woefully as if to say, "He must have been a wise chief of White Indians."

Once in a while prisoners were brought back from these raids, but they were low-grade material: children to replace Indian kids who had died of whatever pox was currently making the rounds, or toothless slatterns who were shagged once or twice by visually impaired braves, then turfed out of the tepee to act as slave labor for the meager industrial concerns of the Red man. You would see them huddled round a campfire in the suburbs, chewing on buckskin and bemoaning their fate when they came off the bite. I generally avoided them, and I could tell their braves half hoped they would have enough initiative to run away so their embarrassment would end.

CHAPTER 14

The Old World Drives the New World

It had been raining that morning, so I did not see the prisoners come in. Anyway, it was hardly as if the circus had come to town (in other words not worth getting dressed and wet for). But Brown Squirrel, the squaw who had decided to be my best friend, came rushing unannounced into my quarters, telling me to get up and come see the commotion.

"White Eyes squaw, very…how you say? Hoity-toity. She is making big trouble for herself. Spits on Red man—very foolish. Big Wing has tied her up, but she is like a rampant she-wolf and tries to tear his eyes out." She made a sign of throat-cutting. I nodded. This was unusual, because all the prisoners were commonly cowed by fear of becoming an Indian's breakfast and were on their best behavior to avoid this fate.

The lady in question was quivering with a mixture of fear, hatred, and arrogance; taut as a bowstring, hands tied behind her back, thin, and brave. Seldom have I seen such doomed pride. A brave came up and cut her bonds. In reply she spat in his eyes and tried to scratch his face. It says much for the self-control of those Indians that he simply shrugged it off. She started flouncing around, and I mean flouncing, for she was dressed in what was once a Parisian gown and making a great hullabaloo about not being used to being treated this way. The funny thing was she upbraided all and sundry in French and English, then as a service to her hosts gave a very rapid-fire translation in their tongue. What is more, it was accurate, with subject and verb in agreement and correct case usage, not with the fits and stutters that marked my essays into their argot.

She turned round to damn the eyes of all present and tell them where to stick their noses. And the years swung back on their axes, and I was standing in my hallway in Sheepy. For there in all her snobbish majesty stood Mary-Anne Dixie, the doyenne of Bosworth Hall, pretending to ignore me as per the good old days when some better treat was in the offing; but then I had changed more than most. I looked again and she slowly metamorphosed into Snowbird. Homesickness, that most malignant of ailments, is something we have all suffered in foreign climes. A coach passes with somebody you went to school with. You didn't like her much then, but she will be your best friend now. You rush up to the coaching inn, embrace her enthusiastically as she steps down from the running board, and end up apologizing to an astonished stranger.

I rubbed my eyes, and verily it was Mary-Anne again. Take away the dark coloring of blackberry juice, imagine her former ivory complexion restored by confinement in the Mingo's lodge, and there you have the squire's daughter in all her high and mighty snootiness. She recognized me all right, for she gave me a very English flounce and swerve to let me know I was snubbed. If she had been wearing crinoline and panniers it might have come off, but her dress was but a sad relic of its former glory, and instead she appeared merely silly with all her frumping about. A further look told me she was definitely Indian; how I knew I couldn't say, but I knew.

She turned to me, shouting hysterically in the fluent English of Shakespeare country, "He was no damn Frenchman! After he swived me stupid, he took off his clothes, and I saw the mark of the cuts across his back from the climbing competition. That puffed-up poseur from Paris was none other than that stinking outsider, He-Who! *Et il m'a foutu*!"

After due consideration, I was left wondering whether the cause of her wrath was not the deception but the consequent ditching, for it was the outcast who tipped her out of the tepee and not the other way round. She wasn't exactly clear on this point, but it seemed that when the rampant Indian wasn't seeking his pounding of flesh, he was searching for a recipe that was not from mother's cookbook. Yes, she was absolutely positive on that score, and sure it was neither pudding, pie, nor crumpet he was after. But what it was she never did find out, for he rifled through every possible pocket, frill, and flounce; unpinned her petticoats till she looked like a ragamuffin; and then, when satisfied that she was sans recipe, turfed her out of the tent onto the cold hard ground outside. When she came to in the frosty morning he had packed up and gone, with ne'er a twig out of place nor any trace to show he had camped and ravished her there.

She was rabbiting on as if bewitched by hatred, but she must have possessed some vestige of self-control, for through the anger and spitting bile she insidiously planted the idea that it was my fault! For a while I wondered if the outcast had left a souvenir of his passion, but beyond the odd rip and wrinkle in her chemise there were no creepy crawlies nor any anticipated addition to the ranks of warrior braves. I wondered also why he took his clothes off post- rather than pre-coitus, which (so I'm told) is the correct form in polite society. Wasn't that locking the stable door after the horse was gone, or something of a similar metaphorical hue?

A recipe? What recipe was worth tearing all over Western Virginia for? Could it be the one I had part ownership in? But then why would a savage have heard of that? And how could the horrible He-Who masquerade so brilliantly as a French milord? Everyone knows that the frogs are the quite most sophisticated race alive. Not least because they never let off telling *tout le monde* they are. A mystery it will have to remain for now, as there was no lack of interest in the new arrival for more aesthetically pleasing reasons from another quarter.

Someone else was taking her in. I refer to His Majesty King Whingwy Pooshie, standing rooted like a young cowherd smitten by his first dairymaid. One look at his horniness and close observation of a rising breech clout told me that my days as queen of all I surveyed were over, and soon I would be washing the table linen down by the streambed with the other has-beens of the regal seraglio. And she, the clever minx, caught on immediately, so she started mincing around. The mouse went after the cheese—snap!

Things are never quite as bad as you assume they are going to be, and the scenario was not as entirely bleak as I have sketched in the previous paragraph. You might say (as my cousin Jane is sure to) that it's a truth universally observed that the aristocracy, blue-blooded or red-skinned, can make short work of the courting preliminaries the rest of us are compelled to subscribe to, so that before you could say, "More tea, vicar?" she was lying flat on her back in pride of place on the chief's favorite blanket, legs athwart to receive boarders. And while they rutted as happy as pigs in their midden, I had to make do with crouching in a draughty corner of the tepee, studying the interesting geometrical designs on the tapestry hanging in our cozy nest, so much more avant-garde than the Flemish weave that kept the draughts off the walls of the long gallery in Sheepy Hall.

Night after night they were ramming away as if they had discovered a new fashion, and getting the most out of it before it caught on with the hoi polloi. Night after night they howled at the moon, bucking the wild bronco, the floor of the wigwam shaking in tune with their carnal ecstasies till I got quite seasick. Mind you I had little else to do bar weeping in my corner, but as nobody took any notice there wasn't much point.

But how came this amazing turnaround? Had she popped something into his afternoon cuppa? Had she the complete three thirds of the great Stewart Secret? What was the great secret anyway? Was it the recrudescence of the potency of fervent youth? The complacent smirk on Whingwy's face as he strutted round the village suggested that whatever it was had reinstalled the iron in his tadger; and with his totem pole sturdily erect, well might he be mightily pleased. Or was the truth the sad, simple fact that Snowbird was so much more enticing than oneself that any jaded warrior could find a new lease of lust with this exotic mount?

During the day she walked down the lanes between the lodges like a prim little Pocahontas, a trifle flushed from her morning gallop, kicking up dirt in the faces of the subordinate squaws. If no one else was looking when she passed me, she hobbled as if saddle sore, just in case I hadn't got the point of the minor earthquake that had almost ruptured the blanket last night. It was our private joke, which I failed to find funny.

One day I was arranging a basket of fruit for a sick old squaw when she approached me and (quite without a by-your-leave) plucked out an apple from my basket and muttered in my ear, "An apple, an egg, and a nut, you may eat though dressed by a slut"—an old saw no one outside England would recognize. Then she sauntered off in her regal manner without waiting to see the result of her little surprise.

Regarding his indiscretion, Whingwy Pooshie was such a perfectly politic gentleman, dealing with wife and mistress with such equal aplomb he could have been French. At least he could play a leading role in what they were pleased to call their bedroom farces. All he had to do was change his clothes to be convincing. Snowbird may have been the mistress of the mattress and queen of the night, but according to tribal custom and in the eyes of the village elders, I was still number-one wife and she merely floozie of the month. In truth the old grey heads of the village might not like her antics but didn't know how to take her; her position was a constitutional conundrum. There was no point in sucking up to her, as she might be kicked out at any moment to become yesterday's blanket warmer; nor did her attitude endear her to their squaws. And if they decided to lick her moccasins for the sake of

Whingwy Pooshie, the courtiers were in for trouble back home, where sat the "sulky sullen dame, / Gathering her brows like gathering storm, / Nursing her wrath to keep it warm," as Scotch Rabbie was wont to say, and he was the one to have known. These squaws might appear meek and mild around the campfires, but within the circular walls of their wigwams they ruled the roost. I had heard too many raised female voices followed by the noise of splintering pots to have any illusions about this being a patriarchal society.

On ceremonial occasions I was wheeled out as queen consort, approved by the tribe, while backstage the new favorite was kicking up trouble, throwing her weight around, and generally upsetting the folks—just like the court of Henry VIII when Anne Boleyn caught his eye. I was Catherine of Aragon: royal by right, beloved by the people, but lacking that tantalizing spark that makes for bed-worthiness fit for a king.

Despite my lack of pleasuring (which by the by was something many wifies said they could live very well without, thank you very much) and my cold empty bed, my status as queen was demonstrated every morning with little gifts left on my pillow, to wit: a posy of flowers; an interesting stone from the river bed, swimming with purple whorls painted on its smooth surface; and one day an adorable, indeterminate puppy, which I found tearing up my best buckskin frock.

Then things changed. One night I discovered, lying atop my jewel pouch, the most beautiful fox fur I had ever seen, soft as silk and the color of snow. That night, while they were thrashing away with enough energy to drill their way to Botany Bay, I put on the fox with the despairing pride that only the exiled or supplanted can know. When the sun tinted the tip of the village tepees, and while they were dozing in post-coital languor, I walked out disdainful of all the eyes pitying me, the spurned wife, the uninteresting remnant of a spent passion.

I don't know what impression I made on the villagers. But one person deeply affected was Snowbird, looking more and more to my homesick eyes like Mary-Anne, the trollop of Tamworth. For some reason the white fox fur was like the veritable red rag to the bull. I had made my procession round the streets and avenues, had sauntered across the plaza when I encountered her: surfeited from swiving, stumbling out of the lodge, lazily rubbing her eyes. She sneered at me with her accustomed arrogance, then all at once spotting the fur her face twisted till it was ugly with rage. She jabbed her finger at me and rushed screaming back to the great lodge in which the somnolent chief was scratching and yawning to greet the dawn. Why she spoke in French I don't know, as not a soul in the camp had a word in that tongue, but she was so wonderfully expressive in her delivery that we all got the gist, which went like this: "So what I'm good for is getting my arse rogered off, while Madame here just sits on hers and sobs, and for that she gets fine clothes and puppies for playthings, while I am left in rags not fit to be seen outside in the daylight."

Now, so far this was the standard litany that any husband, having taken on the burden of a fancy woman who is far too young for him, has to put up with; and as we know a good quarrel is an excellent hors d'oeuvre for sexual high jinks and (when done in public) affords excellent entertainment for the uninvolved. I will say this for Whingwy Pooshie: He was a good sport, taking all her ravings with a good-natured shrug to his cronies, as if to say, "See what happens when an old man like me gets hold of a cute little vixen." And of course his friends nodded sagely back, sniggered, and made whispered comments about old men and young lasses, the same the world over.

Me, I enjoyed it hugely, counting it a little recompense for all my lonely nights, and I played it to perfection, smiling at her with the open smile of old friends rediscovering each other without a hint of condescending—well, perhaps a teeny soupçon of graciousness, appropriate to one who has done somewhat better in the world than her erstwhile peer. That seemed to add fuel to the flames. Don't ask me why. But now she made a fatal mistake. Her croaking was getting her nowhere, and the usual widows and ancient spinsters who hung around the fringe of the campfires began to titter into their blankets, pointedly laughing at her. Being the mere scrapings of aboriginal society they were normally the objects of her derision, but now with the moccasin on the other foot, so to speak, she exploded, letting her rage overrun reason. Screaming in Indian dialect, she broadcast to one and all the length and quality of the high chief's totem pole. I don't remember what unit of measurement was used; it wasn't rods and perches. Whatever was said, the end product was not flattering. The mighty implement that had sired a race of warriors was no more than a minnow in the swimming hole. This was not a wise move.

Whingwy Pooshie's face went blood red. His hand leapt to his side, and a razor sharp tomahawk was suddenly held aloft. Snowbird didn't flinch. She stared at him with a look that could have frozen hell. I'll say that she had more bottom than a tribe of braves. With a speed off the mark that I would not have credited, one of the old men by the fire leapt to his feet and held fast Whingwy's right arm. "This is not good medicine! It is very bad to kill your own squaw in front of the village!"

He was swiftly joined by other senior citizens, for the public slaughter of wives and mistresses was not on in the Delaware tribe. Snowbird let out a volley of oaths and, laughing like a mad virago, screamed more abuse at Whingwy Pooshie. Standing next to her with mouth agape, Nookeesa was polishing a walnut-handled musket for his master. Snowbird snatched it out of his hands, ran up to Whingwy Pooshie, and stuck the barrel into his waist. For an awful minute time itself froze. This time it was Whingwy Pooshie's turn to display composure. Not a muscle flinched. The braves still clutched him, arms frozen, their eyeballs standing out on stalks. Snowbird clenched her eyes shut, drew her head and shoulders back, and squeezed the trigger.

The pistol clicked. It was unloaded. I laughed in relief. Whingwy Pooshie merely grunted and let the casse-tête slide back to its holster. Snowbird threw the flintlock at him. At point-blank range she only grazed his ear. The moment of crisis was over. Everyone enjoying the spectacle went back to their business, shaking their heads and laughing at her. She burst into tears, ran to the nearest wigewa, picked up a spear, and came charging back. The way she carried the weapon showed she had never held one in her life, so the villagers began mincing around in imitation of her inept spear holding, jeering and snickering. The hooting rose to a crescendo when she rose up and took aim with the javelin; it stopped and merged into a horrid scream when the blade plunged into the chief's midriff. For a moment he staggered around with an uncomprehending look on his face, then fell directly onto the spear shaft. Whingwy Pooshie was dead within the minute. My Indian summer holiday was over.

CHAPTER 15

The Escape

This is one of those moments when everything seems to stand still, like in a horrible Grand Guignol tableau on St. Martin's mass. For a second everyone stood rooted to the spot. Then Red Dog grabbed Snowbird round the waist, whereupon everyone present—braves, squaws, and young boys—jumped on her. The squaws had been waiting for this moment for a long time. Now they had a God-given opportunity to vent their spleen. They thrashed her, then tethered her to a stake, stacked sticks and kindling under her feet, and furiously tore at her beautiful hair, screaming, "Paleface slut! We will make you into an ugly boy." Her hair was ripped out in lumps; dirt and dung were rubbed into her cheeks till she looked like one of those horrible urchins that plague the streets of London. I was confined to a securely fastened wigwam on the tenuous basis that sharing the same man made us accomplices in securing his demise.

Well, it was no business of mine, and when she started crooning hymns she'd learned from me, I buried my head in the blanket like that mythical bird from the torrid zones of Africa. Although I must confess to finding it monstrously difficult to remain philosophical while someone I had grown acquainted with was about to be gruesomely slaughtered. It stripped me of any pretenses that I was a princess and not the unwilling hostage of savages. Staying indoors was unpleasant, for the roof fabric sucked in all the sun's heat, firing the inside till it felt like a baker's oven. I drank water from a bowl put there by one of the domestics, a shabby White woman whose name I can't recall, and splashed the water on my forehead and wrists to cool down. Shaking the water from my fingertips, I thought shades of Pontius Pilate, when Snowbird began crooning the slow dirge known as "Loch Lomond."

"If ye'll tak the high road, and I'll tak the low road…"

The music's spell hit me with a bittersweet thud in the stomach. It was Mary-Anne to the very tee on that day when she interrupted me in my study, and I knew I couldn't stand aside.

My father had always said that when I put my mind to it I could do most anything; so this normally unthinkable rescue plan could be an enormous piece of plum duff, or so I tried convincing myself. I summoned up all my cowardly resolve, trembling like a leaf, and with my bowels skirling to the Highland fling I made up my mind. Handily some lazy brave had left a dirty hunting knife beside a pile of dirty pots for his wife to clean. I checked: Nobody was looking. As quick as a flash I grabbed it and tucked it in a fold in my skirt. There was no going back. I had to make believe I was appealing despite my late husband's lack of ardor. Meanwhile the great chief's earthly remains were at that moment being prepared for cremation in a separate fire from that awaiting his murderess. Whingwy Pooshie, surrounded by keening squaws and joined by silent braves in an ancient ritual befitting a great chieftain, was laid out with great ceremony atop an embroidered blanket set out in the council house. Accompanying him to the hunting grounds in the great beyond were the symbols of his sovereignty—pipe, tobacco pouch, tomahawk, and feathered headdress—arrayed round his body.

There were two guards outside my tent, both stupefied with tizwaz, a large vat of which lay upturned by the site of tomorrow's execution. I whistled a merry tune to get their attention, popped my head out, winked sportively, and in my most winsome manner said, "Who would care to walk in the woodlands with me, my fine young braves? What is it that naughty girls do that makes a brave...brave?" I put on a look I remembered from seeing trollops courting in the various bagnios I had visited. In case my Delaware grammar was not up to speed and they didn't get the message, I kept on with the winking and, overcoming a lifetime of domestic prejudices, hitched up my kirtle to the knee, giving them a swift glimpse into the great beyond. I could see them slavering, tussling in their minds between the course of duty and calling on cock robin, and the little bird won as it always does.

They nodded at each other. One said, "What's the harm? It only needs one of us on guard."

"Who is to be the first to take me a-walking?" I nodded at the bigger of the Red men to get properly outfitted to be a lady's escort. Not being one to hang around and get acquainted, he decided to skip the first step and rushed into the tepee, not giving me time to sit up properly before leaping on top of me. He plunged straight onto the dagger held there erect, a dildo in reverse. His jaw opened in astonishment and he gave forth a groan worthy of an orgasm. *Ah, my lad, if only your mother could see you now*, I thought as I rolled him away, *she would have warned you not to get under the blanket with strangers without a proper introduction.* I smeared the blood away as best I could. He was a very messy bleeder and had ruined my best buckskin skirt. No amount of scrubbing on the stones by the river would get these stains out. Then I smiled inwardly. By a strange irony I had achieved my ambition to become a femme fatale.

Doing away with the other one was as easy as stealing the sugar from granny's tea. He had his back to me. In anticipation of good times ahead he was stoking his engine before the fire, leering at the not uncomely form of Snowbird in her fetching graveyard shift. A spurt like that of a fire hose came out of his red pole. He was totally absorbed in his childish ecstasy when I leant forward to cut his throat. If he was lucky he wouldn't be able to distinguish his tiny orgasm from his death spasm. As he leant over, his throat gurgling and gushing merrily away, a contented smile covered his face.

She recognized me now, to be sure. In mortal trepidation she had dropped her regal arrogance and was wailing in heart-wrenching tones about the good old days (by which she must have meant the odd casual remark passed between us by the Seneca camp fire) while I was frantically chopping at her bonds, which the squaws had soaked in vinegar to make them tighter. Normally I'm all for nostalgia, but this wasn't the time. "By all the saints, madam," I chided, "let's go! Quickly!" And I snapped free the last knot.

Here I was a fallen Jezebel, halfway through a campaign of abduction and murder, in deadly peril of joining her ladyship on the stovetop, and she chose this moment for reminiscences. Given half a chance she would get out her pressed leaves and hornbook. A warning glint through the trees in the eastern sky told us that any moment now squaws would be emerging to bang pots and pans around in preparation for their usual stomach-churning breakfast. Who could say if a warrior wouldn't get up and hose his plants. I saw a suspiciously green geyser streaming out of a nearby tent, whose smelly steam hung lingering in the air; the lazy bastard in residence was too idle to roll outside from under the buffalo skin fabric.

By dint of tugging and kicking I got her moving out of the village, passing on our way another bonfire in preparation. The Guy was not Fawkes but the forlorn Nookeesa, who always seemed to be at the receiving end of Punchinello's baton and was now accused of being an accomplice because he was a friend of the other accomplice, but whose only crime was to have loved and lost while making a spectacularly bad choice of woman. His sad countenance as he mutely followed our progress could have moved a stone.

"Let's release him," I said.

"Forget him." Snowbird's innate snobbery was back in full swing. "He's just a stinking Indian. Let him die. Leaves one less to pollute the earth." Whichever way you looked at it, she wasn't a nice person, and by now I was wondering about the wisdom of rescuing the lady. Evidently loyalty did not come high on her list of cardinal virtues. I had no doubt that if I had been stuck on that stake she wouldn't break stride to help, while I could guarantee that where'er she wandered trouble would follow her like Mary's lamb. Common sense told me that having a man of the woods by our side was going to be an asset, so I stopped and got to work hacking at the straps biting into his flesh. It was tough going, as the leather had been hardened in brine. Nookeesa winced as the strap was released, massaged his wrists and ankles (which were horribly bruised and seeping blood), then spat at Snowbird for good luck. She spat back at him. Weren't they just a proper pair?

We were still near enough to hear the camp dogs howling fit to wake even the most drunken dead. I told the pair of them to shut up and cut along. The lady looked indignant at being spoken to in such a sharp manner, especially by such as me, but for once saw reason and for a while (a very short while, mind you) was to all outward appearances cowed. We made our way out by another muddy track into the hills and soon began panting heavily up the slope, twigs and bracken crackling under our heels, sounding to me as loud as thunder. Reaching the top of the ridge we could just make out the squaws opening the tent flaps, shaking the dust out of their eyes and taking their first steps into the open. In a minute there would be a hue and cry and hot pursuit. We put a spurt on, cursing our way through the thicket of thorn bushes at the apex of the ridge, then plunging down through the brambles and bushes on the other side. We could hear in a faint distant whisper the disappointed cries of people deprived of a greatly anticipated entertainment. The chief's funeral wouldn't be the same without its gruesome supporting acts.

Running through the woods like a frightened rabbit was getting to be a familiar part of my routine in the Americas. With the dawn came a steady drizzle, turning our trail into a sucking morass, slowing us down and making our progress miserable, but it helped mask our tracks, a small blessing of which we were unappreciative at the time. I moaned and cursed in good old-fashioned English. My comrades kept their heads down and slithered onward in stoic silence. To baffle our captors we headed north away from the area of White settlements toward the great sweetwater seas and the wilderness of Canada.

The village and all its sights and smells were soon left behind. For a day we ran and ran through giant meadows of prairie with grass so high we had to jump to see into the distance, then plowed our way across broken red shale cliffs, torrents, and endless forests, whose trees were as high as church steeples. Every now and then impenetrable thickets with razor-sharp thorns forced us down into streambeds in the bottoms, where the mosquitoes bit at us furiously for disturbing their territory. Following the rocky streambeds was easier than sliding along on the muddy paths, and being set deep down in hollows we were far less visible.

There was not a sound of pursuit, not a whisper. Whenever we stopped to take stock there was total quiet, and it's an eerie experience hearing nothing but the clock whirring in your brain. Whenever a deer or bird broke a twig I about jumped out of my moccasins, for I had learned never to underestimate the ability of the Indian in anything to do with woodcraft. That first night we tucked ourselves into a hollow log, crammed together for warmth and invisibility. And very uncomfortable it was too, what with insects whose home we had stolen attacking us and the dampness of the wood creaking into our bones. Somehow I managed to grab a few hours sleep, but the dawn chorus woke me in panic, so I shook the others to get them up and away before first light stole through the trees.

The second day, with no danger appearing, we began to drop our guard. "Hey nonny no!" and "Ring a ding-ding!" we laughed and sang and generally prattled about lightheartedly as you do when danger disappears over the horizon. Snowbird and her one-time lover even began to chuckle together like Jack and Jill, as if no shadow of trouble had ever clouded their salad days on the plain of Arcady.

"Hush!" I whispered. "Wasn't that a dog barking?"

"It's only a wolf or coyote," said Snowbird, pooh-poohing my anxiety without conviction. As soon as she said that we heard an uncoordinated chorus of barking that could only have come from a pack of Indian tracker dogs. Their tracking skills in the wet were better by far than ours in eluding pursuit. Panic! We ran, our frolicsome mood flown, slipping and sliding in the sludge, holding little illusions of our fate if recaptured.

It must be obvious, even to the most Olympian bluestocking reading this in the calm of her study, that a well-trained heathen in the prime of fitness, on his own turf, and enjoying the rudiments of woodcraft education, would be more than a match for a pair of drenched and tired females, one of whom was encumbered by a bundle of wet rags whose masquerade as a farthingale frock was but a memory, and that it was only a matter of time before their recapture. This was a logic I was in no hurry to accept.

The hallos and huzzahs of the savages were coming ever nearer. They caught sight of us, and their shrieks soared up an octave so sharply that Mozart would have been impressed. I raced as I had never run before, flying over broken branches and stones as if they weren't there, lungs bursting and heart thudding in my seated ribs against the use of nature, knowing that shortly our caper and life's pleasure-ridden jaunt would be making that curtain call. I burst into a clearing. Suddenly there was blue sky ahead, nothing in front of me. I cast my eyes down to see I was standing on the edge of a cliff. About a hundred feet below me a torrent raged through a rocky streambed. Nookeesa and Snowbird had disappeared into a thicket on my left that, sure as eggs is eggs, would lead them back to their hunters. Well, good riddance; they could shift for themselves. I turned around. A huge warrior about twenty yards away from me was steadying a javelin preparatory to take aim. As he let fly the javelin, I shut my eyes and leapt to certain death, offering up my soul to the foaming torrent.

I hit the water with a wallop. For an instant I was rendered insensible. My first thoughts on coming to were that I had passed through the Great Veil and had been returned to some preternaturally cold womb or been delivered up into Purgatory, but in a very modern Enlightenment version of it, as if I were being churned around in Mr. Cort's puddling furnace. Here, instead of being a slag amidst the molten iron, I became part and parcel of the ingredients of freezing coffee (of the Italian frothy variety, all the rage in London during my short sojourn there), for I was bumped around in a great frou-frou of effervescing living water, luckily not breaking any bones against the many rocks that punctuated my passage.

As I tumbled to the surface for the umpteenth time, I espied the Indians running along the bank, leaping as stags do from rock to rock far above my head. Occasionally arrows came swooshing through the water, but I paid them no heed. After a few more bends in the river, with me bouncing off the rocky banks, the maelstrom calmed down; soon I was swimming through a peaceful millpond, the cries of the barbarians having receded into the distance. Presuming me killed in the fall or drowned soon afterward, they called it a day.

I gave myself up to the ebb and flow of the current and found myself floating like driftwood into a mossy cave far from my original tumble. I doggy-paddled to the shore, stood up, and found the stones underfoot sharp and painful. Balance was difficult to maintain for a couple of steps, and I found it easier if less dignified to scramble up on all fours like the beasts of the field. The biblical phrase brought back memories of my father, and for no accountable reason I started to cry. Pulling myself together I stumbled up the muddy bank. "Our Father, Who art in heaven, what further horrors have You got in store for me, Your humble servant? Yes, I know I have not been in church for a while, but it was lack of opportunity not lack of faith," I said to myself, thinking *that's taken care of the spiritual domain. Now all I have to do is keep myself alive till I am able to cite the Athanasian Creed in an appropriate setting.* Then I collapsed flat onto the mossy cave floor and drifted off to sleep.

CHAPTER 16

A Strange Sir Galahad

I woke up to the vista of a steamy exhalation filling the cave with a cold Stygian gloom pierced by shafts of muted grey light. I was stiff with cold; my shift was completely sodden, and a feverish chill was running through my bones. I prayed mightily to the Lord whence I was instructed to count my blessings; viz, I was alive, safe for the moment at least, and that was that. Warmth, food, and little folderols like ribbons in my hair were unwarranted boons. I struggled to the front of the cave to discover a waterfall curtain hiding me from the outside world. I peeked out carefully through the curtain of falling fountains in case an aboriginal spotted me. I was alone. Briefly I wondered about the other pair. Of their existence there was not a sign, and did I care? I have to confess I was but briefly troubled by their absence.

My overnight domicile lay on the shores of a lagoon of opal green water from which, like a witches cauldron pouring forth steam, the dawn mist was evaporating in a twinkling, unveiling a bright blue sky. In any other circumstances I might have enjoyed this solitary splendor, but today there were other things on my mind than poetic fancies. Luckily it was a warm day, so cautiously I let myself dry out on a rock, spreading my shift on another boulder while keeping a wary eye out for copper-hued elders at

Susannah's well. A dog barked. Grabbing my shift, I leapt back behind the watery drapes and huddled in the farthest recess of the cavern, shivering with fresh terror when I heard steps approaching coupled with yelping of hungry dogs.

I knew my number was up when a ferocious hound, a very Cerberus, rushed up to me, barking as if it was rounding up lost souls on the banks of the River Lethe. This entrance was followed by that of a tall bronzed figure wearing of all things a beaver hat adorned with plumes following the fashion of St. James's Palace, quite the ragged macaroni. I couldn't take any more. I gave up and lay down to die.

The howling dog stopped in its tracks, contemplating a good rump chop; then instead of biting it nuzzled its face against my cheek and started licking me affectionately. I opened my eyes and saw another dog lining up to take its lick. The huge fellow stared at me with that penetrating, thousand-yard stare which is the prerequisite of the frontiersman, and I realized he had blue eyes. Then to my amazement he spoke in English, "See, here he likes you already, and I think I do as well. He's cleaning you up, and reckon—given a bath and some clean clothes and you'd be mighty purty unless I am sore mistook."

I wished I could return the compliment, but there was something about my new champion that had nothing to do with the stink that announced his presence in the cave. The frontier aroma—a concoction of bad body odor, tobacco, and elements of horse—was something you simply had to get used to or suffer to be labeled one of those croaking lime juice drinkers who couldn't take the heat. His dogs: well, you wouldn't find them in Cruft's pedigrees, but they had an affectionate robustness about them that made them endearing. This gallant, now heralding a new chapter in my life, was a proper Jack o' Lent, a scarecrow without straw. His breeches were strung up with a tatty piece of old tow, in which were stuck two well-oiled muskets, a knife the size of a butcher's chopper, and a tomahawk. In one hand he carried a saber, which doubled as a walking stick; in the other he held a primed long rifle. His teeth were great buck horse's teeth, and he gazed at me with the old familiar lecher's leer. *Here we go again*, I thought. With him to squire me, my social contacts (exactly nil for the moment) would be severely curtailed, but hey ho, any port in a storm. As soon as he sat down with a heavy belch, I reminded myself not to introduce this one into Aunt Dolly's drawing room. In the circumstances these thoughts may seem highly inappropriate and ungrateful, but they were the only reasonable way for me to keep a grip on my sanity, pretending all was normal in a properly hierarchical world.

"Well, let's see, shall we?" He placed a horny hand under my chin and tilted it for inspection. "She's a looker and no mistake. Aye, Rastus, what do you reckon?"

The slobbering dog barked in friendly agreement.

"You was hidin' from them Red varmints?"

I nodded.

"Well, let's get us up and away."

I'll say this for Simon Girty (and there's not much you can say on a positive note about the most celebrated renegade on the frontier), he knew his onions as far as tracking and eluding pursuit went—necessary when you are hated on either side of the Alleghenies by both Red and White. He got us out of the cave and onto the trail back to his cabin expeditiously, even while bands of Indians were hunting the fugitives down on the ridges to either side of us. My memories of the route to safety are confused and sporadic, but I recall hiding behind trees, under carpets of leaves and underbrush, and in some nasty hollowed logs, always careful lest the crackle of leaves underfoot or a sneeze might give us away; and all the while brown bodies were sniffing the ground not too many feet away.

We were lying low, nestled on a riverbank, nervously watching while packs of Indians scattered to and fro, scratching at upturned leaves and splintered twigs in the search for our spoor, when I recognized one of them: a big evil-faced fellow with a nose like an eagle's beak, sporting the hem off my undercoat as a war bonnet and looking pleased as punch with his fashion statement. All the time a leaf was tickling my nose (and I dared not sneeze), while Girty was licking his knife, hungry for the kill. He at least was not nervous, but then murder was his only true passion, a snippet of trivia that he passed on to me on more than one occasion. Funnily enough this revelation, although hardly reassuring, did little to unsettle me. You see, I knew he wouldn't do me any harm, foolish virgin that I was. "Ah just love killing, just like you love needlepoint," was the way he put it, which did have its own logic, alarming though it might be. At this particular moment his philosophy was not available for the proper kind of attention, and David Hume in Edinburgh would have to wait before evaluating the ethics and rationality of the proposition.

On our second day an Indian sprang up in front of our path. I screamed in terror that quickly changed to horror as Simon sliced off his head with his saber as blithely as you or I might lop the top off a boiled egg. Then, with his long knife he peeled off the brave's scalp, and if you please offered me the hairpiece, bowing slightly just as one's beau at home might proffer a posy of poppies before the ball. I shuddered and wished I could faint and wake up in Sheepy, far from this horrid continent.

It was on the third day; we had just turned the flank of a hill, and there nestled in the back of a hollow with a waterfall spilling on the rocks beneath was home sweet home, which consisted of a lean-to lolling against the cliff at a drunken angle. There was little light or view, as it had been erected in the middle of a ravine, and facing north it never caught the sun; but being tucked in under the roof of a great red sandstone cliff, it was easily defensible, and that was all that mattered.

I had pictured for myself a charming woodland cottage nestling in its own clearing amidst lofty sweet-smelling pines hard by a clear running brook where the lady of the cabin could wash out the plain but freshly scrubbed tablecloths. I soon realized my imagination was too generous.

The ugly ramshackle exterior of the hovel gave only an inkling of things to come—a gentle prologue too kind by half. The interior would have made Mrs. Cyclops blanch and then plume herself with sweet housewifely pride upon her own cavern dripping with bat droppings. My eyes scouted this outpost of Rhadamanthus, hoping to settle on some ornament, some item that spelt home not hell; and to my surprise, amidst all the accoutrements of the dungeon they lighted upon a posy of wildflowers arranged not unimaginatively in a rough earthenware beaker traded from some wandering sept of Mingoes or Delawares. This was set in the middle of a rough, unpolished oaken table, where in wild abandon the implements of his trade—a stone casse-tête, a knife the size of a cutlass, a cutlass, bits and bobs of musket, a flintlock, a matchlock, a powder pouch, and an antiquated fowling piece—had been laid to rest. I thought, throw in a death's-head, a sand clock, and a dead hen or two, and Gainsborough or one of his confreres could paint a very tasteful still life that would sell for a pretty pence on the London art market. You might title it *When Husband Does the Housework.*

Over against the windeye (actually more of an embrasure for musket or rifle than a port of entry for breezes or sunshine) a fragment of shawl of expired Honiton lace, which had been swagged out as a curtain by some not-too-dexterous hand, fluttered unenthusiastically. In contrast to most of the decor and refurbishments it had the merit of being clean.

"Cooee!" Simon cried out. "We've got visitors."

"Well, tell them to wait."

"Why my love?"

"I'm taking a shit, that's why, and I ain't got no dry moss. So bring us some pronto!"

Simon grinned. "That's the wife. She's an original. Don't take no sass from nobody: me included." He chuckled and amended his statement.

"Fact is, me especially." His face dimpled in the bliss of simple domestic happiness. "Fact is, she's a lovely lass. Takes a bit of getting used to though." I could hear the lovely lass crashing down the hillside.

"Got me some birch bark. Bit rough, and it tickles when I walk. Kinda excitin'. About all the excitement I'm gettin'." The door was bashed open, and I was pushed aside as a great whale of a lady thumped her lover affectionately on the chest.

Simon wheezed out, "This here's…sure, but I don't know who. But them Injuns seem mighty keen on renewing their acquaintance with her."

"Mrs. Girty, I presume?"

"Presume yersel. I'm Mad Annie. What's your jug and handle?"

"Eh?" was all I could manage in reply to this unorthodox introduction.

"Your name! Pretty little thing." There was an edge in her voice, which I recognized later as a warning call, about as friendly as mother bear's growl when protecting her cubs. "Amelia is it then? Not much meat there, is there, Simon? Looks like scrag end of joint when butcher's dog's finished wi it." I assumed this was her idea of a joke and managed an uneasy smile.

In the time I was their guest I got to know a little bit about these two lovebirds. Even though Simon had saved my life, even though they kept me warm and fed, I can't say I ever warmed to either. I say "fed," but hunting must have been lean that year for they dished out small helpings of fatty meat made just about palatable when sprinkled with sugar and salt. For a specific, we drank tree roots boiled in water, which, although bitter and nasty to the taste, they insisted would do me good; sure enough the sparkle returned to my eyes, my blood felt cleaner, and I began to feel the old sap surging through the system.

But to return to my landlord and his lady, there was something about them that made me feel not just ill at ease but a wee bit frightened withal.

It was (and this is the only way I can find to describe it) as if they were forever experimenting with Benjamin Franklin's kite, so that convulsions of lightning were jumping through their bodies. The first time this happened their seemingly jovial mood suddenly snapped, and they became demons of the flesh, screaming at each other and talking of me in not too friendly a manner, not caring that I was within earshot. Simon opened the door; both of them gave a look as if I were a highly succulent delicacy—a fancy pudding, methinks. Such a look as the missionary sees before he supplements the cannibals' broth. They said nothing, carried on stomping around, rearranging furnishings, cleaning their guns, and moving stuff that didn't need moving, as if telling me I was in the way. It gave me the feeling of the guest who has overstayed her welcome—tinged with a nameless, unmistakable fear.

"Do you get many visitors, Mrs. Girty?"

"Na." She went on pretending to dust. I hate it when somebody you are talking to refuses to turn around, and you are faced with nought bar a bobbing bum.

"Is it because you are so off the beaten path?"

"Na!" And this time she did turn round, giving me a significant look while nodding toward his nibs. "It's because he's off the beaten path." I got her meaning right away.

That night they attempted coupling. I can only describe the seismic uproar as on a par with those misbegotten attempts to put a steam engine onto a carriage to give us horseless locomotion (as sure a piece of folly as Icarus's attempt to imitate the birds). Their bunk creaked and groaned. I could hear splinters snapping off, and just at the moment I expected the bunk to snap in half, Annie let out a scream that stopped the owl hooting outside in his tracks and scattered the timid creatures of the forest to the winds.

"Lover boy, that sure was somethin'." The voice was deep, soft, and satisfied. I felt happy for both of them. The next day Anne was mellow, mooning continuously against her lover's side, while the man responsible for this ecstasy walked around with a self-satisfied smirk upon his face.

It was then she told me. Like the village gossips at home, she knew all that was happening for miles around and was dying to spread it around, particularly if it contained bad news for the recipient. How she picked it up, I confess I am at a loss, unless it was listening to the winds soughing through the branches of the trees and sending the leaves all of a flutter. She sat down beside me as if we were old cronies, and then began in that hoarse, mannish voice of hers to impart the gladsome tidings.

"Your Nookeesa has been recaptured and is chained up like a dog to a post, and sleeps outside in rain puddles. The squaws make him wash the clothes by the river and look after the papooses. All day long they have him fetching and carrying water from the river, shifting shite in the night, that sort of thing."

I knew how humiliating the abandonment of masculine role was for any Indian, and my heart briefly bled for Nookeesa.

"Squaws shout at him, 'Nookeesa, come here, clean up this diaper rag,' and they throw their dirty babies at him while they's laughing their tits off."

How abandoned these females must be, I thought, *giving up their instincts as a mother to a male, and a despised outsider at that.* Then I remembered my mother country—the constant stream of drunken wet nurses and dubious governesses who acted as proxy parents to the sons and daughters of the gentry—and kept my thoughts to myself.

"Nights he's their plaything. They force him to bark like a dog, then tether him up and widdle all over him. And then, when their brave bucko hubbies come out to kick him good and proper for the grand finale, they wet themselves laughin'. And wot do ye think is really hilarious is him as having to sleep on the freezing ground outside while they are tucked under their buffalo robes, gettin' their arses shagged off them and havin' a lazy lie in. Come morning he has to cook a good breakfast for all and sundry."

"And if he burns the porridge?" I said, acting unconcerned.

"Ow! You are a proper caution, you are!" And she biffed me on the arm just to prove what mates we were.

"And Snowbird, the Red and White woman? Nobody's sure. She's under a probationary death sentence, but you wouldn't know it. The braves are frightened of her. They think she's a witch, and of course the squaws hate her but hang on to her every word. She is pampered and petted. I suppose if you're brung up that way people git trapped into treating you the way you always git treated. She always gets to wear fine things: fine buckskin and leather, mink and fox fur. No, our smelly clothes be too good for her." She snuffled, and I detected a whittle of jealousy there.

"Trust Snowbird to end up smelling of roses."

"How would you know that? Every day the other squaws take it in turns to powder and pamper her. Spray her all over with rose water. These chiefs don't want any smelly old slag stinkin' up their wigewas."

"I thought they would kill her immediately after what happened in the camp."

"They's a waiting 'cause."

"Because what?"

She paused meaningfully. "You see, them Injuns have got the oddest idea of what makes Christian folks tick. They say as how our God is a three-in-one monster—that's their way of explaining the Trinity, like, and how Christ was crucified in a threesome. Which were right in a way: the Lord plus them two brigands. They're looking for you, my pretty, for three's a charm, and they're a-going to hang you out to dry on Good Friday. You see, they're taking it very personally that you of all people managed to escape their clutches."

I glanced at the raggedy almanac lying on the sideboard shelf and saw Easter was not so far off.

"Yep, I sees them in their village settin' up the crosses, and the squaws gotten to weaving a fancy crown of thorns. They are a-comin' to get you, and I ain't standing in their way. No siree! They's a-goin' to stick you in the middle. Makes you the best at last!" She cackled in her monstrous way. My stomach went cold, and I could feel my bowels churning like a mill race.

"Yep, they reckon a sacrifice to the Christian God in triplicate is the only way to ward off heap big evil and get you good and dead without haunting them afterwards. Paleface, him have big powerful magic." She stopped, then spoke matter-of-factly. "Honey, go fill them buckets and don't worry. We won't be trading you for a good while yet."

"Doan' talk trash, girl." This was Simon, breaking in on women's talk for the first time.

"Howzat?"

"You know there's no Injuns hereabouts no more."

"How come?" I said, and my face must have registered a great big question mark, for he went on.

"Ain't you heared? All them Injuns was smoked out by Colonel Logan and his long knife soldiers not long back. Burnt all them townships down—Wapatomika, Moluntha's town, Tarhe's town. Killed everyone thar. Those that 'scaped took off following sunset. Seems their big chief Moluntha were first to git sliced through. 'It were like cutting through a carrot cake'—that's what the trooper said. And he done it wi a tomahawk, too," he added pedantically.

"Who told you that?"

"A Scotch hunter."

At this point I decided to faint.

When I recovered I put on my tattered robe and stumbled down to the stream, feeling (amongst a passage of other emotions) happy. Like everybody else, my skin was my very first concern, but after the relief I felt a great sadness. I had lived there as a temporary queen, walked its narrow paths and glades, talked, made friends. Some of my best friends were Red men and women, and where were they now? Perchance Goldsmith's "The Deserted Village" best sums up my melancholic mood, viz:

Sweet smiling village, loveliest of the lawn,
Thy sports are fled, and all thy charms withdrawn;
Amidst thy bowers the tyrant's hand is seen,
And desolation saddens all thy green.

The air was clean and fresh, and the animals that I joined by the clearing were free to wallow and guzzle away at the water. There were lynx; there were buffalo: huge, shambolic, and monstrous, pawing the ground and defecating with splendid abandon, like the ancient things that once covered the Earth (according to the controversial Lord Monboddo, who assures us we are all descended from the same minute mollusk whose name is Adam). But they were peaceable and made room for me at the water's edge. Sometimes a wolf would sneak up the bank, looking for rich pickings, and finding none slip unobtrusively away. Some, like Rupert, the deer who always ran up to me for a quick nuzzle, seemed to think of me as their friend. That it was cupboard love (and had more to do with the titbits I stole from kitchen to give them) didn't enter my head. Some creature liked me and that made me feel better. The two buckets that I had dropped into the pond had glugged full of water, after which I had no excuse to linger.

"You mentioned a Scotch hunter. Who might that be?"

"The famous Lewis Wetzel. He wouldn't fancy a scrag end like you." Annie did tend to jump the gun in conversation; as this was the first time I had heard the name of this frontiersman I could hardly be credited with intentions toward him. Nonetheless, being in an expansive mood, her words flew off like cotton broadcloth from the flying shuttle of a skillful weaver about this individual who was apparently famed for his exploits in the backcountry. This intrepid backwoodsman was much talked about amongst men for whom courage was the salt on the porridge of their character. A wily Scarlet Pimpernel of the Ohio glens, plucker of captive damsels from under the Indian noses, he was both feared and loved; feared because he was a dangerous person to cross, and loved not only for his pluck but for being a handsome White hunter to boot. Clearly from the way she rhapsodized on about the wonderful Wetzel, Mad Annie had a girlish crush on the man who could charm the Indians and talk his way out of trouble for himself and others.

"You make him sound like Robin Hood."

"Who? He's not the one from Maryland?"

At this point I gave up, and let her relate to me a very recent anecdote that happened after my rescue.

A particularly nasty band of Tuscarawas caught Girty out on a hunting expedition south of the river in the Kentucky region, an area sacred to the Indian, and would have had him dispatched but for Wetzel, who happened to bump into them just as Girty was being readied to be burnt at the stake. After a long desperate monologue he managed to talk them out of it and get him released. However, their magnanimity was dependent on one condition.

They told Lewis that they wanted to touch and taste the milk-white girl they had espied frolicking around Girty's cabin with the mighty mountain warrior woman who was not a squaw. They were from a different tribe than Whingwy Pooshie's and had not heard of my sojourn there. Girty's continued freedom and attachment to his scalp depended on Lewis managing to chivvy or prize her out of the former's hideaway. Lewis, not having a clue about me, was happy to give his promise on the sensible premise that today's rescue is worth any nebulous promise for the morrow. However, not entirely at ease with his conscience in this matter, Lewis decided to go visit the Girty homestead and find out about the milk-white maid before the Indians came a-courting. I was unaware of any of this, although I do remember a hunting trip where Simon was overdue and came back in a sulk, continually glowering at me, which made me very nervous for a while, and then I forgot about it. With all this going on I must have been a guest chez Girty for longer than I remember. They do say time passes quicker when you're having fun.

CHAPTER 17

Cannibal Caprices Chez Mad Annie

Fall was harsh and bitter. Blasts of snow and biting winds, harbingers of a hard winter, whistled in through the eaves of our cottage. Even with the fire permanently lit, I still couldn't get warm. Girty would be out all day but often returned home empty-handed. "Game's gone to ground. Poor bull this year." Naturally our portions got smaller and smaller. I daren't ask for seconds and could feel Annie's sullen look boring into my back when I filled my platter.

"Put some back! Little mice don't need no big plates." She wasn't joking.

It must have been a month or so later; I woke up to hear them muttering, thinking I was out of earshot. It was Annie doing all the complaining. Simon, who I presumed had the power of veto, kept saying, "But she's such a sweet little thing, like a chunk of candy."

"That piece of candy's eating us out of house and home."

"She don't get much. You see to that."

"She does. You don't see her pinchin' pemmican biscuits out of cupboard in middle of night. You're too busy snorin' house down."

That was an impertinent lie! As if I would stoop to such a thing!

"I don't snore. Do I?"

"Never mind snoring. Look, this winter's goin' to get worse before it gets better. Let's chop her up and be done with it. Chuck her out in't snow and cut slabs of meat off her as needed, all nice and frozen fresh. Didn't need her before she came, and don't need her takin' up space now." She was eaten up by jealousy, of course, and it occurred to me that that was the real reason for adding me to the stew.

Simon to his credit didn't endorse this proposal. "But...but...but..."

"Never mind 'but, but, but.' Simon Kenton was telling me settlers down in Bottoms was starving last year and chopped up their daughter. Said she tasted real nice fried tender, tasted just like a pork chop; real sweet they said it were. Would do it again if they had any more children, they said."

I was being sick with fright and disgust so didn't hear the next bit, but I heard Girty say, "Well, I am right partial to piece o' pork meself." I could just see him, stroking his beard as if he were Archimedes. "Well, let's wait see if needs must. And we best wait till there's plenty snow on the ground to keep her fresh."

"It's you that's fresh, and I'm talking about pork not porking. I see's you lookin' at her, licking your lips, and you're not thinking of dinner." She made a tremendous guffaw and thumped him in the ribs.

Simon wheezed and let out a belch. "Sure am hungry, me," he said, which together with the vocal accompaniment was to be read as a vote in favor of the proposition.

The horror of it was beyond contemplation, and I made sure I got up early every morning to check if snow had fallen. Just a few snowflakes meant at least a temporary reprieve, and you can imagine I was on tenterhooks wondering how they defined snow aplenty. Was it a snowstorm so heavy that you were wading thigh-deep through the stuff, or was it just enough to cover one's moccasins? The question was more than academic.

It was late February, that bleak period when bitter winter never looks like ending. We had eaten nothing bar moldy bread and hardtack biscuits for a week now. Our coffee grind and tea leaves had been boiled so often we had to add acorns to give the hot drinks any semblance of flavor. Even Simon, whose cheeks were by now even more gaunt and haggard than normal, was hauling himself around slowly, paring out his energy like a miser searching his purse for groats. Mad Annie still had some reservoir of fat, but it was all slipping downwards till she looked like a sad, sagging pear. Me, I stayed in my cot most of the time to keep warm and not use up precious energy. The one bright point was that the snow had so far never fallen in quantity and had ofttimes been substituted by freezing rain, which didn't count.

And then one morning I woke up to see a thick blanket of snow on the ground and all the trees heavy with white fluffy cotton. This put Mad Annie in a jolly mood, singing as she went on her daily round that song from *The Grub Street Opera*, "The Roast Beef of Old England." I recognized it and shuddered.

"You getting some ideas, Annie, me old love?" Simon said.

"Aye. I'm thinking. This one 'ere." She gave a significant nod in my direction. "I'm seeing her all chopped up and fried with onions and diced carrots. And bits we can't eat we can freeze."

"Aye, and what about a couple husks o' Indian corn slathered wi butter. And marinated in that, er, sauce."

They were positively slavering at the mouth at the prospect. It's not an everyday occurrence to hear yourself discoursed upon as the main event at a banquet, so I leave you to imagine my feelings.

"Glad we kept her nice and fattened up."

"Nice and fattened up! Is that what you call it? She's still all skin and bones."

"Stop complaining. There's enough chops there to feed an Injun."

"And his squaw and his papoose."

"That's better."

"But we ain't got none o' them fixin' things, have we?"

"Nope."

You could almost feel them drop to earth with a thud, as if they were French chefs who had lost their sauces. They both looked crestfallen.

"We can git some garlic from plants on riverbank."

"Yep, and sprinkle on top them old herbs in cupboard from last year. That'll give her a bit of flavor and take away her smell," he said, ending on a personally offensive note. How I could stand still and listen to their macabre conversation without fainting is beyond my comprehension. I do remember that I was praying frantically. They discussed it dispassionately—just two chefs looking over that day's menu.

Annie rolled up her sleeves. "Now's the time! Grab her, Simon!"

I ran to the door, but a grim-faced Annie was there in front of me. I jumped back to grab a kitchen knife but was caught in a pear-shaped bear hug, and the knife slid out of my grasp and fell to the floor.

"Now then, my little forest doe. Leave the silverware alone. You've done enough eating us out of house and home. Time we got some back." She lifted me up as if I was a feather, then threw me over to her common-law spouse. "Git her 'n' hold her tight!"

Girty grabbed me round the waist; I bit his wrist. He yelped, "Bloody bitch!" then sucked at it. I had drawn blood.

I wrenched myself away but got no further, as he grabbed me again and pinned my arms to the side. I screamed my head off. "Help! Mother! Father! Dick! Oh Jesus, they're all dead!"

"Stop feeling her up, Simon! And put her on the table!"

"Can't. It's full of things."

With one sweep of her arm Annie disposed of the wreckage of plates, knives, and muskets littering the table. "Now it ain't, so git her up and shut her up."

I was kicking and screaming fit to wake the dead if there happened to be any cemetery within hearing distance. Girty took one hand away to rip at the hem of my petticoat for a gag. I kicked out and broke free. I got to the door, slipped the bolt back and pulled it open, screaming, "Help! Help me! I'm being murdered!" There was nothing out there but the forest. I ran out and promptly banged my foot against a stone and fell over. Girty grabbed me, seizing me painfully by the armpits, and dragged me back into the hut. I went limp. Resisting would only prolong the agony, so I let them throw me onto the table like a rag doll. He held me down till Mad Annie wheezed her way up to the table and leant on top of me. Lord, it was like being run over by a buffalo. With the one hand she kept me bound while the other was stretching out for a bale of greasy twine. She had me tied up in a trice. Simon wasn't doing anything beyond staring and grinning, quite the happy husband in a scene of domestic harmony, patiently waiting for his dinner.

I kicked and struggled to no purpose. She laughed a great big cheesy laugh; gusts of fetid Brie engulfed me.

"We had better take her clothes off before we carve her into joints." This was Simon.

"Well, don't be thinking you's going to do it, ye child-snatching scally!"

Incredibly they started arguing about the propriety of him cutting my clothes off! Annie must have been a Puritan in her childhood. The blissful scene of domestic harmony gone like smoke, they argued long, loudly, and bitterly, with me the centerpiece of their debate, trussed like a turkey on the dining table. And they went on interminably. The issue was still the propriety of Simon, a man, stripping me down. In the end Annie relented. "All right then, ye can have yer little candy treat while I'll hold her down."

Girty went off, fetched the sharpest knife from the drawer, then began sawing at my bonds and then my bodice. It mustn't have been that sharp, as he was making little headway. Although when I look back on it now that could have been deliberate. I don't think he was as mean as Madame, but he was slavering at the gills, wearing that cruel, lecherous look that told me he was making free with another appetite.

Suddenly the door burst open. A musket report banged, deafening everyone in that little box. The buckshot flew across the room so near to Simon's head that tremors from the flight tickled his hair, and the ball crashed into the looking glass set against the mantelshelf. The man who fired the musket stood athwart the doorway. With the sudden light coming through the door it was impossible to tell if he was friend or foe. Nevertheless his entrance put a stop to all activity. Simon just gawped, while Madame froze, legs akimbo in her usual gross manner. A great big chopping knife the size of a Roman sword sped across the room and planted itself in Annie's plaid, pinning her to the wall of the shack.

"Hiyar there! Anyone at home?" Whoever this was, he came along at a very propitious moment.

Then, to my astonishment, a bright pink blush lit up the face of the mad butcher. In a trice she had turned from being a murderess cannibal into a simpering sweetheart. I was too terrified to be amazed at the turn of events. "It's Lewis!" she cried. "Lewis Wetzel come a-visiting!"

A laughing cavalier wearing clean buckskin strode wide and easy with an open-faced smile into the pigpen they called the kitchen. It was his idea of a joke. "Sorry if I frightened you," he said, confident that his charm would overcome any objections to his homicidal mode of delivering his calling card. "How's the redecoration of the chateau coming on, then?" He checked out the ragged drapes before taking in my figure, disheveled and semi-naked, adorning the center of the table. "Ah, preparations for dinner if I am not mistaken. Can anyone join in? Ah, it's a young lady," says the observant fellow. "How-de-do? You must be…and why not. I thought I would look in and see this milk-white cherub that's got all the Indians in such a tizzy, whom I promised to deliver fresh as the snow and rosy-cheeked as the dawn wrapped in a parcel. And here you are with the wrapping still on. The Red men are all beating their tom-toms about this ravishing beauty that they are going to roast into a tender, juicy steak. And to think I promised you sight unseen for Monsieur Girty here, who comes back uncooked. Not a great trade I would say, now I see the merchandise. It would need a heap of soap to make you pretty." He laughed again. Mr. and Mrs. Girty echoed the laughter but not heartily.

The musket was held lightly in the crook of his arm. The knife throw had been to impress us with his dexterity, which it did most satisfactorily. Our gatecrasher had a quiet smile on his face as he reloaded the weapon, a complicated task, but he had it done all in a jiffy—powder and ball inserted, tamped down, and hammer recocked; then, as if he had all the time in the world he lifted the gun till it found its mark in the faces of my tormenters.

"Before we get any further in the matter of introductions, which I must say you two have been mighty slow about, might I suggest we disarm, and let me see the lassie's face," continued this extraordinary joker.

With a reluctant grunt Girty dropped his knife to the floor, where it embedded itself noisily, then gestured with his thumb to his wife, who turned me round to meet our visitor.

"Girl, this here is Lewis Wetzel. Lewis, this here is our girl. Don't rightly recall her name, though the Injuns call her Milk-Face Woman, so you can stick that on her baggage."

I was inspecting my ankles. Long ago I had been taught that the proper way for a maiden to make a good impression was to act as meek and demure as was consistent with not being totally witless, and in particular not to stare boldly, as that marks you for sure as a brazen hussy. I had long since learnt that appearances are a woman's only calling card. In passivity is strength; never show trumps in the first trick.

"Come, bonny lassie, let's see what makes you such a sought-for delicacy by the genteel lord and his lady of the Green Woods." The intonation was frontier with a dash of the Scotch dialect that seemed the normal run of things round here. He spoke in jest, but the harridan was flattered by the courtesy title, for she dipped a curtsey and simpered coyly, sounding like a hog in childbirth, which was her honest attempt at mimicking milady.

"Oh, Lewis, you are the one," she whimpered archly, while he wrenched the deeply embedded blade out of the wood. I couldn't help noticing how clean and well maintained his gear was in comparison to mine host's rag and bone collection. Then he turned to give me his full attention. "I knew the Girtys had a guest, but I never realized she would be sae bonny…"

"What's up?" shouted Mad Annie, for as I raised my head slowly in what I had been assured was an interesting manner, she saw that we were staring at each other.

He stared at me as if I was the last thing he expected to see in this troubled world. I looked up at his face, and suddenly the whole nightmare of North America dropped away and I was back in dear Old England, the timid mouse in the corner while Mary-Anne was demonstrating her dance steps. Then the room did a whirligig as I fell into a swoon. This stew of disagreeable circumstances ending in a hallucination was all too much.

I don't know how long I lay on that floor senseless, till an acrid odor pulled me back into the land of the living. A worried frontiersman was holding a damp handkerchief under my nose and making me sniff at some pungent stuff smelling of pish. Whatever it was, Hungary water it was not.

"I'm sorry. I thought you was someone else," I said, now somewhat embarrassed, as if I had made some dreadful faux pas in a duchess's drawing room. I became aware that Lewis What's-his-name was giving me such a going over I wondered if he were in need of a pair of Mr. Franklin's eyeglasses. His buckskin jacket was wrapped in the plaid of a clan proscribed back in its homeland. Would I never be rid of these damn Scotch Jacobites? I was sure these people had been sent to haunt me. Yet there was a ring in his speech that was familiar, that had nothing to do with the peat-sodden glens from whence he indubitably came. Perhaps the familiarity of the stories that hung about his name like an old cloak deluded me into thinking I kent its owner. You know the phrase "I've heard so much about you I feel I already know you," a phrase so frightening in its promise of early disappointment, when the base metal of reality replaces the golden legend. But there was something more to it. The face I had never seen. It was too strong, too sure, too steady. Yet it could have been hewn out of another face: a face that was soft, cherubic, given to occasional sulks, yet honest, often reddened with embarrassment, a face well remembered from Old England. Meanwhile the frontiersman's eyes were fixated upon mine, staring wide-eyed as if he had seen a ghost. Then, warming with dawning comprehension, his mien softened till he was quite beaming down at me.

"Why, bless my bottom dollar! If it ain't Amelia, the vicar's daughter!" The lad smiled. "You're right on the mark, though, Amelia. I am someone else, and you ken me fine," he said in absurd Lallans. "Don't you remember your James Cameron MacPherson, tutor to the snooty Mary-Anne."

"Who in bejeebers are you both?" Simon and Annie chorused in astonishment. "Whose's daughter?" The pair jumped apart, as in a silly village comedy when the squire, bursting in from behind the sackcloth curtains, catches them at it.

"Therein lies a long tale," James said, whereupon he delivered an admirable synopsis of our histories as briefly as would maintain the sense, as well as maintaining my sensibilities.

"And to think we was goin' to chop you up into tasty slices, eat you, and make you into stew," said Mad Annie calmly.

Her irreverent partner added, "Yep, but knowing this: We went without during Lent. Should have filled pickle barrel then." He chortled at his whimsy, but no one wanted to share. For now we had settled down to stare at each other, me puzzling out how James MacPherson—the effete milksop who liked to curl up with a book and play depressing Gaelic laments on his fiddle—had been transmogrified into this steely backwoodsman, and him no doubt wondering where I had got to after we parted company at that dreadful tavern.

My musings were interrupted by Girty's rough voice, which now had a nasty edge. "We found her here. She's ours. We can do anything we want to her. She's our slave, and we know the law of slaveholding holds good here in the wilderness just like it does in the states." He growled, unnecessarily defiant for no one was arguing with him, Wetzel least of all, who just went on grinning.

"Sure, Simon, but there's a buffalo in my larder says you won't do nothing."

"A whole buffalo? Simon asked, not believing, still being stubborn.

"Sure, and a side of venison."

"It's been a hard, hungry time. Grub's so scarce we soon'll be eating tree bark." This was Annie, aiming to soften up Girty's pointless defiance. The pair of them were inspecting me, sizing up my comparative culinary merits with those of the animals just mentioned. I lost.

"Well, she's worn out, and only a couple of suppers left on her."

"And a bit of scrag end of chop to go to bed on. We've got a bargain here, Simon. Let's take it before this donkey changes his crack brain."

Simon changed his mind and, turning to the newcomer, shook hands with him. "Done, Lewis. She'll makes you a right capital housemaid; mind youse, not as good as a Tuscarawas squaw but better than having to light yer own campfire, reckon."

So there I was, an item of goods again. I couldn't help thinking my market value had declined drastically since Angus pulled me off the shelf from Mother Carey's establishment, but a buffalo plus a side of venison was surely better value than five bob dead or alive, which was all I was worth to the Bow Street Runners back in Old England. Maybe Adam Smith could help me understand the ups and downs of the market in English maidenhood and its comparative value as dead or living flesh. Ugh! What a gruesome thought! I chased away that disagreeable line of cerebration and returned to the interesting present.

In terms of squalor, ill treatment, and shuddering fear on waking up every morning not knowing how their worships' temperaments were going to be that day, this had been the worst of my trials. Escape from it had been the easiest. For the sake of a side of black beef and a haunch of venison I was sold down the river and ended my time in hell. Mad Annie made me cry by giving me a farewell gift, a posy of pressed flowers, plus, wrapped in a swag of cloth, her very own wedding ring. I think the poor unlovely soul nurtured hopes of being a bridesmaid or a matron of honor. The last I saw of that well-matched pair was Girty hacking away at the buffalo preparatory to salting it for the days ahead and her standing at the door of the wretched cabin snuffling as she waved me goodbye. As someone once said, "There's nought so queer as folk." I gave her a wave, for there's no sense in holding a grievance in this wild country. You never know whose help you may need. Then I turned to the path ahead. I never saw them again.

CHAPTER 18

More Ancient History

On the way to Wetzel nee MacPherson's cabin I had plenty of time to examine my new captor, for whatever else can I call this succession of men eager to take me over? He didn't say much on that first day as we were still in Injun country, with an urgent need to "vamoose," as he said, which I soon found out meant to exit quickly, a definition I would be surprised to find in the Doctor's Dictionary. We camped within the sound of beating tom-toms, covering ourselves with a grubby mix of leaves and flora to escape detection, then left quickly before sun came up over the ridge. About an hour after dawn he sniffed at the wind and said, "We is safe. Oh sorry, Amelia, I can drop the rough frontiersman camouflage. Whatever! Let us breakfast here in this pretty sylvan glade."

For once the poetic mode fitted. As if all my troubles were over, the sun came out and warmed the forest. "What's the date today?" I asked.

"I don't know exactly, but judging by the trees and the flora it's near middle of April. Aha! Amend that to March." He shivered as a chill breeze struck up out of nowhere and then died away. Spring had arrived with hardly a whisper. Then I realized why the winter had seemed so long. Girty's cabin had been built at the end of a long hollow facing north. It was always about ten degrees colder in the depths of these tree-clad hollows. Now we were entering a sun-washed, rocky box canyon at whose back a waterfall tumbled and sparkled in the sunlight. From there a stream chuckling and frothing flowed over boulders, then shirred smoothly through reed beds till it finally plunged silently into a placid pool whose blue waters reflected the surrounding hillsides. On both sides of the stream were bonny bunches of early daffodils creeping up amidst melting snow patches. Even the grass here was thick enough to rest on. Lewis got out a flint and some moss from his pocket. After a few rubs the moss started smoldering, and by deft management he set alight some tinder; soon we had a boisterous fire to cook upon. Like all the pioneers he preferred to drink a mug of tea in the morning, despite its lack of patriotic credence, but because supplies were short he had to make do with coffee. This he took with a strong dose of sugar to help it on its way. One cup he claimed was not enough to get him started, so breakfast consisted of six cups of this very strong stimulant, a couple of biscuits, a rasher or two of bacon, and to top it all off a pipeful of his foul tobacco. However, the drug in the coffee must have been inefficacious, for he began to doze off.

"This here's a fine spot. Let's rest up here till evening when moving is safer anyhow."

"Mmm," was all I could manage. My nerves were all so giddy after all my misadventures, I could no more make myself look ahead to the next day or two's program than fly. I too dozed off, dreaming of summer in Sheepy when the hay was ripe and you could hear the lowing of cattle in the fields and the regular chiming of the clock in the church tower, assuring all that all was well in that small, insular, and now infinitely desirable world.

I awoke to the late afternoon sun tickling my cheeks, and the fragrance of wood smoke in my nostrils. "Is it really you, James, or should I call you Lewis? Do I pick the name of the man I love, or the name he is currently playing under?" I suppose it was a strange thing to say, but how else do you recommence a friendship so dramatically interrupted.

This was while he was gutting and boning trout freshly caught from the lakeside, so "Mmm" was all I got.

We ate in silence. More to be socially correct than honest I said, "Delicious! My compliments to the chef. The best ever I have tasted. Mind you a pinch of salt would have scarce gone amiss."

"Women!" He smiled, shaking his head. His hair under the coonskin cap seemed more coppery than I remembered, and then: "Yep, it's really me, and I have changed. Call me what you want, when you want." He even moved differently, more assuredly than the dithering scholar of the manse. "Here, make a sandwich with this bread."

The bread was so hard I feared I might break my teeth, so I was attacking it gradually from the flank to minimize dental damage when he gave me the first surprise, coming straight out with it instead of dancing around as James would have done.

"Your father is still alive."

No words can express my shock, my surprise, my sublime minute of giddy ecstasy, all feelings rolled into one terrible moment of bliss. Suffice to say that I swooned anew. When I had recovered my senses: "But how can that be? I saw him swinging from the gallows tree. You were there; you saw it as well."

"Yes, and I made sure it was me that strung him up. 'Stand out of my road, bold boys. This is my party,' I cried. Do ye remember? 'I will do this bastard of a swine in, for how he has corrupted that beautiful girl and my hoped-for ladylove, Mary-Anne Dixie. Let him go, lads, for he hath the rage of a worshipper of idols, and all the Powers of Darkness.' It was that little touch about the dark that had them all afeard, and they stepped well clear of me. 'Give him to me and I will deal with him tenderly.' And so I hanged him."

I stared with amazement that my protector should be a murdering villain without a hint of apology. Then an impudent grin stretched his features. He laughed. "Sure I did, but I tied a thick muffler round his neck before

I put on the rope, and fixed a belt round his shoulders under his jacket, which I tied to the rope above the knot so that it took all of the strain. No, don't ask me how I did it, and with the entire village watching from a distance mind you. Only remember the quickness of the hand deceives the eye. I waited till after dark, and then cut him down and put him in your mother's clothes. If you recall, it was midsummer, Beltane, when the tombs open up and the dead can walk amongst us. To the villagers 'she' was your dead mother, a ghost and now a witch out to drag them through the fires of hell; so they took themselves off, ran home to rattle their locks and bolts shut and put old crosses (kept hidden from the heathen papist days) over their thresholds. It was as easy as taking pence from poor old Simple Simon. I must say those dotards could run. Must have been something they put in the ale." He laughed again, the innocent laugh of James of old.

"But the crows?"

"Your imagination, dearest."

"And the handsome country maid and squire's daughter that you and I know was the cause of it all?"

"Aha! That is another story all in itself, and I believe you know the end of it."

"I do?"

"It seems that Mary-Anne has a way of sticking to anyone she has set her cap on like a briar bush. There she was at the foot of the gallows, greeting away like she was Mary Magdalene, which, come to think on it, is not too inappropriate a comparison. She saw through my tricks, and managed to switch off her tears to lay a threat. She sang, "Hey diddle diddle, the cat and the fiddle. This cat will be let out of the bag, if you dare not dance to *my* fiddle!"

"I wish that cow had jumped over the moon!" said I with unladylike bitterness.

"When he was cut down, Mary-Anne laid out her intentions most specifically. Your father was given a simple choice: dance the Tyburn hornpipe or trip the minuet with Mary-Anne." He hesitated. "You know, he even considered seriously the first option, but he had enough troubles ecclesiastical to be adjudged a suicide and buried on unhallowed ground with a stake through his heart.

"Then he thought of you: 'Ah, my precious Amelia, an orphan? 'Tis too much to bear!' He looked at the beautiful but vicious wench. 'Goddam, my ill-luck charm must come here with us.' Nothing could shake her off. He asked me, 'James, my staunch lad, where is the worst hell on Earth, for I must suffer it for my multitude of sins?'

"Well, I said, that doesn't take too much thinking about. Africky, and second by a short stroke the Indies. White folks can't survive there more than three weeks they reckon.

"'I'd consider it,' he said, 'But I have too much on my conscience to appear to be condoning slavery.'

"Well, I said, that leaves the Americas. They would meet your demands. The climate is horrible. You will be lucky to survive the first six months; most English folks don't. The food is unimaginable, the people rough, forever spitting and chewing tobacco and knocking you off the sidewalk without a by-your-leave. The natives are the most horrific savages on God's green Earth, who'll send you to heaven with a haircut soon as look at you.

"'Perfect! That's the place for me,' says he, 'and maybe there I'll get rid of this cross I have to bear.' He nodded at the mincing Mary-Anne, who was looking at the old vicar like a cat at a mouse."

"Why didn't you tell me then?"

"Dunno. Too much on my mind. Anyway I arranged passages for three across the Atlantic, one way."

"With that horrible sea-captain?"

"The very one, and he don't get any better on further acquaintance. But even after all that he can't give her the slip, and she plagues him and plagues him till he goes plumb loco and escapes to the forest, pretending to be a simpleton, an ecstatic preacher wandering in body and mind, preaching to the Indians, frontier folk, and the trees for all that I know. And guess who followed him through thicket and forest? By the way, when you see him expect changes," he said with a note of caution.

"How do you mean?"

"For starters don't call him Parson Wathes. That was someone else, someone previous. Now he has come to the Lord with a new name to go with his reincarnation. Like we all do here: a new life in the New World. He is now the great…ah, the name slips my memory just now, but he has become a legend in this Second Great Awakening thing, on this side of the briny."

"Second Great what?"

"*Awakening.* A religious revival ye would call it, I suppose, like when John Wesley rode through our villages, preaching to all and sundry, but never allowed to darken the insides of a proper church. If you had been out and about with White folk you would ofttimes have heard of him."

I was far too tired to make anything of this, so said nothing, but when the time came to curl up by the fire I instinctively hunched up near him and felt my toes go warm. There were wild animals out in the forest, and this man was sent here to protect me. Just before we dropped off to sleep in that delicious no-man's-land that is neither slumber nor awakening, he mumbled to me, "Amelia, me dear…"

I tensed up, half expecting a declaration, and had no way of knowing how I was going to react to it. "Yes, James?"

"Sorry. Forgot to mention this, but rumor hath it that your dad eventually managed to cast off Mary-Anne. Dumped her off with some Indians in Virginia, in a place—I think it's called the Monongahela Valley. Poor them, I say."

"No! You don't say? It's not by any chance under Seneca Mountain?"

"Sure is. How'd ye know?"

Now it was my turn to say "Mmm."

Having tossed off that grenade he drifted off calmly in the arms of Morpheus, but I couldn't sleep—well, hardly a wink. I must have nodded off though, for I was woken up out of sorts and unrested by the dawn chorus.

"You know, I was rather looking forward to that buffalo myself. This year game's been pretty lean. Had to take my belt in a couple of notches."

"That's a strange greeting to start the day!" I said, but he just laughed in that ingenuous, boyish way of his. "And now you're wondering if I'm worth that hunk of venison," I remarked, hoping to get a response.

There was a pause long enough for me to get the hint: I was dealing with an untutored backwoodsman. At least he didn't stick some straw in his mouth. "I think you're worth it."

Later, when we had struck camp and hit the trail, I took stock of him: the way he held his gun, the way he stalked his prey, the way he hushed me when Indians passed close on us. All these things said he was from the same cabinet as Girty, but a different drawer. The wilderness had made him ruthless, abrupt, and efficient; yet his early upbringing still left its mark in his personality. All in all an admirable mix to excite the admiration of the hard-bitten Mad Annie. According to him I too had changed. "You used to be quite the mouse, Amelia. But there's a touch of steel under your velvet." I wasn't wearing the teeniest smidgeon of velvet so this was just a lazy, well-worn figure of speech.

"Now. You've told me about my father, but what about yourself, man of mystery? Where did you pop up from? And how come you are here, and why are you not James, the timid bookworm? And how did whoever you are take possession of your body?"

"Whoa!" James alias Lewis took a deep breath. "It's a long story." We were both sitting snugly on this tree trunk which nature had thoughtfully molded into a sofa. The temperature was perfect, on a perfect day in spring, the wonderful season that is a celebration of life starting afresh. "It's not as if we're in any hurry." He scratched the ground with a twig. "I never knew my real parents. But that wasn't unusual after the Forty-Five for those whose folks was out. My father probably died out on the gallows at Carlisle, or of the sweating sickness on a plantation in the Bermudas. My mother was probably stirked to death by the Redcoats." How he said this all without any external show of emotion will ever be a mystery to me.

"I was brought up in a black house on the Isle of Skye. Talk about choking on your own fireplace! It was black on the inside with all the smoke that had no way to escape." He shuddered at the recollection. "You needed the smoke to keep the midges down, far worse than your black flies. I had been left to an old childless couple. There were orphans aplenty then, and I was lucky to find stepparents, never mind such good ones. From them I took the name Cameron. I had no idea what my real family name was, but I couldn't have had a fairer start to life. My stepfather was a fisherman, a strong, practical man with a great love of books—not so uncommon a juxtaposition up there as you might think. He told me my father fought like a tiger at Culloden and my mother, a rare island beauty, was a fine harp player, nothing more. Nothing could be gained remembering those days, he told me. They sent me to St. Andrews, where I garbed myself in the scholar's red gown like a braw gallant. I learnt English there"—I noted that he was speaking proper English now—"and then to Edinburgh, just at the time that Gaelic poetry was quite the mode. I could recite enough to gain entrée into the best houses, where I learnt that I didn't much care for the ton and their vapid airs. Maybe that's why I had little enthusiasm for your Mary-Anne. But I also learnt how to cut a caper on the dance floor, make chitchat when handing round the hot chocolate and fancy cakes, that sort of thing—useless here but the passport to success in Edinburgh's New Town, which if you visit you will find a happy marriage of Bath's elegant crescents and a hint of Athens in its days of glory.

"When my adopted parents died I was a lost soul. However, my father had given me a letter of introduction to Doctor Johnson, whom he had entertained when the great Doctor made his pilgrimage to the Highlands and islands. So off I went on the High Road south, stopping in Market Bosworth to get a bit of background about him as a young man. Samuel's patron there was none other than your Sir Wolstan Dixie. There I added the name MacPherson. It was just a coincidence that was the name of the notorious Ossian scholar." He chuckled. He knew I knew he was telling a little fib. "The rest I'll leave to your imagination till later, maybe..."

My curiosity was only marginally abated, but things had to wait till we arrived at his homestead. From the outside it was not promising: about the same dimensions as the Girty abode although more sturdily constructed, with the saving grace that the inside was clean. Still, a woman's touch wouldn't harm it. The cabin was finely situated on a hillside facing the Ohio River, overlooking an extremely lovely swathe of meadowland the early French settlers called Belle Pre, or "beautiful prairie." Here we had no need of hiding from the footfall of Indians, for the local ones were friendly. Their main interest in White folk was to trade with them or scrounge off customers emerging from the village tavern. Any who were in any way hostile were so incapacitated by drink (sold to them by renegade traders) as to provide no serious menace. The settlement was by the confluence of two rivers with the exotic appellations of Hocking and Ohio, but how different from the poetically lisped Thames and Anker which graced and watered the meadows back in Sheepy. And how different in size, for the latter were but mere rivulets compared to these mighty streams, which could have taken on Father Thames himself at full tide.

A frequent visitor to our cabin was a Bathsheba Rouse, who dwelt on an open stretch of hillside not ten minutes from us in the school house—the first in the Ohio Territory she told us, not without a modest drop of humble pride. Far from being a bespectacled, secular version of the mouse-like vicar's daughter (me, in other words), she was a remarkably tough daughter of a gun, whose major hobby was slaughtering wildlife to feed the poor, starving little nippers in her charge. This she did with an immense long rifle powerful enough to blow a turkey to smithereens at five hundred yards, effectively reducing its value in putting meat on the table if you didn't like mince. An interesting lady indeed, full of contrary quirks, such as a peculiar and absorbing passion for religion that was quite at variance with her belligerent nature.

There being no church in the neighborhood she had to wait on the odd wandering preacher dropping in on the village. She had opinions about all of them, and although all were equal in the eyes of the Lord, some failed to measure up to this severe judge's scrutiny. Amongst their ranks were false prophets and charlatans flogging the gospels merely as meal tickets, who in her estimation should have been tied to the tail of a wagon and dragged from village to village with the letter V burnt in their backs. On the other hand, there was one who (according to her stringent evaluation) acquitted himself splendidly respecting knowledge of the book, charity, energy, charisma—all channeled into an intoxicating maelstrom bellowing forth from the pulpit.

Such was Lorenzo Dow, a self-styled Old Testament prophet—down to raggedy cloak, long grey beard, and wild piercing eyes—who according to her boast could take on John the Baptist, Peter the Hermit, and John Wesley together, and win hands down. His visitations were awaited with the fervor of children listening for the footfall of gift givers on St. Nicholas Eve.

He was expected any day now, and she was in a lather of excitement, worrying her catechism and worn out bible whenever a moment could be spared from picking shotgun pellets out of splattered birds. That day I was strolling through the meadow, reflecting on the beauty of the lilies and Solomon in all his glory, when I heard a cry. Bathsheba was frantically waving her rifle and jumping up and down. "The preacher Lorenzo Dow has been sighted on the water!"

We rushed to the bank, and there standing in the bow of the foremost vessel was an imposing figure—part Moses parting the Red Sea, part Washington crossing the Delaware—leading a flotilla of canoes filled with sleek, rhythmically rowing Indians bearing palm leaves and singing out Hosannas as they swept into our little harbor nestled within the mouth of the Hockhocking River.

From the prow the great man embraced us all in his benediction. Forgetting she was a schoolmarm, Bathsheba rushed to the water's edge and hurled herself screaming upon the preacher. Lorenzo took this salutation in his stride. He had many passionate admirers amongst the fair sex, who were wont to express their devotion energetically and sometimes unambiguously, and for this reason the Indian rowers doubled as bodyguards.

The preacher looked at me; then, without turning his head, having probably decided I was not worth the trouble, began expiating upon his own woes and tribulations. "I was lost, but…" He paused to floss out an obstinate chunk of venison from between his teeth with an Indian scalping knife. "But now I am lost again, yea, amongst the heathen in the wilderness. I was a sinner that dwelt on the Arminian alignment of the altar, of chasubles, of vestments, and on the commutation of tithes."

Of those present it would be fair to say that only I had the faintest notion of what he was talking about. But what with his magnificent delivery and imposing presence, all were gripped by his words. "Of sinners going on the downward path to hell I was witness to many." His voice came out like thundering Jove. "For them I gave not a jot." Then it softened. "I cared more for the beasts of the field, for they had greater souls than the people in that dank Sodom of England. Yea, my tiny village had more sinners than Gomorrah!" He rallied for that peroration. Finished, he let out a weary sigh, and now his eyes flickered over me again in the way of saying, "I am sure I know the face, but the name escapes me." I thought I detected a spark of interest in my physiognomy. Inwardly I flattered myself that he had lit upon an innocent flower in this unkempt Eden.

Finally he spoke to me, but not in the exalted tones he had used for his audience, just in the normal conversational tones you might use for discussing this year's potato crop. "A lass of the manse if I am not mistaken. You, my child, have come far from the homely hearth of the vicarage, but withal you have goodly preserved that which, once taken, means you can't wear white anymore."

I blushed thinking of the numerous instances when I had tried to offload that wearisome burden, but was glad I had come through my trials unsullied, for those eyes of his seemed to have an uncanny knack of flushing out the truth.

"But ye are a lamb, shorn yet unshriven." Then he chanted, "*Agna dei, quae peccata mundi tollit*" (Lamb of God who bears the sins of the world), and stopped and stared for the longest time. "Or are you plucked from a great sheep?" He really hammered home the word *great*. "You know your Latin, my child?"

"Yes. In Latin that would be *Magna*! Sheepy Magna!"

When I spoke the last two words he positively jumped like a Jack-in-the-box. This couldn't be true? Now it was my turn to stare. The formidable features of the preacher had softened and, if I was not mistaken, were about to be liquidly happy; I saw there my own father, my flawed, favorite person on the globe!

I cried out, "Surely not!" The crowd was buzzing, not comprehending save that something momentous was happening, providing enough material for gossip to blether the whole of next winter away. Or perhaps they were witness to a miracle? But there was no mistake. The great Lorenzo Dow was none other than my father transformed from the retiring, abused figure of my memory, now barrel-chested with exuberant hair and beard fluttering in the breeze, standing like a proud, battle-scarred Achilles. Truly America had worked a transformation on all of us. Oh, brave new world!

"Amelia!" But more words were lost as I threw myself upon his bosom in the first truly happy moment I had been blessed with since my innocent life had been so roughly snatched away from me. The orphan lamb had found its shepherd! The vicar had sought expiation of his soul by renouncing the High Anglican Church, all the conveniences of manse, and two bottles a day to go and preach in the untamed wilds of the Americas with all its attendant perils, growing a beard as thick as any John the Baptist in the desert. From being meek, scholarly, and canonical only on Sundays he took on a bold countenance, compelling respect from frontiersman and savage alike, laboring in the vineyard for seven days a week. The once sheep-like voice plaintively calling the foot-dragging parishioners of Sheepy to morning prayers now thundered imperiously over ridge and hollow, threatening the sluggards with the fiery pit and other sanctions too lurid for Sundays at the vicarage.

When I called out his name his eyes brimmed with tears and he hugged me, and honest old dad came through. After we had hugged each other quite long enough we retired to the cabin. In front of a crackling fire he confessed that he longed to drop the firebrand missionary pose that had people fainting in front of open-air altars, to stop inventing miracle cures and planting apple seed and buckeyes along the settlement trails. He hankered to return to the peace and solitude of an English study, dinner and a bottle with the squire, and afterward a quiet game of euchre, playing footsie with the ladies under the table; on Sunday a tedious sermon to the accompaniment of honest English snores, followed by the true worship of the Lord, pink-coated and tallying-ho following the hunt.

"Oh, Amelia, my heart, my only joy, would that I could cast off this role! If only I could get rid of these togs!" He added in a less ecclesiastical tone, "What would I give for a side of honest roast beef, Yorkshire pud, and a firkin of honest English Ale!"

That would have to wait. Outside our cabin a crowd of disciples, manifestly baffled by the tender scene they had just witnessed, were hanging about eager for a reappearance of their charismatic preacher. The door crashed open to reveal a man restored. Bathsheba cried out, "Say a few words, preacher man!"

His alter ego, Lorenzo, resumed his role with relish. "Let me then sing for my supper. Consider this then the bread which the Christ did break." He held up a scone from my pantry. "We share this as a reminder of his fellowship with the disciples when he was surrounded by his enemies, and our fellowship here in the wilderness surrounded by savage men and beasts." Then, taking a large bite at the scone and with scarce a moment's respite for digestion, he recommenced saving souls. The lesson today was the parable of the widow's mite, the one where she gives away her last penny, which was worth more in heaven than the amassed troves of her scoffing, skinflint neighbors. The hint was taken. The instant he dropped his hat onto the ground, a torrent of coins poured into it from far and wide: livres and écu from France, florins from Florence, nobles from Venice, shillings and pence from England, doubloons and pieces of eight from Spain, and the ubiquitous dollar of Maria Theresa.

I think it may have been this unexpected cornucopia that convinced father to linger awhile and cut short his progress round the continent so he could sponge off our hosts. My suspicion was that the firstfruits were not so plentiful elsewhere, the savvy frontiersmen not buying his message as easily as our gullible villagers. But no, for as he said, "I despair of you, Amelia. Your rough passage through the Americas has made you a cynic. Remember those who come to scoff and yet remain to pray!" He pointed a very hard finger at me. "Beware! Lest ye become a Pharisee!"

I had it wrong again. What he was doing was called consolidating the message of the Lord.

"Now let us get on our knees and praise the Lord."

And that was that. I just hoped he would abandon his sales patter and learn to speak normally again.

CHAPTER 19

Round and Round the Lovers Go

So it came to pass that in order to while away the season pleasantly, Lorenzo began making much of Bathsheba. For instance, "Bathsheba, my dear, fair daughter of the crystal Mersey stream, may your soft siren voice cool the villainous ardor, the savage breast of the beasts around us, just as your pumpkin pie eases the pang of hunger from our stomachs." All lies, but the species of harmless stuff and nonsense your roving preacher need practice if he is to going to freeload off of his flock. He probably had caught a whiff of a Scouse accent lingering 'neath her American voice, and improvised from there onward. Bathsheba preened and primped herself, giggling with pleasure and casting coy glances at the preacher. Naturally it was all done in the interest of consolidating—if not the Word of the Lord, at least his own position as resident apostle and prophet, and (not to put too fine a point on it) his own meal ticket.

All in all the winter, that most dismal of times, was passed most agreeably in front of Bathsheba's hearth. Whatever else you might say about him, my father could tell a good tale, and he never wore out his welcome in any of the village cottages. He was astute enough to move along the street every day or two. At Thanksgiving we were almost submerged in pumpkin pies, breast of roast wild turkey, and a mess of Indian corn; and at Christmas we went a-wassailing, sang carols, and played blind man's bluff when we were not too well stuffed to move. Just to show our hearts were in the right place we doled out mince pies to the starving Indians that came begging, and we didn't ask them to do a forfeit.

'Twas in the blank and endless days of pitiless January and dreadful February, when we had time on our hands and Jack Frost on our fingers, that we all began hankering after home.

"What do you think Mary-Anne will be doing now? Some mischief I imagine." James, a fellow sufferer, mentioned it casually, but father stiffened at the mention of her name, which prompted discussion of the identity and whereabouts of the mysterious Snowbird and her friend. We frittered away hours forming half-hearted, unrealistic plots to rescue Snowbird and Nookeesa, till it became a pastime almost amounting to a parlor game. Then in that strange way that truth has of astounding fiction, we heard that everything was going to be easy. News winged across the prairie that the Indians were prepared to have an accommodation with the Shemanese and exchange prisoners. By the Auglaize Greenriver Treaty all prisoners White and Red were to be returned to their homes. Snowbird, regarded as an honorary White, had been discharged together with her faithful Achates, Newquay as he was called now, and the pair of them were wandering around the settlements both White and Red, searching for me, since without yours truly as their English Sybil they were as lost as the nocturnal shades flitting restlessly through the dark forests of Virgil's underworld. You see, without me as their—what?—sponsor, guarantor, they would just be considered renegade half-breeds and kicked around the settlements.

Then one day they did turn up. They were soaking wet, miserable, and looking more like babes in the wood than highborn, noble savages. It was all a bit of an anticlimax. We took them in; they settled in, and for a while we became one big happy family. Even Snowbird/Mary-Anne was agreeable, helped with the domestic chores, and spoke pleasantly to everyone, even neglecting to kick Newquay. That wouldn't last long.

One night, sitting in front of the warm glow of the hearth, tankards of nut brown ale foaming sporadically on the hickory stool between them, the two men of the house began a long overdue conversation.

"Lewis Wetzel, scourge of the frontier, more fearsome than the small-pox to the Red man: Why do I see in front of me the shadow of a shy Scotchman? The quill was mightier than the claymore then, but now look upon you: a man of flint, powder, and steel."

"Lorenzo, the fearless preacher to the savages, is revealed as the soft-spoken and learned Vicar of Sheepy, the St. Francis of the Lichfield diocese, who preached to the pigs and the cows. Tell us again how you came to be here in the wilderness."

"As you was the one who brought me here and had the happiness to pull me off the gibbet, my explanation would be superfluous; such strange tides there are in the affairs of men."

"I got you to the Americas and then lost sight of you. A strange change." James nodded as if saying to himself, "But then, look at me."

"There is a mystery about your origin that may be explained soon. Sir Wolstan, whom you call your patron, was no benefactor of yours. Beware of the treachery of the English upper classes. I know, for once I rode with that blue-blooded claque and was up to all their tricks. In a sense you was their hostage, not their guest."

Cameron's jaw dropped. The great trapper, Gaelic scholar, and sturdy yeoman was at a loss for a policy. "What about his wife? Was she in on the plot?"

"No, but there is a sorry tale lurking underfoot there. She was brought to his mansion as if she were an indentured laborer and treated like a house whore, a situation she does not enjoy. He is a naughty piece of work, and she is poor sweet goodness itself."

"But why were you always on neighborly terms with him, father, if he was so awful?" This was me pitching in.

"The curse of the English social system, my dear: everyone prancing and scraping to their social superiors, who are ofttimes their moral inferiors. For who is the gentleman then, when Jack is as good as his master?"

"Or you might say, when everyone is as good as their gun." This was Jamie, the pistolero par excellence, who believed democracy was the survival of the quickest on the trigger and had quite forgotten about Socrates, Pericles, et al.

We still missed England. Many of your frontiersmen, while immensely good fellows, had a lot lacking with respect to the social graces. Take their habit of spitting and hawking. Sitting round a spittoon and seeing who could gob the bull's-eye could hardly compare to a night round the table with Dr. Johnson at the good old Pineapple, discussing the authorship of Shakespeare; never mind an evening at the salon in Versailles. Marksmanship must have been at an all-time low with no Indians to shoot, for many a pretty dress of mine was ruined, the hem bespattered by self-styled sharpshooters having an off day.

Three or four to a bed for travelers made me cringe. And then, in what they called American hotels, that communal pot in the center of the table made for starvation for dainty eaters like myself. No wonder I became swan-like in slimness, watching the greedy gobblers with their elbows outstretched like winged Pegasus as they belched and trumped away at the table, surfacing for the occasional breath to comment heartily on the good chow. That this was done in our faces was reckoned to be the very essence of attic salt and of a fine, honest, all-American character. In fact, food was the staple diet of many of their conversations. As a result their mouths were always occupied either with practicing or praising gluttony.

If you think my earlier good opinions mealy-mouthed hypocrisy, I had been there for a while, which is enough to take the sheen off any place. As Jamie said, "Darling Amelia, Your views are as stable as dandelion wings dancing on the breeze." But then when you are grumpy and homesick nothing is right and to your satisfaction.

One misty morning in March before the sun did its work, Newquay surprised us all by waking us up with morning chocolate. He had been rummaging around in some old cupboards and discovered an old set of footman's clothes, giving him the inspired idea of setting up an impromptu costume party (with him as the frog footman in Cinderella's silver coach) to chase away the chills from this gloomy time of year. And so for a lark he let out his hair, transforming it into a passable manservant's wig, and now dressed up, hey presto, became the prince's valet. And there stood a man of fashion, all figged up with cotton hose, knee breeches, and as fine a frilled collar as ever graced a damsel's petticoat.

"Good morrow, dear ladies," said he, bowing foppishly. With a little white lead work to remove his suntan he might well have been the polished macaroni.

"Allow me to admit Aurora's rosy fingers into your boudoir to warm your ivory limbs and quicken them to Apollo's rhythms." He had been learning to read, but used as his texts the Augustan poets such as Alexander Pope, thus giving his lexicon more sparkle than was needed to simply pass the message on. Translating this rococo into plain English, he was opening the curtains. We both giggled over our chocolate at his vaguely absurd apparel, and he departed mildly miffed. My laughter was choked off with pangs of homesickness, which his vision of England had induced. All at once I wanted to see Mary-Anne in her customary abode; I wished to marry Jamie in the only fit setting for us: in an English country church, and where better than in Sheepy? And who better to perform the ministration but my own dear father, the true vicar of that parish? And so it was Newquay's freely adapted version of *The Rape of the Lock* that brought home to us a yearning to stand once again on England's soil and let honest English ale pass down our throats. And so it was this that finally spurred us into action.

And I did not have to stamp my feet to get their attention. It was surprisingly unanimous that we should leave this sainted land and go back to silly, sinful England with its winding roads, more taverns than churches, and couldn't-care-less attitude to others' problems.

After the decision to return home was made, it was accepted that Lewis and I were a twosome, a discreetly courting couple. I respected Lewis for his gentlemanly behavior and wished that the commonality of mankind shared his restraint; for if that were so there would be no need of the wretched Speenhamland system that was impoverishing the countryside, so that Man at large could keep Old Adam tamed and trussed in his trousers, and not litter the countryside with bairns to burden the parish. But at the same time, the Old Eve was gently awakening in me, reminding me that I was of the female gender, and I felt it was time to take the initiative before time took away the inclination.

On the taffrail of the ship back to Liverpool, kisses flew between the star-crossed lovers as the seabirds squawked overhead. Our arms were intertwined, but I longed for more, for the meeting of minds in marriage. We stood hand in hand, watching over the westering sun dying on the horizon, telling us that the past was behind us and each new dawn pointed us nearer home. Home, the bittersweet paths of childhood. And now, as England hoved to on the skyline I could feel the quickening of my pulse, but as my heart was filled with longing my stomach was heavy with foreboding, for I was aware that nostalgia is but a doomed reenactment of a past that never was.

The nearer the ship approached England, the less we saw of Snowbird and the more of Mary-Anne. "Surely, my sweet Amelia, you must not have forgotten your oldest and dearest friend with whom you used to gather daffodils on the banks of the Bonny Sence in blazing June," says she, laying claims on my amiability with a fake reminiscence; she even got the month wrong. She had just made one of her entrances into the main cabin, all swirling skirts and flirty glances, with its usual side effect of turning hardy men of war into gaping schoolboys. That settled it for me; she was Mary-Anne, but for old times' sake she would occasionally put on the Snowbird act to keep the increasingly homesick Newquay in line. But these switches were more party tricks than a serious role change, and when we landed she was definitely a lady of the manor (judging by the peremptory way she dealt with the postillion, who was dilatory in fetching up a coach and pair for us and our luggage).

As we rolled down the winding English roads, thick with hedgerows and birdsong, toward Sheepy, every vale and hillock brought long-dreamt-of sights and smells back into our ken, and excitement quickened at every turn as our horses hooves drummed along the old Roman road of Watling Street, still in good shape. Atherstone was unchanged, still as it was on the day Henry Tudor came to town. And there was Fenny Drayton, home to that other peripatetic preacher, George Whitfield, cofounder of Methodism. We stopped in at Ratcliffe Culey, whose rival spire could easily be espied from our dining table, in order to gain breath for the last mile home. Across the sluggish Sence, on whose meadows I had danced in carefree childhood, the mists were unwreathing round the old cottages of Sheepy. "Oh Golden Jerusalem, thou art here in my bosom of home!" We took to the high road in high trepidation and excitement.

However, the nearer home we got the more the landscape seemed set on confusing us, for the ground beneath our feet didn't correspond with our maps or our memories. Instead of the old strips and vistas rolling way into the next county, the fields were arranged in a prim checkerboard fashion; and where before lay good honest English openheartedness, these were surrounded by fussy Dutch hedges, fences, and dykes. As if any stout yeoman of England had anything to hide. It was odd also that instead of little clumps of the lower orders pausing from their toil in the fields to wave at the passing quality, there was just this trim emptiness. Turning a corner in the lane, I was relieved to see a lone figure waving at us. I waved back only to descry the tattered sleeves of a Jack o' Lent scarecrow flapping in the breeze. Everywhere we were greeted by silence, broken intermittently by the mournful bleating of sheep. Father's brow was sad and thoughtful; the pulse that had quickened when the purer evangelist spirit had galvanized his wayward soul now was as slow as one of our sluggish streams.

On the outskirts of the village a clump of dispirited cottages stood in sore need of a lick of paint, their cobbles and front steps resigned to their grimy and unkempt condition. No carefree bairns were playing hopscotch. One withered crone did look up at our footfall and give a rheumaticky wheeze in lieu of a salutation. It wasn't much of a welcome back to home and hearth. The old village's three great fields were swallowed up in a baffling patchwork quilt that cut across the old right of way, and so we were compelled to trudge round three sides of a square, clomping through bilberry hedges and noisome dollops of horse dung to reach the church lych-gate.

Just before approaching the threshold of the Black Horse we stumbled on the familiar figure of Woody Oakroyd—the sobriquet a pun on name and on brain—a squatter who worked (if that is not too energetic a word) a couple of strips of land on the outskirts of the village and scraped a thin living off the common, augmented by thievery of small livestock. He was a ne'er-do-well, whose place of habitation veered between tavern, stocks, and workhouse. In the social hierarchy of the villagers he filled the lowest position, but had been eminent amongst those who had disturbed the peace outside our house, making quacking or other farmyard noises at the time of our previous troubles. Nevertheless we were glad to see him. We had been a long time away.

But it was a broken man we saw in front of us, cap in hand, begging for a mite for his little tiddlers.

"A penny, your lordship. My poor mites is starvin'. A penny given is a penny saved. Save the parish havin' to gie me handout. Farmer Giles, he don't give me nuff, seein' as how it's made up by parish. He says I stole a goose from the common. I says he stole the common from the goose." The penny would never see his children but we hadn't the heart to turn him down. He was that pathetic. "Since he and others like 'im teamed up wi his Great Lordship Sir Wolstan and pushed through Enclosure Act. Gave us notice, he says, wi a tiny scrap o' paper stuck high on church door. He knows nane of us can read, and schoolmaster lost his specs, so we've all been kicked off land and now are begging on parish."

"I'll talk to Giles and knock some sense into his head," said father.

"Mustn't dae that, reverend sorr." Woody was alarmed. "He'll do for me, he will. Anyroad it's too late for all that. Those days are over."

Just at that moment, like a spiteful deus ex machina farmer Giles appeared round the corner brandishing an ebony cane. "Woody, git back to work! Stop loafin' around. Drat that Speenhamland. Us honest folks is squeezed dry paying them poor rates just to keep your kind idle."

Now, we had just witnessed one of those strange reversals of fortune that life is prone to make, for Woody used to torment the said Giles. And now, instead of delivering a robust punch in the eye and sending him on his way, Woody meekly accepted the boxing of his ears and hauled himself off to the fields—those fields of gleaming corn he used to trample over in scorn, running his scraggy cows over Giles's long-suffering crops and laughing when Giles vainly railed at him. Truly something strange had happened. The once-middling Giles now wore the sheen of prosperity. A beaver-skin hat, rakishly slanted as if he were the very item of a bravo, topped his knobbly skull; in his hand he flourished a gold-knobbed cane instead of an old gnarled stick, the traditional sidearm of the yeoman. Truly the meek had been exalted. What we didn't realize was that we were witnessing a manifestation of the great Social Revolution, which was even now transforming the English countryside and which would propel us all—the greedy, the artful, and the downright lazy—helter skelter into the modern age, belching smoke, steam, and knitted stockings from Nottingham.

As I said earlier, the fields were unrecognizable so it was impossible to say who owned what, for the old strips were swallowed up by those square, hedge-boxed fields. No longer could we gaze at the shimmering horizon from the old sycamore at the back of the church and see the cottagers of Ratcliffe Culey, Norton-Juxta-Twycross, and Fenny Drayton; for every distant prospect was impeded by this dull vegetable uniformity. No longer did the village green ring to the cries of children's games or the yokelish "arghs" of old men slurping their pints over skittles. They had all gone to Brum or Manchester, or been seized by the press gang and were now on the high seas in hearts of oak, having their bottoms reamed by Bosun MacBuggery.

Father cried out, "*Salve, Magna Mater*!" as I am sure the prodigal son called out to his father when returning from the bender to end all benders. His eyes were filled with tears, and looking upon him I could not but join in his bittersweet sorrow. We had learned the bitterest lesson of all for the exile, that to preserve your homeland in pristine shape it is better to return in memory only.

Still, it was nice to be home and in a country where the ducks are… well, ducky. And the swans…well, frankly you can say what you like, my dear, but how can you expect a regal bird to flourish divested of its glorious monarchical plumage and fitted up with all the dull feathers of republican dowdiness in a country (let me remind you) where "plain" is considered an accolade.

Ahead of us stood the church set in its green sward, dotted with mossy tombstones tilted and toppling in uneven rows, nestling under the ancient oaks planted in this Saxon plot before the Conqueror came. The door creaked open, and musty air redolent of England's greatness rolled past our nostrils. There were the massy pillars of Norman stone that had weathered the centuries, and the stout oak and ash of the brilliant Tudor century that held up the roof and made up the pulpit, pews, and reredos that gave our churches their singular flavor. What in America's new land could compare with these treasures of the simple English village? For a moment we stood there and stared at that well-remembered scene while memory's imperfect gloss was wiped away by our presence. In that moment all our misadventures abroad were swallowed up, and all that mattered was this place, the heart of Old England. And yet it seemed smaller than when I went away.

I looked at my father. He tried to walk toward the aisle, faltered, and turned to me, eyes swollen and stained with tears. "I have waited so long for this, it's almost like the coming to Glory." Then we looked again at the church. The interior was a wasteland. Squatters had taken possession of the building, leaving the squalor of their animals' muck in every pew and corner. A covey of mice scuttled up the curtains, releasing puffballs of dust from the ancient fabric decorated with the escutcheon of the great families who had sat in these pews since the day of the Conqueror. A hen was roosting in the font, as immobile as if it were waiting for the Day of Judgment. A great mud-encrusted porker muddled its way up the aisle, rubbing and wiggling vigorously against the pews as though performing a well-established routine for our entertainment. Then a homing instinct took over, and she went straight up to father and grunted at him imploringly before settling down to muzzling against father's thigh. *New congregation, but old habits die hard*, I thought sadly. Father stroked and patted the pig while the rest of us stood around feeling awkward. This was not the homecoming we had reckoned on.

A fussy little man, bristling with bossiness, stumped his way up the aisle toward us, wearing an officious expression that conveyed little cordiality. Unfortunately for the sexton's gravitas, his dignity was diminished by the numerous animals running through his legs, tripping him up. "Hey, git out from under," he cried, whacking a pig with his clerical staff of office. The porker had been making his progress less furious than farcical, and the sexton kicked it out of his way. "Gerraway, you useless slab of fatty bacon." Then he boomed at us, "And what do you think you be doin' here? This be private property. All locked up for t' knacker's yard." Then he stopped, the wind quite knocked out of his sails. "Vicar? Reverend? Is that bein' you back from dead?" Then, belatedly, "Welcome, welcome back!" He bent over with a creak in a countryman's version of a Whitehall salute, grabbed my father's hand, and kissed it, much to father's discomfit. Then, in an astonishing outburst of emotion the old sexton wept unashamedly.

Sadly, however, this display of warmth was not shared by all. There were protests to be sure when the vicar returned. Life in the country is history becalmed, and so an event such as the impugned marriage of man to beast was not easily forgotten. After our arrival, we were entertained more or less nightly (with breaks for inclement weather) by groups of village hobbledehoys gathered outside the vicarage for choral evensong, mimicking the husbandry that father had supposedly passed the time of day with.

However, the respectable majority of folk were inclined to let bygones be bygones, and this rehash of ancient history, which they disliked intensely, reinforced their support for father as rightful vicar, who strictly adhered to the timeless rituals of the Anglican Church, untarnished by the heresy of Methodism, Quakerism, and any other deviant forms of worship. They were ashamed of the disgrace brought on by the scandal, particularly the murdering of their much loved priest, whose modest eccentricities had been so feloniously misinterpreted by the village riffraff. They were especially aggrieved that the cause célèbre and consequent lack of ordained priest had brought to an end Sheepy's independence as a parish, which now resided tucked away, a mere appendage of Atherstone's large but dull village church, too dull even to make an entry in the Domesday Book.

Now an old family name was restored. Now a new Golden Age was promised for Sheepy and its adjacent country. When the pastor was reinstated there were only a few muttered protests from some of the die-hard squatters residing in meager state by the duck pond. When he first ascended his rightful pulpit he faced a few gasps of disbelief from lowly sectors of the pews, which I immediately ascribed to his rejuvenation in the great American outdoors, whose fresh mountain air had more invigorating potency than all the concoctions, brews, and herbal essences honest money could buy (with the singular exception of the alchemist's great elixir still tantalizing us).

Here we were back in the church again (quite unlike the previous occasion, when the air surrounding choir and congregation was rent with a cacophony of braying and quacking as donkeys, ducks, and their mimics raised to the heavens their hymn of protest, all of whom had been returned to their fields and ponds by the scrupulous sexton). This was the day appointed for father to be reanointed and his defrocking rescinded. As the living had lain vacant for years now, the original sin had been wiped off the slate by the ecclesiastical authorities; the decisive factor was Mary-Anne's confession that she had been bemused by moon magic. Cameron, considered a reliable witness (being a dour and sober Scot), was able to confirm that the said matter was all mischief, malice, and misunderstanding, which the vicar was graciously able to forgive.

His crimes against nature (buggery and black magic), however, had entered into local folklore. The most suspicious and backward of the rustics, commonly the very old, still muttered, "It were devil's work, him coming back from the dead." And mischievous yokels taking advantage of their grandparents' superstitions were out in force to remind him that even if the church had found it in its bosom to forgive, they were not prepared to grant absolution so easily. But he quelled them when he thundered forth like an Old Testament prophet, "Yea, even the beasts of the field..." This was a new vicar; this was the terrifying Lorenzo Dow, tempered and forged by the Great Awakening of the American soul. His insipid earlier embodiment was a mere shade, a naughty timid shadow. He smashed the front of his pulpit with a meaty fist hardened by hard labor and not from tracing the etiolated lines of effete archaic poets.

"Nor could the hosts of Mideon...!" He bashed the pulpit reading desk. How they quailed, those staid stay-at-homes in their neat little vegetable plots, their unadventurous gardens. They had never seen the forests rolling into the blue yonder, never espied the smoke of the savage hutments far off on the infinite prairie, nor witnessed a scalping.

There was a great trumpet from the back of the church, which shook some of the frailer spirits and momentarily distracted the rest of us so we couldn't help but look backwards. There stood the village idiot in all his idiot costume, guffawing at the preacher. Beside him was his donkey, whose braying was even now drowning out my father's stentorian tones. Lorenzo never even broke stride. Pointing to the moron and his animal he said, "If this be my rock, here I will build my church." As it happened the idiot was called Peter. But the point, reflecting the stumbling intellectual advances made by the village (which, a century after Newton, did not understand why the apple fell on his head), was taken up by the literate few, and they hurried the fool and his ass outside.

With the donkey braying and the fool laughing, Cameron and I had an important conversation. Just to make sure I heard the question right I insisted Cameron repeat it, and with the patience that is his hallmark he did. The second time was even more thrilling than the first.

CHAPTER 20

Amelia's Wedding Day

"It's only a month till thy wedding day, Amelia, and we still have not found the perfect satin. I do despair." This was Mary-Anne's silent stepmother, who had emerged from her shell to act as the bride's mother; and odsbodikins, but she could croak and worry like any real mum. Despair or not, Mary-Anne and I were having fun, and you know what we girls are like. My bedroom was a whirlpool of different materials: satin, silks, sarcenet, and taffeta of wildly differing shades to form panniers, petticoats, negligees, bodices, bonnets, caps, and chemises; stays, hats, feathers, ribbons, and shoes everywhere. The only despair was felt by the maids who had to pick up behind us, but that was their lot in life, and there was no use thinking of changing it. Even Mary Wollstonecraft is compelled to acknowledge that a social structure firmly based on equality of gender can't be built upon the shifting sands of democracy or Babouvism. My whole life revolved around menus, guest lists, flowers, who to place next to whom, and making sure that Aunt Edna was not put beside Cousin Alfred after that remark he had made about her bosoms being built of pomegranates.

There was so much to do that I wondered how ordinary people without our capacities get through it all and manage to arrive at the church gate in best bib and tucker and on time. Of course, if the truth be known a lot of them don't, and that is why there are so many little orphans popping up on doorstops to burden the parish. For once in her self-centered life, Mary-Anne turned out to be a brick, arriving on the doorstep every day to give a hand. Noticing that I was swamped by the daunting task of inscribing perfectly scripted letters of invitation to the various ranks of worthies in want of a free feast, she offered her help in writing them. The efficiency of this arrangement superseded the ethical dilemma posed by the acceptance of a gift solicited from a forged note of hand. Whatever.

During this frenetic period when all the *belles dames* were busily bustling, Cameron was doing what any man with a lick of common sense would do: going for long walks and staying out of the way. On rainy days he retired to the library and once again immersed himself in his beloved classics, renewing that long dormant passion, so totally wrapped up in his books, drifting far away on the wine-dark Aegean sea, that when our fabrics spilled over into the library he was oblivious, which was fine for all concerned.

Father, enthused by this sharing of interests and foreseeing a dynasty of classicists holding forth at the vicarage, broached the topic: "If you love the ancients it is but a short skip and step across the aisle to take up the cloth. Then this house will be truly yours, so that when I retire to my study and make my life's work *The Odyssey*'s influence on the voyages of St. Paul, you can be sitting just there"—he pointed to an old fashioned upright chair, its polished walnut gleaming from the sunlight pouring in from the study window—"preparing your Sunday discourse, simplified of course for the benefit of the laboring poor." So you can see all of us were set to live happily ever after.

Gowns had to be made and altered. Mary-Anne and I were trying on the first draft of our dresses. She looked heavenly in taffeta and satin. *A bit too luscious*, I thought, making a mental note to get the seamstress to make a botch of it and replace it with brown sackcloth. But ruefully I reflected that you could pull her through a hedge backwards and she would still come out smelling of the roses growing therein, or some such muddled metaphor. She was prancing around happily when suddenly she went "whoops," slipped onto her back, and up went her panniers and furbelows to display, together with a gorgeous set of satin pantalettes, a long Indian knife.

"Mary-Anne, why ever have you got a hunting knife stashed into your unmentionables? There are no Indians skulking behind the hedges in their war paint here, you know!"

Hurriedly she leapt up, brushing her dress back into respectability, and said, "True, but old habits die hard, and I get terrible nightmares. Just one look at Newquay in the dark gives me the heebie-jeebies. Also," she continued in a jesting vein, "'tis for a quick release from me stays if I happen upon a randy plough boy I fancy. Then there's this mystery guest to your nuptials, and I might get a hankering for him to take me for a riding lesson down Lover's Lane." It didn't sound too convincing, but I let it go. "And if I changes me mind halfway through the gallop, the knife will persuade him to pretend to be the gentleman and dismount with the utmost expedition."

And now it was the day. Far off, wedding bells were ringing. All dark and dismal thoughts flew away, chased on the wings of our mutual happiness. And so it was we arrived at the church. There was Mary-Anne, the quondam Snowbird, eyes bright with belladonna, waving lovingly at us. She was sniffing. Sentimentality was so rarely a feature of her character that I too felt a little tug of the heartstrings. She managed to pull herself together in order to bouffant out my dress and train, making a great to-do over it. Then the great organ groaned into life with an explosion of dust, and we proceeded down the aisle accompanied by Purcell's "Trumpet Voluntary." Again Mary-Anne began crying, which was strange and comforting. For a cynical moment I supposed she was putting on a performance to impress the quality, who had turned out in gratifying quantity; more likely than not she was envious of me getting to the altar before her in a justifiably white dress. But on such a day harsh thoughts are banished, and I was gratified to realize that she was as sentimental as the rest of us.

Naturellement I was beautiful. the *Atherstone Trumpet* focused on my swan-like neck, for which my pearl-ivory silk gown was a superb complement. I kept glancing at the adorable Adonis at my side and kept my fingers crossed that in not so many hours I would be at last embarked on the irreversible voyage from maid to wife. There were no embarrassing incidents or silly moments to laugh at or cherish in our dotage. All went off without a hitch.

And, no sir, although we did sing a couple of hymns simply because we liked them, there was no dabbling with Methodism nor with Enthusiasm, baggage discreetly left behind on the shores of America. I think that you will agree that hymns do help liven up the traditional service, which can sound a teeny bit dolorous, particularly if the vicar's sermon is plodding and the congregation is out of sorts. For those wanting further particulars of my pearl-ivory gown, my silver slippers, my veil of Nottingham lace woven by seven spinsters (a year in the making), the radiance of my complexion, the gasp that greeted my arrival in church, etc.; I will leave you to ferret out further details from the many witnesses to this happy event who remain extant and the relevant issue of the *Atherstone Trumpet.* The groom was dashing, handsome, and also uncommonly nervous; for myself, I did not betray a tremor.

Mary-Anne looked passably pretty, though her man-of-war coiffure, a miniature version of one worn by Marie-Antoinette, was a whit excessive. I whispered to her, "Take care you don't get keel hauled."

"How so?" She whispered through her posy. For answer I cocked an eye at her hairdo. Was I being a trifle catty? Today she didn't take it amiss, but gave me a look that said *one day the honeymoon will be over.* During the signing of the register, she sang an aria from Mozart's *Cosi Fan Tutte,* all the rage in London just then. I had it on report that she was up to all her range of tricks, eyes fluttering and bosom to the fore, trying to draw the attention of anything even middlingly worth snatching in breeches. When I asked her about this later she said, "That's the way 'tis done at Covent Garden, silly."

A few premonitory wheezes, puffs, and groans—accompanied by a cloud of dusty droplets sparkling in a kaleidoscope of colors, lit up by the sunlight streaming in from the stained glass windows—gave notice that the old organ was about to burst into full-throated voice, and with a splendid rendition of Handel's *Water Music* we all trooped out into the bright sunshine. There the local portrait artist dashed off a quick sketch of the happy couple, which was to be later filled in with oils and framed as a present from the MacPherson Clan.

A line of freshly painted white carriages was waiting outside the churchyard to transport the whole merry band to the ancestral home of the Dixie family. There was a minor hitch before we could embark. Highlanders are mighty high-minded by nature, and the established order of precedence is as dear to them as their birthright. Consideration of this protocol had been insufficiently weighted by our master of ceremonies, the best man, now busily paying court to Mary-Anne. Consequently a kerfuffle ensued in the carriages allotted to our Celtic cousins over who had been allotted the best seat and which chariot should lead this mighty caravan onto the high road. Rusty swords that had not seen the light of day since Culloden were hauled screeching from their scabbards. As the disputants were conducting their business in the Erse tongue, the subtler details were lost on the rest of the guests, but judging from the din and the ensuing theatricals the basic message was grasped by all.

I was about to burst into tears, my wedding day ruined, when an old family retainer, stumbling up to Cameron's side, said in his heathen brogue, "Aye! Whit guid is a wedding wi oot a guid fecht?"

To my astonishment Jamie replied, "Aye, Donhail, they say, 'A serene wedding maks a richt poor bedding.'"

"Aye, Maister. We pit it mair like, 'Wed wi'oot a fight, yer life'll be shite.'"

"Wheesht, Donhail, this is England. You dinnae say these things. No in the mistress's hearing."

"I'm sorry, your lairdship." He made a mock bow, and to me a steeper obeisance, saying, "Your humble servant, ma'am," and retreated to claim his ancestral rights to brawl with his clansmen foes.

So it was all right then. I staunched the flow of lamentation (which to be honest was largely theatrical, me playing the part of the fragile fresh flower of a bride) and settled down to enjoy the spectacle. This was of short duration, as honour was speedily paid its due, for a higher priority was allotted to getting their hands on the vittles (particularly those of a liquid nature); so they speedily stuffed themselves into the carriages any old how, and ancient houses sat cheek by jowl with nouveau upstarts, even with some who had stood on the opposing side of the line in the Forty-Five.

As our horses clipped-clopped through the splendidly manicured parkland, I reflected on the last time I had visited here as a simple lass and all the events set in train by that fiasco. Now, here on the doorstep to greet us was our old persecutor, and now amiable patron once again, looking very much the same as he did on that former occasion, except that he wore that childlike rosy visage untouched by troubles or experience that extreme age often shares with extreme youth.

"Ah, Amy, my dear, welcome, welcome, welcome!" He chuckled out threefold this fulsome greeting. "Bless this benighted building with the bounty of your beatific beauty," he burbled, the air thrilling with the billing of his *b*'s. I made a graceful little curtsey (not too low though, mindful of my teasing décolletage).

"No need, Sir Wolstan; your bounty billows on the breeze," I replied. This thing was catching. Before the momentum should flow to a torrent and create a babble of even more busy bees I decided to cut it short, sensing my newly minted in-laws' patience getting shorter. And although they were behaving remarkably well by their own admittedly Broad Church standards, one never knew when they might decide to cut a rug and go on the rampage. After all, a spot of reiving might help to warm up what must be to them a very tame affair.

Sweeping through the magnificent entrance hall, I could see many a sidelong glance as the clansmen made silent inventory of the potential for loot; and then, when we all sat down for the wedding breakfast, the wine poured out in an ever-running stream like a Highland burn run rampant, while the talk, ever more loquacious, attempted to keep pace with the liquid torrent.

Was I joining in the race? How else can I explain my sudden lack of sensibility and sensation as that sweet, seductive wine went straight to my head, causing the table to start spinning like a whirligig? When it settled down the room was transformed into a china shop and the table occupied with China Wedgwood figures. And at the head of the table sat a Staffordshire figurine kissed into life by some rustic Pygmalion, none other than Mr. Toby of the Jug to the very tee. No—I rubbed my eyes and looked again. There again, sitting as pleased as pleased could be, was Sir Wolstan Dixie, a bumper of wine to the left of him and a firkin of ale on his right flank as scepter and orb, his insignia of office. The time-worn incident which had driven us from the land of our birth was picked up, lightly alluded to, and tossed away as a matter of no consequence by both sides. The ancient rake, whose wish was our command and whose unslaked lust had set us on our fateful voyage as surely as Agamemnon sacrificing his daughter launched the fleet against Troy, now stood up, glowing in this the vinous sunset of his life. Our happy return was his good fortune, and his good fortune embraced us all. He toasted us in a bumper, arms outstretched in symbolic embrace, his words delivered in the manner of Garrick invoking the Bard: "The happy couple, may you be blessed with many offspring to make your old house ring with life and laughter; so may our Sheepy sheep more safely graze." He sat down beaming with the pleasure of his own oratory, his countenance already heated from its usual excess of wine.

CHAPTER 21

Cagliostro

It is a truth commonly acknowledged that an occasion wanting in music cannot truly be called splendid. So we had a band, a string quartet no less, in deference to the solemn urbanity of the celebration. This was no yokel's nuptial. And so the band arrived glittering in their quasi-military costumes, readied their music, and with their bows en garde waited for the signal to commence. Alas, we counted only three performers. The harpist was tardy. There was an embarrassed shuffling around of plates and tinkling of cutlery, for we had anticipated dining to the accompaniment of sweet airs and nimble finger work to mask the sounds of eating. Now the organizers of the music were frantically running around, bowing and scraping apologies to all and sundry, declaiming "Alas, alack," to the ceiling. Fingers were being drummed on oaken tabletops, but even these invocations failed to summon up the missing player. As we found later via village gossip (always reliable in matters not commonly discussed at high table), the harpist, a lady blessed with considerable fluidity of social grace, was at that particular moment (when she should have be boning up on her cadenzas) ensconced in a hedge with the best man—Sir Malcolm himself, temporarily bereft of plaid—her limbs athwart to receive the doctrine of Jacobitism while being educated in the noble Highland art of stirking.

Well, it was good that someone was having fun, but our food was getting cold, and the Highlanders' tempers were hardly being improved as they waited impatiently and hungrily while the office of groomsman was being honored in the bush. However, there's ne'er an ill wind, etc., for it turned out that one of our guests, who up till now had been sitting in a corner unheeded, had secreted in his luggage his own bagpipes; and now, when the appeal for a harpist had not borne fruit after the third call, he stepped forward, his face shiny and puffed as a ripe apple from blowing up his bag in preparation, a genteel modesty having kept him in his seat till the third trump.

After a few hideous preparatory shrieks (which the cognoscenti say are a necessary prelude to incite the blood but which to me mimic the cries of the wounded and dying in some forlorn battle), he quickly tuned up, and a more melodious noise emerged. With pibrochs, airs, sets, reels, and even dirges executed with festive brio, belting through this hall redolent with Englishry, he marched up and down the serried ranks of revelers. At first the three-quarter string quartet skirmished with him, but unable to match his strident sounds they retired, slowly slinking into the hinterland in stately dignity just as the Enlightenment has retreated before the rude, rugged thrusts of Romanticism.

The mystery bagpiper stepped down the hall till we could only hear the drones recede into the distance. I sent for someone to fetch him and ask if he would honor us at the high table.

He was somewhat swarthy for a Scotsman, and at first modesty precluded him from giving his name. Instead he made a great charming bow and told me on the spot how entrancing I was, and could he have the honor of being seated near to such ravishing enchantment? Well why not. There was a spare seat nearby, and this was swiftly summoned up and a place set for the mystery guest.

"You have many talents I am sure, sir. Whom do we have the honor of receiving?"

"The honor is mine alone," he murmured sweetly, bowing steeply as if before royalty, and introduced himself. "I have the honor to be but a humble count of the nobility of the Holy Roman Empire." This was none other than the mysterious noble whose name oft appears as a footnote in the *belles lettres* of the high and mighty, and who was making a grand tour in reverse, from Italy to England—in fact from the Pretender's court at Rome, by way of Versailles, where (it was spoken with bated breath) Madame de Pompadour was *enchantée* to make his acquaintance. His name—and he softly whispered it—was the infamous Count Cagliostro, Chevalier d'Albany.

He made the sort of pause that presumed a short burst of applause would follow, but we were such rustics that none of us had heard of this man, the most notorious trickster of our time. He overcame the silence with an urbane flick of a lace handkerchief, which was then swiftly repocketed in a voluminous mauve sleeve, itself contrasting radically with the cerulean blue of his frockcoat. Altogether it was an ensemble dazzling enough to arouse comment in any court in Italy or High Germany. One look told me he was the type of inconstant rake—forever swearing gallantry and eternal love—that mothers warn their daughters against. Another bow and he sat beside me. His hands touched the lap of my dress, accidentally I was sure. At once a most peculiar force charged my body, and I felt my cheeks glowing hotly.

Cameron noticed. "My dearest, are you feeling tired by today's excitement? Perhaps you should rest for a minute or two?"

"Wheesht, my naughty lad." I slapped his knee playfully. "Patience, patience; you know I'll get no rest when you rip off this dress as though it were a paper frock." I was well pleased with my witty retort. But once again my attention was drawn by action on my starboard bow. Quite undeterred by this aside, the naughty count's hand was pressing down upon layers of tulle, taffeta, satin, and lace, unmistakably kneading my inner thigh betwixt my knees. I turned to face my frotteur. His face, like the sphinx in the desert, betrayed no sign of embarrassment or indeed any emotion, while I was caught up in a thunderclap of unaccountable agitation.

"Ah, my sweet lass, don't be affronted. I was merely endeavoring to steal a favor from so luscious a bride," he said, not affronting but impertinent nonetheless. He was handsome but in a Sicilian, non-English way for which I have little if any taste. My whole body right down to my tingling toes and fingertips was afire with a warmth both sweet and frightening, which I could not name and for which I would fain suffer his embrace here immediately, on this table, publicly before all the ton of the county, notwithstanding the salt and pepper cruets and knives and forks impinging upon my bottom. Reliving this incident later I wondered, was it his hypnotic magic or was I overcome with too much wine and excitement? To this day I have no explanation.

Without anyone noticing it, the count had taken over the function of groomsman and was running the show (perhaps because he was still reasonably sober, a feat to remark upon amongst such bravoes). Anyway, no one seemed to mind his shoving aside of the absent Sir Malcolm. Cagliostro was Wit himself, fluent in as many tongues as were represented at that great table of Babel. *Brindisi* followed *brindisi*, all impresarioed by the mysterious count, and still he stood as sober as any judge. And when the noble count made the toast on behalf of our bridesmaids, I was impressed by how much he knew about me, us, our village, and our peregrinations through the Americas. Most certainly he had done his homework or something. . . .

"*Quelle belle orbs vous avez!*"

This, I thought, *is too much*, inexcusable even in a distinguished foreigner who had spent time at the French court. I slapped him mildly with my bouquet.

"But it is your eyes. Whatever else would I be saluting?"

Perhaps, thinks I, *but* your *eyes seem to be pointing in a different direction*. Then they started roaming like the forlorn Prince over the hills and glens of the women folk. But all these swarthy foreigners are the same, forever polishing their gallantry with the ladies. With all their practiced charm, you might expect their homes would be furnished with gorgeously voluptuous Venuses. Yet what do you see when the door is finally opened? A fat lady enshrouded in black: one of life's eternal conundra.

While lavishing me with outrageous flattery the cavalier was covering his other flank, chatting up Cameron. He praised the poems of Fingal, Dierdre, and the portrayals of the Homeric feuding families in Glen Etive while offering up thought-provoking interpretations of Gaelic bardolatry. "It would be a delight to me to add luster to the land of music, song, and Caesar by rendering your sacred words into my tongue," says he, his hands now above the table, where they were dancing agilely in tune with his words.

Cameron wasn't entirely lacking in business sense, so he said, "We had better sign a contract to make sure we both profit from this exchange." The count was under the misapprehension that my Cameron was none other than the notorious James MacPherson, a remote cousin, the author of the fake Ossianic epic cycle. My Jamie, like every other young man of culture, had flung off a few homespun verses, which at a pinch could be palmed off as neo-Gaelic sonnets, another splendid outpouring of Scotland's Hellenistic revival. I don't think the count was really interested. In many ways his performance was that of the eager-to-please stranger on his best behavior, teetering on the verge of groveling. Outwardly this was clearly the case, but his mien conveyed an assurance that in ways yet to be disclosed we were his to command.

Meanwhile, in the body of the hall the cousins had lain down their knives and spoons (the forks excepted, as these exotic instruments had been pocketed for later inspection in their grim hovels up north). They placed their claymores crosswise on the floor and leapt over them with hideous shrieks and airing of oaken limbs as their kilts swung from side to side, swaying high enough to make a maiden blush. This barbarous activity they called dancing. And what a strange sight it was, ebbing and flowing up and down the aisles, a country dance mated with a prize fight, all this going on in the great hall directly under the portraits of the ancestors of Squire Dixie. Some in these ranks had stood on the winning team at Flodden, and now from their gilded frames they looked down their noses at the skirling of the old enemy beneath them, who had finally made a successful incursion into the very heart of England. Many a grave would be turning in Bosworth churchyard that night. We shall see how this was a mere prelude to a very topsy-turvy evening.

Those able to resist the call to dance and those involuntarily rooted to our seats (me, for example, by the simple fact of the acreage of my dress) were entertained by a culinary conundrum, to wit, the naming of the soups. Many of the chevaliers had perforce spent considerable portions of their lives "o'er the watter," as they called the state of exile. All of them claimed to have passed their time abroad in an extended spree at the French court, rubbing elbows with the Bourbon monarch, his ladies of the couch, and the resident aristocracy. Some may have indeed paid a fleeting visit to Versailles until expelled (when a lightness in the liquor cabinets came to light or the chambermaids complained of the rough wooing of their Gaelic guests), and thus armed with a veneer of sophistication coming to light in outbreaks of French spattered amongst the barbarities of their native tongue, they were attempting to impress the English stay-at-homes.

Lining the tables at an interval of one per head were fine matching sets of Willow pattern bowls, some containing a tomato-colored liquid, some pea green, and yet others a brothy cream paste. The highland nobility pronounced these to be the most exquisite of cold French consommé, the last word in sophistication *de la table*. On these they set to with a will, accompanied by exclamations of delight, much appreciative finger snapping, kissing of digits, muted orgasmic keening, and even elaborate little disquisitions of how their palates, once exposed to the godhead of cuisine *a la belle France*, were spoiled for the bitter herbs that were foisted as fodder for the rest of us. The rest of us stared, for the brilliant bouillon that they were all a twitter over was the mayonnaise: the humble sauce for the salad.

It was a moment fraught with the possibilities of a social Armageddon. The English guests bit their tongues until one idiot started to snuffle helplessly as if about to sneeze, and then a suppressed snigger burst forth. Desperately I hoped someone had inadvertently sat on a set of bagpipes. It was not to be. This was the solitary precursor of the storm. The pent up sniggers of the whole room exploded into a demonic outburst of laughter. The Scotsmen looked puzzled and then red-faced as the light dawned. If you are reckless try stealing a Highlander's sporran; if suicidal try stealing his self-esteem. The Scotsmen's chairs were flung back, and their hands grasped at empty scabbards. A dreadful moment had arrived. Blood was about to be shed.

It was the interval needed to retrieve the claymores from the floor that saved the situation, for it gave an unlikely rescuer that split second to come to the aid of the party. Cagliostro had been sitting at the table, nodding sagely at the inanities of Sir Wolstan Dixie. The count, the perfect gentleman, the very pinnacle of patient politeness, jerked his head up from contemplating the cutlery and took in the hubbub. Before things got to an evil pass, he picked up the sauce dish, dipped his spoon in it, and supping with the aplomb that is the hallmark of your true aristocrat declared, "What's sauce for the goose, is soup for the gander," thus pricking the balloon of our assembled pomposity. Then as if nothing had happened Count Cagliostro exclaimed on the excellence of the "soup": *"Quelle parfaite consommation!"* He spoke with the high, fluting tones of the practiced courtier, the Italian accent adding to the heady mix. He simply oozed savoir faire; there was no gainsaying his authority. Without taking breath the count plunged into a synopsis of the Scottish dilemma, about once tasting the food of the gods and forever after having to walk the earth with appetite titillated yet unappeased. An extraordinary performance, only possible through the magic of osmosis, as he could not even have had half an ear cocked away from Sir Wolstan's lengthy disquisition on the beasts of the field.

Sir Wolstan, knowing where his ancestral duty lay, followed up the standard set by his honored guest, dipped his spoon into the sauce, and proceeded to slurp noisily, declaring, "I declare this an excellent sup, Your Holiness!"

The rustic gentleman, clearly not on nodding terms with the freemasonry of enlightened society, was unaware that the Holy Roman Empire was nothing more than a shadowboxer on the international scene, in no wise connected with the Roman church. Cagliostro was too urbane to smirk, but a momentary raising of eyebrow was masked by an adroit flick of a befrilled handkerchief woven, I observed, by the most expensive Honiton lace makers patronized by royalty.

Lorenzo, not to be outdone, shouted out, "Quite the Lucullan banquet, my lordage!" The cry was echoed to the very walls and rafters by honest trenchermen shouting, "Surpassingly excellent belly timber!" They followed where their squire led, slurping and sighing in approbation, a sound not far different from the sea crashing and ebbing in Fingal's Cave. Thus peace once again reigned in the party, and so began the second French invasion of our English paradise garden, more insidious than 1066 in that our honest plain provender was seduced by this saucy tickling of our palate. If you have ever wondered why your menu is in French, now you know.

Once again our mysterious guest rescued our grand party. Was there no end to his Odysseus-like stratagems? The count was laying on the charm with all the dexterity of one wielding a hefty butter knife. But it was worth the extra plate we had to set out and the approximate gallon of wine he supped like a voluptuary—expensive wine, I should add. We weren't able to fob him off with the cheap rubbish the Highlanders were drinking apace. He explained how he had to make a stop on his progress around the three kingdoms, to pay tribute to my father as a fellow scholar, whose learned articles had excited him so much he simply had to come along in order to salute him at our wedding. Why this pilgrimage to our shores? Why, it was to see the future: the great industrial revolution in the making, the charm of Coalbrookdale, the music of the steam engines in the dark, satanic cotton mills. He wished to wallow in the dirt, the grime, the smoke of the hellish furnaces that most Englishmen, even those who profited from them most, did their best to ignore.

"And that is the main reason you are here?"

"No, *mia cara, naturalmente* that is a mere subterfuge! I have come to worship at the true temple of beauty: not in Rome, not in Venezia, not in Taormina, but 'ere in thees room! And 'ere I am at the very altar of pulchritude, paying my most humble devotion and adoration!" As he spoke, he indulged himself in a big slobbering kiss of my hand, over and over again. Well, he was a foreigner, so I let him get on with it.

Two glowing coals were fixed on me: They bored into my innermost being, penetrated my taffeta layers, scrutinized my heaving bosoms and rising paps, and (dare I say it?) lighted on the moistened bush of my quim. All the while the rascal licked his lips as if he were to leap upon my nuptial bed and displace the now pickled groom. In troth he would make a dashing substitute. You must think me a fickle wench. If I were to be swived while my hubby had tavern droop, by this man or monster who surely had a Tower of Pisa in no wise leaning, and if I were to be seduced by these penetrating eyes I could not be blamed nor accused of enjoying what had been forced from me. It was only later, waking up from his spell, that I realized the devil inhabited his soul.

I'll say this for the count: He was very quick on the uptake. For with that sixth sense already employed in the sauce-versus-soup controversy he picked up on Mary-Anne sitting sober, seething, and dripping with jealousy. I could see no good coming out of this, but never anticipated the depths of her malevolence, never realized I had befriended a Medea. And foolish virgin that I was, I never for a moment suspected the evil she was even now plotting against me at my wedding supper. This being reduced to playing second fiddle was a role she hated.

At the moment when the rest of us were jousting with the good old roast beef of Old England and the roast potato, the count turned to her. "*Mia cara*, how can I have lived until this moment? And who is thees silent Aphrodite? It would be a foolish connoisseur who would not turn aside from the Mona Lisa and cross oceans to admire such an incomparable!" So he put in the necessary spadework there, putting a smile on Mary-Anne's cheeks (no mean feat in itself, although in the interests of producing a true history I have to say the butter was not laid on half so thick as it had been for me). This of course was meat and drink to our bridesmaid, who simpered behind her posy. Beauties don't need to say or do anything, for they are the objects of desire, not the subjects. The swarthy foreigner snapped his fingers in an unmistakable Italianate gesture. "*Pero naturalmente*, I see I have not lived but merely existed until thees day."

"But who are you, you extraordinary man?" Thus from Mary-Anne, her manners unchanged.

He snapped his fingers again. "Alas, I have the misfortune to be a stranger to you. Allow me the honor to present myself as the Count Cagliostro—"

"Yes, I know all that, but *who* are you? Have you perchance come by canoe up the Sence via the Trent, or did you paddle up the Coventry Canal without paying the lock fees? For a second you reminded me of someone." She was struggling to be snobbish but failing dismally, as fascination and Cupid's little darts were prickling away merrily. Only Newquay—seeing Mary-Anne sucked in by the count's charm, his spleen churning mad with envy—could spot the troubled waters ahead. I detected a hand going for tomahawk, which fortunately we had asked him to leave at home for the day, thus sparing the flatterer an impromptu wig trim. I say "fortunately" for convention's sake, as little did we know on that happy day what dire events were to spring from such trivial things.

Minutes after this imbroglio, Sir Malcolm returned from his extra-curricular tutorial; surprised and not a bit pleased to find his office usurped by this swarthy man of the south, he sidled up to Cameron and me. Perhaps he was embittered by Cagliostro's coup; perhaps he was not as dumb as he pretended. At any rate he muttered what follows into the uncomprehending ear of my beloved.

"That 'Count Cagliostro' is a false knave of the first water, so false he wakes up every morning not sure who he is supposed to be that day, so every night he puts upon his chair a clue as to his identity on the morrow (e.g., a feather for an Indian, an earring for a pirate, an ace of diamonds for a gamester). This strategy, fine if he goes to bed sober, is mighty fallible when in his cups. Ofttimes His Holy Impudence gets it wrong, and his impersonations are shuffled out of sequence, as for instance when he appears at breakfast as a charcoal-faced Turk after posing for the evening as milady's father confessor, or when a sober Swedish pastor turns into a reckless gamester making off with the family's diamonds, or a Musulman appears who yesterday was a papal legate privately blessing a blushing bride, or a libertine who was formerly an avid Calvinist preacher, or a Whig amongst Tories, and so on and so forth. Then the best he can hope for is a day in the stocks facing the rotting vegetables of the rabble; more often it is an early morning meeting with an enraged husband, thus he always makes sure a speedy horse is on hand to gallop him to the next county."

"Stuff and nonsense!" That was me.

Cameron demurred, spluttering, "But surely his gold-trimmed hat, that excessive lace collar, the black beard and ferocious moustache, earrings, scarlet velvet jacket, and splendid yellow breeches are simply too outré for a gaming coxcomb to carry off? And how would you know this anyhow, you who have been toasting us in absentia?"

"Yes, he is quite the bird of plumage," said Malcolm, who himself was not without sartorial splendor. "Let's just say I know." He winked and tapped his nose significantly.

It was at this moment that the subject under discussion closed upon the three of us. The color schemes of the groomsman and the count clashed so violently I was in danger of having a headache, but luckily Sir Malcolm elected to be in the huff because we doubted his warning; he made a great show of storming off. None of which the count took the slightest notice, for he then proceeded to take over the conversation. He spoke with a soft, sibilant, beguiling sort of whisper that recalled (for those who had undertaken the Grand Tour) the languid lapping of wavelets across the Mediterranean strand—persuasive, seductive, yet with an enticing element of the dangerous. I saw him for what he was: a charming, unabashed womanizer spreading his flattery widely amongst all the ladies like the sower of seeds in the parable, wasting it amongst the stones and thistles of those fated never to become swans, setting up a fluttering, whispering storm amongst the silken petticoats.

He hinted that he was a wandering distant cousin of Charles Stewart, an *amicus curiae* at the august court of the Cause in Rome. "I was nobly knighted by His Eternal Highness, the Prince Over the Water, to encourage me to pay a call on yourselves at the nuptials bonding two dauntless supporters of the true regality. *N'est-ce pas, davvero.* Of course I needed no encouragement to pursue this mission, no wind up my backside," said this astonishing person, lying fluently, forgetting he had already admitted another rationale for his venture into middle England. He was bowing to Jamie, but his eyes were fixed on the silver heraldic brooch of the wildcat, of Clan Chattan, suspended betwixt my bosoms—a gloating stare to make clear that no petal would remain unravished by this bold buccaneer. Once again the force of his gaze did work marvelous strange things within me. I sensed my body awakening to the lewd call of his lechery with an intensity it never achieved for my poor dear true love, a feeling I hasten to add I had never encountered in the hallowed halls of the Sheepy vicarage.

CHAPTER 22

The Girl is Stabbed by Cupid's Arrow

Stumbling through the ranks of dancing couples came a rough, unkempt person wearing the unmistakable air of the hermit scholar (the shaggy beard spumed with white, the glittering eye, and so forth) that the philosopher Plato had in mind for his cave. He stomped right up to Dad and parked himself uncomfortably close, so that Lorenzo involuntarily took a step backwards. Gesticulating with his finger, he made no bones about his lack of introduction or the discourteous violence of his interruption.

"I know all about you, mister vicar o' the parish. And I ken things aboot ye, ye dinna ken ah ken. An' I'm gan ti pit ye to the test." He spoke in a savage, scarcely intelligible version of the King's English.

Dad's eyes popped out on stalks, dreading that he was about to be interrogated on animal husbandry (and not in the sense understood by Turnip Townshend; that scholarly anchorite merely wished to joust with him over some disputed passage in Homer on which father had written a commentary in those far off sunny days when he tilled in the groves of academe).

The ancient turned to me and smiled with an air of familiarity. In a mild fit of hauteur I stared at him for his presumption and put it to him: "And who invited you, good sir?"

Unembarrassed, even though quite obviously uninvited, he continued smiling. And then he winked, and I saw he wasn't so ancient after all. It was slow coming, but at long last recognition dawned, for there standing in front of me was none other than Angus McOgg MacPherson, returned from the land of the dead.

"But…" I stuttered, "are you a ghost?"

"Nay, my bonny lass, and I'm nae deid neither." That gravelly voice could have come from no spectral gullet. I was convinced and rushed forward to be crushed in those great strong arms. Of all those I wished returned from the other side of the grave, he was first in the queue after my father. "You great big bonny bogieman!"

"You thought I was deid." He laughed. "Well, those Indians knew on which side their corn cob was buttered, and after saluting me as a bonny fechter they realized they needed me for trading more than they needed my scalp; as soon as I persuaded them the culprits weren't in the cabin, relations returned to normal. Course they drank me out of house and hame. But I lost my best housekeeper." And he chucked me under my chin like a cheery drunken uncle.

Meanwhile, Mrs. Dixie had turned deathly white. What with the outré behavior of our Scottish guests and the sudden irruption of unexpected company, it had all been too much for this shy, retiring lady. She let out a quiet scream and swooned there and then in front of us all. Sal volatile was quickly applied to her nostrils. She coughed, and then with eyes still shut murmured the tune of the song popular in any household in the kingdom in possession of a harpsichord: "Will ye no' come back again? My Angus, my bonny Angus has gone awa…" Then in tones more Englished for the present company to comprehend: "If I open my eyes will you still be there? You that was stolen frae me on Drumossie Moor."

The music hushed; every eye in the place was turned to this strange encounter. Angus stood stock still, his eyes registering a rapid sweep of responses. Then he drew a deep breath, and although his voice was obviously struggling with emotion he spoke, but it was a voice quieter and more soulful than I had ever heard from that strong man's lips.

"Aye, ma wee bonny burd, ma wee Hielan Fiona. I kent you was here. I am back again frae the plantations, whaur I thought of ye every day frae dawn tae gloamin', and wi every stroke of the overseers lash I thought on ye. Better loved you will never be!" They threw themselves into each other's arms like newlyweds to the great applause of the rest of the company, who enjoyed this fairy tale climax to a delightful day, with the exception of one very prominent character whose reactions must be recorded in due course.

What a wonderful conjunction at my wedding! But that was by no means the end of our surprises. The honest, marvelous Angus approached us to congratulate the groom. "Yer a lucky laddie. She can shoot deer and cook it. She will keep your hoose bonny and blithe. She's a dab hand wi the sweeping brush, and she can dash awa wi the smoothing iron and keep you well supplied wi loaded muskets when the Injuns come a-calling." He looked down the table at the polite husbandmen and polished squirearchy of middle England. "Aye, well, ye might need all of those competences here." He was (as might be expected from a Scotsman when free drink is on hand) in an expansive mood and swaying only slightly, but as always with Angus his faculties were alert. "Whaur did ye get that wee medallion, sonny?" He pointed to a teeny miniature of an effete gallant that Cameron had pinned to his cravat, which I had assumed was there to prevent the cravat lace from ruffling when we were kissing. In truth I had never noticed it before, which is as unusual for me as for any maid checking her lover's turnout. "I hae one the very dab o' it," and he pointed at his collar where sat a button with an intaglio of the Young Pretender in one of his better days, identical to Cameron's. "My, but is that no remarkable? The Prince didnae hand these oot like groats at a souter's wedding."

Was I the only one who saw the distinct resemblance between the seed and the parent branches? Why had his mother not drawn any maternal conclusions when they shared the same roof? But then, she was kept as a recluse, and he resided apart in the servants' hall.

Once again Mrs. Dixie was the first to spot what later seemed obvious. "Angus!" she screamed in a voice far louder than her normal soft whisper. "It's oor laddie, our bonny wee Hamish. Look at him and at yersel in the looking glass. Twa peas frae the same pod, and does he no' hae the lugs o' my great aunt, Maire?"

"He doth. Hamish, my wee puddock!" My husband was assaulted by affection on both flanks, leaving me to pull my wedding gown out from under their feet. Maybe it was the Gaelic blood link; maybe it was the usquebaugh that was flowing fit to drown us all. But it seemed as I glanced from Angus to James that the weather-beaten, craggy brow was faintly mimicked in the noble, scholarly forehead of my husband.

Hamish, Cameron, Lewis, James! All was confusion. Might he have another name before breakfast tomorrow? I had better find a pet name for him and stick with it while I remembered who he was. Meanwhile Mary-Anne had fainted. At first I assumed it was from lack of attention, then I remembered that she too had ambitions towards whosoever he was who was now her brother, at least by half. For a moment it was touch-and-go whether I should join the ranks of the swooned; then it struck me that I had been just a nip and a tuck away from being the surrogate mother of my own husband. Luckily I had stayed as a housekeeper and left as a friend, and had not gone the whole hog in that cabin, for then I would have been Oedipus's stepmother. So I pulled myself together and concentrated on looking as beautiful as a bride should be at any normal wedding. This one was rapidly turning into a lady's novelette with all these characters popping up all over the place, but then they do say that truth is stranger than fiction. Not unnaturally I wanted to pull back everyone's attention to the most important player at this event, namely: *moi.*

Angus bowed to me (I think he sensed I was mildly piqued by the changing focus of the day) before turning his attention to our host, who by now was puffed up beetroot with anger. He had just recognized the unwanted guest.

"Do ye know me?" Angus bellowed, "For I ken you, ye skulking redcoat. Ye were one of Butcher Cumberland's mercenary murtherin' minions. Not so fat then. Sirrah! You were the English officer whae stole my wife, whae imprisoned me in Carlisle jail and deprived me of my only begotten. Come, Englishman, let us dispute Culloden again. Or dae ye deny it, ye cowardly captain? And if it weren't for the spoiling o' this joyous occasion, now wid be the time of reckoning."

"Deny it!" Sir Wolstan bellowed like Beelzebub. "It would take more than you and yer raggle taggle skirted army to deny anything. Aye, I remember you! Skulking under your lady's petticoats after that skirmish, you was. Couldn't take your medicine like a man, could ye? Well, she has a man now. Where there's a thrashing to be done, you won't find Wolstan Dixie skulking." He pulled off his jacket and rolled up his sleeves, ready for combat, then stopped and stared as if he had sudden second thoughts. He threw his jacket at the wife under discussion, moved forward into battle, and then stumbled. "Indigestion," he mumbled in a quiet voice quite unlike his usual bellow before hitting the floor with the thud of a fallen oak.

Angus held his fist back. "The man's ill." This was an understatement. Sir Wolstan Dixie was dead: seized by a fit of apoplexy, which had killed him as surely as a claymore skewering his guts.

So sadly the feast ended on a melancholy note after the servants picked up Sir Wolstan and trundled him out of the room to be borne off to a far, far better land. Like many another he never played a better part in life than his parting from it. He had paid for the wedding feast. I have to confess I had the greatest difficulty in appearing grief-stricken. Mary-Anne screamed and collapsed in a heap, but as nobody was watching she ostentatiously swept away to re-powder her nose, overcoming her filial grief in double-quick time when she realized she was mourning alone.

I have to say, a very sad thing it is when no one grieves for someone for whom grief should have its due.

When she came around, Mrs. Dixie was also relatively unfazed by the sudden demise of her second husband. Years of neglect and abuse had worn the insubstantial vine of her affection to the very root. "Oh, what a pity!" was all she said, and with this valediction Sir Wolstan had to make do, for now she rushed upon my Angus crying, "My one true love!"

And Angus, as grief-stricken as a man could be who sees his favorite enemy fall in front of him, hailed, "Aye! Thon was Culloden. Tonight it was Bannockburn!"

Poor Newquay was sitting at the end of the top table being ignored, the feathers perched above his ears unequivocally labeling his fashion statement out of touch, and what was more grievous, seriously un-English.

"Much badness!" he said, the Englishing of his tongue momentarily disrupted by the emotional turmoil of the evening. "He is bad! Very bad medicine!" No one took any notice. "He no who he say he is." And then he got completely confused with his word order. "He-Who he is! No who he say he is!" It was a sad, pathetic little display of petulance, and I perforce thought it best to instruct the servants to ration any further firewater. I turned to the butler, nodded toward Newquay, and then made a chopping motion with my hands. He understood perfectly. These savages lacked the emotional stability of the Saxon, and clearly his pettish mood was caused by our surprise guest's extravagant courtship of Mary-Anne, who was at this moment signaling to the Italian with big belladonna-infused eyes, a most provoking display for anyone, never mind one whose bowels were knotted with jealousy. Yet even though he had exchanged targets, the Italian's glittering eyes kept flashing over the ballroom to me—on and off, on and off—like the Pharos lighthouse of olden times.

Despite sensing the menace of his gaze, or perhaps reacting to it, I danced in a dizzy cloud of ecstasy with my husband, a title I bestowed on its worthy holder as many times as I could thrust it into any sentence, banal or witty, as per: "My darling husband, 'tis not the finest of days." He remained mute. "My husband, have you not noted the splendor of the guests? Surely it is a phenomenal company for Sheepy, husband sweet?" Silence, continued and discouraging, reigned betwixt the couple. "Husband dear! Do you hear me?"

"Amy, beloved wife, please, cease your prattle for a moment. I can either dance or talk; the two I can't do together."

This discouraging rejoinder made me glance away over his shoulder to see the count making eyes at me like a ravening beast. Once again I sensed a rapture almost liquefying in intensity.

Breakfast the next morning and not even my sweetened chocolate in its brilliant Meissen dish could appease my irritation. Would you credit it? At the end of the happiest of evenings, a drunken Newquay had the impertinence to challenge the count to a duel, pettishly slapping him on the face with a flower. Very sensibly and nobly, the count had the savoir faire to misconstrue the Indian's mutilation of the English tongue and declined the aborigine's invitation to dance as he pretended to understand, adding, "Thank you, but my skin is allergic to your petals." The silly man persisted, however, making his intention plain by slapping the count again, this time with his open hand. There was a loud crack. Our table went quiet. The count had no alternative but to decline, and to decline in a manner that firmly put the imbecile savage in his place.

"*Caro amico,* I regret, but socially I must refuse your honorable invitation to fight, as you are *canaille*, that is to say, scum, and I am *noblesse d'épée*. I have not come to this fair land to kill anyone, especially not a person who is so much beneath me, and thus"—he snapped his fingers in a definitive Italianate gesture—"I cannot in all honor notice your presence. If you persist in this ridiculous behavior, I will order my lowest groomsman to horsewhip you at dawn tomorrow at any spot you care to name." The count gave a great sniff, wafted his kerchief magnificently, and strolled off bedwards alone (a unique occasion).

I was furious and told Cameron to boot Newquay out into the cold, which he sensibly declined. As to whether the party was dampened by this unseemly behavior, opinion was divided. The stuffier souls I am sure went home miffed, while many if not the entire Celtic group said that it livened up a too-formal evening, making them homesick for their more unfettered gatherings. But it ruined our mating. I was too upset for lovemaking. Once again fate had intervened to padlock my maidenhead. I even thought, *Why not accept fate and retire to a nunnery?* But one look at my angelic husband sipping his tea and munching on an oatcake dispelled these gloomy reflections. I stroked his angelic locks, murmuring, "My husband."

"Amy, beloved wife of mine, there is a matter which we must rectify if we are to award each other these familiar titles, and that is betwixt the two of us and the bedposts," said he, as calm as calm could be, without any of the irritation a more selfishly impetuous husband would display, which is just one of the reasons he was such a sweet beloved to me.

I blushed and murmured, maidenly yet, I hoped modestly beguiling. "Be patient my amorous stallion; I am but a fragile filly. Tonight."

"Till tonight, then," he said with an underlying—how shall I put it—almost minatory tone measured into the mix of uncharacteristic grumpiness. Outside the breakfast room we heard the sounds of bridles and saddles being mounted up.

"Look, my sweet, Newquay and the count must have made friends for they're off on a morning's jaunt."

"What!" James threw down his napkin and rushed out the door. In the old days he would have said, "*Quid nunc*?" then laughed and used it as a gambit to open up further discourse. I wondered if all these sad tales of swiftly disillusioned, newly wedded wives were true.

"James, cooee! You've left your riding gloves behind." He had leapt aboard a hastily saddled horse. I could see the saddle shifting, for the groom had not had time to tighten the girth.

"James, you positively cannot go in that velvet jacket! It's a breakfast robe!" Then I gave the clinching argument. "What will the neighbors think? Think of our position!" But I said it into the wind. He was off, his horse plowtering through the puddles and the heather, and his beautiful bottom bumping around on the unstable saddle. I sighed. Already we are acting like an old married couple.

I went inside to the parlor, that very room where the sunbeams illuminated all my childish dreams, and attacked my needlework with counterfeit vigor. But it no longer answered. These lovely buckled shoes would be unmercifully mucked up by the mud. The horrible thought struck me that I was turning into my mother! Stitch, stitch, stitch! Was that all we women were fit for, while men go out dueling and rushing into dangerous exploits? We had brains, usually much more than the men I had encountered. We had character. Imagine any man putting up with the pains of childbirth. If it ever became a man's job, it would be banned by act of Parliament as a cruel and unusual punishment, to use the Yankee phrase. I threw down my pointless embroidery in disgust. To cheer myself up I put on my best morning dress, which was in blue cotton, adorned, which is to say made perfection with the finest Chantilly lace cuffs and collar. I practiced a little curtsey in front of the glass in a sarcastic mode for when they returned. No, these stockings would not do. I rummaged through my drawers till I found a pair of the finest, sheerest blue cotton, spun by a Nottingham stocking frame, which would answer nicely. I honestly did not know till long after I unfurled them aloft my thighs that I was making a political gesture. I must write to Mary Wollstonecraft, the queen of the Bluestockings, asking her to recommend where I should go to give my support to our sorely oppressed sisters.

It was a couple of hours later, past two o'clock, when two riders disconsolately drifted back. Jamie had his arm round the count, who was weeping copiously.

"He refused the horse whip. Insisted we fight. Even when I told him I was forbidden to duel in Venice, as I was cutting down all the coxcombs and the ladies were bereft of gallants." The next bit was difficult to make out because of his snuffling. Jamie filled in the gaps, though even he too was stuttering with emotion.

"He insisted the count must fight, and the signore was left with no alternative when Newquay told him he was the son of a great Chippewa chieftain, and thus a gentleman, a person of rank and account."

"*Si, belladonna mia*, I pipped him right through the heart. Peep, peep. When I make fire there is no mistake."

When I had a moment's leisure, I examined both firing pieces; Newquay's barrel was as clean as a whistle. It had not been fired.

The poor misunderstood little lambkin! To die so pitifully on this alien soil, on the wind-chilled moors above Atherstone, and on such a bleak day too! Of course he had no future here, unless some great lady in the height of fashion, indulging a momentary whim, took him up as an exotic pageboy.

When we broke the news to Mary-Anne, she brushed it aside indifferently. "Let's hope that when he makes it back to the happy hunting grounds he learns to control that temper of his, else he challenges St. Peter for the gate key," she said before brightening up to contemplate what to wear for the funeral. "I've had that black outfit for ages and never had occasion to wear it. Do you think it goes well with my skin coloring?" I wanted to say *it goes well with your black heart*, but some things are best left unsaid.

At least at the graveside we gave him a rousing send-off. The calumet in one hand and tomahawk in the other went well with his silk knee britches. It was a most fitting farewell. In full vestments proudly worn (rescued from the depths of an ancient trunk), father dispatched the Indian brave with all the ceremony and grace notes of the High Anglican Church. The deceased had not been consulted as to its suitability, but I am sure he would approve of all the dressing up. He at least had returned home. Mary-Anne disgraced herself by shrieking all the way through the litany and then attempting to throw herself into the grave on top of the coffin. I say "attempted," but I am sure there was not much deliberate intent. Knowing the lady's fashion sensibilities she would never have allowed her best mourning outfit to be scuffed up with mud and earth. I would have happily helped her desperate plunge, but some poor fools with misdirected gallantry held her back from the brink. I was sorely tempted to kick her precious bottom and send her on her way. But pace, Mistress Wollstonecraft, there are some things a lady doesn't do at a funeral.

In truth her attitude was rather on the lines of "Well, with that out of the way, I can set my hat at the main man, the devil may care the count of where." Honestly, if she could just see herself in the looking glass, she would have curled up and died of embarrassment what with all her antics.

"All the signs of the zodiac could not produce such spring-like pulchritude as that of our *preciosa sposa*, Amelia. Say, how old art thou, our youthful bride?" the count asked. I looked at my shoon, how tiny they were. "Such a pretty blush. How could I be so lacking in savoir faire to inflict it. A million apologies to you, Amelia, and your prince amongst husbands. I could swear you will live in an eternal springtime, as if you have quaffed from the *fons juventutis*." And there in that moment the topic of the elixir of the Stewarts was artfully brought center stage.

"Aha!" said several people at once, and then all looked down on the pattern on our Royal Doulton teacups, which now had become very interesting.

"Is there such a thing?" I asked in all innocence.

"Madonna! I have carried about with me a third of the recipe. Everyone knows it was given to me by the gay chevalier with his own hands"—Cagliostro flipped his hands up in the air to lend authenticity to this announcement—"in gratitude for a trifling service I was able to accomplish for him. Angus has another third given for services on that fateful field, and rumor has it that you are the possessor of the last piece."

"We heard your father stole it, count?" This was from me.

"Pff! So much gossip, so much envy from the little people." He snapped his fingers.

"It was in our family and a mighty heap of trouble it has given us. It's so long since I thought about it that I couldn't place my hands on it."

"Think of the service to our great enlightened age, the benefit to humanity, if you could discover it. Or if you choose not to think of that, think this: It would make you and your husband a rich and doubly respected vicarage couple." And with that the topic was laid aside for the time being, the count finally deciding to give it a rest, for it clearly had become an irritant to the rest of us.

It was on the day after Sir Wolstan was laid to rest that his widow, feeling a suitable period of mourning had elapsed, approached the altar for the third time, according to the ritual of the Church of England. Even Angus, normally no latitudinarian where his religion was concerned, was willing to stretch a point. "Ach, I micht as weel drink frae the poisoned chalice—ye ken, yon Anglican communal cup—and dae it here in Sheepy Church. When ye look at it, lass, the Episcopal Church of Scotland is different only by geography. The sands of the Solway Firth are no' a theology." Perhaps more to the point was what he told me later. "It wad tak too much siller to gang back tae bonny Scotland and get re-wed on the blacksmith's anvil at Gretna. Besides, we was in a hurry."

It was agreed that now there would be frequent visiting betwixt manse and manor without any of the condescension that had impeded relations previously. We had plenty to blether about over tea, and so our cups rattled as we chattered about the horrors we had witnessed in the wilderness, now all seeming incredible in this tranquil corner of England.

And so it came to pass that Angus McOgg, of the Clan MacPherson, by right of conquest and marriage became the unlikely laird of the manor. As for any parishioners still wishing to commemorate the bestial frolics of yore, they were swiftly discouraged by the sight of their new squire taking up the senior place in the foremost pew, girded with dagger, musket, and cutlass, nodding in solemn approbation at my father's sermon and uttering a loud, sonorous "Amen" at concluding arguments of obscure points of theology (unlike the previous occupant, whose snores had blended sweetly with the sonority of the sermon).

CHAPTER 23

Honeymoon

It was four happy people who departed the next day for our wedding holiday. The count asked most humbly, "Might I have the pleasure of joining with you? I am no—how you say the fruit, the berry is it?—of the goose. I will leave your courting unspied upon, for I wish to study the life of Maria Reine des Ecossaise during her period of jail time, when she held an establishment at Buxton, tasting of its hot steamy spa and *ancora* in gloomy, *frigido*, damp Tutbury Castle. She is *molto importante* to all the *amis d'Stewarts*, and the Tudors believed in the efficaciousness of the English water torture in wearing her down: I mean the dreadful weather. But of course I also enjoy *la conversazione* of the distinguished scholar here"—and here he pointed to Cameron—"while digesting eyefully such *belle donne*." And he pointed at yours truly plus Mary-Anne, sensibly selecting the peevish one first. "I have in mind to write a monograph on the subject, and of course I will mention you all as an aid to study in hearty acknowledgments."

He was so charming we were ready to believe anything he said, and so the count amused us along the way with his tales of myriad escapes; his meetings with Catherine the Great (on horseback) and the frivolous Marie Antoinette, both of whom claimed to enjoy his body "*moltissimo*, and far too avariciously"; and the Count Potemkin, with whom his shared passion was more cerebral. Only Frederick the Great he did not find simpatico. "He worked so hard at state papers he looked like a goblin filing clerk, not the great warrior of repute. Besides"—here the count waved his lacy handkerchief in his familiar signal of disapproval—"he had no interest in *le donne*, so we had nothing to talk about. And another 'besides,' his poems were an excruciation! Oh how I suffered. Thank Madonna, Monsieur Voltaire was also there. Only his sarcasm saw me through that bleak winter."

We laughed at his outrageous stories, his witty sallies, and even giggled when he took the liberty of playing footsy with Mary-Anne and me in the coach; for truth to tell my darling Cameron, while eminently worthy and stalwart in so many ways, was—let it be confessed—just a wee bit Sabbatarian, shall we say?

If my husband espied a standing stone, we had to stop the coach so that he could rush out to discourse—about the Druids, mistletoe, astral calendars, and such—on top of them. Even the impeccably well-mannered count couldn't suppress a yawn, dropping hints that the charming inn where we had set our hearts on passing the night might, if we didn't move with the utmost expedition, perchance be fully booked, and he personally would insist, even at the point of an épée, that our lovely ladies must be adequately housed and not slumber on straw, as he was accustomed to in many a cold bivouac in the Seven Years War whilst serving in the legions of Frederick the Great. But even so blatant a plea fell on the deaf ears of Cameron, declaiming away like Demosthenes atop a mossy stone, ignored by all except the cow rubbing its rump on the stone, who did in fact show her approbation by mooing very loudly.

The forbidden topic of the recipe was given another airing, even though none of us had a clear idea of what it was all about. Now, after subterfuge laid upon subterfuge, the count finally came clean about his real purpose. "I have been following your stars over mountains, over the oceans, over the *montes veneris* of so many belle donne."

To gain possession of that wretched recipe which has been the bane of our family's life for so long, I thought.

"I want to be able to boast of the longest thong in Rome and live forever, also to make lots of money selling it to the better classes of society, making everyone happy."

I had put the subject, the crux of so much of our family's folklore, out of mind. The topic was so boring, even the thought of it being raised in conversation was enough to bring forth a cavernous anticipatory yawn, on a level with the announcement that Auntie Annie from Ashby was coming for tea this Sunday. And it bore as much a chance of fulfillment as that other pot at the end of the rainbow, the Holy Grail, that I had totally dismissed it from my thoughts. I had a vague recollection of father telling me that mum had kept some family secret on her person, but he didn't know where she had it stashed. He had only half believed it when she told him about it, and with too many other more pressing matters to consider around that time he had dismissed the story as nonsense after she died.

"Forget it, Count. I have no idea where it is. I suspect it got burnt when the house went on fire." Over the years I had made desultory searches for the wretched manuscript, and now wondered if it had ever really existed.

He groaned, "Mia cara, so many dreams are now ashes," and was uncharacteristically down in the dumps for the rest of the day.

We had gone by chariot to the charming Peak District of Derbyshire in search of refreshment in the wilderness, away from the more docile beauties of the English landscaped gardens, their geometric joys and mathematical mazes. We did not realize that our visit to these roughly hewn scenic splendors would set a fashion soon to be heralded by Wordsworth and his followers. So in a dim sense we could lay claim to the title of Authors of Romanticism; and moreover, if the patient reader will pursue our history to the termination of this volume, she will see that we have given the world an authentic (because true and verifiable) supply of source material for the Gothick novel with all its concomitant horrors. The bare crags and the desolate moors had such a somber, chilling beauty that I made a mental note to write to Mr. Horace Walpole to recommend employing these gaunt stones as a setting for one of his Gothick masterpieces. I shivered as we clip-clopped gently through the vale of Dovedale, whose looming rock pillars' long shadows and rain sweeping down the dale added a menacing spice to the placid stream below, where once Isaac Walton fished and declaimed over its watery charms. A better place for unhallowed happenings I couldn't imagine.

We made our base near Bakewell, which allowed pleasantries about tarts and placing buns in ovens. I, dizzy with orange blossom and love, let these jests pass while we sallied forth on our daily excursions. More precisely, we were staying on the estate of the Duke of Devonshire at Chatsworth House and having the free run of his land. I hesitate to mention our privileged domicile, as it might upset some of my readers who have to mind their bawbees and cannot afford anything more than a fortnightly dip in the sea at Brightstonwell followed by a bracing stroll along the Prince's promenade, but there it is. Truth must prevail.

Every day when we had finally abandoned the chariot of Thalamus for a necessary breakfast we took our morning constitutional. After admiring the rose garden and the ornamental fountains (which surpassed those of the Palace of Versailles, so I am told), we would draw breath and gaze at the wild gritstone moors with their ramparts, crags, and flying buttresses—nature's cathedrals looming over all of our little world, as potent and secretive as the silent stones of Cuzco. This we were assured by the count, who had been everywhere.

Of further nuptial matters good taste compels me to draw a veil, although I can say without drawing a blush that my husband was uncommonly loath and a laggard in joining me on the connubial couch. Instead of getting down to the splendiferous combat he sat by the bedside, chuckling over comical passages in *Tristram Shandy*, enjoining me to "listen to this, Melly." Then he would read to me some drollery that tickled me not one whit. Losing patience I urged him not to keep me waiting.

"Cameron, do hurry! My toes are getting cold."

Finally he stumbled to the bedside, and so carried away by the rising tide of passion was he that he was stuffing the bed sheet into his breeks, thinking it to be his nightshirt. Sensing that I was mildly fuming he exclaimed, "I'm coming, Melly. I'm coming, my Melly!"

I could hear chuckles from the next room, the count doing a passable imitation of Cameron, echoing, "I'm coming, Melly. I'm coming, my Melly!" followed by girlish giggles and then a voice suspiciously like Mary-Anne saying, "If you don't arrive soon, I'm going to get there on my own," except it was done in a high-pitched, whining mockery of my voice.

That night at leisure after dinner I studied the count. I already have mentioned how he possessed all the charm of a Frenchman and Italian together, which when properly concocted was a formidable combination able to infuse lechery into a dead nun. It was said in cabalistic circles that one flash of his eyes was enough to moisten any lady's quim, and Mary-Anne, increasingly starved of what she was pleased to call her totem pole, was mad to be pronged by the pole under the silk breeches (although Polish was the only nationality of the Habsburg goulash not represented in the colorful count's bloodstream) and was now quivering on the edge of irrationality. That he even exerted a fraction of his oily charm on me burned her up with ridiculous jealousy, I knew, but I had no reason to suppose she would murder me, or that she had suggested the venue of our next day's outing to enact an insane plot to dispose of me.

When the lads went off for a day's tramping on the moors above the grotesque monoliths of Stanage Edge, Mary-Anne suggested combining a girl's own picnic with a visit to the old plague well at Eyam. While this seemed like a good idea, her suggestion that we both wear our wedding finery struck me as superfluous, but I went along with it as I always did. It was commonplace then to wear the bridal gown at assemblies and other evening receptions for six months after the wedding, but not for a morning stroll. However, Mary-Anne was a trendsetter, and as she said, it would get more use out of an article of clothing that was fated to be stowed away in an old trunk in the attic and finally brought out to light sixty years later to my granddaughter's disgust. The careful reader may have discerned many instances in this chronicle where I have put up with others' daft suggestions with lamblike meekness, all for the want of upsetting people. As the tale unfolds to the last knot in the thread and I become more assertive, you are left wondering why I did not put my foot down here. The only answer I can give (and a feeble one at that) is that I have the lazy lady's way of going along with others' hobbyhorses when the outcome has minimal importance. So there I was, lumbered by a huge skirt the size of a Montgolfier balloon, sweeping it up past brambles and cowpats, all for the sake of *la mode*. But what I couldn't have foreseen was that my tractability was to be my salvation.

After a somber visit to the plague victims' graveyard at Eyam, with its reminders of the fragility of the mortal coil, we decided on a stroll to disperse the melancholy that was threatening to overwhelm us, and thus found ourselves sauntering along the cliff top above the little hamlet of Stoney Middleton, enjoying the vista of limestone clefts and gritstone crags unfolded in front of our feet. I was too nervous to go near the very lip of the abyss, but Mary-Anne was laughing and whipping her skirts into the breeze, egging me on. "Amelia, get some cold airs up over your stocking tops. After all, what with all your swiving you need a cool down, else your quim bursts into flames with the constant friction. Ye are a handsome lass, withal. Now why not give yonder yokels 'neath your gorgeous limbs an incomparable treat. Let them snatch a glimpse of your ankles. Give them something to savour in their dotage." A comical, somewhat mischievous idea, quintessentially Mary-Anne, and I quintessentially complied. I tiptoed cautiously forward, looked timidly over the edge to see an old tavern, smoke spilling from its chimney, but of yokels the scene was utterly bereft.

"Go on. Be not afeard. Step blithely toward the precipice." Her voice had changed. Gone were the fruity vowels of the rustic Midlands; instead a broken guttural creaked out. I looked back and saw, instead of an English maiden, the cruel, hatcheted features of a bronzed savage. "Yes, you are right. It is I, Snowbird. Moneto has sent me here to extract vengeance for all the evil deeds of the Shemanese. Mary-Anne? I give not a single wampum bead for her. She never made it back over the Great Salt Lake. I murdered her, and it was I who killed the chief. Now you too will die as atonement for the rape of my country by the White Eyes."

"It's my husband you are really after," said I, a strange utterance admittedly but one containing a remarkable degree of prescience considering the circumstances.

"That too," she acknowledged unblushingly, and then added, "How could you expect someone like him liking you—you, Miss Mouse in the corner—when he had the chance to spread the Snowbird's loins? Only black magic managed to snare him into your bed. We have walked out today in our bridal outfits, signifying the end for you and a new beginning for me." She drew herself up in all her savage splendor, an avenging Fury, while I simpered like the frightened field mouse she called me, too petrified to even try running past her. "Now, racked by guilt, you take your own life. The suicide note, saying goodbye to all, lies"—she cackled at her malevolent pun—"in your petticoat pocket. Why you think I spend so long copying your sad little scribble? Writing those invitations to your pathetic nuptials filled me with disgust. Neither wonder some of the guests did not turn up after what I wrote." I had been flattered and amazed that she had wanted to copy my handwriting, and now I knew why. She cackled horribly, and even at this desperate impasse I wondered what social ostracism my corpse was about to suffer. "He will assuredly be mine after reading this." She pulled out a sheet of fresh parchment from her own inner pocket. "This is a copy of what will be found on your corpse."

I will not sully this page by quoting it. It was a nasty compilation of horrid, vicious lies destined for the fireplace. Her voice, whiny and pathetic, ended with a malicious cackle. "Now off you go!" And just as she pushed me over the edge into perdition, I caught a glimpse of her in her fluttering bridesmaid's satin, a pretty soft shepherdess pink contrasting weirdly with the mad glitter in her eyes.

Falling to certain death, I screamed, tumbled, spun a merry cartwheel, and then the wind, that gentle zephyr, caught under my skirts to form a giant pumpkin, slowing down my precipitation to a gradual swallow's glide. Just as you have dreamt of making your way down the grand staircase at your first ball with your admirers agape at the foot of the stairs, or like one of Giotto's angels descending to Earth, all shimmering draperies and insubstantiality, I was sailing gracefully into harbor. I wondered at the astonished face of my husband and the count gawping up (peradventure they were precisely below my skirts) till I saw to my dismay that my intimate clothing was on public display. I tried tucking my petticoats in but could not manage to fold them down, as the sturdy scaffold of my hoops and panniers held the balloon rigid. *Oh well,* I thought, *there is a season for modesty and a reason for flaunting.* All the time in the world seemed to be at my disposal. Fluttering down I pondered why all evildoers in the best romances, and this sorry masquerade we call life, feel compelled to gloat and confess all before hurling their victims into the abyss?

Plump. As softly as thistledown I landed in the open arms of Cameron, my skirts subsiding slowly over his head and shoulders as the breath went out of them. "My savior, how apropos!" Gracefully I stepped down to sample the simple but safe pleasures of terra firma. It is still difficult for anyone to believe that this thin silk and satin carapace delivered me from the perils of the precipice, even for my husband, who was an eyewitness; he was bereft of words, mouthing like a goldfish. But then he was the taciturn one, I his chatty better half. She—I say "she," although soft femininity had never visited her soul—the changeling monster peered over the cliff, an expression of well-monitored horror carefully composed on her features, then puzzlement, and finally a different kind of horror took over before she ducked away to be seen no more, I hoped. And good riddance to her, whomsoever she might be!

CHAPTER 24

The Riddle Resolved

Purely as a token rebellion against Mary-Anne's strictures, I had worn my mother's wedding gown instead of my own; it had weathered beautifully, the satin still holding the silky sheen and softness after years folded in an unremarked bottom drawer. Although it could be accused of being just a wee bit old fashioned, say for London Town, for the countryside, where novelty was inclined to create envy if not suspicion, it had stood the test of time.

I remembered what the harpy had said. Forgetting my last minute change of gown, I instinctively felt in my petticoat pocket. There, quite forgotten and forlorn, tucked away in a corner amongst its own crumbs was a crisply folded, tattered piece of parchment that was clearly too old to be Snowbird's valedictory masterpiece, so presumably my mother had concealed it therein. I drew it out, unfolded it, and wondered. The print was faded, so it was not easy to make out the lettering. It seemed at first glance to be cabalistic nonsense, such as witches construe to scare the neighbor's cat or turn her cow's milk sour.

"What is it?" asked my astonished lover. And then: "Why, no—surely it can't be? Yes it is! No! Yes! Yes! Yes! 'Tis surely the missing link, the third piece of the puzzle! As surely as I am a Christian!"

"Put the pieces all together and we will have the wonder of the age in our possession," said the count immediately, and he perked up for the first time since I had given him the bad news of the document's non-existence. "And riches undreamt of outside of Araby," he added as an afterthought.

"The elixir of perpetual youth. Perchance, Count, you may wish to apply for a flagon?" I declared, miffed that my miraculous escape from the jaws of perdition was not the primary topic of conversation.

"And of perpetual beauty for those not fortunate enough to be in possession of it already." This was my husband. "That excludes you, Amy, who is perfection itself." I blushed, just enough to show an appreciation of his gallantry and my own untiring, maidenly modesty.

"And promises a perpetual appetite for swiving," added the count in a surprisingly direct *mauvaise plaisanterie*, finally putting the lid on Cameron's conversational amiability. I blushed again; my innate modesty tinted a delicious rose pink onto my porcelain cheeks, which quite set off the immaculate white of my gown.

You know, when we finally returned home from our venturesome honeymoon, father was not exactly bowled over by Cameron's account of our ups and downs—an unfortunate phrase, but it showed my darling's innocence when he conveyed it. Even the part about my descent from the heavens like an involuntary angel went by scarcely heeded. I think this was the first signal that his sojourn in the great American wilderness had taken its toll. Up in the pulpit he still could take wing like an articulate eagle, but down below he was becoming an old man pottering around aimlessly. He had forgotten what that poke of paper in my pocket was about, assuming it was a recipe for the rhubarb crumble that my mother used to make. "People—quality, I mean—came trotting by from far and wide just for a bowlful slathered wi clotted cream, always finishing wi a flourish, 'My compliments to your goodwife, Sir.' Aye, Amelia, them were the days."

"It's the Bonny Prince Charlie beverage, father. Remember, the big secret?"

"Oh that! No, it can't be. It went to the grave with her. I recall that distinctly. I put it in the underskirt pocket of her wedding dress. She had asked to be buried in it."

"Then what was I wearing on top of Stoney Middleton?"

"Dunno. Summat else. Anyroad, that recipe, or whatever it was, is like an albatross around our necks, attracting the wrong type of visitors to the village and such." He gave a short sharp glance at the count, which told me he hadn't entirely lost his wits. "I wanted it dead and buried, so I buried the recipe in with her wedding dress in the coffin when she died. After all it meant something to her, though can't say as I rightly know what."

"Dig it up!" The count came all over excited and was all for disinterring the corpse; he was that eager to get at the manuscript. "The lady will not mind. We haff no need even to say excuse me. Just open it up, pick it up, and close it down. Is simple. At Pompeii they do it every day."

Cameron stiffened, firmly vetoing this move. "Not in England we don't. Anyhow the chemical processes of the grave will have long blotted out any script and destroyed the parchment." The suggestion gave some indication of the count's insensitivity; the very idea was so repugnant that only a foreigner of his kidney could have put word to it.

Was I carrying then a fake recipe, which might poison all our prospective customers? The mystery was solved after dinner. Food seemed to revive father's spirits. Had the rhubarb crumble I baked (from quite another of mother's old recipe books) helped make the years roll back?

"Nah. Now it's coming back. Where was I? She didn't go to her grave in thon gown." The lady had vetoed the project with almost her last breath. "Said she wasn't sure that St. Peter was happy with her choice of husband." He choked back his breath and paused. It was an old faded memory, but it still hit hard. After two deep breaths, he continued. "Didn't want St. Peter to be reminded of her marrying beneath her rank and dignity when she was standing outside the pearly gates." And so with that mean spirited valediction she left him to go to her proper place in celestial society, shrouded in an old kilt that Bonny Prince Charlie had left as a memento of his visit, the most memorable event of her life.

Father was weeping beyond consolation. Memories are messy things. We tiptoed out of his study, leaving him to his grief.

"So that paper in your pocket?" Cameron was staring at me.

"Must be the real thing."

"The *ipsissima*!"

"Absolutely!"

Angus was waiting for us at home. How he got hold of our discovery, I do not know. But he was as commonsensical as always. "Amelia, how long have we toted round this cabalistic nonsense, knowing it was sacred without kenning its secret?"

I shrugged my shoulders, signifying, I suppose, a long time.

"You ken the Bonny Prince gave me a wee bitten recipe just afore Culloden for services rendered tae the Cause. I surmised it was a recipe for some horrible health drink, like Gregory powder, that I hated, and so I stuffed it in my sporran and forgot about it. I was kind of preoccupied at that time," he said with a wry grin. "I kept the sporran, as it was the last remnant of Culloden and the Cause. I must have it somewhere." He scuttled about in his chest of drawers and with a shaky hand came upon a weathered scrap of parchment. "Here it is. I think. Canna make it out. It's all wrapped in a wee scrap o' cloth, like a bitten bread 'n' cheese after the mice have had first go at it."

"And here is my third of the document." The count placed his portion onto the table with his usual dramatic flourish. We had all the bits of the puzzle: the complete manuscript in front of us. We paused. We were rational beings, products of the Enlightenment, believers in scientific

Newtonian laws, and yet…we were on the verge of opening up one of the great mysteries of the ages, beside which the philosopher's stone is but a rock. Even the count, the Devil's favorite familiar, was silent, awestruck.

"*Andiamo*!" That was the count. We plunged in. Angus's portion was parceled in greased cloth such as was used to keep gunpowder dry, and that was firmly wrapped around with thick-knotted tow. The knots in the rope would have defied an Alexander the Great; but a saw, a claymore hacked heartily by Angus, and a couple of hey-prestos from Cagliostro did the trick.

The prince must have been more of a jester than he appeared from his solemn portraiture, or Father Time had done his busy work; for on opening the parcels, out fell fragments like bread crumbs thrown to the birds. Some contained a whole word, others a fragment of a single letter, an arabesque, a broken horseshoe, a curlicue, a swooping curve, and (most frustrating of all) the crossbar of a *t* or the dot of an *i*.

"It's a desperate puzzle," quoth my father, a sentiment quickly echoed by Angus.

"Aye, it'll be a deil o' a job sorting it oot."

Even Cameron, my intrepid Indian fighter, was deterred. "All the learned professors of Padua and Sir Edward Gibbon himself would have hurt heads putting this into English…or Latin," he murmured as an afterthought. No professor from Padua would deign to put anything into English.

The count, however, screamed with delight and jumped at it. "I can! I can!" He shuffled the papers about with great to-do; the matter of their interlocking was difficult, and soon it emerged too difficult. Even with all cabalistic wizardry at his command, he could make nothing of it and retreated crestfallen. We now had all three portions, all the clues, yet we were clueless.

"Ye may have something there, loon." Angus was stroking his chin, a wizard summoning a genie to the rescue. "Let's assume these twa, three pieces make a letter. See, it's Greek pi, ken. And yon there if I'm no mistaken spells oot "usquebaugh," and here we hae *mel*, "honey" in Latin. *Dolce*: that's Italian if I am no mistaken. Aye, Count?" His voice took on a rising, exultant tone. "It's a mish mash o' languages ancient and modern, and we're the boys—and girl—tae solve it!"

He was right, but it was no child's play. The first part of the job was to put together this huge broken mosaic, a grown up version of the child's puzzle—odd shapes with no known geometrical provenance that have to be fitted together to form a true likeness. The mish-mash of myriad shapes and oddities was spread out on the withdrawing room floor. Our first versions of the solution were more a tribute to hope and imagination than sense, but bit by bit we opened up a veritable treasure chest, a verbal thesaurus. It took two months to resuscitate the formula, but finally the knowledge of the elixir was ours! If you were expecting eye of newt and leg of toad, you are in for a pleasant surprise. It contained, besides its essence, satisfactory dollops of palatable ingredients—such as honey, molasses, fortified wines, brandy, and pure malt whisky—to keep our Angus happy.

"Why don't we make the blessed brew while we are still quick enough to enjoy it, test it on the public, and then make a fortune hawking it? For it cannot be more of a swindle than drinking that water bottled at Bath, pedaled as a recycler of lost youth, or that foul *aqua vitae reginae Hungariae* that people pay fortunes to swig, then complain when they still have the plague. Then we can all live as randy as Roger's bull and as rich as Sir Richard Arkwright, happily ever after."

The scheme had its merits, but in the end we decided not to flog the stuff. Some selfish physiocrat would break down the formula, and everybody would live forever. Then where would we all be? Sheepy would be the size of Birmingham, full of querulous ancients demanding their beer at last century's prices. We were down to two couples, the elder and the younger Highlanders, plus the count, self-elected to be guinea pigs. Father wouldn't touch the stuff. "Playing with God's allotted span," he said it was, and remained stuck with his old pre-Newtonian mental compass.

It was a few nights after making our devilish compact (as father put it) when I heard a faintest tinkling, as of a windowpane breaking, coming from the back of the house. But being dull and drowsy after the fulfillment of ecstasy, I thought no more of it. Contentedly I snuggled up to my beloved and asked, "Was that a window pane going smash, my love?"

"No, Rabbit! 'Twas the Green Man, set to snatch you away from me," he growled sleepily.

"But I am sure I heard something."

"Merely the boughs tickling the windowpane in the breeze. Now go to sleep, my loved one. No, not again, my sweet, me withers can't take any more."

The dawn surprised us, its golden rays playing over our eyelids, and then we awoke. After attending to my extensive toilette, we repaired to our breakfast nook and cranny. But where were the kippers, the kidneys, the cold eel pie, or the cool jugs of small ale? An empty nothingness awaited us. The cook rushed into our morning room all of a dither, an unforgivable intrusion when I had not yet supped my chocolate.

"Ma'am, Mistress MacPherson, there's been an intruder in the night broke into kitchen! It were the Green Man! I'm sure of it."

"Stuff and nonsense, Betty. That's a tale daft old biddies use to frighten their kids with."

"Well, you come see for yourself, ma'am."

"Only after I've sipped my morning chocolate, which I had hoped to see slathered in cream and cinnamon on this table," I said in a properly withering lady-of-the-manor tone. The cook snapped a look at me. It hadn't been wise to put her on a par with daft old biddies. Within minutes she was back, belligerently sloshing an unpleasant muddy mixture into my dish. "Enjoy your dish of chocolate, ma'am." Then, arms akimbo: "You'd best come see, ma'am." Not fancying a domestic uprising and realizing there would be no peace nor kippers till I made an investigation, I stirred myself out of the chair.

"Upon my mother's grave!" The kitchen was a wreck. Someone—something—had swept it into disarray on the hunt for God-only-knew-what. Every cupboard shelf was flung open, broken dishes everywhere. All the clay jars holding herbs, dried fruit, or apples were smashed and the contents spilt all over the stone floor. The vessel containing the essence was split wide open; the mixture (what was left of it) dumped in odd little heaps higgledy-piggledy over the cold stone. Judging by the way the damage was done, that was what they were looking for. There were footprints mixed in with pawprints stamped in the mess on the floor, also an object I could not square with any rational construction: an embroidered scrap of deerskin impaled by an eagle feather.

"Who could it be? What could it be?"

"Let's go back and at least enjoy our chocolate, then take stock." It was the count taking charge of the situation. The muddy brown broth that awaited me was no more attractive than before, especially as it was now cold. I put on my best face and slurped the concoction. Surprisingly it tasted better than it looked—there was a moral in there struggling to get out, but more important things were crying out to be considered. The count got up and strode up and down the room, flicking his handkerchief masterfully at every turn.

"Oddsfish. 'Tis no time to be practicing your Italian gesticulations," I said.

It was then that the count put me right. He sat me down on one of our fine Chippendale chairs in the morning room and patted my hand avuncularly. "My sweet Amelia, circumstances make us...how should I say it...make us do things incomprehensible when we are sitting in the full day's sunlight enjoying our breakfast." He took another turn around the room, pausing in front of the sunlit French window and displaying a haughty attitude so that I could not fail to appreciate his profile, which echoed the bust of Scipio in the Borghese Gardens—an allusion lost on poor, dull, untraveled me. "When I went out for that fatal *rencontre* on the Heights of Atherstone, I did not have the heart to slay the poor booby, the Indian boy. He was led astray by the mad passion of his love for that female Proteus, who changes identity as often as you change your delightful frock."

I demurred, which was exactly what I was supposed to do in my role as passive female.

"He needed to be taught a lesson, but not to die, so I filled my pistol not with ball but with pepper interlaced with wartbane and extract of nitrous oxide, enough to put a horse to sleep but not to kill *una mosca*, a fly. I also, by sleight of hand"—he snapped his fingers imperiously, demonstrating his dexterity—"placed a wad of paper betwixt his hammer and cap. I had no desire to risk being shot. Why should I?" He flicked his kerchief from his sleeve, wafting it thoroughly so that I might enjoy its magnificently expensive perfume, and then blew his nose elegantly (a feat I had never before seen accomplished, but I did not applaud). His breach of gentlemanly conduct in not allowing himself the opportunity to be killed was enough to banish him from all proper society, but the count didn't care. I guess some people make their own rules.

He continued, "I hit him dead center, knocked him off his feet. He 'lived' long enough to not forgive me. He cursed, 'He-Who cheats once, cheats again. You stink with evil. You are a motherless swine, sir!' Then he 'died.' I did not understand a word he said, but did he not look beautifully dead in his coffin?"

"Count, you are by your own admission a despicable rascal, but even admitting that, I cannot for a moment believe a word you say."

Again the handkerchief did its little entr'acte. "*Naturalmente*, but it is a part of my diabolical arts for which I have a European reputation. It is my unhappiness if the news has not trickled down to such a charming rustic retreat as Sheepy Magna and its even more *charmante* denizens." He bowed.

I bobbed a curtsey, for whatever magic arts he possessed, he also had the art of graciously sweetening an insult, a courtly skill I could not help but respect.

"And so I have no doubt that your intruder was the not-quite-dead—or if you like, the 'undead'—Indian. For who else knows of our secret, and who would wish to so untidy the kitchen? What local peasant could be so annoyed at the opulence of your culinary setup?"

"You're saying that Newquay is our burglar? And as for you…"

The count made another of his dramatic pauses, took up a histrionic attitude (bringing to mind, deliberately I should say, *Il Commendatore* about to give Mozart's Don Giovanni the bollocking of his life), and then proceeded to wreck my peace of mind. "Mmm…indeed, my little flower of the Midlands, sadly I have much graver news to impart. And you must remember these things are known only to those who dabble in the cabalistic cosmos."

"For the Lord's sake, out with it!"

"How can I put it? If you do not get the ingredients precisely right, you will be sought after by a maestro di cappella who wants a man who sings like a sweet, unswived girl."

"Oh! You mean he'll be knackered like a bullock?" I said astonished.

"Absolutely. I did not wish to be so heavy-footed, so indelicate, but assuredly he will be able to join with the little boys in the choir."

"A castrato?"

"Precisely."

"Is there anything else I must know?"

"Regrettably. And assuredly this is much the more terrible. If the mix is unbalanced and there is, for example, too much extract of sloe, or a lacking of petal of elderflower or peel of mandrake root, and it is not the season for that, then there is a probability—nay, a certitude—that the mixer will be granted eternal life, but in the shape of a lycanthrope: a wolf man."

"Fiddlesticks," I said, but then I swooned and was not aware of anything till I found myself lying on the floor and my sweet, darling Cameron, eyes bulging with anxiety, applying smelling salts to my nostrils. But the count was shaking his head. I had tried that trick too often.

'Twas hardly a week later when more alarming news came to breach our Sabbath serenity. I was about to plunge my knife into a jar of Blairlogie's marmalade and stab those wanton tendrils. Nay, that is too Shakespearean dramatic. I was toying with my spoon amongst the curlicues of Seville orange floating in the marmalade paste secreted in that characteristic grey pot, musing over Andalusian nights of enchantment, when in bursts Betty all a fever. "Betty," I said, somewhat shocked that she had not taken to heart the severe chastisement of the previous occasion, "are these eruptions to be a continuing feature of our break of fast upon a Sunday?" I was trying to be as light-footed as possible in my admonitions. What with all the happenings in France, not to mention the naval mutinies at the Nore and Spithead, there's no telling what sauce, impudence, and worse domestics are ready to dish out for a careless trip of the tongue. "Or are these one-act plays exclusively for festal days?"

"Oh, Mistress MacPherson, do not mock. There is a terrible hue and cry about the village. Many of our fowl are scattered in feathery heaps round the rose garden, and they say a wolf has been killing sheep in the village. 'Tis a terrific hullabaloo, and the bad ones are saying 'tis the parson's quondam"—that unfamiliar word (meaning "once upon a time") tripped over her tongue as if she were indulging herself in a little verbal treat—"witchery to blame." She nodded the way old wives do when they have something especially furtive to relate. "Begging your pardon, mistress. There's still some in't village with long memories."

"Oh, havers, Betty! The last wolf was killed a good half-century ago in the farthest north of Scotland." Then I stopped. The last time I accused her of talking tripe it was me who was wrong. "Sorry, Betty." Then I did something democratical and American. I invited her to sit down. "Seat thyself down and have a cup of tea." She was a good cook, not given to tantrums and quite often sober. Alienating her would not be a good idea. "Tell us all from the beginning."

"Well, mistress, I don't know how to rightly say this, you not being like us common folk. They do say this one can change its shape and turn into summat half-human, half-hellish that pads about at night seeking its prey. And young maidens is a special treat, they do say."

"You mean a werewolf? Stuff and..." The look on Betty's face told me to try another tack. "It may well be. There have been several well-documented cases in the Harz Mountains of High Germany." Then I thought back to the count's lecture and was struck by an irrational fear. Could he be right? Could Betty and the villagers be right? Here we were in the century of Voltaire, Volta, James Watt and his steam Beelzebub, and Mr. Townshend and his turnips. What right had werewolves and hobgoblins to come and annoy us at night?

That night I got my answer. There was a plaintive howling, rising and falling in pitch outside our windows, a cry no dog ever made. The only other time I had heard such a chilling, strange sound was in winter on the highlands of Virginia when the wolves were starving. I swear that at times through the howling someone was calling out in anguish. In no way could that mockery of the human voice be put down to the effects of the wind. I shivered and stuck my head under the blankets, but even that refused to make it disappear.

CHAPTER 25

The Changeling Returns

What is it they say about the bad penny? Any reasonable person would have thought that the attempted murder of her best friend had put her outwith the bounds of decent society; that she would stay away and go live in Boulogne with the bounders, cads, card cheats, broken down duelists, and the rest of society's flotsam, not to mention old reamed-out whores. And who the h— was she anyway: Indian princess or spoilt child of the squirearchy? This question did not detain me long. I had more interesting diversions to pursue.

It was probably a week after the events just described. The old grandfather clock in the hall had just chimed ten. I yawned. Cameron yawned. That was our signal *di amore*. I put away my needlepoint. We were retiring for the night, and I was slipping into my most fetching night rail, the one with the bonny blue silk ribbons and cascades of lace and satin to swathe my body till it was only almost visible through a shimmering, diaphanous curtain, enticing enough for anyone not singing in the high-pitched section of the choir. A teeny dab of perfume completed my preparations for besiegement. I lay there quivering in quasi-virginal anticipation when a well-aimed slingshot was fired at our window. The second stone couldn't have been a chance meteorite.

"Psst!" A familiar stage whisper had me shaken out of my romantic reverie, and suddenly the night had a bleak chill to it. Only one person had the effrontery to make an unheralded visit at this hour. That one syllable bore her unmistakable hallmark. Was my attempted murderess ready to have another go at me? Would this woman never stop? The voice was a timid whisper. I drew back the drapes, and there she was shivering, all waifish and woebegone under the spreading chestnut tree. "Amelia, my darling," she whimpered, her voice trembling in time with the quivering of the leaves in the chill breeze, as if she were riven with remorse and bearing the weight of some great sorrow on her shoulders. "I have been so worried about you. That day on Stoney Middleton when you tripped and fell, I almost threw myself off the cliff trying to save you. But the Lord and all the saints heard my fervent prayers, and they have been granted," she added complacently, as if my rescue were all her doing, "for amazingly you emerged without a splinter or scratch."

They say that God grants each one of us a special gift. Hers was to lie with utter conviction that black is not black but a darker shade of pale. She knew the simple lie told with false sincerity wins every time. Even today I am not quite sure if I didn't pitch myself over the edge. I actually visited the spot and found a treacherous root at the edge, which might have been the culprit.

"I would even have sold my soul to the Devil to have you restored to life."

That I could believe, but not in the way she intended. She said this while twitching her little bottom, running her fingers through her hair as if she were carding cotton, and gazing at me appealingly, her eyes large with tears. Once upon a time it would have worked. It almost did, but while I was on the brink of surrendering to her acting ability a voice said in my ear, *Amy, have you not learned anything from that cavalcade of twisters and rogues who have been rifling through your petticoat pockets*? "But I heard you plain as day: an Indian talking in Indian behind my back." I heard myself doubting, sensing the white-hot intensity of her gaze gradually overpowering me, willing me to return to my former submissive self.

"Such codswallop! Amelia. Your brains must be in your bottom, what with that randy husband of yours rattling your nethers off. I knew all that rogering would be the death of you, Sheepy's answer to priggish Pamela, the prude who couldn't be screwed." I didn't believe it. She had actually read a book! And this was her delicate way of referring to Richardson's masterpiece. "But once broken and entered, there's no going back to your prim little tea-pouring ways." And there she was wagging her finger at me, admonishing me! The cheeky cow! As if she had been walled up in a nunnery! "Me, a Hindoo! And Old MacDonald's pigs can fly!" She barked out a sarcastic grunt, midway between a laugh and a snarl. "Why, I've never so much as *once* touched a curried egg." And yet how clever of her to pretend to be the wrong kind of Indian. "If you let your fevered imagination take control of you like that, your husband will have no option but to commit you to Bedlam, and I will have to come all the way to London to visit you. And that stagecoach journey is such an uncomfortable ride—splashing through puddles, bouncing in and out of potholes, and grubby hostelries with their unsavory inmates." Very clever she was, the way she turned the tables on me always, even to the self-serving point of moving the subject matter to the topic of her own inconvenience, and now the burden of guilt fell on me! There's no arguing with some folk. By the by, it was the way she pronounced "once" as "woonce"—no Indian from the forests could get their mouth round that unique middle English vowel—that settled it for me. Probably, possibly, maybe…

"Well, come on in then. You'll catch your death out there." I had crumbled. She vaulted over the window ledge like a black panther from the forest. No English lass with ladylike pretensions possessed that agility.

Of course she disarmed me immediately. "We couldn't have done that with all our frills and furbelows, eh, Amy? I recommend six months amongst the savages of the Americas for any dainty English lady. It would be an improving vacation." Then, "Oh, Amy, I have missed you so much. Why did you keep me out in the cold?" As I said before...

The upshot was of course forgiveness. Floods of tears of questionable sincerity and hugging fit to crush my stays brought her back into the fold, and soon she was lording it over everyone, just as in the old times. Come to think of it, if her motive for pushing me off the cliff was her jealous desire to purloin my husband, she showed no sign of it now, no interest in him at all. For she was once again enthusiastically pitching herself at the count, who (no dilettante in the art of teasing courtship) was playing at being a ticklish fish to land.

One thing about Mary-Anne one must admire was the way she moved on. Newquay wasn't dead, just transmogrified into an annoying wail in the night—a nuisance of insufferable volume, but not a problem—leaving the coast clear to go full steam ahead for Cagliostro. My father, in one of his moments of insight, warned her: "Take care. That one's not who he pretends to be."

"Then who is he?"

"Why, he is He-Who. He is Old Nick himself."

She laughed the kind of laugh that says, *you are being ridiculous but I can't be bothered dealing with it just now*, before turning away to more amusing company. What else would you expect from a flibbertigibbet dealing with a decrepit old man? She replied, "Forsooth, who in our little society ever settled in the role allotted to them in God's great scheme of things? To wit: the shy vicar who hocus-pocus became the terrifying prophet of the prairies, Lorenzo Dow; the stooping scholar with a flick of the fingers is hey-presto the fearless backwoodsman; the giddy trollop—oh yes, I know myself—transmogrifies into a princess of the great Seneca Nation. 'Tis only little Amy remains as unchanged as the parish pump." I was not entirely sure I was being flattered, but then the insult wrapped in a velvet glove had ever been her trademark.

So Mary-Anne had returned, bringing in her train her usual load of mixed blessings: the swirling excitement of the merry dance; cacophony and chaos; quarrels, then happy resolutions; stirring up pent-up jealousies like an amorous Pandora in our placid realm. To sum up, Cameron, she conceded, was out of the race; father gave her a wide berth, warding off the evil eye behind her back. Anyway he no longer had any fizz. Swiveling round as if she were picking and choosing produce in the market, she directed all her attention toward the Count Cagliostro. Now he was the very stuff of her dreams: a bravo, outrageous in behavior, who could cut a swagger as easy as pinking someone with his rapier; dryly witty; immaculate in his dress and address; and as handsome as they come. And I almost forgot: The smell of money hung around him like an exotic, enigmatic perfume—enigmatic in that its provenance was as yet a mystery, and no specie had yet been sighted.

However, he was not so easily won over. When once again assailed by her formidable charm, the count did not flinch but, elaborately drawing out his familiar handkerchief, poked around in his sleeve for a pinch of snuff. He paused, a tactical device to intimidate the timid (which Mary-Anne most certainly was not), then in his languid drawl asked, "Mademoiselle, my pretty maid, you have me at a disadvantage. Are you perchance an actress portraying the ferocious savage, or…what? Who then are *you*?"

She very coyly replies, "Who am I? Who are you? All of us here are two people; viz, the pedant and the pathfinder"—she indicated Cameron, shying away from controversy, making himself as small as possible in a corner of the withdrawing room—"the gentle vicar and the fiery Old Testament prophet"—which fiery prophet was fiercely contesting Cameron's corner.

"Who am I?" The count pointed to the star of the Order of St. Theresa on his breast and did not wait for an answer. "I am He-Who can make your dreams come true. I am two-faced Janus. The coin has two sides, and according to the spin of the coin you could enjoy the stuff of dreams or something far beyond your worst nightmare."

"Perhaps I may have the best of dreams with you?"

"Perhaps."

However, after his first flirtation with indifference, the count was nothing loath to accede to her request to be bonded in holy matrimony. My guess was that he was zealously sought after by the police of various European states. There were rumors that the Emperors of Austria and Russia and the King of France, not to mention the Doge of Venice, were eager to have him assist them with their inquiries, making homely Sheepy suddenly more attractive than seductive Paris, sea-girt Venice, and the white nights of St. Petersburg.

The event was celebrated with less pomp and to-do than our own heady nuptials. I was matron of honor, wearing a suspiciously dowdy dress, thus leaving no doubt who was the star. But I didn't care as long as Mary-Anne was safely married off and out of harm's way. There was one difficulty. My father was loath to perform the ceremony. He made all sorts of excuses, each one weaker than the last, till on the day he finally called things to a halt by claiming he had lost his false teeth and therefore could not read the service, and both he and the sexton had lost the keys to the church. I suspected at the time that all was fabrication, and now have a pretty fair idea of why he put the brakes on their unholy matrimony.

For a man with the wiles and resourcefulness of the count, this was no problem. He snapped his fingers at one of the servant lads. "Go tell the blacksmith in Atherstone to prepare the village smithy. We will celebrate the rites *a la Écossaise*—over the anvil."

Mary-Anne was preparing to look miffed over the downgrading of the ceremony when the count said, "Do not worry, my cherub, the Holy Father himself has given me permission to act *in loco sacerdotis*, as a priest, if one is not available in an emergency, which this decidedly is."

Mary-Anne's protests died on her lips. Like the rest of us she was somewhat in awe of the count, to the point of being frightened by him. The fact that she would be wed at least approximately according to the rites and customs of the Church of Rome was also passed over without remonstrance.

"Fret not, my little cabbage, your protestant heresy will be in no danger at my hands," said the count, and that was that.

The Atherstone blacksmith was prepared to have a serious disputation on the aberrant theology of the ceremony ("I'm a good Quaker, milord, and can't countenance your heathen practices, not for any price") till the count pulled forth from his breeches a hefty purse, coming from goodness knows where. This jingled most musically to the good artisan's ears. "Not for any price" must have been a figure of speech, for the price was right, and he instantly managed to overcome his doctrinal objections with "When all is said and done, 'tis all one church under heaven," an admirable position, most fitting for our Enlightened Era.

However, to ward off any last minute apostasy from the lay priest, the count had taken the precaution of ensuring he was well-primed by celebrating the health of the bridal pair before the splicing of the knot. This might have been fatal, for besides being illiterate, the blacksmith was now too incoherent to conduct the service from the prayer book given him by the count. With that self-possession that is his hallmark, the count removed the book from the blacksmith's brawny hands and read out the appropriate passages. I don't think I was the only one to note that the ceremony was not conducted in Latin, but in a tongue unknown to me. Cagliostro was condescending enough to enlighten me afterwards.

"Since you ask, it was Coptic, the language of the early Syriac Church."

Well, that was all right, then, and we all relaxed to enjoy the novelty of the proceedings. Mind you, the hems of dresses had to be paid attention to as we carefully negotiated a path between the traces of the horses' progress, which made the solemn ritual almost like a kids' skipping game. As for the count, I could not begin to describe his look of anticipatory pleasure, "vulpine with a smirk" might begin to sum it up, for Mary-Anne indeed was a dainty dish to set before a king or, in this case, a margrave.

But it was the wedding night that rendered their splicing memorable.

"Hasten, my handsome, *parfait*, gentle knight, for I am impatient," she declared like a haberdasher displaying her goods, lying there on the sumptuous divan, ready to take on boarders.

Cagliostro shrugged and made an unmistakably Italian gesture of *que ser*á *ser*á. "*Bene, mi amore*; getting what you wish for is often the last thing you want. And now you have me." This was his parting shot as he removed himself to the disrobing chamber next door.

"And that is what I want!" Here was the authentic, imperious Mary-Anne of old, draped over the cloth of gold counterpane in delicious anticipation. It was the proud boast of the glorious and ancient borough of Atherstone that the four-poster bed at the Three Tuns was the very one upon which Mary Queen of Scots had once spent the night. Not surprisingly considering her circumstances, that had been a restless night, but it was not in the expectation of a good night's sleep that Mary-Anne now filled the royal berth. She lay like Cleopatra waiting for her Roman gentleman friends. Swags of plush red velvet framed the bride's delectable outline; her skin glistened with softly anointed aphrodisiac ointment, pulsated with mounting excitement as she stroked her mossy mound, which now awakened was gleaming with liquid ardor. "Hasten, Count, a thousand angels could not bring to you the delights you are about to enjoy."

From another room came a distant, boastful voice, slightly distracted with the struggle to remove breeches. "Your promise is a high one. I that have lived a thousand years have enjoyed sleepless nights with…let's see. Messalina, wife of the emperor Claudius. She was such a naughty flibbertigibbet. Galla Placidia, wife of Attila the Hun—my, what a scrape that was getting out of that one! Joan of Arc—but that armor! The poor girl had no fashion sense. It was so unlascivious. 'Twas the only time I needed a tin opener as part of my honeymoon package. I really did that one as a favor to France. And of course the gorgeous, treacherous Lucrezia Borgia, one of the best rides in the Middle Ages. But did I accept as much as a refreshing glass of sack in her palazzo? Not on your Nelly! Which brings me to dear, sweet Nell Gwyn. I kept her bed warm when his majesty was off squiring one of his duchesses. 'Tis no joke, but her bosoms were twin to a pair of oranges. With Flora MacDonald I did not wish to tangle. She insisted I dress up like her servant girl before I gain permission to enter!"

"Oh hurry up, in the name of God's codpiece, my bombastic swive-meister!" said the lady in waiting, her voice arch but falsely so, as if she were trying a bit too hard to master impatience.

The door opened. There was a gasp. Mary-Anne screamed. This was no performance scream, no operatic interlude; this was the scream of one seeing a true fiendish apparition. Here was no Count Cagliostro! Foursquare against the Queen Anne doorframe stood a malignant nightmare. She screamed again—a ghastly, high-pitched screech, an animal shriek—as the monster, adorned in the regalia of a Chippewa chieftain, slithering across the floor toward her in his own slime, was none other than the hideous He-Who. The outcast raised his arm and pointed at her. Along the length of the arm from the shoulder to the nails was an obscenely pulsating rattlesnake. The eyes of the rattlesnake were fixed on the girl's wildly palpitating breasts, as if the creature was about to strike. The apparition's breechclout was distended like a spinnaker in a down-easterly gale.

He laughed. No human being could have uttered such a chilling cry. Here in the very heart of Old England came forth the harsh guttural roar of a creature of the great forest of the Americas. "You had so many warnings, but your vanity was so great you didn't give a prairie dog's bone for them!" Then he straightened up, making his breechclout slide to the side, revealing the tadger of a great stallion as he set to the terrified bride. "At last the great prize. Here endeth the race to Seneca's summit!" The creature beat its chest as if beating the war drums to summon all the Confederation of the Iroquois Nation to council.

Snowbird screamed again. Her shrieks carried to the church graveyard, where the dead stirred in their long sleep. The fiend leapt aboard her like an eagle diving from Seneca's crest plummeting for its prey—his shaft straight, solid and stiff as a tomahawk handle—and rode her and raped her with a savage relentless violence. The drawbridge was open; the moat was dry.

When he finished he took out a well-honed knife and cut a single hair from her head. "Every night I will complete my rapine with this single ceremonial scalping till you are scalped clean, and then…" He let his words dangle in the night air.

We opened the door of the bridal room. She was sitting in a corner, shaking with hysteria. There was no one else in the room. Outside, the count was looking as baffled as the rest of us.

But every night he came to deliver on his promise, and each time after his raping he struck one hair off her head as if he were keeping tally. Mary-Anne reflected bitterly, *So this is what eternal life has condemned me to, being scalped in slow motion and violated in perpetuity by this monster that we have all gone through such trials and tribulations to avoid,* while outside her window her erstwhile true love was howling in an infinite Hades of his own. And the worst part of it was never again to go out in public and flaunt her abundant crop of hair, what with wigs being so unfashionable now.

Of course, as with any tale coming from the lips of Mary-Anne, truth may well be a stranger. Was she romancing because the count, once wedded, forsook the dash and gallantry of his single years just like any other tedious husband? And her hair was falling out naturally, a result of an overly excited life. For ought we saw of him, the urbane count gave no sign of satanic practices. Poor Mary-Anne. Life had turned out to be so dull. Having romanced her way through life, no one would believe that the little man pottering about with the tea-cozy hat on his head could be the diabolical fiend of her fantasies. In the evening he would regale us with tales of his adventures in the courts of High Germany, but these were no sagas of debauchery, of escapes through windows from husbands wearing horns, but of conversations with illustrious kappellmeisters on the art of the fugue; of Frederick the Great, who had stolen the count's best piece for himself, which now was widely known as the monarch's finest flute concerto; of being the favorite pupil of Tiepolo and Canaletto, who vied with each other to get him to fill in the blue skies on their masterpieces.

Marriage had quieted Mary-Anne. Every evening she sat in front of the fire, combing her hair, teasing out every lock so minutely as if she were counting every one, which of course she was. The count had composed a novel about the last days of Pompeii, which according to Dr. Johnson was so imaginatively reconstructed that you felt the author was standing in the very streambed of the molten lava. Currently he is lecturing to the county literati on what it was like to be at Bosworth Field on the very moment that King Richard lost his crown. (By the by, his last words were not "A horse, a horse!") These talks are so popular we have to use all sorts of skullduggery to acquire tickets.

And of course he is still there in Atherstone Town, masquerading as the mild-mannered, somewhat eccentric, scholarly librarian who shuffles between the stacks muttering to himself in tongues incomprehensible to the good burghers of Market Bosworth and its environs. This is the final charade of the chameleon we knew as He-Who.

So after these halcyon years of our youth, everything all about us is calm and restful. But on those bitterly stormy nights, with the wind screaming through the thatch, the boughs creaking and snapping, the leaves weaving and dancing against the window panes, and horrid shapes lit in a flash by jagged lightening…one wonders.

Valediction

"We have each sought our philosopher's stone; each has been tossed around on the billows of the world's oceans, and all have returned home safe, wiser, and wearier. Some more than others." So spoke the vicar, casting a gentle nod at the middle-aged woman sitting by the bay window picking at her needlepoint, wearing a large mutch cap to hide her thinning hair.

Replying to the toast, Angus put a stress on the magic of our return. "Oh, brave new world of Signor Volta's electricity, of vaccination and magic transmutations. And what is most amazing, Amelia: You returned to us unspoilt and chaste, the perfect vicar's wife." He turned to the other woman, "Mary-Anne, the pursuit of happiness is but a naughty chimera. Chase after it and it shall surely bite you rudely. Give it away to others and it will repay you tenfold. Thus you; thus Amelia." This was a bit pointed, but Angus carried on nonetheless, without noticing any embarrassed tremors amongst his audience. The manor hall at Market Bosworth had seen many more tremulous gatherings.

Cameron, to the rescue, leapt to his feet. "A toast, a toast! A brindisi, to all of us. 'All to their own, and God bless home!'"

"Indeed! Amen to all that!" we all chorused.

Indeed, we lived happily ever after, some of us more happily than others. But if I could have seen what was ahead, I might have wallowed less deeply in the wine of eternity.

Amen to the clangor of the well-targeted spittoon; amen to meat soused in sugar; amen to tomahawks, and to savage whooping in the heart-chilling night; amen to every man being as good as his neighbor; amen to the strong hand clasp and the steady eye of the democrat; amen to the wild purple hills vanishing into the great blue yonder.

Hail to the snug cot with the smoke lazily purling out from the chimney, to the tankard set stolidly in its rightful place by the hearth. Hats off to the squire and his lady, the parson, the idle artisan with his pewter mug on the bench by the duck pond, and to God's divinely ordained order. Hail to the wild whooping in the night of the wise old owl, reassuring the world that all is at peace in Sheepy's placid dell. The household gods will sleep well tonight.

Epilogue

The devoted son's letter concluded:

So here I am at the splendid village tavern, a quondam hideaway of Dick Turpin, living like a lord on roast beef and Yorkshire pudding, washed down with tankards of the splendid local ale. Mr. Stephenson would have us propelled round the kingdom in gusts of steam at hectic speeds of fifteen miles in an hour. I prefer the steady clip-clop of my old gelding to enable me to tarry in the still unspoiled vale of Warwickshire astride old Watling Street. If I look over the top of the hill I can see the battlefield of Bosworth, where bad King Richard would have sold his kingdom for a horse. If I turn my faithful old nag around now, I shall still be in time for tea at the vicarage.

But enough of me, who will always remain,
Your most obedient and affectionate son,
Edmund.

About the Author

M.G. Anderson is the author of *On Belay*, *Mons Graupius*, *The Last Jacobite Princess*, and various published short stories. He is the recipient of the prestigious W.H. Murray Literary Prize.

Anderson has been a mountain climber and adventurer from his early teens, beginning with walks alongside his father in the Pentland Hills near Edinburgh. Later, he accumulated a considerable number of classic ascents in North and South America, the European Alps, and on his home turf in all four corners of the British Isles. His ascent of Alpamayo in the Peruvian Andes, "The World's most beautiful mountain," was a boyhood dream come true.

These experiences have lent considerable details and a well-developed sense of reality to all of his written works.

In addition to being an accomplished mountaineer, M.G. Anderson is a former Latin teacher. He was born and raised in Edinburgh, Scotland, but now lives in Columbus, Ohio.

Made in the USA
Coppell, TX
28 June 2026

82798407R00187